SALVATION, BOOK 1

WRANGLED

K.C. WELLS

This is a work of fiction. Names, characters, places, and incidents either are the product of the author's imagination or are used fictitiously, and any resemblance to actual persons, living or dead, business establishments, events, or locales is entirely coincidental.

Warning
This book contains material that is intended for a mature, adult audience. It contains graphic language, explicit sexual content, and adult situations.

CHAPTER ONE

Memorial Day Weekend
Toby

Why does he want to see me?

The bad feeling that had started after Tyler's call was much worse by the time he rang the buzzer. I pressed the button to let him in, then opened the door to my apartment, my heartbeat quickening.

This is not *going to be good.*

Not that Tyler had given me a clue as to the purpose of his visit, but those four little words had filled me with dread.

'We need to talk.'

And then there had been his voice. He'd sounded nervous as fuck, and that wasn't like him. Tyler was young, self-assured, and scared of nothing. I waited for that first glimpse of him on the staircase. I watched as he trudged up the steps, his footsteps as heavy as his expression. He saw me and gave a single nod.

"Hey."

And that right there was another clue. The first word from his lips was usually Sir.

This is really *not going to be good.*

"Get in here."

Tyler lowered his gaze and stepped across the threshold into the apartment. I closed the door behind him to find him standing in the tiny hallway, looking like a lost sheep.

I pointed to the living room. "You know the way."

He went ahead of me, coming to a halt in the middle of the room, his gaze darting, his Adam's apple bobbing sharply.

He wasn't kneeling as he always did.

Then I knew we were done, and my heart plummeted.

This is going to be bad.

I closed the door. "Okay, let's get this over with." There seemed little point in prolonging the inevitable.

What's happened?

Has he found another Dom?

Didn't I meet his needs?

I thought I had. Hell, I thought we were a good match.

He blinked. "Sir?"

I shook my head. "Uh-uh. Too late. That should have been the first thing you said." I gestured to the couch. "So… sit, and tell me what's on your mind."

Jesus, he was shaking from head to toe. I figured he sat down before his legs gave way under him.

Am I making him that nervous?

I put my hand on his shoulder, and I swear, he almost jumped out of his skin. "Look, whatever it is you have to tell me, it can't be that bad—can it? I mean, not bad enough that I'm gonna kill you if you tell me," I quipped.

He swallowed. "Sir… I… I broke your rule."

I arched my eyebrows. "Which one? I do have a few."

Another swallow. "Your number one rule."

Oh God.

Every sub who'd ever played with, or signed a contract with, was told the same thing. *This is just BDSM and sex. We play. We have fun. And if it gets to be more than that…*

Apparently, it was more than that, and I hadn't seen it coming. Tyler was a level-headed, no-nonsense kinda kid.

Not level-headed enough, it seemed. I knew what he was telling me, I just didn't want to believe it.

"I can't give you what you're looking for," I told him in a low voice. "I don't *do* love. I'm not built for it."

His beseeching gaze made my heart ache. "Haven't you ever loved *anyone?*"

"Nope."

"Then how do you know you're not built for it? How can you know unless you take a step out of your comfort zone and let yourself feel—"

"I'm not gonna do that. And do you want to know why? Because you wouldn't want me to."

"Can't you let me be the judge of—"

"Tyler." He froze, and I squeezed his shoulder once more. "I wouldn't be good for you." I lifted his chin with my fingers and stared into glistening blue eyes.

That hurt more than I'd anticipated, and I forced myself to not let his tears get to me.

"Tyler, you're better off without me. If you're looking for love, look elsewhere."

"But Sir…" God, the pain in his eyes. "I… I love you," he croaked.

"No, you don't," I said in a firm voice. "You have this romantic idea of falling in love with your Dom. And don't deny it. I see the shit you read. All those BDSM romances? I don't *do* romance, all right? You knew that coming in. But hey, if that's what you're looking for, maybe one day it could happen." I looked him in the eye. "But not with me."

He said nothing for a minute, and then he stood. "Then I guess we're done." He sighed. "It was good while it lasted."

It had been better than that. He'd been so responsive, so willing to push his boundaries.

"Have there been others before me?"

I frowned. "Other subs?"

He wiped his eyes. "You know what I'm asking."

"Why do you think I have that rule?" Been there, done that, broken a few hearts…

"I see. Then I guess I'll take my stuff and go." It sounded as if the words strangled him.

I gestured to the cabinet I'd allocated him. "It's all in there." I waited as he opened it and removed his toys, his ball gag, the leather cuffs I'd given him when we first began doing scenes together…

So many memories. Good memories.

Except there was now a sour taste in my mouth.

He shoved them into the backpack he'd brought, then straightened. "Will I... Will I see you at the club?"

"I think that's likely, don't you?" I softened my voice. "I hope this isn't going to be awkward, okay? I'd really like an amicable split."

Hell, *I* hadn't done anything wrong, had I? *He* was the one who'd brought us to an abrupt, unsatisfying end.

"Well, seeing as I'm no longer your sub..." He raised his chin and squared his shoulders. "I think it's gonna be awkward as fuck, but there isn't a lot I can do about that, is there?"

I flinched. "Don't be bitter. You knew my rule going in."

"I did," he admitted. "I just didn't expect to fall in love with you."

I wanted to tell him it wasn't love, but infatuation. He was so freaking young, barely legal when we'd first gotten together, but so keen...I'd been cautious about taking on someone so inexperienced, but he'd persisted, and persisted, and little by little he wore me down.

I should've gone with my first instincts. I should've told him to find himself another Dom.

Only, I hadn't. I'd said yes, and God, it had been so freaking *good*.

I wanted to hug him, to tell him there would be other Doms, maybe even a Dom who would love him the way he needed to be loved.

I couldn't move.

"I guess I'll be going." Tyler slung the bag over his shoulder and walked—no, *trudged*—toward the front door.

I followed him. "One day, you'll come to me, and you'll have a glow about you no one can miss. And you'll tell me you're happy, that you're in love. And on that day, I will be overjoyed for you." I studied him. "But looking at you now, I don't see a glow. And do you know why? Because I don't think you're really in love with me."

He locked gazes with me. "For the record? You don't see a glow because you just put the fire out." And with that, he walked out of the apartment, closing the door behind him.

Goddammit.

My chest felt tight, my limbs heavy.

It had been going so well.

I had to get out of there. And the mood I was in, there was only one place to go.

I went into my bedroom and opened the closet where I stored my leather.

I needed a scene to take me out of myself.

To take away the taste Tyler had left in my mouth.

To assuage the guilt that shouldn't be torturing me, because *it wasn't my fault, okay?*

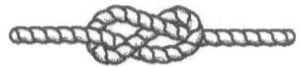

I walked through the door of the club, and several pairs of eyes focused on me.

Oh shit, news sure travels fast.

I headed for the bar, the comments bouncing off me as I ran the gauntlet.

"Aw crap. I really thought you two would make it."

"We even thought there'd be wedding bells."

Really?

"I was hoping you'd collar him."

Yeah, I was sure Tyler had hoped the same thing.

"Can I have Tyler's number?"

I fought the urge to smack Will in the mouth for that. Insensitive jerk.

But it was Sean's comment that cut me to the quick. He gazed at me with narrowed eyes as I sat on the bar stool next to his. "You're a bastard, you know that?"

"Just because you're my business partner, that doesn't give you the right to talk to me like that." I thought we were friends, for God's sake. I glared at him. "*Why* am I? For being honest? Would you prefer it if I strung him along? Toyed with him? The situation wasn't going to change."

"How do you know?"

I kept up that glare. "Because I know myself."

I ordered a lime and tonic water, shutting out the barrage of questions.

This was a bad idea.

It wasn't long before I saw the first one, a twink in a jock and a harness, slinking toward me like a shark circling chum, spotting its next victim.

He dropped to his knees, hands behind his back. "Sir? Can we play?"

That had taken about a New York minute.

He was fresh, eager, pretty… and I wasn't interested.

"I'm not in the mood."

Of course, it didn't stop there, and by the time the second and third sub had made their move, I'd gotten the message.

They saw an opening. A challenge. The chance to get their asses in my sling, and my collar around their necks.

I grabbed my jacket. "I'm outta here."

"But you only just—"

"Later," I hollered as I made a dash for the door.

Much later. Like maybe a month or two. By then something new and shiny would grab their attention, and my break-up with Tyler would be ancient history. And it wasn't as if Sean couldn't run the place without me, right? Hell, that was why we'd gone into business together—this was what he did. I messaged him from the metro, just to let him know not to expect me for a while.

He'd be okay with that. He usually joked that I only got under his feet anyway.

I was still on edge, however, by the time I got home. I had to do something to get my mind off the situation. I flopped onto the couch and grabbed the remote.

A Hallmark movie was someone's idea of rubbing my face in it, and I scrolled away. I flicked onto Paramount. I was halfway through season two of *Yellowstone*. Someone at the club had recommended it, and

I've been hooked from the start. The huge Montana skies, the horses, the blue mountains capped with snow, the rolling green plains…

All of it took me back to my granddad's place in Wyoming when I was a kid. I could still hear his voice.

'The best thing for the inside of any man is the outside of a horse.'

How long had it been since I'd ridden? Long enough that I'd almost forgotten.

When the idea first came to me, I dismissed it. But the more I thought about it, the more I realized I needed a break. It was going to be awful at the club for a while anyhow.

I sat at my table, opened my laptop, and typed three words into the search engine.

Dude ranches Montana.

I've been hooked from the start. The huge Montana skies, the horses, the blue mountains capped with snow, the rolling green plains…

All of it took me back to my granddad's place in Wyoming when I was a kid. I could still hear his voice.

'The best thing for the inside of any man is the outside of a horse.'

How long had it been since I'd ridden? Long enough that I'd almost forgotten.

When the idea first came to me, I dismissed it. But the more I thought about it, the more I realized I needed a break. It was going to be awful at the club for a while anyhow.

I sat at my table, opened my laptop, and typed three words into the search engine.

Dude ranches Montana.

K.C. WELLS

CHAPTER TWO

Saturday, June 11
Robert

Rusty slowed as we neared the creek. "You know where we're going, don't you, boy?" I murmured, leaning forward to stroke his neck.

Of course he did. We'd traveled the same route every morning for the past four years.

The year before that, I couldn't even get within sight of the place. I hadn't crossed the cabin's threshold since 2017. Thank God Dad had passed two years before that. He wouldn't have stood for such behavior.

We came to a halt at the edge of the creek, and I closed my eyes, letting the soothing sound of water trickling over rocks flow over and through me. Except it didn't stay soothing for long. All too soon the memories crept into my mind.

The sight of Kevin, lying face down in the creek.

Lightning standing there, head bowed, as if he'd known his master was dead.

Kevin's body moving gently, buffeted by the water but unable to break free of the rushes surrounding him.

Too many goddamn memories. Closing my eyes did *not* shut them out.

My fault. It was my fault.

Not the first time I'd said those words to myself, and I was pretty sure they wouldn't be the last.

I opened my eyes, and stared across at the log cabin, the stones leading from the front steps, set into a path that meandered to the water's edge where boulders had been placed across the creek.

How many times had I crossed there? I'd lost count since that first time in 2005.

Our place.

Our hiding place.

Sometimes I was convinced that if I walked through that front door, I'd find him there, waiting for me with that lopsided grin, buck naked, standing next to the sling, a bottle of lube at his feet, along with a tub of something suited to the task of putting more than his cock inside me—

Said cock pointing to the ceiling, hard as fuck.

Don't go there.

The two Adirondack chairs still sat on the front porch, a more domesticated sight than what lay beyond the front door. The weather hadn't been kind to them, however: they were in pretty bad shape.

So was I, but on the inside.

No one was allowed inside the cabin. *No one.* And while the ranch hands could be stubborn and awkward as fuck sometimes, they knew better than to cross me.

At least, I hoped that was the case. Because if they snuck a peek at the cabin's interior, they'd see their boss in a whole new light, and I didn't think I could handle that.

I gazed across the creek at the dilapidated porch. *I could sit there for a while.* I had nowhere else to be, right? I grabbed the pommel, ready to dismount…

And then the assault came from out of nowhere.

The memories were more forceful than ever.

'First one to reach the chairs gets his dick sucked.' Kevin's raucous laughter. The sound of his belt buckle hitting the deck. His hands on my head, holding me there while he opened my throat with his cock.

The fact that he wasn't there anymore? *My fault.*

My heart quaked. *I can't do this.*

"Boss?"

I twisted in my saddle to see Zeeb trotting toward me on Thunder. I didn't ask how he'd known where I'd be. The guy wasn't an idiot. Everyone on the goddamn ranch probably knew. And if I believed anything different, I was fooling myself.

I didn't hire idiots. Neither did Teague.

I straightened in my saddle. "What's up?" I acted as if I was just out for my usual morning ride, that it was mere coincidence I'd happened upon the cabin.

Yeah, I was fooling no one.

"The new guests are coming in today."

"I know." I left the day-to-day running of the ranch to Teague, but that didn't mean I didn't know what was happening on it.

"Teague is waiting for you at the big house. Says he wants to go over the new bookings for the rest of the summer. There have been a few cancellations." Zeeb glanced at the cabin, and his face contorted. "Aw, boss… why do you do this to yourself?"

What the everlovin' fuck? "Excuse me?"

Zeeb blinked. "You think we didn't know? A dude would have to be blind not to know."

And there it was, confirmation of my suspicions.

They all know. Because if Zeeb does…

And yet they'd stayed. Not one wrangler had marched off in a torrent of religious fervor. No one had denounced me as perverted, deviant…

Why would they? We're a family.

We were surely that. The ranch hands had different ages, different backgrounds, yet they'd all ended up at Salvation, drawn there, seeking sanctuary, escaping their pasts, ready to leave all that behind them.

And now I thought about it, how likely was it that *any* of them would take exception to my sexuality, given the mix of men who worked on the ranch? There were probably only two straight guys among them—and I wasn't even sure about them.

An awful thought crept into my mind. *A dude would have to be blind not to know* what, *exactly?* That their boss was gay? I could cope with that—maybe.

But as for the rest?

"You telling me you were all okay with… with what was going on?" I needed to hear the words.

"Sure we were. It was your business, not ours."

"And is that why no one said a goddamn word?"

Zeeb's gaze held more compassion than I'd ever seen there. "No, we kept quiet about it out of respect."

I stared at the cabin. "I don't know why I keep coming back here."

"I do. Well, I know why you're here today of all days." I turned to peer at him, and Zeeb swallowed. "None of us can forget that day. And maybe another part of it is you're looking for something you haven't found yet."

I raised my eyebrows. "Oh yeah? And what's that?"

His gaze didn't waver. "Closure."

My chest grew tight. "When did you know? About me and Kevin, I mean." My voice sounded husky to my way of thinking. When Zeeb didn't respond, I rolled my eyes. "Oh, for Pete's sake. You've said this much. Don't get bashful on me now."

He cleared his throat. "I've worked on this ranch for ten years." He paused. "I think I'd been here about two days when I cottoned on."

Were we that obvious?

Zeeb coughed. "Not that it was difficult to spot you two in the barn late one night. You're not quiet when you're getting fucked, are you?" I stared at him, and Zeeb stared right back. "Hey, you were the one who told me not to get bashful. Just doin' what I'm told."

I wanted to tell him he had a goddamn *nerve*, talking to me like that, and then I decided against it. If Zeeb felt comfortable enough around me to speak his mind like that, without pulling any punches, to my mind that was no bad thing.

"Family is where you should always tell the truth," Dad used to say.

"So… you were okay with it? Me and Kevin, I mean?" I wasn't about to ask the burning question. *How* much *did you know about us?*

Zeeb smiled. "You just asked me that, remember? Love is love, right? Ain't that what they say? And who you love is no one's business but yours."

And I *had* loved him.

The only thing was, I hadn't worked that out until he was already dead.

I struggled to drag my attention back to the conversation.

"I had to ask. Not everyone thinks like you, you know." But that wasn't true. I'd had an inkling more of my workers thought like Zeeb.

He waved his hand. "I ain't got no problem with it. Each to his own." His eyes twinkled. "And seeing as we're being so honest… I can't say the thought hasn't crossed *my* mind once or twice."

I stilled. *The thought of what?* If the guys knew I was gay, well, I could live with that. But as for them knowing about my… proclivities?

That was something I wanted to keep under wraps.

"You see it all over the place nowadays, right?" Zeeb continued.

"See what?" I mentally crossed my fingers. *Please, God, let me keep some secrets, all right?*

"Guys having sex with guys. What do they call it, a bromance?"

I forced a smile. "Not sure a bromance automatically means sex. But yeah, it *is* out there a helluva lot more than it used to be." My heartbeat slid down a notch or two. Then his words sank in. "Wait—you've thought about having sex with *guys?*"

"Why not?" he said with a shrug. Then he grinned. "Maybe I wanna see what all the fuss is about."

I blinked. "You know, I'm not sure if you were actually being serious, or just trying to be supportive—in a weird-assed kinda way."

"You take it whichever way you want." His gaze met mine. "But boss, I gotta say…You can't keep doing this."

"Doing what, exactly?"

"Coming here every day. It's… it's not good for ya."

I bristled. "You were right. It's no one's business but mine."

He held up his hands. "Hey, I'm only telling you what you already know deep down, so don't go shooting the messenger. It's been *five years*, boss. You have to move on. You can't keep… torturing yourself."

Yes, I do, for reasons you know nothing about.

Only, I couldn't keep a lid on my guilt. Not on this day. "But it was my fault."

Zeeb glared at me. "No, it wasn't. *You* didn't put him on that horse. And you sure as shit didn't pour that whiskey down his throat before he did."

"Maybe so." *But I was the reason he was drinking whiskey in the first place.*

Except that was only partly true. He'd been drinking before our argument. After it, he just drank more.

Zeeb fell silent for a moment. "You know what? You're right. It's none of my business. This is between you and your conscience. But I *will* tell you this for free." He leaned forward, his hands resting on the pommel. "You know what you need to do?"

"Burn this cabin to the fucking ground?"

He scowled. "I wouldn't do that if I were you. You've got a lotta stuff you have to work through first before you get to that point. But… maybe you should consider going into Bozeman. To Lacey's."

I widened my eyes. "You think I'm gonna cure all my problems in a *bar*?" I hadn't touched a drop of alcohol since Kevin died.

"Wasn't thinking about drinkin'. There's a band playing tonight. Not that any of *us*'ll be there, for obvious reasons."

I coughed. "Yeah, let's not get into that."

"But lots of people *are* gonna be there. Strangers. Maybe there'll even be a guy who catches your eye."

The light dawned.

"Oh, *now* I get it. You telling me all I need is to get laid?"

Zeeb's eyes sparkled. "A little fuckin' is good for a lot of what ails ya. Think about it. Especially since I'd be willing to guess you haven't... *you* know... since..."

I laughed my ass off. "You are such a paradox."

Zeeb grinned. "And there you go, using big words again."

"You're okay telling me a little fucking will cure my ills, and even going so far as to tell me you heard Kevin fucking me, but you can't bring yourself to say I haven't gotten fucked since he died?"

He'd nailed it, of course. I was expecting a letter any day now, demanding the return of my gay card.

Zeeb grinned at me. "Gotta say, boss. Sure was a whole lotta fuckin' going on in that last sentence. *Reader's Digest* has this page about improving your word power. Want me to lend you a copy?"

I merely raised my eyebrows.

"Besides, it wasn't so much the fuckin' part, more about not wanting to bring up—"

I held my hand up. "It's okay. I get it." I grabbed the reins. "I'm going back to the house. Be sure to get the new guests ready to rock and roll tomorrow. This isn't Diana's place. They're here to work."

Zeeb tipped his hat. "Yes, boss." He turned Thunder around and headed back toward the ranch.

I gazed across the creek at the cabin.

Zeeb said I had to move on. Of course, he didn't have a clue what he was talking about, because he didn't know the truth—no one did—but all the same, that hair shirt I'd been wearing for five years was starting to itch. If I let it abrade my skin any longer, I was in real danger of turning into a whining bitch—in my head, at least.

And that just wasn't me.

I stared at the chairs where we'd sat—and done a few other

things too, my heart pounding like a bass drum for fear someone would come along, which was why Kevin had made me do it in the first place, the bastard.

I nudged Rusty's flanks. "Let's go home, boy." We headed back to the ranch.

Enough is enough.

CHAPTER THREE

Toby
Saturday, June 11

I got off the shuttle bus, put my suitcase on the sidewalk, and scanned my surroundings. It had dropped me off outside the Baxter Hotel, as indicated in the email confirmation of my stay. I hoped there'd be food when I got to the Salvation ranch, because it was already getting close to six-thirty and I was starving. The more than three-hour layover in Salt Lake City had made me regret flying Delta—I could've flown nonstop with United, but I had points, so what was I going to do?

I chuckled to myself. *You're just stingy. You could afford to fly first class if you wanted to.*

My dad didn't raise fools. Just because I had money didn't mean I was going to throw it away.

I gazed at the green parasols of the café that was part of the hotel. Main Street in Bozeman was pretty quiet for a Saturday night.

Too quiet. All of a sudden, San Francisco seemed a long way away.

Then I reasoned I wasn't there to have a good time. I doubted I'd have the opportunity to sample the nightlife anyhow. I knew what lay at the root of my anxiety.

I'm not sure if this is a good idea.

It had seemed the perfect solution, back in my apartment. A break from it all, getting back to nature, hard work—

And horses. Couldn't forget that part, right?

That first view online, Salvation had ticked all my boxes. It was a working ranch, with the prospect of a cattle drive to move the herd to summer pastures. The email had said there would only be two other guests apart from myself. From the photos, the ranch seemed kinda rustic, but I was okay with that.

I wasn't going there to live in the lap of luxury—I wanted to drive Tyler from my mind.

Two weeks since the break-up, and it still hurt, goddammit. I *needed* this trip.

I pulled out my phone to recheck the pickup time. They'd said a truck would take me to the ranch. Then I noticed two guys standing in front of the hotel, both with luggage, both checking their phones. They appeared to be in their late forties, although one had a lot more gray going on than the other.

I wonder…

I picked up my bag and strolled over to them. "Excuse me, but are you going to Salvation?"

The older-looking guy extended a hand, and I shook it. "Declan McCarrick. And yes, we're headed there." His hands were smooth, he had a manicure, and he was an immaculate dresser.

I had no room to talk. My clothes weren't exactly Nordstrom. But this guy seemed to belong behind a desk, not riding a horse.

Maybe my incredulity showed in my face, because he smiled. "Son, I've been doing this every summer for the past six years. Driving cattle might be a long way from Wall Street, but it sure drives the cobwebs away."

"Good, because that's exactly what I'm hoping for." I had one big cobweb to clear from my mind, in the shape of an early-twenties pretty guy who went by the name of Tyler.

The other guy held out his hand and we shook. My first impression was that he seemed unsettled, maybe even a little nervous. "I'm Garrett Evans. This is my first time." His brow furrowed. "I'm not sure about this, I have to say. I'm only here because I'm following advice."

It was on the tip of my tongue. *Your therapist's advice, right?* He had the appearance of someone badly in need of breaking the cycle. Lord knew I'd seen enough of those kinds of guys turning up at the club.

I didn't push. It was none of my business.

I gave them a friendly smile. "The name's Toby Merrow. I've never done anything like this either." Except that wasn't true.

Hey, that was a long time ago. I'd been nothing but a kid.

A black truck pulled up, with the word *Salvation* painted on the door in yellow. When it opened, the biggest cowboy I had ever seen got out.

How did he fit behind the wheel?

He was maybe in his fifties, tall, and just as wide, clad in jeans and a plaid shirt, and boots that looked as if they could stomp the shit out of anyone if he chose to do so. A wide-brimmed brown hat was perched on his head, with leather stitching around the edges. His beard was several different shades of gray, but man, those eyes…

And we were being studied.

He peered at us for a moment, then lines wrinkled around his eyes. "You folks for Salvation?" he said, addressing Garrett and myself. When we nodded, he leaned in through the truck window and grabbed his phone. He scrolled, then peered at the screen. "Garrett Evans, Toby Merrow?"

"That's us." I was about to introduce Declan, when the cowboy grinned and thumped him on the arm.

"I knew *you'd* be here. You're nothing but a bad penny." He gestured toward the truck. "Throw your luggage in the back."

We did as instructed and got into the truck. Declan headed for the front seat.

Our driver got behind the wheel and twisted around to greet us with that same grin. "I'm Butch Buchanan. You'll be seeing a lot of me." He turned to Declan and clapped him on the shoulder. "Hey, Dec, how's it hangin'? Good to see ya. How's the big city treating you?"

"Still hanging on in there. You should come visit. I'd show you the sights."

Butch laughed. "No, thank you. I'm not a city boy." He

twisted once more to glance at me. "But *you* sure got the look of one."

"San Francisco," I replied, keeping my tone polite. "Didn't know it showed."

Like hell I didn't. Designer jeans, Gucci shirt… I might not waste money on flights, but I saw nothing wrong in dressing well.

Then it hit me. It was my choice of footwear. I guess nothing screamed outsider like a pair of brand-new fancy cowboy boots.

And maybe I should've chosen a more toned-down outfit.

Butch started the engine and pulled away from the curb. "So, you boys ready for some hard work?"

"I've been thinking about this for months," Declan confessed. "And now I'm here, I know the next two weeks are going to fly by so fast."

Butch stared at me in the rear-view mirror. "Hey, San Francisco? Can you ride a horse?"

"The name's Toby, and it's been a while, but yeah, I can." *Is he really as red-necked and blunt as he comes across, or is it an act?*

I couldn't tell. Then I recalled the questionnaire I'd had to fill in, where they'd wanted to know my experience level.

You already know all this.

That told me one thing about Mr. Butch Buchanan—he was being a dick.

Maybe it's a test. Maybe he does this with all the guests.

I still didn't like it.

"I've never done that." Garrett sounded scared to death.

What's he doing here if he's too scared to get on a horse?

Whoever he was in therapy with had done him no favors, suggesting a dude ranch. Well, maybe not a ranch like Salvation. There'd been another not that far out of Bozeman that might have been more suitable. Luxury accommodation, all kinds of activities, a five-star chef…

"Have you got maybe… a beginner's horse? Something slow and steady?"

"Dude, they don't come with training wheels, all right?" Butch said with a chuckle. "Slow and steady wouldn't be much use around here, not when you're riding hard into the bushes to drive the steers out. But don't worry. We'll be gentle with you."

I thought he was teasing Garrett, but then I realized he'd spoken with absolute sincerity, and with far less attitude than he'd shown toward me. *He recognizes Garrett is a little on the fragile side.*

Okay, maybe he was less of a dick than I'd thought.

"Are you in charge?"

That earned me another derisive snort. "Hell no. I'm the one who gets to babysit you guys until you know how the land lies. I'm in charge of the bunkhouse, which is where you'll be sleeping." His eyes met mine again in the mirror. "I hope you ladies weren't expecting any fancy five-star hotel accommodation."

And just like that, he was starting to piss me off again, until I realized this was still part of his test.

Well, I wasn't in the mood to play.

I locked gazes with him. "Your boss know how you talk to his clients?"

He flushed, and I knew I'd hit a nerve. "Sorry. My mouth kinda runs away with me. But that's how we roll on the ranch."

"I can assure you, I don't need a babysitter." His contrite tone softened my ire. "And you calling me a lady is not about to make me clutch my pearls, all right?" I grinned to show him there were no hard feelings.

He chuckled. "You're okay, Toby." And just like that, the air was cleared.

I guess I passed the test.

Declan hooted. "You do this every year, Butch. It's obvious from the website Salvation is a working ranch."

Butch shrugged. "I gotta make sure they read the fine print, don't I?"

"Who owns the ranch?" I asked. I must have read it someplace, but I'd forgotten.

"Robert Thorston. His dad owned it before him, and his granddad before that. Now, his dad? *He* was a tough old bird." Butch cackled.

That implied the present boss wasn't, but I said nothing. I'd find out soon enough.

"I didn't know you'd been there that long," Declan said.

Butch laughed. "I've been around since before they built the bunkhouse. Hell, when I first got there, Diana hadn't gotten married yet."

"Diana? Are there women on the ranch too?" Not that I minded.

"*Dude Ranch* might be kinda misleading. Dude's a neutral term around here, and yeah, we do get female guests." Butch grinned in the mirror. "Some of 'em have more balls than some of the guys. But Diana is the boss's sister. She don't live there—she's married to Newt Webster, and they run a dude ranch too. Maybe you saw her place when you were Googling this one. Now that *is* one swanky place."

"How long have you worked on the ranch?" Garrett asked.

"Old Mr. Thorston gave me a job in 1989. I was nineteen. Diana was sweet sixteen."

Declan chuckled. "You old dog. Had a thing for the boss's daughter, did you? I never heard about that."

Butch shook his head. "You've got it the wrong way round. She had a thing for *me*. When her dad got wind of it, you'd better believe he dragged her under Newt Webster's nose quicker than you can say wedding bells."

I arched my eyebrows. "So the boss didn't want his daughter getting involved with a ranch hand?"

Butch's gaze met mine once more in the rear-view mirror. "He knew what he was doing. He knew what I was." Then he focused on the road ahead.

Now *there* was a cryptic statement.

We lapsed into silence for the remaining ten minutes, and I

gazed through the window at the rolling landscape surrounding us. One minute we'd been in civilization—or Bozeman, at least—and the next, we were out in the middle of nowhere.

Except nowhere came with fences, sturdy barriers constructed out of hefty-looking logs, enough to stop cattle from straying where they shouldn't, I guessed.

When we reached a gap in the fence, Butch turned into a long, straight gravel driveway. At the end of it were two posts, and balanced on them over our heads was a hefty log with the word *Salvation* burned into it. Ahead of us were three white barns, trimmed with green. In the middle of them was a sand-covered paddock where a horse was running in circles, tossing its mane.

"Oh, would you look at that." It was a beautiful palomino, its coat a glossy light brown, with four white socks. Then I noticed the man standing in there with the horse. He wore his long black hair loose, and he exuded an air of calm.

"Who's that?" Garrett asked.

"Paul Stormcloud. Best goddamn horse whisperer I've ever seen. He's also our wrangler." Butch pointed to the nearest barn. "That's where you'll sleep, eat, piss, shower…"

I glanced up at the hill to the left of us. At its summit was a house, a truly grand version of a log cabin. A porch ran along the two sides I could see, and it had two stories. A stone-covered chimney rose into the air.

"Who lives there? Is that the boss's place?" It had to be.

"Yeah. And don't expect to see much of him. He may own the place, but he leaves the running of it to Teague McKay. He's the foreman. I'll introduce you." He stopped alongside the bunkhouse. "End of the line. Grab your stuff and follow me."

I got out of the truck and went around to get my bag. I couldn't help looking once more at the majestic horse. Such a magnificent specimen.

The guy stroking it wasn't half bad either.

Maybe this will be better than I expected.

I scanned my surroundings. "I don't see any cattle."

Butch chuckled. "That's 'cause the herd is in the north pasture. We'll be moving them to the south pasture the week after next, and it'll take us a couple of days."

"How far is the pasture?" Garrett asked.

"About thirty miles. Not that far."

He gaped. "It takes that long to move them?"

Butch laughed. "Dude, we're talking over a thousand head of cattle. They don't move fast. And once they're on the trail, they might stretch out one or two miles. As it is, we move 'em in two groups. Some of you will set out Monday morning, with seven or eight guys, and the second group leaves the next day. Once the herd reaches the south pasture, you'll get one day to relax at the camp before it's time to head back. The horses will need to rest too."

"How many horses does the ranch have?"

Butch rolled his eyes. "Can we save the questions for later? Because I don't know about you guys, but I'm starving."

Now that he mentioned it...

"I'm pretty hungry too." Not only that, I wanted to get a glimpse of more cowboys. If they were anything like Paul—and into guys—maybe the next two weeks wouldn't be the sexual desert I'd anticipated.

Chapter Four

Toby

The bunkhouse was bigger than I'd expected, comprising three sections. The front part was where the hands watched TV, and ate around a huge table. Every wall was covered in pine cabinets, and there wasn't an uncluttered surface to be found—there were hats, spurs, gloves, even boots… An enormous fridge took up a lot of wall space.

The bunks were in the next section, which pretty much merged with the front part. There were ten bunk beds, four against the outer walls and two at the rear, of which six or seven bunks were in use. Butch told us to grab anything that was going.

"Except that one," Paul said, pointing to a lower bunk on the right as he strolled toward the bathroom. I guessed he was done for the day. I gave him a quizzical glance, and he grinned. "Butch's bunk. Don't touch his stuff. He doesn't like it."

"Quit trying to make me sound like an asshole," Butch groused.

"He doesn't have to try too hard." One of the ranch hands hooted, and Butch gave him the finger.

I dumped my bag onto a lower bunk, then took in my surroundings. It was as if I'd wandered onto the set of *Yellowstone*.

Hey, at least I was prepared.

At the rear of the bunkhouse was the door to the restroom. There were two showers that were nothing more than tiled trays with dark blue curtains across, hanging from plastic hooks. Three sinks lined one wall, and above each was a shelf, loaded with toothbrushes, toothpaste, shaving foam, razors, and combs.

"Do we have time to unpack?" I asked Paul on his way back

from the bathroom.

"Not really. That can wait till after supper." Paul smiled. "This lot are like a pack of wolves when they get hungry, and right now they're ready to chow down." He pointed to a chest of drawers next to the bunk I'd chosen. "You can put your stuff in there." He lowered his gaze to my feet, and coughed. "Nice... boots. They look perfect—for a square dance." He cocked his head to one side. "They the only ones you brought with you?" When I nodded, he patted my arm. "Just be ready to clean 'em every night. Because they are going to get covered in shit—literally."

"Grub's up!" Butch hollered. The door to the bunkhouse opened, and a guy came in, maybe my age. His boot heels clicked on the wooden floor. He carried an insulated bag that he set down on the table.

"It's stew tonight, boys. And there's cornbread too. I'll be back later." His gaze met mine briefly. "Welcome to Salvation." Then he walked out.

I gazed after him. *Well, hel-lo.* I loved a scruffy beard on a guy, and his was dark, matched by his piercing blue, sexy-as-fuck eyes. Muscled thighs too, that stretched the denim so it clung to them. I could *so* imagine them wrapped around me. I hadn't gotten a good glimpse at his package, but what I'd seen thus far was already floating my boat.

Things were *definitely* looking up.

Whoa there, cowboy. Who's to say he's even into guys?

I grinned to myself. I could dream, couldn't I?

"He's not going to eat with us?" I strove not to let my disappointment show.

"That's Matt," Butch told me as he took a seat at the table. "He does the cooking around here." He opened the bag, and the delicious aroma of cornbread filled the air.

If it tasted as good as it smelled, Matt was obviously a treasure.

A hot as fuck treasure.

Then a thought occurred to me. I stared at him. "You have a

cook just for the ranch hands?"

Paul laughed as he returned to the table. "Matt cooks for everyone, including the boss."

Damn, he sounded good when he laughed, deep, and musical.

I could tell the eye candy around the place was going to prove *all* kinds of distracting.

The guy who'd spoken a moment ago snorted. "And *someone* needs to make sure that man eats."

I extended a hand to him. "Toby Merrow. And you are...?"

He grinned as we shook. "Zeeb Nolan. Welcome. And this is Paul Stormcloud." He sniffed. "Damn, that smells good." His eyes gleamed. "What are the rest of you fellas eating?"

Butch gave him a mock glare. He removed large plastic boxes from the bag and popped the lids. Steam rose from them. Paul grabbed large bowls from one of the cabinets, and Zeeb thrust a ladle into Butch's outstretched hand.

"So, what did you think of Bozeman?" Butch asked as he filled the bowls and passed them around.

"I didn't see enough of it to be able to pass a comment. I guess it's a big enough place that you can get anything you need there." The food smelled amazing. "Does Matt drag all the food down here from the house every time you eat? He must be a regular mountain goat."

Butch pointed to a door. "That leads to the kitchen. Runs the length of the bunkhouse. Matt usually cooks for us in there, then goes on up to the house."

"He also shops for groceries and takes care of the house," Zeeb added, helping himself to a hunk of cornbread.

Two more men came into the bunkhouse. One of them was again probably close to my age, but the other appeared younger.

Actually, he looked a lot like Tyler.

Butch pointed to them. "This here is Walt," he said, indicating the younger man. "He's the one who keeps all the fences as they should be so we don't lose any cattle." Butch grinned. "He's also the baby of the outfit."

Walt rolled his eyes. "I'm twenty-fuckin'-eight, Butch."

The resemblance to Tyler was uncanny: the beard that wasn't much more than five o'clock shadow, the dirty blond hair, blue eyes…

"And already a potty-mouthed bastard. You mind I don't wash it out with soap." Butch winked at me, and I recalled his remark about how things rolled at the ranch.

Yeah, I was going to fit in just fine.

"Wash your own out first, you red-necked fucker," Walt retorted.

I burst out laughing. "Are you always this snarky and foul-mouthed around new guests?"

The other guy stared at me, his lips twitching. "Well, that was fast."

"This here is Teague, our foreman." Butch grinned. "He eats with us lowly mortals, but he don't sleep with us."

Teague fired him a glance before addressing me and Garrett. "I have my own place beyond the big barn. Not much, just a little cabin."

Walt cackled. "Yeah, and you don't get to line up for a shower, or the sink, or to use the john…."

Teague smiled, and his face was transformed. The man was gorgeous. "Hey, you can have my place, provided you do all the work that comes with it."

Good Lord, is everyone *working on this ranch a fuckable specimen of manhood?*

"And to answer your question…" Teague pulled out a chair and sat. "We've been doing this for a while now. At first, we played nice, gave the guests a couple of days to settle in…"

"Didn't work," Butch said bluntly. "Okay, it did for some of 'em, but for others, when they got to see how we rolled, they didn't cope, and they left. So now?"

The light dawned. "Now you drop guests in at the deep end

right away, to see who sinks and who swims," I surmised.

Teague grinned. "You're smart. You'll do just fine."

"And to be honest? We've only lost a couple of guests in the last six years," Butch added. "So I guess we're pretty much what people expect to find on a ranch."

I laughed. "I take it you mean *lost* as in they left, not that you lost them someplace."

Butch rolled his eyes.

Teague surveyed the table. "I don't know about you guys, but I'm starving. Let's eat."

I had to admit, the food was great. There were huge chunks of beef in the stew, and *Lord*, they melted in the mouth. The cornbread was perfection.

"Tell me it's always this good," I demanded. "Tell me it's not gonna be grits and beans after this, that you're lulling us into a false sense of security."

Zeeb's eyes gleamed. "Holy fuck, another one who talks like the boss." He glanced at Declan. "Mind you, that's how *you* spoke when you first got here." His eyes twinkled. "You soon learned how us good ole boys talk."

"Maybe Toby'll pick it up just as fast," Teague murmured.

I was intrigued he knew my name.

"Do you go into Bozeman much?" I asked.

"Not as much as we'd like," Zeeb said with a rueful expression. "But that's because we got banned from Lacey's because *somebody* got drunk one night—naming no names, *Butch*—busted a pool cue over Vince Traynor's head and got all of us embroiled in a bar fight."

Butch chuckled. "'Embroiled'. You've been talking to the boss again. You *always* come out with these big words when you've been talking to the boss." Zeeb gave him the finger.

"What's he like? The boss, I mean."

"He's a good man," Teague declared.

Paul sighed. "He's a troubled soul."

"Enough of that," Zeeb flung out. He gazed at me. "He's fair. You can talk to him, for one thing. I've worked for bosses who had a broom shoved up their ass. *He* ain't got no airs and graces."

"That's true," Walt admitted.

Butch helped himself to more cornbread. "You just don't see that much of him."

Declan leaned back in his chair. "I think I've seen him… twice, maybe three times, in six years."

"Isn't that a little strange?" I'd thought a ranch owner would be more hands-on.

"Not really," Teague said. "He leaves me to run things how I like, and I report back to him."

"He must trust you a great deal," I observed. When Teague arched his eyebrows, I smiled. "You look like you're my age. That's a lot of responsibility for a guy in his thirties."

"I'm thirty-four. He's known me since I was sixteen. Made me foreman when I was twenty-nine."

Butch stared at me. "You think maybe an older guy should have Teague's job? Someone like me, for instance?"

I held my hands up. "I'm sorry. I didn't mean to offend anyone."

Butch indicated Teague. "He's younger than any of us, with the exception of Walt. He knows his shit and he don't take no shit either." He snorted. "Zeeb nailed it. I've worked for more than my fair share of assholes in my time. Teague and the boss? They're solid."

Teague gave him a look of obvious gratitude.

"Looks as if you've got a fan," I remarked. I turned to Butch. "You've been here a long time too. Since you were nineteen, I think you said."

Butch smiled. "You just take everything in, don't you?" He glanced at Paul. "He remind you of someone? *Nothing* got past *that* dude."

Paul cleared his throat, and I swore something drifted across his face.

Something that seemed a lot like sorrow.

Then it was gone, leaving me curious as fuck. "Got past who?"

"Don't matter," Teague muttered. "Ancient history." He glanced around the table. "Okay, I know Dec here can handle a horse. Tomorrow we'll find you guys a suitable mount."

"Garrett's gonna need Lucy to start with." Butch flashed Teague a glance.

Teague nodded. "Fair enough."

"I said on the application form I haven't ridden a horse since I was a kid. My granddad had a place in Wyoming. I used to spend my summers there." Heavenly days.

There was a gleam in Butch's eye. "Cattle ranch?"

I shook my head. "Horses. He'd break them, then sell them on."

Butch nodded. "Well, we'd better find you a reliable horse." He glanced at Teague before addressing Paul. "What about Lightning?"

Zeeb stilled. "Hey, no—"

"You hush. He's used to horses. He said so, didn't he?"

"Sure, when he was a kid. Lightning, though…"

I had the feeling I was being tested again.

Teague cleared his throat. "Let's leave this till the morning. Seeing as you'll be getting up at five."

Garrett blinked. "'Five'? That time comes round twice in one day?"

They laughed.

"Matt'll have a good breakfast for you, then we feed the horses. And after that the lessons can begin."

Garrett frowned. "We don't get a day to settle in?"

Zeeb chuckled. "Hell no. Gonna teach you how to rope a steer."

"Don't worry," Declan assured Garrett. "It's easier than it sounds. Besides, you won't be roping a *real* steer, just a metal one they yank along."

Butch snorted. "That's not what you said the first time *you* tried. *How* long did it take you to get the hang of it?"

Declan laughed. "Yeah, okay. I was pretty shit at it. But I got better." When Butch peered at the ceiling and whistled, Declan thumped him on the arm. "Hey! I did."

"Yeah, you did," Butch admitted. "Just yankin' your chain." He peered at Garrett. "And so is Zeeb, truth be told, because we won't get to steer roping on the first day. The first week is always training, where we teach you to care for the horses—feeding, grooming, the whole shebang—plus you'll ride a lot of trails, practice roping…"

"And then the second week, it'll be the cattle drive," Zeeb added. "Gotta make sure you're ready for that."

"I've been telling them about it," Butch commented. "How long it takes, stuff like that…"

"We usually camp out three nights before we head back." Teague smiled. "Most folks like the idea of sleeping under the stars. Then you get a little downtime before you leave."

"How long has there been a dude ranch here?"

"Since 2016. Declan was one of our first visitors. The boss's dad died the year before, and the boss's sister came up with the idea to bring in more income and keep the place going," Butch told me. He grinned. "Then she went and started her own dude ranch, but it's nothing like this place."

I recalled our conversation from the ride to the ranch. "Ah. Would that be the swanky one?"

"Yup. Real fancy."

His comments about Salvation's owner had me intrigued. "The boss's dad…Was he more hands-on than his son?"

Crickets.

Zeeb broke the awkward silence. "Yes, he was, but so was the boss—before."

"Before what?"

"Bed, I said." Teague's voice rang out.

Butch arched his eyebrows. "Someone put you in charge of the bunkhouse when I wasn't looking?"

Teague got up from the table. "Then I'll leave you to your job. Goodnight, gentlemen." He walked out of the bunkhouse.

"Goin' for a smoke." Butch followed him out the door.

Okay, that felt awkward as fuck.

Walt caught my puzzled glance. "Don't mind those two. They butt heads once in a while."

Zeeb cackled. "That ain't all they butt." Walt fired him a warning glance.

There seemed to be quite a few of those exchanged that evening.

"Do we have Wi-Fi here?" I hadn't checked my phone since I'd arrived in Bozeman.

"Sure." Paul pointed across the room. "Code's on the fridge."

"Excuse me." Garrett got to his feet. "Call of nature."

Walt waited until he'd left the room. "Okay, guys? You don't need to tell us if you need to take a leak, all right? We all piss in the same two pots, anyhow." He pointed to the rear of the bunkhouse. "I wasn't joking. That bathroom is pitiful small when you've got six or seven guys in there first thing in the morning."

I glanced at Declan. "Is Garrett okay?"

Declan sighed. "He just needs a break, that's all. He's been through a rough time." He smiled. "Don't you worry. This place is exactly what he needs. He'll be a new man by the end of his stay."

"Did you know him before this?" Because it sure sounded like it.

Declan shook his head. "We were on the same flight from New York. I guess I have the sort of face that invites conversation."

It must have been one hell of a conversation.

He stood. "If you'll excuse me, I'm going to go outside and stretch my legs before bed."

Then there was only me, Zeeb, Walt, and Paul.

Zeeb flopped onto the couch. "Now Teague's gone, I'm gonna find something to watch. He's not gonna tell *me* when to go to bed. Who does he think he is, my mom?" He picked up the remote.

"I'm gonna go check on the horses." Paul grabbed his jacket and headed out. Walt was on his phone, scrolling.

"Hey Zeeb." I went over to the couch. "Have we met all the hands?" Six men didn't seem like enough.

"There are a couple more, but they're out with the herd. Usually we have more guests. When we move the cattle, it normally takes eight to ten of us with each group, so we take on more hands, guys who've done this before."

I glanced at the bunk beds. "So where do they all sleep?"

He pointed toward the ceiling. "There's another floor. No bathroom up there, though, so this one gets awful busy sometimes."

Another floor made sense. The barn was huge.

I walked over to the fridge, found the network, and typed in the password. When I saw the Scruff icon on my screen, I couldn't resist. I clicked on it—then blinked when it told me I was only feet away from a couple of guys.

The first guy to pop onto my screen was Walt.

The second was Matt.

Walt chuckled. "Well well well." I looked up from my phone to find him grinning at me. "Ain't *you* full of surprises?" He scrolled. "Hot damn." His eyes glittered. "You ever get lonesome, there's a great spot I can take you to. Where a couple of guys can…" He lowered his voice. "Fuck each other's brains out and no one will see."

Holy fuck. He really did remind me of Tyler.

I coughed. "Fraternizing with the guests… is that allowed?"

"*I'm* not gonna tell anyone." He grinned. "Are you?"

"No, but I'll pass. Not that it isn't a tempting offer."

Walt chuckled. "Hey, no harm, no foul. Pity though. I'd have liked to get up close and personal with some of your… equipment."

He kept scrolling, and his eyes widened. "Jesus. You really are gonna fit right in around here." Before I could ask what he meant, Butch came back inside, and he clammed up.

"Come on, guys. Bed." He glared at Zeeb. "Because if I have to dig your ass outta bed in the morning, you'll be sorry."

Zeeb grumbled and switched off the TV. "Fine."

I pulled up my Scruff profile, curious to see what had brought about such a reaction. There were my usual torso shots, thinly disguised dick pics… and a lot of images of me in leather at the club.

Now I really was curious. *Who else around here is into similar… activities?*

As I shucked off my clothes, I went over some of the evening's conversation. There'd been more than a few cryptic remarks, and I had to admit, I was intrigued.

This could prove interesting.

I had no idea what time it was, but something had awoken me. Then I realized the room wasn't dark. I leaned out of my narrow bunk and scanned my surroundings, my eyes adjusting to the dim light that came from Butch's lower bunk.

It was a night light.

Then I realized I could hear sounds too. Butch was clearly in the throes of a bad dream. He tossed and turned, moaning. I was debating getting out of bed and walking over there to wake him up, when he sat upright with a speed that made me jump. I froze.

Butch put his feet on the worn rug, rubbing his head. Then he got up and padded toward the bathroom. I caught the splash of water in the sink. When he came out, he squirmed into jeans and boots, and grabbed his jacket and hat. With a stealth I couldn't help but admire, he crept out of the bunkhouse.

A smoke? At this hour?

"You saw nothing, okay?" Zeeb's whisper from above startled

me.

"What's with the night light?" I whispered back.

"I don't know, and I don't ask. *No one* mentions it, not since a former ranch hand teased Butch about it about nine years ago. He ended up in the hospital. All I know is, it helps Butch ward off whatever comes in his nightmares." He peered over the edge of the bed at me. "And he gets those a lot."

"Where's he gone?"

Zeeb shrugged. "Where he always goes when he wakes up from a bad dream. To Teague's cabin. Not that he needs an excuse, but yeah…"

I arched my eyebrows.

He rolled his eyes. "They fuck, all right? And you don't know that either." He narrowed his gaze. "And don't go reading more into it than that, okay? It's—what does the boss call it?—a symbiotic relationship. They both get what they want—what they need—and no questions asked."

The boss knows? That was one hell of an understanding, broadminded boss.

Zeeb glanced at me. "I hear you're from that side of the church yourself."

I bit back a smile. "News sure travels fast."

Zeeb snorted. "Around here? You bet your ass. Now get some sleep." He grinned. "You're gonna need it." Then he disappeared from view.

I lay down, my fingers laced under my head.

The springs above me squeaked, a noise that settled into a rhythm, and I knew exactly what Zeeb was doing.

You have got *to be kidding me.*

"Cut it out and go to sleep," I whispered.

"Hey, I'm going as fast as I can," he replied, a little breathless. "Wanna help me rub one out quicker?" I snorted, and he let out a rough chuckle. "Then shut the fuck up and leave me to my fantasy."

I couldn't resist. "Who're you fantasizing about?"

"Sometimes it's Scarlett Johansson, but tonight?" Another ragged chuckle. "It might be you."

Salvation was growing more interesting by the minute, and while I was conscious of having a helluva lot dumped on me the first day, I was determined.

Let them try their sink-or-swim routine.

This was one dude who was gonna swim.

CHAPTER FIVE

Robert

By the time I'd lain awake for a few hours, I realized it was a pointless exercise. I got up, pulled on my robe, and went downstairs to the kitchen in search of that tea Matt had bought for me once. He'd claimed it would help me sleep.

I was skeptical, so skeptical I'd never even tried it, but I was also desperate. I didn't function well on less than six hours' sleep, and lately I was lucky if I achieved that.

Outside, it was still dark, but I could see down the hill to where white lights illuminated the barns and the bunkhouse. I filled the kettle, and pretty soon its noise shattered the quiet, growing ever louder as it neared boiling. The box of chamomile tea had been shoved to the back of the cabinet, gathering dust.

Maybe it was about time I tried it.

As I dropped a tea bag into a cup, my phone buzzed on the table, and I peered at the screen. It was a text from Diana.

Hope you were okay today.

I should have ignored it. No good ever came of middle of the night conversations. It obviously wasn't urgent. It could wait until morning.

Except… I needed to talk. I laid the blame for that at Zeeb's door. He'd started this ball rolling.

I clicked on call. "What are you doing awake at this hour?"

"Haven't been to sleep yet."

I huffed. "That makes two of us." The kettle beeped, and I poured water over the tea bag.

"You in the kitchen?"

"Uh-huh. Making tea."

"Okay, where's my brother? What have you done with him?"

I read the instructions on the box as to how long I needed to leave it to steep. "What the hell are you talking about?"

"If you ever need a transfusion, they're gonna be in for a shock. What runs through your veins is pure coffee."

"Any particular variety?" I quipped.

"Yes, Colombian."

I decided the tea had steeped enough, and squeezed the bag against the side of the cup. "Okay, you've established we're both insomniacs. And by the way, I hope you're not in bed. I'll be on Newt's shit list if you wake him up talking to me. Why did you text?"

"Relax, I'm in the kitchen too. I was going to call you. Kept meaning to do it all day." She paused. "But I kept putting it off too."

I picked up my cup and wandered into the living room. I set it down on the coffee table, and switched on one of the lamps, flooding the dark room with warm light. "You call me every day. What makes today so different?"

"Because of what today is. Or *was*, given the time."

Of course she knew. "I see," I managed to squeeze out. "Not sure why you felt the need to call."

"Robert Thorston, just because you didn't come out and tell anyone officially, that didn't mean Kevin wasn't the closest thing to a brother-in-law I'm likely to have."

Oh shit. First Zeeb, now Diana.

I retreated into humor. "I didn't *come out?* I see what you did there." Except I couldn't joke with her. "It… It wasn't like that with us."

"Then why don't you tell me how it was? Lord knows, it's about time." Another pause. "If it helps, I'm not as oblivious as you might think. Because to my reckoning, you and he were getting it on for maybe… thirteen years?"

"'Getting it on'? You've been hanging out with those young things who work at your place. And for your information… fifteen years. You're not as observant as you think you are." I managed to sound relaxed when inside, I was anything but.

Maybe I'd nailed it earlier. Maybe everyone *did* know.

"Well shit. Looks like you were better at keeping secrets than I thought." She lapsed into silence for a moment. I was about to speak when she cleared her throat. "So... how *was* today?"

There was no getting away from it.

"I went for my usual morning ride, and ended up down by the creek—at the cabin."

"Oh Rob." Her voice cracked.

"You stop that, right this second, you hear? You are *not* gonna start crying." I could stand a lot of things, but my sister crying was not one of them.

There was a smothered gasp.

"Now, let me finish. Zeeb turned up and gave me shit. I mean, he was talking about me and Kevin, about how I needed to move on..."

"Tell me you didn't fire his ass." She sounded more in control of herself.

"I didn't."

"Wow. I'm impressed. And I gotta say, I have a newfound respect for that man. Good for him." Yeah, there was the Diana I knew and loved.

I'd clearly felt the same way. "Maybe him bringing it out into the open, talking about it... Maybe that was the catalyst. Maybe that's why *we're* talking now."

Why I hadn't hung up.

"Then I'm glad."

"But you wanna know what *really* burns me? Why say it now? How come no one said a goddamn word for *five years*?"

Diana coughed. "Speaking for myself? I felt guilty about that. I had my own ranch to run, my own life... And I figured you'd talk about it when you were ready. Except you never did. And here we are. I got tired of waiting, figured you to be healed by now. As for the rest of them? I can hazard a guess why they kept their mouths shut."

"Zeeb said it was out of respect."

"Possibly, and maybe because... You're the *boss*? They respect you, they like you, but maybe they're more than a little scared of you? Being honest, I knew you weren't ready to talk about it, and it killed me to see you suffering."

"But you still called." Part of me was relieved to have broached the subject at last.

"Maybe an alarm went off in my head. Maybe it said, *it's time*." Another pause. "So talk to me."

"Isn't that what we're doing—talking?" I knew I was being facetious.

I also knew Diana wasn't likely to let it go that easily.

"Hell no, we've barely touched the surface. Think of me as your therapist."

I laughed. "I had no idea you'd taken up a second career."

"Hey, don't mock. I've done a lot of reading around this."

"Oh really?"

"Personal stuff—and not something I want to talk about."

"Gotcha." It sounded as though Diana had troubles of her own.

"I think you're dealing with a lot of unresolved grief and regrets. Now, that's some powerful stuff right there. That takes a lot of time and effort to work through."

"Okay, thanks for the analysis. I'll send you your fee."

She ignored my attempt at humor. "Did you love Kevin? Did he love you?"

I went quiet for a moment. "This morning, Zeeb said who I loved was no one's business but mine. I didn't tell him the truth. That yeah, I loved Kevin, but I didn't know that until they laid him in the grave. And with every spadeful of earth they dropped onto his coffin, that realization weighed in on me, heavier... and heavier..."

Except what had weighed me down hadn't been love, but

guilt.

That hair shirt was going in the trash, first thing in the morning, swear to God.

I sighed. "So yeah, I loved him. And he loved me." That was true... kind of.

"And neither one of you came right out and said the words?"

There was nothing to say.

Her sigh echoed mine. "Lord, I hate the damn strong silent types. That means you were... thirty-two when you two got together?"

"Quaint way of putting it, but yeah, we snuck around for a while. Couldn't let Dad know, right?"

Silence.

"Diana?"

"You think he didn't?"

My heartbeat quickened. "Guess I've been fooling myself."

"Okay, he might have known about the sex," she conceded. "I don't think he cottoned onto the rest."

"Excuse me?"

No. No. No. My little sister—I didn't give a shit that she was forty-nine—was *not* talking about...

She coughed. "Okay, I might not have known about *everything* you two got up to, but I certainly recognized the... er... power dynamic in your relationship."

"'Power dynamic?'" I could almost hear the air quotes.

Yeah, she knew more than I'd expected—or had ever wanted her to.

"Robert." Her voice was soft. "It's okay. You don't need to go into details. I'm a woman of the world." With a note of pride, she added, "I've read *Fifty Shades*."

In that moment I was *so* grateful we were having this conversation over the phone instead of face-to-face.

"And no, I don't think Dad knew. Some people can be unaware of what's going on around them. I'm married to one of those. Others—like me and Zeeb—tend to notice too much. All Dad saw was the ranch."

"Maybe because that was all he wanted to see."

"I'm glad we finally talked," she said quietly. "I'm sorry I didn't get the opportunity to know Kevin better."

"You two would have really gotten along. You had the same sense of humor."

"You mean, twisted?"

I sighed. "Go back to bed, sis. Cuddle up to Newt and have some sweet dreams."

"Now we've got this out into the open—finally—I just might."

I said good night and hung up. I took a cautious sip of the tea and grimaced.

Hell no, Matt.

A little night air and a stroll would probably have more chance of sending me off to sleep. I went back upstairs, removed my robe, and got dressed. It wasn't until I was heading back downstairs that it hit me.

I felt a little better.

Maybe I am finally healing. I knew one thing for certain—Diana had nailed it with her talk of regrets.

I should have told Kevin how I felt. How much he meant to me.

Except I was kidding myself. He wasn't the love of my life, and what I regretted wasn't the stuff I *should* have said—it was all the stuff I did say.

If I'd just kept my mouth shut… If I hadn't have pushed…

I opened the front door and stood on the porch, breathing in the crisp, cold air.

What I *wanted* to do was yell into that expanse of night sky, to whichever dimension Kevin Porter was watching me from, and tell him "I'm done with the fucking guilt! You hear me, mister?"

Out of the corner of my eye, I spotted movement. I knew without looking it would be Butch leaving Teague's cabin. That was no surprise.

It was also none of my business.

Then I reconsidered. If whatever those two had going on went to shit, then it *would* be my business, especially if it affected the smooth running of the ranch.

Kevin might have coped well with fucking the boss *and* running Salvation, but he'd been a little older than Teague. The trouble was, most of the time I didn't see Teague as a responsible guy in his thirties—he was still the scared kid I'd found in the barn.

The memory was so sharp, it could have been yesterday.

Kevin and I had met up in the barn like we always did in the days before we made the cabin by the creek our own special hideaway. I'd texted our usual signal—*need you*. It was still dark, and we had maybe a couple hours before the hands would get up.

Funny thing was, I had no recollection of what had prompted the text. I only knew my need had been acute, and his response swift. We'd met, stripped, and he'd taken whatever it was that had troubled me, and made it melt away with a combination of ropes, fingers, tongue, and cock. When we were done, he kissed me, and told me what a good boy I was. Then he'd headed out to his cabin to get ready for the day, and to shower off any remnants of our encounter.

And then I learned we'd been observed...

2004

As I was leaving the barn, I heard movement. Whatever caused it was way bigger than a rat, that was for damn sure.

We've got an intruder.

"Who's there?" I picked up the rifle that stood against the barn door and cocked it. "Get your ass out here where I can see you."

"Please, don't shoot."

It was a young male voice—a scared voice—and I lowered the rifle. A scrawny kid walked out from behind the bales of hay. "I'm sorry. I only came in here for a warm place to sleep." In the dim light I saw he wore jeans, a T-shirt, and a dark jacket, sneakers on his feet.

"This isn't a hotel," I told him. Then a thought came to me. "How long have you been there?"

He coughed. "Long enough."

Okay, now I was pissed. It was bad enough that Kevin and I had to sneak around. The last thing we needed was someone spying on us. Someone I didn't know. I picked up the flashlight I'd brought and shone it in his face. My anger dissipated when I saw the bruises. "Holy crap, what happened to you?"

He swallowed. "How about…I got in a fight with a barn door?"

I arched my eyebrows. "Wanna try that again?"

Another sharp swallow. "I ran away from home, all right?"

"Someone at home do that to you?" When he didn't answer, I took a step closer. "I'm not gonna hurt you, okay? Now talk to me, kid. Who did this?"

Christ, his eyes… So much pain.

"My dad. I'm used to it. It… it happens every day."

"Your mom does nothing about it?"

He snorted. "Fuck no. She's too scared of him. She gets the same treatment." His chest heaved. "My dad always said I was too chicken-shit to run away." He squared his skinny shoulders and raised his chin to look me in the eye. "I guess he hit me one time too many."

He sounded like a smart kid. Brave little bastard too.

I put down the rifle. "You come with me."

His eyes widened. "Why? What are you gonna do with me?"

I cocked my head to one side. "How about I give you some breakfast? When did you last eat?"

His stomach chose that moment to erupt into a loud growl.

"Guess that answers *that* question. Okay, let's go."

He stared at me. "I don't know…"

I bit back a smile. "Well, you can either stay here and wake everyone up with that grumblin' belly of yours, or you can come with me up to the big house, and fill your face. We've got eggs, bacon, pancakes, biscuits…"

I figured the menu was what finally got to him. He nodded.

"You got anything with you?"

He scanned the ground, then picked up a backpack.

"Okay, follow me." I headed for the door, and as he stepped out of the barn, I stopped him. "What's your name?"

"Teague. Teague McKay."

I patted his shoulder. "I'm Robert Thorston. My dad owns this ranch." And he was probably awake by now.

"Thank you," Teague murmured.

"We'll talk more when you've got some food inside you."

He followed me up the long path to the house. As soon as I opened the back door, I heard Dad humming to himself in the kitchen. He never could wait for the cook to make him coffee.

We walked into the warm room. Dad stood in front of the coffee pot, his back to us. I cleared my throat, and he spun around. "Lord, you almost gave me a—" His eyes widened when he caught sight of Teague. "Christ on a cracker, what happened to you, boy?"

"You can ask questions later, Dad. Right now he's real hungry."

Dad caught on fast. He pointed to the coffee pot. "Grab yourself a cup."

"I don't drink coffee, sir."

Dad narrowed his gaze. "Then start. Coffee builds character."

I chuckled. "My dad says a lot of things build character, like eating sprouts."

Teague grimaced, and Dad laughed. He sat at the table, his gaze locked on Teague. "What's your name, son?"

"Teague, sir."

"And how old are you?" His brow furrowed. "Don't even think about lyin' to me."

Teague swallowed. "S-sixteen."

He frowned. "And are you bringing trouble to my door, Teague? Anyone gonna come looking for you?"

Teague shivered. "No, sir. He don't care. And he's too far from here for me to worry about."

Dad glanced at me. "Where'd you find him?"

"In the barn."

He arched his eyebrows. "And what were you doing in the barn at this hour?"

"I woke up, went outside for some air… and then I heard a noise, so I investigated."

Dad studied me for a moment, then pointed to the fridge. "Grab the bacon. There's biscuits in the freezer. I think Lou put some sausage gravy in there too."

Another loud growl filled the air, and Teague's cheeks were scarlet.

Dad chuckled. "I think you'd better hurry." He pointed to a chair. "Sit, son. Robert will sort you out."

Teague sat, his hands clasped on the table.

Dad leaned forward, his chin resting on his laced fingers. "So what are we gonna do with you, Teague? Do I send you home?"

He shivered. "No, sir. Please don't do that."

Dad flashed me a look, and I mouthed *Later*. He nodded. "Okay then. You can stay here. But you're gonna earn your keep."

Talk about a transformation. Teague's face lit up. "I will. I'll work night and day, I promise."

Dad cackled. "We don't work at night here, son, but the day starts awful early." He cocked his head. "Can you ride a horse?"

"Only the big old mean bastard my dad used on our farm."

"I'll take that as a yes." Dad glanced at me. "Find him a horse." I nodded. Then he addressed Teague. "He will be *your* responsibility, you hear? You feed him, clean him, exercise him—"

He nodded so vigorously, I felt sure his head was about to come off. "I understand. Thank you, sir."

Dad fired me another glance. "When he's eaten, take him to the bunkhouse. Butch'll find him a bunk." He pushed his chair back, and picked up his cup of coffee. He gave Teague a warm smile.

"Welcome to Salvation." Then he walked out of the kitchen.

Teague watched him go. "That's your dad?"

"Yup." I set the pan on the stove, then grabbed three eggs from the basket on the countertop. "Scrambled okay? Except it'll have to be, 'cause that's all I can do with 'em."

"Scrambled is good."

I cracked them and dropped them into a bowl, then whisked them with a fork.

"He doesn't know, does he?"

"Know what?"

There was a pause. "That you like guys." The words came out in barely a whisper.

I dropped the fork into the bowl with a clatter, and whirled around. "And what makes you think I like—Jesus, how much did you see?" My heart hammered. *And are you going to tell anyone?*

Except I wasn't thinking of *anyone.* I was thinking of Dad.

"Like I said, enough. Well... most of it." Teague regarded me with a thoughtful expression. "He doesn't know, does he?"

"No, he does not. And I'd prefer it if it stayed that way."

"Then I won't tell a soul."

I studied him. "You watched us fucking and you didn't make a sound. Why?"

Teague's Adam's apple bobbed. "I liked it."

I blinked. "Well, you're honest, I'll say that for you."

"But watching him tie you up like that..." He tilted his head. "Didn't he want you to get away? Because for a minute there, I thought he was, *you* know, rapin' you. But then you started making noises... and I knew."

"Knew what?"

He looked me in the eye. "You like it."

There seemed little point in lying to the kid, not after all he'd seen. "Yeah, I do." I peered through the window to where the bunkhouse sat. "You're gonna be sharing with a bunch of cowboys. It might not be such a good idea to let 'em know you like guys."

"It might make them nervous about having me in there with them?"

I snorted. "No, they'll just beat the crap out of you." I placed my hand on his shoulder. "They're not that bad. You'll be okay." I peered at him. "Does *your* dad know you're into guys?"

Teague said nothing but pointed to his face.

I sighed. "Guess I have my answer." I went back to my task.

"I won't tell a soul, I promise. I can keep a secret."

I might have only just met the kid, but I believed him.

2022 - the present

The wind picked up, and I shivered. *Maybe I should just go to bed.* I peered toward Teague's cabin.

Or maybe I should go talk to Teague.

CHAPTER SIX

Robert

I turned my collar up against the stiff breeze whistling around me, and walked along the path to Teague's cabin, my boots crunching on the gravel. It had been a while since I'd paid a visit to the foreman's cabin. Then I realized just how long that had been.

I haven't been here since it was Kevin's place.

There was no need. Teague reported to me up at the house every day, and if I needed him, there was always the phone. And as to why I was on my way there in the wee small hours?

This had to be a face-to-face conversation, and I knew he was awake.

The cabin stood apart from the barns. My granddad had built it back in the day. He'd wanted to afford the foreman some privileges, and not having to share the bunkhouse was one of them.

'He's in charge. They don't get to watch him take a leak or stroll buck naked out of the shower.'

It hadn't taken long for Kevin and I to realize we might attract some attention if I was forever visiting him, and after that we'd been on the hunt for a meeting place, far enough away from the house, the barns, and prying eyes. The cabin by the creek was the perfect spot. My dad had built it for my mom when they were first married. It had been her sanctuary.

And then it had become mine.

I approached the front steps of Teague's cabin. Despite the hour, there was a light on inside, as I'd known there would be. I climbed up to the front door and knocked.

Teague opened it, wearing nothing but a towel. His eyes widened when he saw me. "Anything wrong, boss?"

"Can I come in?"

"Of course." He stood aside to let me enter, then hurriedly closed the door to shut out that chill wind. "We might be in for some bad weather. Forecast don't say shit, but you've only gotta look at those clouds. And that wind…"

I trusted my dad's barometer in the hallway of the big house. I'd checked it out of habit as I'd left. "We'll be okay. This is gonna blow over."

I glanced at the interior. Little had changed since my last visit. I was pleased to note Teague was a tidy man, not that I'd expected anything less.

The cabin was one big space, comprising a living room, tiny kitchen, and open stairs leading up to a mezzanine where the bed stood. A small window sat over it at the apex of the vaulted roof. One door shut off the bathroom from the rest of the cabin. Everywhere there was the smell of pine.

The place was warm, and I soon realized why—a fire burned behind the grate. Two empty glasses sat on the coffee table—along with a bottle of lube.

I was pretty damn sure he'd have been mortified if I drew attention to that last item, so I averted my gaze, looking up to where he'd slung a colorful throw over the railing around the bed area. "Is that new? I don't recollect seeing that."

"Boss?" I turned to find him staring at me, his eyes dancing with amusement. "You didn't *really* come over here to discuss my interior decorating, now did you? So what's wrong?"

"Nothing's wrong," I assured him. I cleared my throat and gestured to his towel. "Just getting into the shower, or out of it?"

As if I didn't know.

"Out." He cocked his head. "You want something to drink? There's juice in the fridge, and iced tea."

"Tea sounds good." I fixed him with a stare. "But if you're planning on going back to bed, I'll get out of here." I grinned. "Lord knows, you need all the beauty sleep you can get."

Yeah right. Teague was stunning, not that I was interested. With our history, that would've been plain *wrong*. His square jawline was dark with stubble that was permanently there—he hovered in a perpetual state between five o'clock shadow and scraggy beard. Not that there was any trace of hair on that wide, firm chest or sculpted abs, no sir. I hadn't met many guys with green eyes, and his were amazing.

Lord, but you sure grew up pretty. Nothing remained of the sixteen-year-old scrawny kid who'd sheltered in our barn.

Except those hauntingly beautiful eyes with those long black lashes.

Teague laughed. "I wasn't planning on it, no. I'll get dressed. Help yourself to the tea." He headed for the bedroom.

I went into the small kitchen and opened the fridge. It took up most of the room. "You got yourself a new fridge?"

"You told me I could, remember?" he called out. "Three years ago."

I'd forgotten. I spotted the iced tea and removed it. "You want some tea?"

"Sure," he hollered.

I found two glasses and filled them. "So it's cold enough for a fire, but warm enough for iced tea?"

Teague joined me, dressed in jeans and a red shirt that he buttoned as he approached. "I was freezin' my tits off."

I had to laugh. Teague always felt the cold worse than any of them. I handed him a glass. "I think you're safe. They're still there."

He drank a little, leaning against the countertop. "If there's nothing wrong, then why are you here? Couldn't whatever's on your mind wait until a more reasonable hour?"

"Can't seem to get a decent night's sleep these days." I peered at him. "Did *you* get any, before he came a-knockin'?"

Teague shrugged. "Couple of hours." He frowned. "That's not why you're here, is it? Because of me and Butch?" He snorted. "Course it isn't. You'd have said something before now. I mean, how long has it been going on?"

I'd forgotten that too.

I gestured toward the couch. "Can I warm these old bones in front of your fire?"

He let out another snort. "You ain't old, but sure."

I sat on the worn fabric couch, covered with another colorful Indian throw. I held my glass in both hands, elbows on my knees.

"How come you're not sleeping?" Teague asked as he sat in the room's only armchair. Then he almost dropped his glass as he scrambled to grab the bottle of lube, and stuffed it down the side of the chair.

I pretended not to notice.

"If I knew the answer to that, I could do something about it."

"Maybe the doc can give you something."

I snorted. "And maybe I don't wanna take pills." I peered at him. "Can we get personal for a second?"

Teague's lips twitched. "I guess that depends on *how* personal."

"You were wrong, by the way. This… thing you've got going with Butch…"

He blinked. "*Thing?* You're not usually this coy."

I rolled my eyes. "Fine. You and Butch are fuckin'. We both know that. Hell, *everyone* probably knows, even if they don't say as much."

He laughed. "Yeah, *that's* the boss I know and love. So… what about us?"

"I wouldn't presume to tell you your business, but—"

"I knew there was a but coming."

I put my glass down on the table. "What you two do in this cabin is nothing to do with me or anyone else, okay? It's not my responsibility—*unless* it goes tits up, and suddenly you two can't work together anymore."

He fell silent.

I leaned back. "At the end of the day, you're the foreman. I want you to see to the smooth running of this place, and if you and Butch—"

"Robert."

I gazed at him. He only ever referred to me by my name when we were alone, when it was important.

Teague sighed. "It's not that kind of relationship, honest."

"I know it didn't start out that way," I fired back. "I get it. You both have itches, and you get 'em scratched. That *was* how it got started, right? I mean, that was what you said." He nodded. "And I've stayed out of it. I didn't pry. Like I said, it's nothing to do with me. But for all I know, things might have moved on since then. There might have been... developments..."

Teague stared at me. "Are you asking me if I'm falling for him, or him for me? Hearts 'n' flowers kinda stuff?" He snorted. "You've got no worries on that score. We're strictly platonic. Besides, he's not my type." He smiled. "I mean it, Robert. Don't be thinking we're gonna break up one day, and sour the atmosphere around here."

I sagged into the couch. "I had to be sure."

"I know, and I get it. Hell, if I saw two of *my* cowboys sneaking off to play hide the salami, I'd want to know whatever they had going on wasn't gonna spill over into their working life." He gazed at me earnestly. "And it's not, all right?"

"All right." I was satisfied. I shook my head. "Remember that time I came into the barn late one night? And caught the pair of you—"

"Please, don't remind me," he begged. "I swear, every time I saw you after that, you could've heated the big house with the fire in my cheeks. Took me a whole three days to get over it."

I grinned. "Maybe it was payback for the night we met." I gave him a fond glance. "You kept your promise. All these years, and you never told a soul." What came to mind were my conversations with Zeeb and Diana. I huffed. "They found out anyway."

"And so what if they did?" Teague chuckled. "What does it

matter when you've got the gayest bunch of cowboys this side of the Rockies?" He speared me with a look. "Do I exaggerate?"

He had a point. Among the regulars, Matt was the only straight guy, and I wasn't even sure about him. He kept a lot under his hat. Walt and Paul were bi, and as for Zeeb? I'd have said he was straight until our chat.

Now? I wasn't so sure.

Teague smiled. "They don't care if you're gay."

I picked my glass up and drank. "When Butch came to Salvation, I'd have sworn he was straight. I thought I could tell back then if a guy was gay." I laughed. "I was nineteen, what did I know? But no, I didn't think he was gay."

Yeah, back then my gaydar was for shit.

"I don't think he is now," Teague murmured. "I don't flatter myself."

I frowned. "What do you mean?"

"I mean, I'm a convenient hole. Not that I'm complaining. Like I said, it works out just fine." I blinked, and he coughed. "And I just said way too much, didn't I?"

"Your secret's safe with me." I regarded him with interest. "You never thought of settling down? You're still young."

He chuckled. "Got my hands full with this place." He fell silent.

I stared into the flames. I knew what lay at the root of my insomnia. Salvation was my life… and it wasn't making me happy anymore.

"What's wrong?"

I glanced at him. "Hmm?"

"It's just that… lately… Well…"

"Spit it out."

He looked me in the eye. "If you want the truth? Your heart doesn't seem to be in it anymore. And I'm not talking about yesterday—that day was always gonna be a shit show." He winced. "Sorry."

I waved my hand. "You're the third person to mention what day it was. I'm kinda getting used to it being common knowledge." That was no lie, which came as a surprise. *Maybe Diana was right. I'm finally healing.* "But let's get back to my heart not being in it anymore."

What struck me was how much Teague *saw*. He always had, right from the start.

"I'm talking about how you've been acting for more than six months. When you first started this venture, you were excited. Anyone could see that."

"I was," I admitted. "Then I lost him." I heaved a sigh. "That kinda took the shine off. What was the use in being excited if I had no one to share it with?"

Then I realized the only sound in the room was the crackle of the logs.

Teague was so still, his gaze unwavering. "You... You're not thinking of selling up, are you?"

I frowned. "What makes you say that?"

Damn. That had crossed my mind for the first time less than twenty-four hours ago, then vanished from it as fast as it had arrived. The man was uncanny.

"I hear things on the grapevine. Seems like every day a business folds, a ranch dies..." Teague cocked his head. "We're doing okay, aren't we? I mean, you haven't said anything, and I know we've had a few cancellations, but—"

"We're doing okay," I said in a low voice, hoping my tone reassured him. "Well, the dude ranch is. There are always cancellations when money gets tight. And it *is* tight for a lot of folks right now. But no, I'm not thinking of going anyplace else." I gazed at the window. "This place is in my blood, my bones." Somewhere out there in the dark was the ranch cemetery, where generations of Thorstons lay below ground. "And part of me is buried here." I turned to look at him. "I'm not saying that to get a pity party started, just stating the God's honest truth."

Teague nodded. "Time you moved on—emotionally

speaking."

I smiled. "You sound like Zeeb."

He smirked. "We do end up on the same page now and then." He stared at me. "Did he tell you the same thing?"

"Just yesterday."

Teague shook his head. "His timing is for shit." Then he grinned. "You know what that is, right?" His smile grew smug. "It's a sign."

I laughed. "Sure it is." We fell silent, and I stared into the fire.

"I'll always be grateful to you and your dad. You know that, don't you?"

I shrugged. "We just took you in. That's all."

He shook his head. "No, it was more than that. You made me feel like I was part of the family. "

I smiled. "That's because you are. Like I said, you keep my secrets. Except after talking to Zeeb and Diana, I don't think I have any left."

"Diana too?" Teague whistled. "You sure had a red-letter day, didn't you?"

"What are the new guests like?" I hadn't paid them much attention, other than scanning the paperwork. Three was a lot less than we usually dealt with. The average was five or six.

"You remember Declan? Money guy from New York?"

I smiled. "Regular as clockwork every June. He's okay?"

"Yeah, he's fine. Better now he's here, I think."

"He just needs to feel the wind in his hair and on his face. Except as I recall, he was losing the hair last time I looked."

"There's Garrett Evans, a newcomer…" Teague stroked his chin. "I think we need to keep an eye on him."

"Why? You think he's trouble?"

"Not what I meant. He's kinda… fragile. Put it this way, Butch is handling him with kid gloves."

I widened my eyes. "Whoa. Did Hell freeze over, and no one told me?"

"I know right? Maybe he'll settle down once he gets into the swing of things." He paused. "And then there's Toby Merrow."

Something in his voice got my attention. "Why are you smiling?"

"Oh, no reason. I think you'd like him though." I arched my eyebrows, and his smile widened. "Not gonna say more than that."

I searched my mental logs. "He the one from San Francisco?"

"Yup. Says he's at home on a horse—or used to be, when he was younger. Guess we'll see tomorrow."

I chuckled. "It *is* tomorrow." Saturday had slipped *into* Sunday while I wasn't looking.

Teague leaned forward, his elbows on his knees. "He reminds me of Kevin."

And just like that, he had my attention.

"I see. We talking a physical resemblance?"

"Yes, but… it's more than that." I peered at him, and he shrugged. "Just a feeling."

"What kind of feeling?" I pushed.

His gaze met mine. "The kind of feeling I used to get about Kevin when I watched you two together."

Now that was *all* kinds of interesting. In that moment, I wasn't sure if I wanted to get a better look at Toby Merrow—or keep my distance.

"Color me intrigued." I pulled my phone from my pocket and noted the time. "I'd better get back to the house. Maybe you *should* try to grab another hour's sleep—you have work to do."

"Yes, sir."

I got to my feet, and he followed suit. When I reached the front door, he stopped me. "Hey, Robert… You know where I am, right? For anything." I rolled my eyes, and he smiled. "Look, the offer's there whether you take me up on it or not."

I did something I hadn't done in years—I gave him a hug. "You're all right, kid." Then I opened the door and made my way back to my own bed.

I could *try* to sleep, right?

Chapter Seven

Sunday, June 12
Toby

A hand grabbed my shoulder and gave me a rough shake. "Come on, Princess. Rise and shine."

I opened one eye. Zeeb stood by my bunk, a cup in one hand. I blinked. "It's still dark."

"Not for long. Up and at 'em. Breakfast is in ten, and the line's already forming for the shower." He walked away.

I got out of bed, shivering, then grabbed my bag of toiletries and headed for the bathroom. The room was already full. Both showers were in use, and Butch, Paul, and Declan stood in front of the sinks, busy washing, shaving, brushing teeth… There was no sign of Garrett or Walt, so I figured they were the ones in the shower.

What struck me was the lack of conversation. I stood for a minute, observing the scene.

Zeeb glanced toward me. "Wanna take a picture?" he asked, scraping a razor over his scalp.

I had to smile. "You're not morning people, are you?"

Butch turned to glare at me. "If you are, we are *not* gonna get along. I ain't worth shit before my third cup of coffee."

From behind the farthest shower curtain I caught Walt's voice. "Where's my razor? I left it in here."

"Wanna borrow mine?" Zeeb inquired.

"No, I do *not*. I know where it's been. And can I just say…Ew?"

Zeeb cackled. "Dude, I'm shaving my head, not my balls. And even if I were, what do you want a razor for in the shower, exactly?"

The others cackled too.

Walt stuck a hand out from behind the curtain. "Give it here."

I opened my toiletries bag, grabbed a fresh disposable razor, and slapped it into Walt's hand. "Here. Brand-new."

"Aw, thanks. I'll give it you back after."

I laughed. "No, you can keep it. I've got more." The rest of the guys laughed with me.

The other curtain drew back, and Garrett got out, a towel wrapped around him. "The water's not all that hot, is it?"

"You want a hot shower, you need to be first in line," Butch told him. "Most of the guys were showering while you were still dreaming."

I dove into the shower enclosure. I didn't think I could face a cold shower.

After what seemed like the fastest clean-up ever, I walked into the front room, dressed in my designer jeans and a plain blue shirt. The aroma made my stomach growl. The table was laden with eggs, bacon, ham steaks, pancakes, syrup, sausage, biscuits, gravy…

Damn. Matt was a wonder.

I headed straight for the coffee. I knew what my priorities were. Then I found an empty chair, sat, and filled my plate. No one spoke while we ate, but by the time we were on the third pot of coffee, the conversation started to flow.

"So what's first on the schedule?" I asked.

Butch leaned back. "Finding you a horse. Then making sure you can ride him." He peered at Declan. "You okay on Charger again?"

Declan smiled. "That big old boy? Sure. He's a sweetheart."

Butch cackled. "Well, I wouldn't have put it quite like that, but whatever fills your bucket."

"What's Lucy like?" Garrett asked. "That's the horse you thought might be a good match for me, right?"

Butch's smile was kind. "Yeah. And she *is* a regular sweetheart. Gentle as a lamb. You won't have no trouble with her."

He went up in my estimation. *You can be a sweetheart too, can't you?* Not that I'd say as much to his face.

I imagined those big fists could land quite a wallop.

I finished my coffee. "Can I go look at the stables?" I grabbed my jacket from where I'd left it on a hook the previous night.

"You can't go out like that," Paul said, his eyes wide. "You're naked."

I blinked. "Excuse me?"

Paul grabbed a hat from the wall. It was then I noticed for the first time that there were a great many hats. He flung it at me. "That should fit you."

I put it on, checking myself in the mirror. It was white with a leather trim.

Zeeb snorted. "Quit preening. We got work to do. And about that hat…"

"I know, don't put it on the bed."

Butch and Zeeb glanced at one another, and intoned simultaneously, "*Yellowstone.*"

I gaped. "How did you—"

"We get a lot of guys coming here who watch that show," Walt informed me.

"It must be good for business," I reasoned.

"It's sure good for property prices," Butch remarked. "They've soared since that show aired."

"But that's gotta be good for the economy, right?" I persisted.

"Wrong. It ain't good when folks starting out can't afford to buy their own place, because a lot of city folk push the prices up by coming out here to 'live the dream', Butch air-quoted.

"It's too early for this shit," Zeeb complained. "Get off your high horse, Butch."

"You know I'm right." Butch gave me a nod. "You go ahead. Paul'll sort you out with a horse. I need to check in with Teague before we get started."

I followed Paul out of the bunkhouse, and we crunched our way over to the stable.

"Welcome to *my* world," he said as we stepped into the light, airy space, filled with the smell of wood, straw, and horses.

God, I'd missed that smell. "Been a while since I was last in a stable."

He smiled. "Don't suppose they have many of these in San Francisco." I watched as he went from stall to stall, checking on each horse, stroking their noses and talking quietly to them. Paul was a handsome guy, tall and willowy. His hair hung in a glossy black curtain down his back, and a cream choker lay snug around his throat.

I did a count up. "Ten horses? Is that all?"

"These are the ones we use to make sure you can handle yourself. There's a corral of horses in the north pasture. Most of them will go on the cattle drive. You might ride three or four different horses during that. That's my job—to take care of the remuda."

"The what?"

Paul smiled. "That's what we call a team of horses. I make sure they're all fed and doctored. I also help Matt out with rustling firewood."

"How long have you worked on the ranch?"

"I've been here since '99. That was the year the boss's dad found me in the river, drowning, and saved my life."

I gaped. "Seriously?"

He nodded. "He jumped in and pulled me out. He looked after me. And when he learned about my… circumstances, he gave me a job." He smiled. "I was this seventeen-year-old kid with a chip on his shoulder, who resented the fact that a white man had built this ranch on land that had once belonged to my people." He grimaced. "I'd been fed that since I was old enough to listen. *Then* I got to know these people—and suddenly they were family." His voice was warm, deep and rich.

I didn't ask what his circumstances had been. It was none of my business.

I glanced around, searching for the beautiful horse I'd seen him working with when we'd arrived. There was no sign of it.

"Where's the palomino I saw yesterday? That was a real beauty."

Paul arched his eyebrows. "You recognized the breed? That's more than a lot of guests do when they first come here. And that was Rusty. He's the boss's stallion. You don't see him because the boss took him out early this morning."

"He often goes out riding at this hour?" Dawn was only just breaking.

"Usually, except this is early, even for him."

I surveyed the stalls, recalling the conversation of the previous night. "So what's the deal with Lightning?"

"What do you mean?"

"Butch suggested you might have me ride Lightning." I grinned. "I'm not blind. *Something* is going on. I figured he's the ornery one, who usually throws people off. That's probably how Butch gets his kicks."

"It's not that. And he's only thrown someone once, but those were exceptional circumstances." Paul regarded me, his expression grave. "By the way, you'd better know one of the boss's rules. You don't go near a horse if you've had so much as one drink."

"Got it. I wouldn't do that anyway. Drunk in charge of a horse doesn't sound like a good scenario. So what's the deal with Lightning then, if he doesn't send riders ass over tea kettle?"

Paul bit his lip. "No one has ridden him in a while, that's all."

"Is that because he's old?"

"Not really. He's fifteen. He's a good age." He pointed to a stall at the end of the stable. "Go see for yourself."

I wandered over there, and peered into the stall. A black horse with white socks and a flash of white on his nose came closer to inspect me.

"I can see why he got the name." I stroked the little white flash, and the horse pushed his nose into my hand. "Hey there. You feel in the mood to take me for a ride?" I leaned into him, aware of his size and strength.

Paul watched in silence for a moment. "He likes you. That was fast."

"How can you tell?"

"He's relaxed. See how he cocked his back leg? How he sighed?" He grabbed Lightning's halter. "Let's get him outside." He walked the horse out of the stall, then inclined his head toward the rear of the stables. "See that saddle at the end, on the left? Bring it."

I went over to the rack, and grabbed the dark brown leather saddle. The smell was heavenly. I lifted it from the rack, and Paul grabbed a blanket, throwing it over his shoulder. He pointed to the bench. "Know what they are?"

I glanced at the items laid out. "Brushes and combs for removing dirt, tangles, and burrs." He gave me an approving nod, and I laughed. "Did I just pass a test or something?"

His dark eyes twinkled. "Maybe? We don't need those, by the way. I groomed him before you were even awake. Plus, I checked his hooves for stones. But you need to do that every time you take a horse out." He led Lightning out of the stable, heading for the paddock.

I followed. There was no sign of the others.

"Where is everyone?"

Paul chuckled. "I know they tell you it'll be work right from the get-go, but it really isn't, not the first day at least. They like to take their time, make sure the guests are happy before they throw them into the deep end." He grinned. "Then it's like you said—sink or swim time." He closed the gate behind us, threw the blanket over the fence, then dropped the reins. "Now show me how you saddle a horse."

I grinned. "Sink or swim time?" I placed the saddle alongside the blanket.

He returned my grin. "So what's the first thing you do?"

"Tie the horse. He needs to stay put." I searched my memories for everything granddad had ever taught me. I took the lead rope, slipping its tail through the loop of a quick release knot. "In case Lightning knows how to untie knots," I said for Paul's benefit.

He chuckled. "And he does, so good call."

Then I checked the area where the saddle would be for any sores or wounds. There were no lumps, bumps, or swellings either. I glanced in Paul's direction, and he smiled.

"Doing good so far."

I grabbed the blanket and placed it on Lightning's back, putting it a little higher on the withers, then slid it back into place just behind the mane.

"Tell me why you did that," he demanded.

"So the hair on his back lies flat under the blanket and the saddle." I made sure it was even on both sides, then grabbed the saddle. I stood on Lightning's left side, and flipped the right-side cinches and stirrup over the seat of the saddle to keep them from getting caught under it. Then I swung the saddle over the horse, rocking it back and forth into position, unfolding the cinches and stirrups, and ensuring the center line lay over Lightning's spine.

"Yeah, you've done this before."

I slid two fingers under the curve of the saddle just under the horn, and made sure I could fit three or four fingers between the horse's withers and the cinch. I marveled at how it all came back to me.

"Now what?" Paul asked.

"I need to secure the main cinch. Can't ride without that." I pulled it under Lightning's belly toward me, slipping the strap through the cinch buckle and ensuring it wasn't twisted. Paul watched without comment as I untied the horse, then walked him around for a minute or two, letting him relax to the saddle before I finished tightening the cinch. Then I loosely secured the back cinch, attached the breast collar, and latched it to the saddle's cinch and front D-rings.

Paul beamed. "Very good."

I smiled. "I guess some things you don't forget." I walked the horse over to the fence, climbed onto it, and mounted him.

"Wow. Now I'm impressed."

I blinked. "By me getting onto the horse?"

"By the *way* you mounted him. Most guys just put a foot in the stirrup and throw their leg over. You know, like they've seen in the movies."

I frowned. "Mounting a horse like that puts undue pressure on him, my granddad used to say."

"Your granddad obviously spent a good deal of time around horses." He folded his arms. "Okay—show me what you can do."

As soon as I tried to get Lightning to move, it became obvious he was going to be a bit of a handful. "You said no one's ridden him in a while. Exactly how long are we talking about here?"

Paul's face tightened. "Too long. Persevere. He just needs to remember, that's all. He's a good horse."

It took me about twenty minutes to get him to do what I wanted, and I spent the next ten minutes after that trotting around the paddock under Paul's watchful gaze. We picked up a little speed, slowed, sped up again, and then I brought Lightning to a dead stop in front of him.

Paul smiled. "Yeah, you know your way around a horse."

It occurred to me that if we weren't in a hurry to get started, there was something I wanted to do while I had the chance.

"Can I go for a ride?"

Paul shook his head. "I can't really go out right now. I need to sort out a horse for Garrett."

I wasn't about to be dissuaded that easily. "You don't have to come with me. You've seen I can handle him, right?"

Paul stared at me. "You want to get my ass fired? Guests aren't allowed to go out on their own."

I tilted my head to one side. "Another of the boss's rules?"

He chewed on his lower lip. "More of a… guideline, really."

Aha.

"Paul," I said in a coaxing tone. "I just need to be alone for a while, okay?" No observers, just me on a horse for the first time in years, enjoying a little solitude, communing with nature.

There sure was a helluva lot to commune with. Meadows stretched out before me, swelling into hills covered in trees, and farther off in the distance, snow topped the blue peaks.

His brow furrowed. "I'm not sure about this."

"Look, you've seen me on a horse. You said I'd be safe with Lightning, didn't you? I mean, you can see he's fine with me, right?"

"And what if you're out there and you come across a rattlesnake?"

"Then I'll keep him away from it." Paul bit his lip once more, and I took it as a sign he was wavering. "Just a little time to myself, please?"

Paul sighed. "I guess I know how that feels." He gazed at our surroundings, as if trying to come to a decision. "Fine. You've got thirty minutes, tops. If you're not back by then, I'll come looking."

I beamed. "Thank you. Wanna suggest a way I could go?"

Paul pointed. "Head that way. There's a trail that leads down to the creek. Nothing that should prove difficult terrain." His frown hadn't disappeared. "I'm still not sure about this."

"If you get into trouble, I'll make sure they know it's my fault, all right? I'll say I insisted."

At last he waved his hand. "Go on, get out of here before the others arrive. I'll deal with the fallout—if there is any."

I gave Lightning's flanks a slight nudge with my knees, Paul opened the gate, and we trotted out of the paddock. I bent forward. "Isn't this better, boy?" I took care not to go too fast. Lightning was in no shape to be galloping anywhere, and besides, I didn't know the land. There could be any number of unexpected obstacles ahead of us. We trotted through the meadow, his mane flapping.

I'd forgotten how exhilarating it was, even at this slow pace

I'd forgotten the feel of a horse under me, strong and sure-footed, the wind on my face, through my hair, the feeling of being so fucking *alive*.

We maintained the steady pace, and it wasn't long before the meadow disappeared, and I was in tall grass, the sound of running water nearby. Ahead of me was the edge of a forest, and through the green leaves and brown trunks, I spotted a structure.

I wonder what that is?

I headed towards it, and found myself at the edge of the creek. Across from me was a log cabin. It appeared to be in dire need of some TLC.

Does anyone live in it? I didn't think it likely—it had the look of a place that had been long deserted. Two chairs sat on the porch, beaten and weathered, the varnish long since peeled away. And now that I peered closely, the deck of the porch had seen better days too.

"Someone must have loved you once," I murmured.

And then I heard it—the sound of a horse approaching, getting louder and louder. I glanced up, and coming toward me was a man riding a palomino. He was a good-looking guy in jeans, a blue-and-white plaid shirt, open at the collar, and a brown hat. His beard was mostly gray, his mustache darker.

I knew instantly who was staring at me with wide hazel eyes.

So this is the boss.

I opened my mouth to greet him but he got in first, his gaze like steel.

"What are you doing on that horse?"

CHAPTER EIGHT

Toby

A shiver trickled through me, and my next thought was definitely more carnal.

No one told me he was sexy. Better yet, *my* kind of sexy.

I gazed at the curls of gray hair showing at the open collar of his shirt. Tyler might have been a pretty young thing, but handsome older guys lit a fire under me every time.

Except *this* handsome older guy was staring at me as though I had two heads.

I gave him my brightest smile. "You must be Robert Thorston."

I wanted to run my fingers through that mat of salt and pepper chest hair, to tug on that amazing beard. Except I knew better than to get my hopes up.

Why are all the sexy men I lust after, always straight?

Okay, not *always*, but enough of the time that I was convinced there was an immutable law of nature few people were aware of—women always went for gay men, and gay men went for straight guys. Oh, and bisexuals pretty much liked everyone.

Sure, they were stereotypes, but stereotypes often existed for a reason.

That hard stare hadn't wavered. "You haven't answered my question. Who told you you could ride that horse?"

The weird thing was, I didn't think he was pissed, but in the grip of some other strong emotion that I couldn't get a handle on.

That unflinching gaze told me he expected an answer.

"Paul did. He vetted me first, mind you, and made sure I could handle him." I trotted over to him. "I'm Toby Merrow, by the way."

He didn't thaw an inch. "Well, Mr. Merrow, you shouldn't be out here alone. Paul knows better than to allow it."

"I'm afraid that's my fault. I kind of insisted. I just needed—"

He straightened in his saddle. "I don't want to appear rude, but your needs don't come into it. No guests are allowed to ride unaccompanied. That's one of the stipulations of our insurance."

Nope, he wasn't about to bend, not one goddamn inch.

"Then I'd better head back." I trotted past him, tipping my hat as we came within a few feet of each other. To my surprise, he moved Rusty to trot alongside me. I arched my eyebrows. "I see. You're escorting me?"

"You bet I am."

"I managed to get here all by myself, you know."

"Happy to hear it. I'm still riding back with you."

We rode along the creek, leaving the cabin behind us. I wanted to ask him about it, but figured the mood he was in, I was unlikely to get an answer. His back was stiff as he rode, and I couldn't help wondering what it would take to loosen him up. I waited for him to say something, even if it was to reproach me again.

Stony silence.

This sucks. We were almost at the ranch, and I couldn't bear it anymore.

"I love the ranch, by the way."

Crickets.

"It's my first time on a dude ranch."

Crickets.

"You've got a great team here."

Crickets.

When it became obvious being polite wasn't going to get me anywhere, I resorted to good old-fashioned bluntness.

"Are you always this quiet, or is it just me? Because if we're going to ride the whole way back in silence, I may have to resort to humming show tunes." I gave him a sweet smile. "And trust me, you wouldn't like it. I couldn't carry a tune if I had a bucket."

He stared at me, his lips parted, and just as I was beginning to despair, he chuckled.

"You're right, I'm being rude." He glanced at Lightning. "To be honest, it was more the shock of seeing you on this horse."

Really? He was all bent out of shape over me riding Lightning?

"Paul said no one had ridden him in a while."

Part of me was dying to know why that was. Because Paul's manner, Butch's suggestion that I ride Lightning in the first place... There was a mystery here, and I was a sucker for a good mystery.

Robert

"Paul was correct." I couldn't take my eyes off him. Toby Merrow sat high in the saddle, so at ease on Lightning that anyone would have thought he'd ridden the horse all his life. He appeared to be in great shape. His dark beard and blue eyes were very attractive.

Those same eyes were locked on mine.

"He also said it was less of a rule and more of a guideline," Toby continued.

"Okay, he's right about that too," I admitted. "I leave stuff like that to his discretion."

"Then the part about the insurance was—?"

"Only partly true." I coughed. "Okay, it was me being a hardass."

His eyes twinkled. "You know, you have that down to a fine art."

Oh, I like you, Toby Merrow. He had this I-don't-give-a-shit-air about him, that reminded me strongly of—

"Declan—he's one of your regular guests, apparently—says he's only seen you twice, maybe three times in six years."

"As many times as that?" I quipped.

My attempt at humor rolled right over him. I couldn't blame him for that, not after the way I'd yelled at him, charging over to confront him when I'd spotted Lightning.

And that had been the real shocker, seeing Kevin's horse standing beside the creek, across from the cabin—with a man astride him. A familiar-looking man. And for a minute there, I'd really thought…

Then I'd come to my senses. I didn't believe in ghosts.

"So pardon me for asking, but what do you do all day if you're not dealing with the guests? You leave all that to Teague."

I blinked at his forthright manner. "I have meetings with the cattlemen's association, buying and selling livestock, paperwork, the accounts…"

Toby snorted. "Paperwork? Seriously? If I were in your shoes, I'd hire a bookkeeper. Why be stuck in an office, working, when you have *this* office?" He gestured to the breathtakingly beautiful landscape surrounding us.

I smiled. "That's why I come here every morning—to enjoy my office." *And I was doing just that—until the sight of you almost gave me a heart attack.*

"Do you usually ride this trail?"

"Most of the time." I frowned. "Why?"

He shrugged. "Just wanted to know if I was going to run into you again, that's all."

I remained silent, not trusting myself to speak. I'd had the same thought.

"It's okay, I get it. You're the strong silent type. That's fine. I'll talk to Lightning instead. Except the conversation could be dull as ditch water, because I suspect all he'll want to talk about is hay, flies, and when his next feed is."

That broke the ice. I laughed. "And he'll also say 'don't forget the oats.'"

Toby grinned. "He only gets those if he's a good boy."

Dear Lord. I had to bite my tongue. *And what do I get if I'm a good boy?* Then I smiled. *You need to meet my sister. She has a few words to say about strong silent types.*

His eyes gleamed. "Is this you appreciating my sense of humor, or did I say something funny?"

"You just echoed something my sister said on the phone last night."

"Would that be Diana?"

I stared at him. "And you know that how?"

"Butch mentioned her when we were driving here. Married to some guy called Newt, I think he said?"

I gave him another hard stare. "Did Butch give out any other information while he was driving you? My shoe size, for instance? The combination to my safe? The size of my—assets?"

We stared at each other for a minute, then both of us laughed.

I couldn't believe I'd said that. *Since when do I dabble in double entendres?* Especially with a guy I'd just met.

"He was just passing time, I think. I have to ask, though. His parents named him after Newt Gingrich?"

"No idea, but when he was a teenager, the name really suited him. It was more of a size thing. You should've seen him when he and Diana first started dating. He's got bigger since. Thank God." I peered at him. "You're from San Francisco?"

"Yup."

"What do you do there?"

He bit back a smile. "Yeah, that wasn't one of the questions on the form I had to fill in online. Because good Lord, it wanted to know everything else. I wouldn't have been surprised if it had asked for my… measurements."

Looks like I'm not the only one talking in sexy riddles. Because yeah, I was thinking about his dick. And when was the last time I'd done that?

"You didn't answer my question."

"I'm half-owner of a club."

"What kind of club?"

"Just a… social club, for guys only."

I arched my eyebrows. "I see. And do you let someone run it for you, or do you like to get your hands dirty?"

His eyes glittered. "I like to get dirty."

Yeah, there was nothing ambiguous about that statement, and we both knew it.

Heat flooded my face, and I was thankful we were almost at the ranch.

Toby cleared his throat. "So… Maybe we might meet up one of these mornings and ride the trail together?"

"You never know," I said with a shrug. "Anything could happen."

"In that case, maybe I'll make *sure* it happens."

And maybe I'd make sure of the same thing.

We trotted over to the stable. Paul's eyes widened as we approached. In the paddock, Butch and Zeeb were talking with Declan, and a few feet away, Teague was with another guest. That had to be Garrett.

Butch and Zeeb broke off from their conversation to stare at me, and I gave them my most cheerful smile. "Morning, boys."

Zeeb grinned. "And a good morning to you too, boss." Then they resumed talking.

Paul gave me a cautious nod. "Hey boss." Then he addressed Toby. "So, how was it?"

Toby beamed. "It was great." He stroked Lightning's neck. "Great horse too."

Paul opened his mouth to say something else, but I got in first.

"Whose decision was it to put Mr. Merrow on Lightning?"

All conversation dried up, and the only sounds were the birds chirping in the bushes, and the screech of buzzards circling overhead.

Paul swallowed. "Well, someone suggested it last night… And then Toby asked… And Lightning clearly took to him, so…"

One glance at his startled expression had me regretting my

sharp tongue.

I held my hand up. "It's okay. They're obviously a good fit. Maybe *I* was the one at fault, insisting no one else ride him."

Judging by the shock on the faces of my ranch hands, anyone would have thought I'd just informed them of the Second Coming.

Toby broke the silence. "Does that mean I can ride him again?"

Paul looked at me for a response.

I nodded. "Sure. And just so we're clear, you're okay to go out alone." The thought of meeting up with him again sent a shiver through me. *How long has it been since I even noticed another man?*

My mind went back to where I'd found Toby.

"One more thing, Mr. Merrow…"

He arched his eyebrows. "I thought we were past being polite." His gaze locked on mine. "Call me Toby."

Those eyes… I was grateful to be sitting on Rusty. If not, I think my knees might have trembled.

I smiled. "Okay, then, *Toby*—"

"And what do I call you?"

My heartbeat quickened. "Mr. Thorston. And I do have one stipulation, with regards to your solitary rides out. Don't go any further than the creek where we met." I wanted to say, *And stay away from the cabin*, but that would have aroused his interest.

And now that I'd set a boundary, I waited to see if he'd question my decision. When he said nothing, he went up in my estimation. Toby's maturity only added to my overall impression of him.

There was definitely something about him that made me want to know him better. I watched him ride Lightning toward the fence where he dismounted, and I smiled. A man who treated horses with such regard…

Toby Merrow was improving by the minute.

I rode Rusty toward the mounting blocks, and clambered off him. Paul led him and Lightning toward the stable. Teague was still standing by the fence, talking with Garrett.

"So I guess this means you're going back to the house now," Toby stated in a flat voice. He stood with his thumbs tucked into the waistband of his jeans, and whether intentional or not, my gaze was drawn lower. I jerked my head up in a hurry. The guy was perfect. Good on a horse, not too hard on the eyes, sassy enough to grab my attention, considerate...

Before I could respond, Butch strolled towards us. "Hey, San Francisco. I guess you were telling the truth about knowing your way around a horse."

"I reckon so."

Butch grinned. "No Gucci shit today? Oops, my bad. I see you've decided to slum it in Nordstrom."

I knew there was no malice in Butch's words—it was just his way—but I watched with interest to see how Toby reacted.

He studied Butch in silence for a minute, then cocked his head to one side. "Butch, I don't know if anyone has ever told you this, but you can be a real dick sometimes."

Oh my God. It was all I could do not to laugh out loud.

A stunned silence followed his words, followed by an eruption of applause.

Zeeb was laughing his ass off.

Butch let out a mock gasp. "What do you mean, *sometimes?* I must be doing something wrong. I was aiming for being a dick one hundred percent of the time."

Toby chuckled. "Yeah, well, keep working at it. They say practice makes perfect, right?"

There was something very attractive about a man who exuded confidence and not arrogance, who appeared comfortable in his own skin.

Did I say by the minute? Toby was growing more attractive by the *second.*

Now I got why Teague thought I'd like him. He was *so* like Kevin, it was uncanny. I remembered when Kevin had been made foreman. He'd possessed a similar confidence, and that confidence had spilled over into the bedroom… the barn … outdoors… anywhere there was a flat surface—and sometimes when there wasn't.

Against the front door had been a particular favorite position.

"There's coffee in the bunkhouse," Butch told Toby. "Grab some. We're not done finding a horse yet for Garrett."

"Sure. I could do with more caffeine." Toby gave me a nod. "I'll be seeing you."

As he walked away, I was dying to ask, 'Is that a promise?'

Garrett joined Butch and Zeeb, and I saw my chance to grab Teague. I beckoned him to follow, and we walked away from the small group.

I lowered my voice. "The herd goes to the south pastures next week. Is he gonna be ready by then?" I didn't have to mention Garrett's name.

Teague watched Garrett. "He'll have to be."

I thought fast. "You know what? Maybe it would help if I spent more time with the guests."

Teague arched his eyebrows. "Really? And why would you do that?"

"After what you said about Butch taking it easy on Garrett, it might help if I was a little more… hands-on this time. Especially when we've got a guest who might benefit from a little one-on-one attention."

Teague's eyes twinkled. He glanced to the bunkhouse where Toby had just gone inside, and then back to me. "Sure. Whatever you say, boss." As I walked away, I caught his whisper.

"Of course, you didn't specify *which* guest would be doing the benefiting."

CHAPTER NINE

Toby

From the door of the bunkhouse, I watched Robert stroll up the path toward the big house, a cup of coffee in my hand.

Damn. That was one fine-looking man. Then it occurred to me. What else did I know about him, apart from the ranch hands telling me he was solid, troubled, fair… *Is he married? Divorced? Widowed?*

Yeah, I knew diddly squat. I smiled to myself. Inquiring minds needed to know. He'd requested that I call him Mr. Thorston, but in the safety of my own thoughts, he was Robert.

And Robert was something of an enigma.

Teague was headed my way, and I walked over to meet him.

"So… what's the plan?" I knew he'd have one. Teague struck me as an organized, efficient kinda guy.

"Paul wants you to groom the horses before lunch."

I blinked. "What—*all* of them? That's a lot of horses." I'd counted at least nine that morning, and that didn't include Rusty.

He grinned. "All part of the experience, right? Besides, he didn't think you'd mind being around the stables."

Paul caught on fast.

"Sure." It would be hard work—I recalled that much from doing it as a teenager—but I didn't mind that.

"And while you're at it, you'll be cleaning out the stalls too."

I arched my eyebrows. "I see. Anything *else* you want done? Maybe I should shove a broom up my ass and sweep out the stables too." Then I grinned right back at him, to let him know we were good. Hell, I knew what I'd signed up for.

Teague batted his lashes. "Would you? That'd be great."

Well, what do you know? Teague also had a sense of humor.

"And what will the others be doing while I'm shoveling shit?"

"Declan's coming with me. I need to check on the herd. Had a call this morning from Hank Quaid. He runs helicopter trips out of Bozeman for tourists. Said he spotted part of the fence was down in the north pasture, and some of the cattle had gotten through. Declan's done this before. Walt'll come too."

"What about me?" Garrett demanded as he approached us. "What will I be doing?"

"We're gonna put you on Lucy," Butch told him as he walked up behind him. "But… you gotta relax, dude. Horses sense that kinda shit."

I stared at Butch. "'Kinda shit'?" I rolled my eyes. "Yeah, I'm sure that's *really* going to help him relax."

Butch narrowed his gaze. "If he gets on a horse and it senses he's nervous…"

"So he falls off a few times. It's part of the process." I addressed Garrett. "Can't tell you how many times I've fallen off a horse. And look, I'm still here. It won't kill you."

Behind Garrett, Zeeb flinched.

"And you say *I'm* not helping?" Butch retorted.

Garrett's wide-eyed stare darted from Butch to me, and then he walked into the bunkhouse, slamming the door behind him.

Teague glared at us. "For fuck's sake, guys. This might be asking a lot, but can you guys *not* butt heads around him? And don't talk about him when he's standing right in front of you."

Butch gaped. "Who are you, his mom?"

"No, I'm the guy who's here to make sure he has a good experience. You know, so he leaves a five-star review on Trip Advisor, and makes this place look good?" Teague glanced toward the bunkhouse door. "I've been watching him. Conflict makes him uncomfortable. He was the same last night when you were dicking around." He squared his jaw. "*You* might not have noticed, but *I* sure did. And right now I'm guessing he's feeling uncomfortable as fuck, which is why he just hightailed it back to his bunk. So in future…" Another glare. "Cut the locking horns crap, all right? At least until he settles in. I'll go see how he is. Paul, you take Toby to the stables and make sure he has everything he needs."

"Hey," I called out as he walked toward the bunkhouse. "I'm a guest too. Aren't you supposed to kiss my butt?"

Teague came to a halt and turned to face me. "You don't need support—he does. And no, I'm not about to kiss your butt."

"Why not?"

His eyes glittered. "Because I get the feeling you'd enjoy it too much."

Teague caught on fast too.

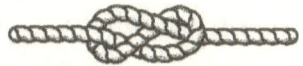

I knew it was almost time for lunch by the rumbles coming from my stomach. I'd cleaned out all the stalls and groomed all the horses except for Rusty. I figured Paul would've done that before Robert had taken him out that morning, but I was going to do it again, because hey, the boss's horse needed that little extra, right?

Maybe it would correct Robert's first impression of me too. Lord knew we hadn't gotten off on the right foot. And then it hit me.

I want him to like me.

Why his opinion should matter, I wasn't certain—I only knew it did.

I walked into Rusty's stall, and he moved toward me, those big brown eyes focused on me.

"Hey there," I murmured. "Let's get you in tiptop shape."

I ran my hand down his foreleg, the hoof pick ready. I cupped his hoof, slowly leaning in until he shifted his weight, allowing me to pick up his foot. Supporting it in my hand, I used the pick to gently remove the pebbles from the inside of the shoe. Paul had told me how to check for signs of thrush. When all his hooves had been picked and inspected, I used the curry comb to loosen the dirt from his coat. I worked from ear to tail, avoiding the head, mane, tail, and lower legs, taking care when I went over the bonier sections. Rusty flattened his ears, and I eased off, currying with more care. Then I grabbed the dandy brush and used short, flicking motions to remove the debris from his coat. Finally, I applied the body brush, using long, sweeping strokes to smooth down the hairs.

His coat groomed, I picked up a dampened sponge and wiped around Rusty's eyes, ears, and muzzle. Then I wiped the dock area beneath the tail, being especially gentle.

The mane took some detangling, and I worked through it with my fingers before using the mane brush to straighten it all out. When I did the same with his tail, I made sure to stand off to the side, so as not to be in kicking range if he got spooked.

"Nearly done," I said in a soothing voice. "Yeah, you're a beautiful boy, aren't you?" I smiled. "Come to think of it, your master's no slouch in the looks department either."

From behind me came a cough. I stiffened. "And he's right behind me, isn't he?" I turned slowly to find Robert leaning against the wall, grinning. I tried not to stare at his open collar. Seeing a guy's chest hair like that was a turn-on for me, always had been, and I didn't want Robert to catch me looking.

He pointed to the fork standing against the door frame. "So what did you do to end up shoveling horse shit?"

I chuckled. "Still trying to work that one out. I reckon it could be Butch's revenge for me calling him a dick." I went back to my task, conscious of his gaze.

Well, if he's going to watch…

I dropped the brush. "Oops." I bent over to retrieve it, feeling the denim stretched tight over my ass. I might have imagined that hitch in his breath, but I couldn't swear to it.

"You're good with horses."

I straightened. "I used to be. When I was a teenager, maybe

thirteen or fourteen, we'd spend our summers at my granddad's place in Wyoming. He put me on horse detail. It got so I could groom a horse blindfolded."

"Did you have a favorite horse?"

I smiled. "Yeah, Willow. She was a beauty, a chestnut mare. You should've seen her kids too. I was there when her second foal put in an appearance. The birth got a little tricky, so Granddad and I spent the night with her in her stall."

"You and he were close, weren't you?" I gave him an inquiring glance, and he smiled. "I could hear it in your voice."

"Yeah, we were. Losing him was tough." I hadn't thought about him in a while. I guess being around horses made the memories more acute.

"You said *we* spent the summers... You've got siblings?"

"One sister, two brothers. I'm the youngest. We don't get to see much of each other, we're kinda spread out." Which was no bad thing, given how the last family meet-up had gone.

"You're not close to *them*, though."

I arched my eyebrows. "You're good. They... We had a falling out, a while back." That was as far as I was willing to go. He didn't need to know about their nasty little minds.

"Anything that can be fixed?"

He wasn't asking out of politeness. I knew that from the warmth in his voice.

This guy cares about people. Probably what made him such a good boss, because it was plain to see his hands looked up to him.

"It's a nice thought, but no, not really. They're not gonna change, and neither am I. Let's just say... They disapprove of me— well, of how I earn my dollars."

They'd tossed out the word deviant once or twice, along with a few other choice phrases.

"This club of yours that you co-own, is it successful?"
Robert held up his hands. "You don't need to tell me any more than that."

"Yeah, it is. San Francisco is the perfect location for it too." Plenty of kinksters who liked to have a place to hang out, shoot the breeze… among other things.

"Then if it's successful, what they think doesn't matter. It's *your* life—not theirs. You live it how *you* want."

I bit back a smile. "Do you write for a problems page? You know, kind of *Ask Agatha* sort of thing?" His face darkened, and my stomach clenched. *What did I say?*

"I try not to dole out advice. Sometimes it can backfire." He cleared his throat. "Your granddad sounds as if he was good people. How did he die?"

"We lost him to pancreatic cancer four years ago." *And you just changed the subject.*

Compassion filtered into his gaze. "I'm sorry. We lost my dad seven years ago. And you're right—it *is* tough."

"The men still talk about him," I remarked. "Your dad, I mean."

Robert's eyes twinkled. "I can imagine."

"'Tough old bird' I think was the phrase Butch used."

He laughed. "That sounds about right."

"So it's just you and Diana?"

Another twinkle. "What—didn't Butch fill you in on my family tree? Yeah, it's just me and my little sister."

Zeeb strolled into the stable, and came to a halt when he saw Robert. "Hey, boss. Thought you were up at the house." Then he smiled at me. "You know, if this guy's distracting you, you only have to say, and he's outta here."

The fact he felt comfortable enough to come out with stuff like that said a lot about his relationship with Robert.

I returned the smile. "What if he's a welcome distraction?"

Robert's eyes widened.

Zeeb blinked, then coughed. "We're riding the Shafthouse trail this afternoon, boss. Figured Declan and Toby here might like a little challenge after their laid-back morning."

Laid-back? I rolled my eyes. "Of course, I've been sitting on my ass since breakfast. Not sure I can fit in a trail ride—I *was* thinking about getting my nails done."

Robert burst out laughing. If I'd thought Paul's laugh was great, Robert's was on a whole different level. I couldn't help but think he didn't laugh enough.

Judging by Zeeb's dazed expression, I'd nailed it.

Robert patted Zeeb on the shoulder. "Sounds as if you've tailored the trail ride to the clients. Good job."

Zeeb waited, but when it became clear Robert wasn't about to say anything else, he tipped his hat, and ambled out of the stable.

"This trail Zeeb is talking about—what's it like?" I was looking forward to getting on a horse again. My brief morning ride had only served to whet my appetite.

"Put it this way, you'll get a fantastic view. It can get a little rocky the higher you go, but nothing you can't cope with, I'm sure."

"Sounds awesome." I bit my lip. "Hey, if you want to give your paperwork a rest, you could always come along."

And why did I say that?

I knew why, of course. Robert was a hot older guy who ticked all my boxes, and was sexy as fuck on a horse. The prospect of riding a trail with him?

Put it this way, I wouldn't be admiring the fantastic landscape. "Don't tempt me."

"Why not? Don't they say temptation is good for the soul?"

Robert's eyes danced with amusement. "I think you're getting a little confused. Don't you mean confession?"

I grinned. "Temptation sounds like more fun."

And why am I flirting with this guy?

Robert

I cleared my throat. "If you'll excuse me, I need to go talk to Teague."

Like hell I did. I just needed an excuse to get out of there. Toby was a particular kind of trouble, spelled H-O-T.

"Well, think about it." Toby's eyes met mine. "And I'll keep my fingers crossed."

I strolled out of the stables, aware of heat rising inside me. Paul was in the paddock with Garrett and Lucy. Teague was watching from the fence, his arms resting on it.

I wandered over to him. "So… how bad was it? The fences, I mean." Anything to get my mind off the sexy-as-fuck dude who was grooming my horse.

"There was a gap, sure enough—God knows how that happened—but only six or seven cows had gotten through it. We got 'em back and Walt patched it up."

I nodded towards Garrett. "How's he doing?" He was standing at Lucy's head, stroking her neck.

"Paul got him to feed her. Nothing like a little food to create a bond, right? I reckon we'll have Lucy eating out of his hand by the end of the day."

I loved Teague's confidence. "Is Paul okay to work with Garrett for as long as it takes?"

He nodded. "And when Zeeb takes Declan and Toby out on the trail, I'll stay here and keep an eye on things. I think Butch is gonna lend a hand too. You know, for moral support. If we can get Garrett relaxed enough to get on the horse, that'd be a bonus."

"I wonder what the deal is with him," I mused. Not that I had any intention of finding out.

Don't get involved. Don't offer advice.

"No clue. Declan seems to think he just needs a little breathing space."

"Hell, we all need that, now and then." When the thought slipped into my mind, I jumped on it. "In that case, I might go riding with Zeeb and the other guests." I kept my tone nonchalant.

Teague arched his eyebrows. "Yeah, I can *totally* see how riding out with them is you being more hands-on with Garrett."

"Hey," I remonstrated. "There'll be you, Butch, and Paul here. Don't you think if I stuck around too, that would smack of overkill? Besides I'd just be in the way."

Yeah, that sounded plausible. Logical.

Teague grinned. "Sure, boss. Whatever you say."

He sees right through me, doesn't he?

I wasn't sure if I found the thought irritating—or comforting.

Toby

"No one wants this last piece of chicken, right?" I said as I grabbed it from the basket in the center of the table.

Butch snorted. "If anyone does, it looks as if they're shit out of luck."

"Hey, I've been working all morning, remember?" I retorted.

"He's got a point," Paul admitted.

I beamed. "Then I claim the right to the last piece." Matt made the best fried chicken I'd ever tasted. The man was a national treasure.

I listened as Declan and Walt discussed the pros and cons of barbed wire fences as opposed to log fences. Teague and Zeeb were on their phones, and Paul was flicking through a horse magazine.

Butch was watching me, however.

I arched my eyebrows. "What's up? I got ketchup on my face or something?"

He grinned. "I was just thinking how you rolled up and fitted right in, that's all."

"I'll take that as a compliment."

"Compliment intended."

He lapsed into silence, and I ate my chicken, enjoying the

peace and quiet. What came to mind was the cabin down by the creek. There had been something... sad about the place.

"Hey, guys? Can I ask you something?"

Walt broke off from his conversation with Declan, and grinned. "Eight inches without choking."

Splutters and violent coughing came from around the table.

"Christ, warn a guy before you say shit like that," Teague growled, wiping his phone.

I rolled my eyes. "Funnily enough, that wasn't the question." Then I grinned too. "But I have to say... I'm impressed." Walt laughed his ass off. "No, what I wanted to know was... this morning when I went for my early ride, and—"

"And got your ass escorted back by the boss." Paul's eyes twinkled.

"Yeah, okay. I followed the creek, and I ended up at this cabin, all on its own."

The room fell silent, and the hairs stood up on my arms.

I frowned. "What have I said?"

"What about it?" Teague asked.

"Does it belong to someone? I mean, the trail that led me there was a well-used one, so I figured *someone* must've used it."

"It used to belong to the boss's mom," Zeeb told me.

"You looking forward to the trail this afternoon?" Teague helped himself to the last piece of bread. "I think you'll really like it."

Declan gazed at the faces around the table, his brow furrowed.

He feels it too, as if they just shut down the conversation.

But why?

CHAPTER TEN

Toby

We rode in a line, Zeeb leading us, Declan behind him, then me, with Robert bringing up the rear. We'd been out of sight of the ranch for the last twenty minutes, but my surprise at his decision to join us hadn't faded.

Did I persuade him? Or did he just need a break from his paperwork?

Whatever his motivation, I hadn't been able to hide my smile when I caught sight of him strolling down the path toward the stables.

Beside me, Zeeb had cackled. "Now, what do you suppose made the boss decide to join us?" He nudged me in the ribs. "Except maybe it's not a what—it's a *who*." Then he'd sauntered away.

The implication had been obvious. Robert was there because of me.

I was curious to know why.

I was also a little peeved that he was behind me. How was I supposed to get a glimpse of his ass when I couldn't see it?

Toby Philip Merrow, did it ever occur to you that you might be staring at a straight *man's ass?*

It was uncanny how my inner voice sounded so much like my mom.

We maintained a steady pace as we trotted across the prairie, a carpet of yellow- green grass, the trail pointing like an arrow toward dark green trees ahead. The sky was an expanse of blue, dotted here and there with wisps of white clouds, a perfect June day.

"Where are we going?" I called out to Zeeb.

He pointed to a ridge ahead of us. "Up there. The trail takes us through the woods, past the lake, and then it starts to climb.

That's when the terrain gets a little rocky."

Robert was right. There would be a fantastic view from that altitude.

"Are you going to show him the wolf den?" Declan asked.

Zeeb twisted around in his saddle to give him a mock glare. "Will you quit giving the game away? Maybe I wanted to surprise him."

"I'd say that boat has sailed," Robert said with a chuckle.

There we were, riding through a huge open space, and for the first time I understood what was meant by the phrase *big sky*. I didn't recollect noticing the skies when I was a kid. As an adult, I'd watched a few sunrises and sunsets from the beaches in San Francisco, looking out over the water at the horizon, but that was as nothing to my reaction to the staggeringly impressive vista before us.

I felt so fucking small and insignificant.

"Kind of overwhelming, isn't it?" Robert's voice drifted forward.

"It's so peaceful out here." Except that didn't even come close to touching the landscape's effect on me.

Ahead, Zeeb nodded. "And that's why I'm here. This is a place where a man can appreciate the simple life." He gestured to the view before us. "Kinda fitting, don't you think, that we're up here on the Lord's day, enjoying His creation. *This* is living the dream. I get to see new faces, create the life I want... Because make no mistake about it, life *is* what you make it." Conviction rang out in his voice.

"How long have you been at Salvation? Ten years, I think you said? Where were you before that?"

"Idaho, and don't go there."

I chuckled. "I have no intention of going there. What reason do I have to visit Idaho?"

"No, I mean, don't go there. Not gonna talk about life before Salvation."

"Fair enough."

Good Lord, does everyone *who works here have a past they're escaping from?* Not that anyone had come right out and said as much, but there sure had been hints of it, first from Butch, then Paul, and now Zeeb…

Prairie gave way to trees as the trail headed into the woods. On either side of us, tall, slim trunks rose into the sky high above our heads, and here and there trees had fallen, some sawn off near the base, others more jagged in appearance.

"This is where we get wood for the ranch," Robert told me.

There was a different smell in the air, a musky, earthy kind of smell. The trail was covered in dirt and leaves, and it was fairly easygoing for a while. After about twenty minutes, the trail started to slope downward. The air grew fresher, and at last we emerged at a lake, its perimeter lined with trees. The water was so goddamn clear.

"Okay, time to give the horses a rest, and let 'em have a drink." Zeeb pointed to a tree stump. "You can use that to dismount."

"I get the feeling you've been here before," I quipped.

Declan laughed. "I guess Zeeb has lost count of how many times he's done this trail with guests."

I walked down to the water's edge, staring at its calm surface, at the reflection of the tree line. *So still…* Declan had his phone out, and was taking photos. Zeeb saw to the horses, their reins tied around a tree.

Robert joined me. "I always forget how beautiful this is," he murmured.

"How often do you ride the trails?"

He gave a rueful smile. "Not as often as I should."

Holding back was not in my nature. "Have you never heard the term, work-life balance?"

"What's that?" he said with a chuckle. Then he sighed. "I had one, once."

"Then what happened? Was it because you lost your dad? You had to run the ranch?"

"Yes and no. Dad had been gone a year when Diana came up

with the idea of a dude ranch. Till then, I was... struggling. I mean, we just went on as before, because he'd got everything set up for that, but..." He let out another sigh. "I don't think I was ready to run the ranch—or to be without him." He gave me a quizzical glance. "And I have no idea why I shared all that. My apologies. You didn't come here to listen to my life story."

"No need to apologize," I assured him. I didn't tell him his confession only made him more... human, I suppose. "We all have to share sometimes."

"Ready to move on?" Zeeb called out.

Robert looked at me, his eyes sparkling. "Now *that's* a good question."

We got back on the horses. Zeeb led off, and we followed the trail into dense woodland. After about fifteen minutes, he came to a halt.

"Something I wanna show you." He pointed to a mass of fallen trees. "This is a wolf den. I think it's been abandoned, but I can't be sure. Different packs use different dens. But this is a perfect spot, a great rendezvous point. It's away from the road, from people, and there's plenty of shade. No one messes with them."

"Are there many wolves around here?" I inquired.

"Montana Fish, Wildlife & Parks have permission to 'manage' them," Zeeb air-quoted. "Last estimate gave the figure at one thousand one hundred and fourteen wolves, but that was the end of last year."

"And despite more aggressive hunting and trapping, those numbers remained stable," Robert added. "Everything changed in February this year."

"What happened then?"

Zeeb snorted. "They were declared a protected species, that's what. Which is not so great when three or four of 'em go on the hunt, and you wanna protect the herd."

"Am I likely to see one?" I liked the idea of coming face-to-face with a real live wolf.

Zeeb shrugged. "Maybe you might get a glimpse of one." He smiled. "Okay, so they can be a menace. There was this one time, though, about three years ago. I was out on a trail, and there were maybe fourteen wolves, running down the hill in front of us. It was an awesome sight." He pointed ahead. "Let's keep moving."

We continued on our way, still deep in the woods. Suddenly Zeeb came to a stop, and held up one hand. We all came to a halt.

"What is it?" I called out.

"Toby… quiet," Robert advised in a low voice. "Look to your left."

I followed his pointing finger, and my breath caught at the sight of a brown bear, standing upright—watching us.

Holy shit. The size *of it.*

I hadn't expected it to be so big. Then I caught rustling coming from my right, but there was nothing to be seen.

"Look up," Robert whispered. I did as instructed, and saw—

Oh wow.

A bear cub was up the tree, lurching down backward.

"Stay very still," Robert murmured. "We're between a momma bear and her cub, and that's not a good place to be."

The cub reached the foot of the tree, and ambled across the trail in front of us toward its mom, as if we weren't even there. When it reached her, the bear dropped to all fours, and led her cub away.

Wow. I took a deep breath.

Zeeb turned to glance at me. "Exciting enough for ya?"

I couldn't stop smiling. This was turning out to be a phenomenal trip.

We continued along the trail, and the trees grew less dense. Finally, we emerged into open grassland. Zeeb twisted around to look at us.

"How about we pick up the pace?"

I was all for a gallop. "A short one, though. Lightning's a little out of practice."

We rode fast, the horses' hooves thundering over the ground, and after the steady pace we'd maintained thus far, it was a welcome change. It wasn't long before the trail started to climb, winding up and up, and we slowed down until at last we reached the ridge.

I soon spotted the tree stump that served as a dismounting block. I got off Lightning and held onto his reins as I stared at the landscape spread below us, a carpet of green, yellow, and brown. Around us were stark, bone-white trees, no life left in them. It was windy up there, and I held onto my hat. I watched the shadow of clouds rolling over the hills, and once again I had the feeling of being so insignificant.

Robert walked up to me, leading Rusty, and I gestured to the patchwork quilt of land. "Now *that's* what I call an office."

He stood beside me, staring out at the scenery, lost in his own thoughts. Then he smiled. "I need to do this more often."

Zeeb chuckled. "I've been telling you that for two years, boss."

"Okay, okay, I've heard you. Satisfied now?"

Zeeb's eyes gleamed. "Nope, but I reckon I will be."

It struck me that nearly everyone on Salvation was given to cryptic remarks.

Declan sighed. "It's sights like this that make me rethink my life. I have no family, it's just me... Who am I'm working for? Two weeks a year out here... It's not enough."

"There's still time. You're young enough to make a change," Robert observed. Then he stiffened. "Never mind me. You do what works for you." He walked off a short distance from us.

I followed. "Hey." When he turned to gaze at me, I looked him in the eye. "It's okay, you know. To give advice, I mean."

"We should head back. We need to be home by supper time."

Before I could get another word out, he led Rusty over to the tree stump, and mounted him. Zeeb and Declan soon followed.

There was an uneasy feeling in my belly.

What just happened?

We reached the grassland again, and I was ready for another gallop.

"Hold on there," Robert called out behind me. "There's a—"

Lightning bucked, and I held onto the reins as he bolted, charging along the trail, almost running into Declan.

"Whoa there." I jerked the reins, and the next thing I knew, the ground came at me, and *fuck*, it was hard.

"Are you okay?" Robert was off his horse in a heartbeat, handing the reins to Zeeb before kneeling next to me. I sat up, wincing. "Have you broken anything? Sprained anything?"

"I think I bruised something," I muttered. When his eyes widened, I gave another wince. "My pride." I met his gaze. "It's okay. Not the first time I've fallen off a horse. What made him bolt like that?"

"There was a horsefly on his rear. I think it took a bite." Robert helped me to my feet and brushed me down.

"I can manage," I told him. "It'll be worse later."

Zeeb came over. "You all right? You scared the livin' shit outta me. Fuck, you're one lucky man. You could've hit your head on a rock or something."

"Then isn't it a good thing he bolted *now*, and not up on that ridge?"

"Are you *always* this calm and philosophical?" Robert asked.

I smiled. "I like to keep my calm." It was a good trait, one that was appreciated when I was in charge of a scene.

Robert helped me back into the saddle, then mounted Rusty once more. "Okay, we're going to take it at a steady pace from here on."

That was fine by me.

As we trotted along, I became aware of developing aches.

I swore I could hear my bunk calling my name.

CHAPTER ELEVEN

Robert

As we rode into the ranch, I spied Garrett ahead of us in the paddock, sitting on Lucy, and Paul was leading them around.

"Well, there's progress for ya," Zeeb said with a chuckle.

As we drew closer, Garrett saw us, and grinned. He waved. "Hey, look at me."

"We're looking," I called out. "Keep both hands on the reins."

We trotted up to the fence, dismounted, and tied up the horses. I gave Garrett a smile. "Looking good there." Garrett stuck his chin and his chest out, his shoulders held back. I wandered over to where Teague and Butch were watching from the fence. "He been on Lucy since we left?"

"Yup." Butch cackled. "He's gonna have aches where he never had 'em before."

He was right. Most folks ached like a son of a bitch after their first time on a horse.

Toby joined us. "He's not the only one." He winced.

I gazed at him with concern. "Are you okay?" He'd come off Lightning with an awful wallop.

He grimaced. "My ass is complaining. Apparently, there's a hell of a difference between a short morning ride, and a trail. That fall didn't help."

Teague gaped. "You fell?"

"Lightning had an encounter with a horsefly," I told him. "It didn't end well."

"What I *really* need right now is a soak in a tub." Toby rolled his eyes. "Except there isn't one, of course."

I don't know what made me say it, but the words were out

before I could stop them. "You can use one of the bathrooms up at the house."

He blinked. "Really?"

"Sure." I acted like it was no big deal.

Then why is my heart racing?

Butch grinned. "That's a great idea. Garrett could probably use a soak too."

Well crap. It was only then I realized I'd made the offer out of an ulterior motive —which had just been thwarted by Butch.

"Why not? There's no shortage of bathrooms up there." I grinned at Toby. "So you won't even need to share a tub."

"Hey, Garrett," Butch hollered. "You wanna soak your ass? I got a packet of Epsom salt with your name on it."

Garrett gave him a look of pure gratitude. "Oh wow, that'd be great." He glanced down. "Once I get off this horse, of course."

"I'll put the horses back in the stables," Teague said. "You go on up to the house."

"And I'll go to the bunkhouse and grab a clean change of clothes for after my soak." Toby met my gaze. "Thank you for this. If you only knew how much I need it."

"Hey, maybe the boss can find you some bubble bath," Butch said with a grin.

Toby laughed. "I think I can manage without it." He walked stiffly over to the bunkhouse.

"What happened to him?" Garrett asked as Paul led him toward us.

"He had a little mishap, that's all." I didn't want to put him off, not now he'd finally gained some confidence. "He's okay though." I gazed at Garrett. "And as soon as you're comfortable on Lucy, you get to go on a trail too."

He smiled for what seemed like the first time since I'd met him. "I'd like that." Paul led Lucy out of the paddock and over to the mounting block, where he helped him climb down.

"We had a bear encounter," I murmured, keeping my voice

low.

Teague's eyes widened. "Serious?"

"Thankfully no. Zeeb had his rifle, of course. And she was fine as soon as she had her baby back."

"I don't think you should share that with Garrett. It would likely freak him the fuck out."

I'd had the same thought myself.

Teague grinned. "So… you running a bathhouse now? This a new sideline?"

I coughed violently. "Will you *not* say things like that?" Garrett was walking toward us, stiff as hell. "If you grab some clean clothes, I'll take you and Toby up to the house."

He beamed. "I'll be right back." Then he winced. "Once I can figure out how to quit waddling like a goddamn duck."

I laughed. "All part of the experience. And trust me, it'll feel much worse tomorrow."

"Does that mean I get a day off?"

Teague chuckled. "Hell no. Tomorrow you get right back on that horse."

Garrett said nothing, but walked toward the bunkhouse.

"You did good," I muttered.

"Thanks, boss. And how was the trail? I watched you ride out." His eyes sparkled. "Looks like you had a great view."

I knew he was talking about Toby's ass.

"The trail was just fine, thank you."

"And will you be doing that again?"

I smiled. "Possibly."

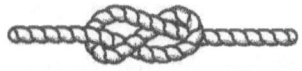

Toby

Garrett and I trudged up the path toward the big house, both of us with a bundle of clean clothes under our arm. As we reached the summit of the hill, I got my first real good view of it.

"Wow, look at this place." Garrett whistled.

Up close, it was bigger than I'd expected. Thick stone-covered posts supported the porch, but the rest of the exterior was nothing but dark logs. Rocking chairs sat on the veranda, and I could imagine sitting there, enjoying a sunset, or an early morning cup of coffee.

The front door opened, and Robert stood there. For a minute, I wasn't sure what was different about him, until it hit me. It was the first time I'd seen him without a hat. He was bald, and the total absence of hair told me he'd shaved it all off.

I smiled. "You should go without a hat more often."

He ran his hand over his scalp. "Well, I'm not about to wear one in the house. Come on in."

He led us into a large open space, and I had to admit, it took my breath away. The vaulted ceiling made it look almost palatial. Around three sides, about twelve feet off the floor, was a mezzanine gallery, surrounded by a balcony. The gable end of the room was an expanse of glass, letting the light flood into what was a dark interior. There were more windows underneath the gallery on two sides. The balconies above were framed with neat rectangles of wood, but infilled with natural boughs, giving it a rustic feel. Through them, I could see couches and lamps, and paintings on the walls. Some were draped with throws. Below, the heavily varnished floor was covered here and there with warm-looking rugs, on which stood several couches. Lamps sat on small tables, and the huge fireplace dominated the room.

I imagined growing up in this house would have been interesting. Lots of places to hide, to explore. I glanced around me. "How do you get up there?" I pointed to the gallery. "I don't see a staircase."

Robert indicated the hallway that led off from the room. "The stairs are back there. That's where the kitchen is too, and the dining room. I thought I might make some coffee for when you're done."

Before I could tell him he didn't need to go to such trouble, Garrett butted in.

"How many bedrooms does this place have?"

"Five. And three baths."

"You don't have to make us coffee, you know," I informed Robert. I didn't want to put him out.

He arched his eyebrows. "You think I'm gonna kick you out with your hair still damp?" He led us through the house towards the staircase. When we reached the second floor, he pointed to a door on the left. "Garrett, there you go. Soak as long as you like."

"Thanks."

As he pushed open the door, Robert added, "And my apologies for the color scheme, okay?" When Garrett gave him an inquiring glance, Robert smiled. "My dad chose it for my mom. When she passed, he didn't have the heart to change it, so I hope you like pink."

Garrett smiled, and went into the bathroom, closing the door behind him.

Robert let me farther down the hall and pointed to a door on the right. "And this is yours."

We went inside, and my mouth fell open. "Wow. I could fit my whole apartment in this bathroom." The large tub sat in the corner, with windows above it on two sides. The floors were marble, as was the tile surrounding the tub and the sink. "Never mind that— you could hold a square dance in here."

Robert laughed. "That was granddad. Small was *not* in his vocabulary." His eyes gleamed. "By the way, if you *did* want some bubble bath..."

I chuckled. "I'm good, thanks. And I won't let on to Butch. I'll keep your secret."

He bit his lip. "I appreciate that. Everyone around here knows too many of my secrets already." He paused. "I'll leave you to soak in the tub." Then he walked out of the room, and closed the door behind him.

I stared after him. *And what secrets are those?* Not that I was about to learn them anytime soon. Those guys in the bunkhouse were a loyal bunch. And whatever secrets Robert was keeping were none of my business.

I opened the faucet, and undressed while the hot water gushed into the tub and steam filled the air. I don't know what gave it away, but I had the feeling I was in Robert's bathroom. I glanced at the tub, and the first thought to cross my mind was that it was plenty big enough for two.

Robert

The coffee machine beeped. I removed three cups from the cabinet and set them on the countertop before shifting to the window to gaze out at the ranch below, inhaling the coffee's rich aroma.

I glanced up at the ceiling. *Why did I make the offer?* I've never done anything like that before. And I just *knew* Zeeb and Teague would make a mountain out of a mole hill. It was just a kind offer, that was all.

Who was I kidding? I'd wanted to see more of Toby.

Does that include seeing him buck naked, getting out of the tub?

Oh dear *Lord*, the image in my head. An image I had to banish before he came downstairs. I did *not* want to be staring at him, picturing him in the tub, water swirling around his shoulders, his hair wet, drops of water clinging to his beard…

I opened the fridge, gazing at the squat beer bottles I kept in there for when Teague and I hung out. Once a week we'd sit on the porch of an evening, shooting the breeze, talking about the ranch, me with my iced tea, him with a couple of beers. On impulse, I grabbed the nearest bottle, and headed out the kitchen. As I climbed the stairs, my heartbeat quickened.

I shouldn't be doing this.

He's a guest.

And since when have I let a guest take a bath in my house?

I walked over to his bathroom and paused outside. I raised my hand to knock on the door, still debating the rationality of such an action. From inside, I heard him humming, and I had to smile.

Decision made.

I knocked gently on the door, and he fell silent. "You weren't kidding, were you?" I called out.

"Excuse me?"

"You really can't carry a tune." I paused. "Don't suppose you'd like a beer while you're in there?"

"Are you kidding? Now *that's* what I call great customer service."

I laughed and went into the bathroom. Toby lay sprawled in the tub, his head resting on a folded towel, his knees poking through the surface of the water.

He was every bit as sexy as I'd imagined—and a damn sight less hairy. His pecs were smooth, his nipples set in dark bronze discs of pebbled flesh. His abs were well-defined, his torso lean. The only thing missing was a treasure trail leading down to his—

Oh my God. Now *that* was a thing of beauty.

I averted my gaze, and he laughed. "Dude, we've got the same equipment, right? I'm not shy." As if to reinforce the point, he spread his knees, allowing them to fall back against the sides of the tub, and my attention was drawn instantly once more to his crotch.

"I've noticed that about you." There was something else I couldn't help noticing too. It bobbed in the water, and I had to wonder. *Is he usually this hard, or was he jerking off?* Maybe the humming was to cover the noise of splashing.

I held the beer bottle out, and he grinned. "You need to come a little closer. I can't reach it from here." He grabbed the sides of the tub, half lifting himself up. "Unless you want me to get out—"

"You stay there."

He grinned. "If you say so." He sank back into the water.

I lurched forward, placed the bottle in his hand, then stepped back.

Toby pointed to the stool at the foot of the tub. "Sit a while. I could do with some company. I was getting a little lonesome in here." His gaze locked on mine. "Unless you've got somewhere else you need to be?" His lips twitched. "You might have some… paperwork that needs seeing to."

I sat, trying not to stare at the sight of Toby's nude body stretched out before me. "Did you enjoy the trail?"

"Yeah, right up to the point where I fell off Lightning." He took a drink, then glanced at me. "Can I ask you something?"

"Sure." My pulse quickened. I couldn't get a handle on this guy. I had no idea what would pop out of his mouth next.

"Is it just you in this house?"

"Yes. Matt sleeps in the bunkhouse."

He frowned. "He wasn't in there last night."

"No, he had to go see his mom. He'll be back tonight."

He nodded. "That's a lot of house for one man."

"When my granddad built it, he was planning on having a large family."

"And did he?" He drank some more, and I took a moment to admire the bob of his Adam's apple, the line of his neck, the flush on his chest from the warm water…

"He and my grandma had five sons. Only one of them stayed around here—my dad."

"What happened to the rest?"

I shrugged. "They married, they left—the house, the county, the state… Most of them didn't want a life on the ranch."

"Except for your dad, it seems." He cocked his head. "You haven't mentioned your mom, except to say she died. When was that?"

"When Diana was born. Childbirth complications, they said."

"So your dad raised you both on his own?"

"Yeah. His sister-in-law—my aunt Phoebe—moved in for a while, but it didn't work out. They kinda brushed each other up the wrong way."

"How long was she living here?"

I smiled. "A week." We both laughed. "Put it this way, no one was surprised she and my uncle didn't have kids."

Toby dipped his shoulders beneath the water. "Damn, this feels good." He peered at me. "You didn't mind me asking?"

"Not at all," I assured him.

"It's just that...I know so little about you. Not that I have a right to know anything. I'm only a guest, after all."

There was no *only* about Toby.

He glanced around. "Aw crap. I didn't bring a towel."

"That's okay. I have a linen closet full of them. I'll get one for you." I stood, and hurried out of the bathroom before he could object.

Outside, I leaned against the door, my heart pounding. It might have been my imagination, but I had the feeling Toby was flirting with me. Then I recalled the casual way he'd spread his knees, his cock poking up.

No, it wasn't my imagination.

I don't know much about you either, Toby Merrow.

But I wanted to know more.

CHAPTER TWELVE

Toby

Supper was over, and I headed toward the door of the bunkhouse. It was eight-thirty, and judging by the amount of clouds, it promised to be a glorious sunset. I left the others playing cards, and by the sound of it, Butch was on a winning streak. Teague had already gone to his cabin.

I wandered down to the paddock and leaned on the railing, gazing at the changing hues of the sky. Considering I'd only had one full day on the ranch, a lot had been crammed into it: the ride out to the creek, and that lonesome little cabin; meeting Robert; cleaning up the horses—and talking to Robert; going on the trail—and talking to Robert; not to mention soaking in the tub—and talking to Robert. That last part had been… interesting. And cute too, the way he scooted out when I said it was time to get out of the tub.

Yeah, Robert figured pretty heavily in my day, not that I was complaining, far from it. And while there was no denying he was hot as fuck, there was more to him than that sexy gray beard and those gorgeous hazel eyes.

What is it about him? I couldn't put my finger on it, but he intrigued me. I doubted there'd be as much interaction for the rest of the two weeks, but I'd take what I could get.

"Hey."

I turned my head to find Zeeb strolling across to join me. "You finished losing?" I teased.

Zeeb rolled his eyes. "That fucker has the luck of the devil." He held out a squat brown beer bottle, the cap already popped. "Here. Thought you might like one of these." There was another in his other hand.

I frowned. "I thought there was no alcohol allowed around here." Except if that were true, then why had Robert given me a beer?

Maybe the rules were different up at the house.

He cackled. "Where in the hell did you get that idea? Sure, we ain't allowed to drink during the day when we're working, but after supper? We can do whatever the fuck we want." He grinned. "As long as whatever it is, we don't do it to excess." He snorted. "Excess is what led to us gettin' our asses barred from Lacey's—well, Butch's excess, if we're being honest."

I took the bottle. "Thanks." We clinked.

"Happy trails," he intoned before we both took a long drink of cold beer.

I matched his grin. "This is my second today."

He widened his eyes. "You don't say. You got a secret supply?" When I didn't illuminate him any further, his eyes gleamed. "Oh, *I* see. You're not gonna tell me, are you?"

"Nope."

He leaned on the fence. "You feel better after your soak?"

"Yeah, but I know it's temporary. I'm not looking forward to the aches I'm going to wake up with." I smiled. "They'll pass."

Zeeb snorted. "I hate to break it to ya, but your arms are gonna hurt like a son of a bitch tomorrow. Grooming one horse? That's not so bad. Grooming ten?"

"And whose idea was that?" I retorted. "In whose bed do I leave a little surprise as a thank you gift?"

"What kind of gift were you thinking of? A scorpion? A turd?"

I grinned. "I was thinking more along the lines of a toy snake. Nothing dangerous, but it'd give 'em a fright."

Zeeb cackled. "I like the way you think." He stared out at the horizon. "Sure is beautiful."

I had to agree.

"Tomorrow afternoon I'll give you a lesson in roping. Gotta get you ready for the cattle drive, right?"

I was looking forward to it. Then I reconsidered. "You're not expecting me to throw a champion-class lariat, are you? After the day *I've* had?"

Zeeb gave a hoot. "If you can throw it just once, that'll be something. I'll take whatever you can give me." He pointed to the landscape before us. "You think this looks good? Wait till you see the valley where we take the herd. Right about now, it'll be lush and green, with the river snaking through it. Under the trees it's cool and shady. Of course, we have to keep a watch for wolves, but you don't need to worry about that. Most of us are a crack shot." He flashed me a grin. "Matt can't shoot to save his life, but we don't mind none. He'll be there to cook."

"So who'll feed the boss? Or does he come too?"

Zeeb's smile faltered. "He used to. He hasn't been on a cattle drive for a few years, though. But he sends Matt so we don't starve. We take about ten guys with us, but most of us only stay two, three nights up there. The others will stay with the herd until it's time to bring 'em home."

I was dying to ask why Robert had stopped participating.

We fell silent for a while, both of us gazing at the horizon. Except now that I had him alone, there *was* something I'd wanted to ask.

"Zeeb… That's kind of unusual. Is it your real name or a nickname?"

That got me another snort. "I don't tell *anyone* my real name. Zeeb is all they get."

I grinned. "Now you *know* I've got to take a guess."

He returned my grin. "Give it your best shot."

I went with the first thing that came into my head. "Zebadiah."

His eyes widened. "What the fuck?"

"It's the name of a character from one of my favorite books. Zebadiah Carter from—"

"*The Number of the Beast*, by Robert Heinlein."

I chuckled. "I nailed it, didn't I?"

"It was my mom's favorite book too. I think it came out a few years before I was born."

"Have you read it?"

He pulled a face. "Hell no. I don't read shit like that." His eyes sparkled. "I'm more your one-handed-reads kinda guy." I sprayed beer over the railing, and he cackled. "I know. Shocker, ain't it?"

I wiped my lips. "In the book, Zebadiah's nickname was Zebby. You could have had that as your name."

He arched his eyebrows. "Now, do I look like a Zebby to you?"

I chuckled. "Maybe not. I'd have thought Zeb was closer to Zebadiah, though."

"Sure it is, only I didn't want to *be* a Zeb, okay? Zeeb was more... unusual."

We drank, and as I watched, the clouds changed color, from pink to orange to red, as the sun sank slowly.

I raised my bottle. "Here's to the end of my first day. May the rest be as interesting." I tipped it up and drank what was left.

"I'll drink to that." Zeeb followed suit.

I wasn't ready to go inside yet. Having Zeeb alone was too good an opportunity to miss.

"Something else I've been meaning to ask—not you specifically, but seeing as you're here... You remember we were talking at lunch time, and I mentioned that cabin by the creek?"

Zeeb stilled. "What about it?"

"I got the feeling I was missing something. Almost as if you all shut me down." I turned to face him. "Now, don't deny it. Declan noticed it too. So you wanna tell me what *that* was all about?"

Zeeb stared at me. "That wouldn't be my first choice, no." He sighed. "Besides, it's a long story."

"And I've got nowhere to be except my bunk, and it's too early for that." I stared at him. "So start talking." I folded my arms. "Not gonna move from this spot until you do, so you might as well get it over with."

Zeeb gazed at the horizon. "The cabin belonged to the boss's mom, right enough. But then it got new owners. And the reason we don't talk about it is because *one* of those owners is dead."

"I see. Who took over the cabin? And how did one of them die?"

"His name was Kevin Porter. He was the foreman here for years, way before I got here."

"And when did he die?"

"Five years ago. Got drunk one night, climbed onto a horse, and went for a ride. We found him in the creek. His neck was broken. The horse was still standing there. Hadn't left his side."

"Oh my God." I stared at him. "He was riding Lightning, wasn't he?"

Zeeb's gaze met mine. "Yup. That horse was his baby. Never thrown anyone before or since."

"Is that why Robert has the rule about no drinking on a horse? Not that it isn't a sensible rule."

Zeeb regarded me with sparkling eyes. "So it's *Robert* now, is it? What happened to *Mr. Thorston?*"

Oh shit. I feigned ignorance. "Don't guests ever refer to him by his first name?"

"No sir, they do not. Even *we* don't—except for Teague, maybe. But as for why *you're* on a first-name basis with him..." He grinned. "Garrett said he thought he heard the boss in the bathroom with you, up at the house. What was he doing—helping you find the soap?"

"We were just talking."

His eyes lit up. "And *now* I know who gave you that first beer."

"Don't change the subject."

He sighed again. "Yeah, you're right about the drinking part."

"Is that also why Robert doesn't allow anyone to ride Lightning? For fear he'll throw one of the guests?" That made sense.

Zeeb shook his head. "No, that isn't it at all." He took a deep breath. "You see...the other person who took over the cabin? That was the boss. He and Kevin, they were close. I mean, *real* close. I guess they were what you'd call an item."

My jaw dropped. "Robert is gay?"

"As a nine-dollar bill. Not that he's ever... *you* know... come out and said as much. But trust me, we all knew." He chuckled. "The way those two carried on, it wasn't hard to miss."

"How long were they together?"

"Don't rightly know. They were already at it when I got here. I suppose some of the others might know, but... you see, the thing is, we don't exactly discuss it. It's like the worst-kept secret on this ranch."

"So everyone knows, but no one talks about it?"

"You got it."

It explained Robert's manner when he found me at the cabin. It also explained the cabin's dilapidated state.

He leaves it alone because it has too many memories.

Then a thought struck me. "Why are you telling me all this? Doesn't sound like the kind of thing you'd blab about with the guests."

He opened his eyes wide. "We don't tell the guests a goddamn thing."

"But here *you* are, telling me..."

Zeeb studied me for a moment. "You're... different."

"How? What makes me different? Is it because you know *I'm* gay?"

"That's part of it, but... I've never met a guest who elicited the same kind of response from the boss that *you* got... And then I saw you had the same reaction to him."

Robert reacted to me?

"You don't think you're imagining things?"

"Nope, I don't think so." Zeeb counted off on his fingers. "He never interacts with the guests. He doesn't just stroll into the stables when a guest is mucking them out, and strike up a conversation. He never goes on a trail with any of them. And as for offering the use of his bathroom? Woo boy. That's something I *never* thought I'd see in my lifetime." He locked gazes with me. "And then *you* arrived."

"Hey, Garrett got to use a bathroom too, remember. Does he have a thing for Garrett as well?"

Zeeb snorted. "That was all Butch's doing. And *you* might not have seen the boss's face when Butch suggested it, but *I* sure did. He looked as if someone had pissed on his fire and put it out. Now, maybe he just wants the company of a good-looking dude—and don't deny it. I know a good-looking dude when I see one. But then again, maybe he wants more than that."

I was torn between dismissing it all as Zeeb's flight of fancy— and wanting it to be true.

I arched my eyebrows. "You like to speak your mind, don't you? Tell me again why I need to know all this."

"Look… I've got this idea, okay? The boss has an itch that needs scratching—and the scratcher just walked onto the ranch."

"And what makes you think I'd be interested in scratching his itch?"

Because *damn*, he'd got me thinking about it.

Zeeb's eyebrows shot up. "Do I *really* look that stupid to you?" He lowered his voice. "He's been alone since Kevin died. For some reason he feels guilty about Kevin's death, though I don't see why. And I'm telling you all this because I'll swear there's been no one in his bed since Kevin passed. We'd know. Hell, we get to know *everything*."

"Let me get this straight. You want me to make a move on your boss?"

"At least make him an offer. See what he does." Zeeb's face tightened. "We want him to be happy again."

"Kevin made him happy?"

"Like you wouldn't believe. But his death seems to have sucked the life right outta him." Zeeb gave me a thoughtful glance. "Maybe getting you between the sheets is the first step to him getting his life back."

I gaped at him. "Dude, I've been here *one day*. You don't think this is all a little fast?"

"You're here for two weeks. Make him live again for those two weeks. That's all I ask." He cocked his head toward the bunkhouse. "They don't need to know. And if they do find out, they won't say a goddamn word, at least, not to Declan and Garrett."

I didn't know what to say.

Zeeb was studying me again. "I didn't imagine it, did I? You like him?"

He'd been honest with me. I could be that honest too.

"Yeah, I like him. But you need to bear something in mind. He might not be interested in *me*."

Zeeb smiled. "Oh, he's interested, all right."

"Hey!" Butch hollered across to us. "Lights-out time."

Zeeb tugged my arm. "We'd better get in there. But I'm glad we had this chat. I guess I've given you something to think about."

We headed toward the bunkhouse.

"You sure have." I had a feeling I'd be thinking about it long into the night.

"So if I wake up in the early hours to find you beating your meat, I won't have to ask who *you're* fantasizing about, will I?" I jerked my head to stare at him, and he grinned. "Yeah, I got your number." He sounded smug as fuck.

"No one likes a smartass, Zeeb."

He just laughed.

When we reached the door, I glanced up the hill toward the big house. Maybe that was what I hadn't been able to put my finger on.

Robert was lonely. He hid it well, no doubt about that, but the conversation with Zeeb confirmed it.

One thing was certain. I wasn't about to march up to the house to find out if Zeeb was on the money. I wanted more than his hunches.

I wanted an invitation.

CHAPTER THIRTEEN

Monday, June 13
Toby

I stared at the cardboard box Zeeb set down in the middle of the paddock.

"Is there a cow in there?" I quipped. "You telling me you get your cows delivered by Amazon? They're awful small, if that's the case. Catching one should be no problem." The jokes were my way of delaying the inevitable. I ached like a bastard.

Zeeb glanced toward the fence where Robert stood watching us. "Hey, boss. Looks like we got ourselves a fuckin' comedian."

Robert grinned. Then I watched as Walt, Butch, Paul, Declan, and Garrett joined him. I was used to being the focus of attention—I'd given God knew how many demos at the club over the years—but this particular audience did little for my nerves. I'd hog-tied plenty of guys in the past, but *throwing* ropes was something new. I smiled to myself. *If I'm any good at this, I might do a demonstration at the club. 'How to deal with runaway submissives.'*

Zeeb returned his attention to me. "When you're starting out, you can use any number of things for a target—a post, a roping dummy, a plastic steer head, and yeah, even an Amazon box." He handed me the lariat, maybe forty feet of coiled poly rope. "Now, stand about fifteen to twenty feet away from it. You need space to swing your lariat."

"Yeah, you don't wanna accidentally catch the target before you throw it," Butch called out.

"Ignore him," Zeeb told me.

"What makes you think I'm going to be able to get it up?"
When the guffaws erupted, I realized what I'd said. I rolled my eyes.

"Jeez. Guess I've found *your* level."

"Hey, if you've got problems getting it up, you might wanna see a doctor," Walt hollered. He leered. "I'd be willing to lend a hand, if it came to that."

I gave them all a mock glare. "Trying to throw a lariat here."

"Yeah, shut the fuck up," Zeeb added. He returned his attention to me. "And you? Just give it your best shot. It's your first time, after all."

"Yeah, Toby's a lariat virgin," Butch called out, amid chuckles.

"Okay, that's enough." Robert's voice cut through the laughter, and everyone quieted down. "Zeeb, get on with it."

"Sure thing, boss." He addressed me. "Lean your weight on the balls of your feet, like you would if they were in stirrups. Now, make a loop in your lariat—you're right-handed, aren't you?" I nodded. "Okay then, hold the loop in your right hand. See that eye at the end of the rope? That's called a honda. That slides the loop open and closed."

"How big does the loop need to be?" I asked.

"That's up to you. Some folks prefer to start small and let it grow while they twirl it overhead. Others prefer a bigger loop— maybe seven feet across—and keep it that size while they twirl it." Zeeb grinned. "I don't figure you for a guy who does anything on a small scale."

I rolled my eyes once more. He showed me how to hold the excess coils of lariat in my left hand, leaving enough slack to give myself room to lift the loop above my head, twirl it, and throw it.

"You ready to start swinging?"

"As ready as I'll ever be."

"Yeah, you look like the kinda guy who enjoys swinging," Walt called out.

"Let him concentrate," Robert admonished. "Or do I bring out the video of *your* first time doing this?"

Walt gaped. "You said you'd deleted that." The others snickered.

"I lied. Now leave him be." Robert flashed me a smile. "You can do this."

Damn, that made me feel good.

"Okay, when I have your attention?"

I jerked my head to look at Zeeb. "Focused."

He gave a nod. "The twirling is the hardest part to master, mostly 'cause folks try to make it happen by moving their whole arm. But you're only gonna move your wrist, all right? Think of it as an axle. The rope is a wheel revolving around it."

I started twirling, my heart hammering, and Zeeb hollered words of encouragement as I maintained the speed of the loop.

"Fuck, that hurts," I groused.

"You just give me one good try, and we'll leave it at that. You gotta choose the right moment in the swing to throw the lariat," Zeeb told me. "Wait till your swinging wrist makes its way from back to front, then take a step forward, and bring your hand forward and down to shoulder height." I did as instructed, and suddenly he called out, "Now! Extend your arm and release the loop."

The lariat landed on the box, and I jerked it taut.

Applause burst out from the audience, and I took a bow.

"Nice job," Butch told me. "Don't get cocky, kid. The goal is to do that while you're riding a horse, and you're a long way off yet."

"Don't you listen to him," Garrett said warmly. "I think you were awesome."

I smiled, then glanced at Robert. "What do *you* think, boss?"

"Looks like you're a natural with a rope."

Beside him, Walt erupted into a violent cough, and Butch patted him on the back.

"Boss?" Teague rode up on horseback. "We've got company."

And just like that, I knew he'd be out of there.

Well crap.

Robert

"Who's here?" Then I saw Diana's car pull up beside the barn, and just like that, I knew I was in trouble.

For God's sake, it's been one day, sis. I'd forgotten to call her Sunday night. When our dad had been in the hospital, we'd gotten into the habit of calling each other once a day. I hadn't spoken to her since the early hours of Sunday morning, and while technically that *was* Sunday, I knew it wouldn't cut any ice with her.

Teague's phone rang, and he answered it. "Aw shit, where?... I'll be right there." He disconnected. "I'll be back soon, boss. Got a problem to sort out." Then he rode off at a gallop.

I didn't move from my spot by the paddock—if she wanted to bawl me out, she'd have to come to me. Garrett and Paul headed to the stables, Walt disappeared God knew where, and Butch joined Zeeb in the paddock, showing Toby how it was done, much to Zeeb's amusement.

I didn't think Toby needed the extra help. He'd done just fine. Watching him in action had been a revelation. Lord, that man's body didn't move—it *flowed*. *And he did all that after all the work he put in yesterday.* I appreciated a guy who gave one hundred percent.

I didn't turn around as I heard footsteps approaching.

"I guess the mountain is coming to Muhammad." Diana rested her arms on the fence.

"Hey, sis. Good to see you." I glanced at her. The afternoon sun lit up her face, making her white hair glow. The gray had started showing right around her twenty-seventh year, and by forty she'd given up coloring it. I liked it. I'd lost count of how many times I'd wondered if Mom would've looked like her, if she'd ever gotten to Diana's age.

"Don't you give me that. What's going on?"

"I haven't got a clue what you're talking about." I could play dumb when I wanted.

"I've sent you texts, I've called—you didn't answer." She pointed to the paddock. "Zeeb doing his thing with the guests?"

"Yup."

She chuckled. "I remember Dad showing me how to throw a lariat. I was damn good at it, I do recall."

"And modest too."

"I'd say fuck you, but I'm too much of a lady." I burst out laughing, and she whacked me on the arm. "Hey."

Butch spotted her, and waved. "Hey, Diana. What brings you here?" He sauntered over to join us.

She smiled. "Oh, don't mind me. You keep doing what you're doing. I'm just enjoying the show."

He cackled. "And what would Newt say about that?"

I cleared my throat. "Why don't you go help Paul feed the horses?"

"Sure thing, boss." He tipped his hat at Diana, then strolled toward the stables.

"Such a crying shame," she said with a sigh.

"What is?"

She nodded toward Butch. "If Dad hadn't gotten so fixated on having Newt for a son-in-law, me and Butch might've been something."

I didn't have the heart to tell her the truth. Teague had it all wrong, to my mind. Butch wasn't burying his dick in another guy's ass because of convenience—he was in goddamn denial.

I waited until the stable door closed. "Okay, you've seen me. I'm still alive. Now, unless there's something urgent we need to talk about…"

Then I realized she'd gone quiet. I glanced at her, and found her staring at Toby.

She grinned. "And who is *that?*"

"He's one of the guests, from San Francisco."

She fanned herself. "Wow. Maybe I need to go there sometime. If only to see if there are any more like him." She glanced at me. "Don't *you* think he's good-looking?"

"Stop that."

"Oh, come on. He's freaking *gorgeous*." She nudged me with her elbow, then leaned in close. "It's okay, you can say it. Nobody else can hear."

"We're not going to have this conversation," I said through gritted teeth. "And this is a fast turnaround, don't you think?"

"What do you mean?"

"Yesterday you acknowledged my relationship with Kevin for the first time. And today you want me to start noticing *guys?*"

Diana glanced at her watch. "Isn't it lunchtime?"

"Is this you changing the subject, or inviting yourself to lunch?"

She chuckled. "I always said you were smart."

"Come on up to the house. Matt'll have something for us."

She let out another sigh. "One of these days he's going to walk into your kitchen and announce he's met a wonderful girl, they're engaged, and he's going to work out his four weeks' notice. *Then* where will you be?"

"Hungry, and looking for a new housekeeper." I put my arm around her and squeezed. "People move on. It's part of life."

We strolled up the path to the house, and she paused now and again to gaze at the ranch. "Looks smaller than it used to."

"*You* were smaller back then. Remember the first time you wandered down the path on your own?"

She laughed. "No, but Dad used to talk about it. He said I'd wanted to go riding."

"You were four years old." We reached the house, and went inside.

"Matt, there's an extra mouth for lunch," I called out.

He stuck his head around the kitchen door. "I know. Teague called. It's all ready for you in the dining room."

"You are a treasure," Diana gushed. "And someday you're going to make someone a wonderful husband."

His cheeks reddened. "Good to see you, Diana. How are you?"

"Doing just great. And after getting a look at one of the new guests, I'm thinking of leaving Newt and running away with him."

Matt laughed. "Which one?"

"The gorgeous one from San Francisco. He'd put a spring in anyone's step."

He gave her a sympathetic glance. "Sorry, Diana. I think he's spoken for."

She pouted. "Pity."

Matt met my gaze. "If you'll excuse me, I need to go feed the boys."

I gave him a wave. "You go do that." I led Diana into the dining room where a huge bowl of salad sat in the center of the table. Handfuls of lettuce, chunks of tomato, cucumber, and onion lay beneath pieces of chicken and Parmesan shavings, sprinkled with chopped walnuts and drizzled with a creamy dressing.

Diana pulled out a chair, then helped herself. "I think it's time." She took two hunks of bread from the basket next to the salad, then poured us both a glass of water.

"For what?"

"That you told me the truth."

My chest tightened. "And what truth is that?"

Her eyes focused on mine. "Whatever it is you haven't told me—or anyone else—about Kevin's death."

My stomach clenched. "You know all there is to know. He got drunk, he got on a horse, he went for a ride, he broke his fool neck. End of story."

She leaned back in her chair, a piece of chicken speared on her fork. "If it was that simple, guilt wouldn't be eating you alive."

I stared at her. "How… How did you know?"

"One, because I'm your sister. Two, because I've seen what guilt does to people. I recognize the signs." She put her fork down on her plate. "So tell me, what on earth do you have to feel guilty about?"

Maybe she was right. It was time for the truth.

"It's my fault he's dead," I confessed quietly.

Her eyes widened. "How can it be *your* fault?" When I swallowed, she got up, walked around the table to me, crouched beside my chair, took my hands in hers, then looked me in the eye. "Talk to me, Robert."

God, this hurt.

"Kevin… Kevin was very close to his family. He had a great relationship with all of them, especially his younger brother, Chase. And then something happened…"

"I'm going to guess it wasn't something good."

"Chase went out on his first motorcycle. He'd only had it two or three months."

"Oh Jesus. I think I know what's coming." Her expression grew pained.

I nodded. "A car took him out on the highway."

Tears welled in her eyes. "Oh, his poor family."

"It hit Kevin awful hard. And then he got upset, which led to him drinking. And he drank. And drank. I tried to get him to talk about it, to bring his feelings out into the open, but he just wanted to be left alone." I could still hear him.

Not everyone is like you, okay? Some of us are shit at showing our emotions.

"And then one night, I obviously tried too hard." Another hard swallow. "We had a fight. Kevin drank a shitload of whiskey, then stormed out of the house, I went after him, but he wasn't listening."

She pulled out the chair next to mine, sat, and squeezed my hands. "You didn't kill him because you had an argument. He'd been drinking."

I pulled free of her. "You don't understand. If I hadn't tried to get him to open up… If I hadn't tried to comfort him… help him… he wouldn't have run out on me. He wouldn't have gotten on that horse. If I'd just left him alone, it wouldn't have happened and he'd still be alive."

Diana stared at me for a moment before taking a deep breath. "Okay, now you need to listen to *me*. You remember when Dad was dying in the hospital, I'd go there and sit with him why you were taking care of the ranch?" I nodded. "Well, I got to talking with his nurse. I was feeling guilty—"

"What did *you* have to feel guilty about? You were there with him. I wasn't."

"I just felt I should have spent more time with him. But there was all kinds of shit going on at our ranch. Anyhow… The nurse said something to me. She said… 'I've seen people do nothing when someone they love is dying, and they feel guilty about that. I've seen folks who did *everything* to help their loved one, and they still feel guilty when that loved one dies. *Everyone* feels guilty, but nothing good ever comes out of those feelings. You can't change the past. You *can* forgive yourself, even when you feel there's nothing to forgive. Adding guilt just makes everything worse." Her eyes glistened. "And you just talked to me about this for the first time. Was I right? Have you ever told anyone what you just told me?"

"No," I admitted. "I kept everything bottled up inside."

"Well, you finally let it out. And maybe now, you're ready to deal with your loss. Because you know what? I *finally* understand what's been going on."

"You do?"

She nodded. "All this time, I thought you were mourning Kevin, that you'd been madly in love with him. But that wasn't it at all, was it?"

I pushed my plate away from me. "I've thought a lot about this the past few days. When I said I loved him the other night, that wasn't a lie, but you're right, we weren't madly, deeply in love. What we had was a very symbiotic relationship." I huffed. "This seems to be the ranch for that type of relationship." Except I thought Kevin and I had been close, whereas Teague and Butch?

Yeah, not so much.

Hey, it works for them, right?

Then I remembered. It had worked for me too, years before Kevin showed up.

Good Lord. I haven't thought about him in decades.

He was still there of course, in the dark recesses of my mind.

I guess you don't forget your first time, right? Especially when it had set me on the path I was to tread years later.

Diana squeezed my hand, and I dropped back into the conversation. "When I reflect on how I've been feeling these last five years… Were my feelings logical? Rational? Not really, but I don't think that matters. Everything was twisted up in emotions— grief, anger… Okay, none of that is very healthy, but at least now I can *recognize* that, and I can start to deal with it. Because letting my guilt overwhelm me? That's unsustainable. It sucks the pleasure— the happiness—right out of living."

Tears trickled down her cheeks. "You will not believe how happy I am to hear you say all that." She hugged me. "And now you can really move on," she whispered, her tears dampening my cheek.

When she pulled back, I wiped her face with my napkin. "That was the intention. I've even done some things this week I've never done before."

"Such as?"

"I went on a trail with two of the guests and Zeeb."

She widened her eyes. "No shit."

"Really. We went up on the Shafthouse trail."

Diana cocked her head. "That gorgeous specimen of manhood out there, the one who caught my eye—was *he* one of the guests on that trail?"

Damn her. "Yes, yes he was."

She grinned. "Okay, I like the sound of this new Robert. And what else are you gonna do that you haven't done for a while?" Her eyes twinkled.

"Stop that." I pointed to her plate. "Now sit back down and eat your lunch."

"Whatever you say."

She was still grinning, but I'd take that sassy grin over her tears any day.

I gave Diana a hug. "Thanks for stopping by. But please, don't come running if you don't hear from me for a day, okay?"

She bit her lip. "I guess I can relax a little now. Especially since we got it all out into the open." Her eyes twinkled. "Well, as much of it as I needed to hear."

"So… no more stopping by to check on me if a day goes by and you haven't had a call?"

Diana grinned. "If a *week* goes by and still no call, I'm turning up with a whip, and your ass is in for it."

"Duly noted."

She kissed my cheek. "Do something new every day, no matter how small."

I waved her goodbye as she went down the path, back to her car. She passed Matt on his way up the hill, and they exchanged a few words.

When Matt reached me, I put my hands on my hips. "Okay, what did she say?"

He chuckled. "She thanked me for lunch, that was all." When I blinked, he laughed. "I know right? That's awful tame for her." He headed for the door. "I'll make you some coffee."

"Matt? Hold on a sec." I gave him an inquiring glance. "How would *you* know Toby is spoken for? I didn't think you'd spent all that much time with him."

"I haven't. I just… know."

I arched my eyebrows. "And what is it you know?"

Matt coughed. "Diana's barking up the wrong tree."

"Oh, I see. Toby's not into cougars?"

"Not exactly. I just know he's not into… mares." He flushed.

It took me a second or two to catch on. *No way.*

"Don't stop there. Tell me how you know all this. And if *he* didn't tell you, should you even be telling *me*? Or anyone, for that matter?"

Matt sighed, then got his phone out. "It's not exactly a secret, boss." He showed me the screen, pointing to an icon. It was a black square with a white letter S.

I frowned. "What is that?"

"It's... an app, boss."

I rolled my eyes. "Yeah, that much I got."

"It's a site for gay men, called... Scruff."

"Oh. I see."

And there went any thoughts that Matt was straight. *Damn it, Teague was right. Gayest bunch of cowboys this side of the Rockies.*

I pointed to the icon. "Are *you* on there too?"

"Yeah." He started to scroll.

I laid my hand on his arm. "Hey, don't show me. I don't wanna see."

His flush deepened. "I wasn't gonna show you *my* profile, boss—just his." He held his phone up once more, and there was a headless torso shot. Not that it mattered—I'd seen those abs less than twenty-four hours ago. Then Matt scrolled, and I saw something else I recognized, only, it was thicker than it had been in the tub. Granted, it was an underwear shot, but hell, the outline was clear enough to make my dick twitch.

Maybe the water had been a little on the cool side.

Then Diana's words came back to me, and I laughed.

"What's so funny?"

"Diana got it right, you know." Matt tilted his head to one side, and I grinned. "You *would* make someone a wonderful husband. Except she doesn't know that someone would be a guy."

He chuckled. "One day, maybe. I'm only thirty-six. There's still time. And I'm not in any hurry. Rushing into things can be a huge mistake." Before I could ask if he spoke from personal experience, he smiled. "So... we're good?"

I returned his smile. "We are. Can't say I'm not a little surprised—I had you down as batting for the other team, but I wasn't certain."

"I figured you'd be okay with it. Just checking." He gave me a speculative glance. "*You* would, too."

"I would what?"

"Make some guy a wonderful husband." Then he dashed into the house, leaving me staring after him open-mouthed.

It wasn't that he knew—hell, I was reconciled to the fact that everyone knew by now—it was that he felt comfortable enough to share the thought.

Then I let the rest of his revelations sink in.

Toby is gay.

I got the feeling Teague had known that all along. What had he said again? '*I think you'll like him.*' He'd been right about the whole Kevin vibe too. Then I got to wondering what else was on that app Matt had shown me.

I pulled my phone from my pocket, and typed in the search engine.

Scruff.

Chapter Fourteen

Robert

I sat in my rocker on the porch, waiting for Teague to arrive. When he'd called to ask if he could come on up, I figured it wasn't anything serious. The man didn't do drama.

What a day this has been.

Talking with Diana had been cathartic, discovering Matt wasn't as straight as I'd figured had been a revelation, and what I'd seen on Scruff had been an education.

My face tingled when I recalled some of Toby's photos. Not that I'd found full-frontal nude pics—I hadn't seen any of those anywhere on the site, but I was sure they existed... somewhere. What had floored me was how he had a way of making love to the camera lens.

To be looked at like that...

I heard the sound of boots on gravel, and I glanced up.

Teague spied the bottle of beer standing on the table next to me, and grinned. "Now *that's* what I was hoping for."

As he climbed the porch steps, I gave him an inquiring glance. "This *is* a social visit, right? Or is there something we need to discuss?"

"Social. Unless you're all socialed out after Diana?"

I chuckled. "Have a seat and a cold one."

He sank into the empty rocker and reached over to pick up the bottle. I picked up my bottle of peach iced tea, and we clinked. He sagged against the loose cushion, the bottle raised to his lips. "Just what I needed."

"Wanna tell me why you had to dash off like that when Diana arrived?"

"Kyle called. Said he'd found a calf caught up in the thicket. Only, he couldn't free the little guy. I went to give him a hand."

"So all is well?"

Teague smiled. "All is most definitely well. Especially now." He took another drink.

I gazed at the sky. "Another beautiful sunset," I murmured.

"So… How was *your* day?"

I laughed. This was usually how our porch conversations began. "Well, let me see. I learned a couple of new things, and… I guess you could say I made a breakthrough."

Teague's eyebrows shot up. "Okay, that last part sounds kinda serious. Let's start with the new stuff."

I enjoyed the sensation of iced tea sliding down my throat. "For one thing, I discovered Matt's into guys."

That earned me a blink. "He told you that?"

I shrugged. "In a roundabout way. Turns out he's on this app, Scruff. You heard of that?" He nodded. "Well, *I* thought it was a dating app—until I saw the pics."

Teague laughed. "It's more of what you'd call a hookup app."

"And you know this how? Are you on it too?"

He smiled. "No sir. I don't have any need for such a thing. Why go looking, when I've got all I can handle right on my doorstep?" He shook his head. "Good Lord, another one. I confess, I didn't know about Matt, but then he's a real private individual."

I pointed in the direction of the gatepost at the entrance to the ranch. "Is there a sign hanging over this place that I don't know about? One that says Queers Welcome Here?" If there was, it had been there since I was a teenager.

Teague burst out laughing. "I know what you mean. Zeeb reckons it's like in that movie, *The Hobbit*."

"Excuse me?"

"You know, when Gandalf drew a sign on Bilbo's door, and only the dwarfs could see it, so they all walked right on in there?" He peered at me. "You *do* know what I'm talking about, don't you?"

"Of course. I saw it too. It's just…" I bit my lip. "Never had you down as a *Lord of the Rings* kinda dude."

"Boss, there's lots you don't know about me. Man's gotta keep *some* secrets, right?"

I snorted. "I would *love* to keep some secrets." Except I did have one secret left, didn't I? Butch had been around the longest, and I didn't think even he knew about Clay. If he did, he hadn't said a word to a soul. I stroked my beard. "So if there *were* one of those invisible signs, what do you suppose it would say?"

Teague grinned. "Queers Welcome Here."

I laughed.

"But I guess it says something else too."

I frowned. "Like what?"

"Think about it. Is there *anyone* working on this ranch who has any issue with guys not being straight?"

He had a point. I smiled. "Then maybe the sign also says, 'If you're gonna hate, well, there's the gate.'"

Teague laughed. "My boss—the poet."

"Anyhow, back to this app. There was a familiar face on it." I coughed. "Except that's a lie. There was everything *but* his face." I stared at Teague. "Did *you* know Toby was gay?" I waited for the confirmation I felt sure was coming.

Teague let out a wry chuckle. "Hell, *everyone* knew that the day he arrived. Walt pretty much spread the word."

"But how did *he* know? What did Toby do—offer him a blow job in the bunkhouse bathroom?"

Teague guffawed. "Now *there's* an image. Dear Lord, he could have a line forming, if he's any good at it. But no. Walt found those pics you just mentioned."

"I see." I shook my head. "Whoever invented that app is probably a millionaire several times over."

Teague studied me for a moment. "And you do like him, don't you?"

I played dumb. "Sure, I like Walt just fine."

That got me an eye-roll. "You know *exactly* who I'm talking about."

I cocked my head to one side. "You see that movie, *Fight Club*?"

"Yeah."

"Okay then." I gestured to the porch. "As far as you're concerned, this is Fight Club."

Teague gave me a knowing glance. "And rule number one is, no talking about Fight Club."

"Got it in one. Whatever we say here—"

"Goes no further, I get it."

I nodded, then took a swig of my tea. "Okay then. Yeah, I like him." I took in the cocky tilt of Teague's head. "And you don't have to be so smug about it."

"I knew you would."

I stared at the sinking sun. "You know what I think? If he'd arrived here a month ago, I'd have looked at him and thought, 'Now there's a good-looking dude.' But now? Something's changed."

He frowned. "What?"

And now that I was finally there, I wasn't sure how to proceed.

"Robert…" Teague's voice softened. "You don't have to tell me, okay?"

Hell, I'd gotten this far.

I coughed. "Well you did say if I ever needed to talk…" I finished my tea and set the bottle on the table. "It's as if… The best way I can explain it is… A whole lot of things happened at once, like *bam bam bam*. Zeeb confronting me about my holding onto the past. Diana doing pretty much the same thing. Finding Toby at the cabin, and thinking just for a second that—"

"Yeah, that part I get. I said he reminded me of Kevin, didn't I?"

"You had a part in this too," I told him. "Telling me everyone knows I'm gay, they don't give a fuck about it, and I need to move on. And then today…" I took a deep breath.

"I guess we've come to that breakthrough you mentioned."

I nodded. I wasn't ready to share my revelations about feeling guilty. He didn't need to know that. "What it all boils down to is… You were right. Diana is right. Hell, even Zeeb is right. It *is* time to move on."

Teague became very still. "Fight Club, Robert."

I wondered what the hell was about to come out of his mouth. "Gotcha."

"You wanna know what I think? Toby brings all these feelings and emotions out in you that would have been there regardless of the circumstances. So I guess what I'm telling you is…" He drained the rest of his beer. "If anything were to… happen between you and… a guest, no one would say a word. Shit, they probably wouldn't even bat an eyelid. And ethically speaking, I don't see a problem in you and him—"

I held up one hand. "You don't have to draw a diagram."

He gave a shrug. "Just saying, if it's permission you're after…" He looked me in the eye. "You don't need it. Do whatever the fuck you want. Because you know what? You've *earned* that right. You spent five years in hell, and someone just let you out. And it's about fuckin' time."

I blinked back the tears I felt sure were about to put in an appearance.

Then he grinned. "Just don't go crazy, okay? I don't wanna find you in the middle of the paddock one dark night, riding some guy like he was a wild stallion."

Be still my beating heart.

"Oh my Lord, now *there's* a vivid picture."

Teague stared at me. "Oh my God. I just put that idea into your head, didn't I?"

I laughed. "Trust me, I'll steer clear of the paddock." I smiled. "I realized something else today. Diana really was sweet on Butch way back when." I glanced at him. "You know the story, right?" I was pretty sure Butch would've filled him in.

"Yeah, that wouldn't have ended well." He stroked his stubble-covered jaw with his index finger. "Can I ask you something?"

"Sure."

"Do you think your dad knew about Butch? I mean, did he have some sixth sense or something?"

"Are you asking if Dad didn't want his daughter getting involved with a gay guy? I know—you don't think he is, but…"

"Is it possible? Your dad was a pretty good judge of character."

I thought back to those years. "I was nineteen when Dad gave Butch a job. Diana was sixteen. And right from the start, I liked him. He was a laugh, a real character."

"Hasn't changed much, then," Teague remarked with a smile.

"And yet… I noticed how Dad watched the two of them. It wasn't long after that, he brought her and Newt Webster together."

Teague scowled. "You think he didn't want his daughter married to a hired hand? I didn't think your dad was that kinda guy."

I shook my head vehemently. "No, it was more than that. Fight Club, okay?" Teague nodded. "Because I have never told a soul what I'm about to tell you."

Teague's expression grew solemn. "You got my word."

"One time, I confronted him about it. I was this zealous nineteen-year-old kid, burning with the injustice of what he'd done. Because he *had* split them up, make no mistake." Except I'd been sure the attraction was mostly on Diana's side.

"What did he say? When you confronted him?"

"I'll never forget it. He said, 'Son, you don't invite a wild animal into your house. You keep it outside where you can see it. Where you can aim a shotgun at it if you have to.'"

Teague paled. "He said that?"

I nodded. "I told him I didn't understand, and he said, 'You look into his eyes. Trust me when I tell you, you look into a man's eyes and you can see into his soul. There's something in Butch's past that haunts him, and whatever it is, it's not good. He's only here because I gave him the benefit of the doubt. That boy is looking for atonement, and I don't know if he'll ever find it.'"

Teague stared at me. "Okay, we both know Butch might be lacking in a few social graces—"

"A few?"

"Yeah, all right. But... *wild animal?* What did your dad know about him that no one else did?"

"I don't think he did know anything for certain, but whatever else he suspected, he took it to his grave. Want to know something else? Diana was bitter about it for a while, but Butch? He took it on the chin. Never badmouthed my dad about it, not once."

Teague got to his feet and walked to the edge of the porch, staring out at the ranch below us. "It's almost as if Butch knew your dad was right." He turned to face me. "It makes you think, doesn't it? We have all these guys working here, and we know nothing about their past before they arrived at Salvation. Who knows what baggage they carry with them?"

"Their baggage is *their* concern, not ours. It only becomes ours when it comes knocking on our door." I knocked on the wooden table. "And so far..."

We lapsed into silence as the sky shed red and orange and took on purple.

"I wonder what tomorrow will bring?" I mused.

Teague leaned against one of the posts that supported the porch. "Whatever is coming right around the corner at you, it's best to be prepared. Practically speaking." His face flushed. "And if you need... anything, just holler. I mean, whatever you still have lying around must be out-of-date by now." He cleared his throat. "I'd better be off to my bed. Thanks for the beer."

He stepped off the porch, and crunched his way down the path.

I was still puzzling over that last remark when it hit me.

Did Teague just offer to procure some condoms?

CHAPTER FIFTEEN

Tuesday, June 14
Toby

Breakfast was finished, and I needed a ride to get my head on straight before Zeeb continued with his roping lessons. My arms ached less than they had the previous day.

What day is this? Tuesday? I'd lost all track of time. The following week would be the cattle drive, and once that was over, there'd be a day to chill out a little, and then I'd be out of there, back to San Francisco.

The prospect of going home didn't fill me with enthusiasm, not when my mind was focused on other things.

Okay, one thing in particular—a certain sexy rancher. I could still hear Zeeb in my head.

Maybe getting you between the sheets is the first step to him getting his life back.

Make him live again for those two weeks.

That got me thinking. *If I did make a move, what would be my motivation? Altruism—or lust?*

Maybe a little of both.

I smiled to myself. Who was I kidding? It was lust, all the way.

Butch and Walt were laughing at something on Butch's phone, and Zeeb had the radio on. Garrett and Declan were huddled in a corner, lost in conversation, and Paul was already heading out to the stables. Teague wasn't around.

I needed a moment of peace and quiet. I grabbed my hat and jacket, and followed Paul into the stables. "Can I take Lightning out?"

He smiled. "Sure. Seeing as you've got permission now."

"Thanks." I grabbed Lightning's saddle, and went into his stall. "Hey boy," I said in a soothing voice. "Wanna go for a ride with me?" I got him ready, aware of the first rays of sunlight creeping in through the open door. It had to be around five-thirty, the perfect time for a morning constitutional on horseback.

I knew exactly where I'd be headed too.

Paul unfastened Lightning's reins and handed them to me, and I mounted him. He led us out of the stable. "Remember what the boss said. No farther than the creek."

I had no intention of going past that point—I wanted another look at that cabin.

The day was shaping up to be a good one as Lightning trotted through the meadow, heading for the trail. The sky was an unbroken blue, the pink and red hues of dawn already dissipating as I reached the creek. I rode along it, enjoying the sound of water trickling over rocks, a happy sound that seemed to fill my soul with contentment.

I could see why Zeeb loved this place.

Eventually, the little cabin came into view, and I brought Lightning to a stop at a hitching post. I hadn't noticed it the first time, but I guessed they'd had to have somewhere to tie up the horses. The grass grew tall around it, camouflaging the mounting block beside it.

I stared across the creek at the little cabin.

Now I understand why this seems such a sad place. It was covered with an air of neglect. I tried to imagine how it might have been, full of laughter, and maybe other sounds too, sounds its occupants didn't want overheard.

What's that saying about getting back on the horse?

Maybe no one came here because there were demons—Robert's demons—and he needed to face them.

I heard the sound of a horse approaching, and without turning around, I knew who it was.

Robert came to a halt next to me. "When I saw Lightning was gone, I had a feeling you'd be here."

I smiled. "Maybe I came here expecting to meet you."

His eyebrows went up a little at that. He glanced at the cabin. "Have you been over there? Did you go inside?"

My stomach tightened. "I wouldn't do that, especially now I understand its... significance—and your reaction to finding me here the other day."

Robert was like a statue. "I see." He blinked slowly. "Who told you?"

"Does that matter? What's important is that I know." I lowered my voice. "I'm so sorry." I'd never lost anyone in such tragic circumstances, so I couldn't begin to have the slightest idea how he was feeling, or how badly Kevin's death had affected him.

Robert dismounted, looped Rusty's reins around the hitching post, then picked his way across the boulders with great care.

"You haven't done that in a while, have you?" I called out.

He reached the other side. "First time in five years." He approached the cabin, and climbed the steps with a caution I now understood. I watched, my heart racing.

He stood in front of the porch steps, staring at the front door. Then he turned his head and beckoned. "Come on over."

"Look, maybe I should just leave you to—"

"Come over, I said." He smiled. "I... I want you to. Don't worry, we're not going inside." His smile faltered. "Don't think I'm ready for that yet. But I'm not about to holler across the creek."

I nudged Lightning closer to the mounting block, and dismounted. Once he was secured, I crossed the creek, stepping with care onto each boulder, feeling as if I was walking a tightrope. "If I fall into the creek—"

"You'll get wet, that's all. Clothes dry." He walked back to the water's edge, and extended a hand. "Here."

I grabbed it, and he hauled me onto the bank. Robert returned to the porch steps, and just when I thought he was going to turn tail and leave, he climbed them, taking his time. When he reached the deck, he turned his head to gaze at me.

"I haven't stood on this porch for five years."

"Since he died."

He nodded. "This was our hideaway." He smiled. "We got caught once too often in the barn for my liking. This was Kevin's idea. Dad never came here—too many memories of Mom, I guess. I didn't have enough of those to make this an awkward place to be. I was three when she died."

I breathed in the delicious, fragrant scent of pine. "It's a peaceful spot. I can see why he chose it."

"It was the *perfect* spot. No one came here. I used to marvel at that. How come not one hand ever happened across us?" Robert smiled. "Now I can guess why that was."

"They all knew, didn't they? About you and Kevin."

He nodded, and then to my surprise, he peered at the Adirondack chairs.

I took one glance at them. "I don't think that's such a good idea, the state they're in. If you want to sit, then sit on the porch. Except if that breaks, you're going to end up with splinters in your ass," I warned him.

He chuckled. "I think you're right about the chairs. I'll take my chances on the porch." He sat on the top step, his elbows resting on his knees. "And if the worst happens, then I'll just have to find someone to pull the splinters out, won't I?"

I had the feeling he was talking about me.

I joined him on the porch. "What was he like? Not that you have to tell me. It's none of my business."

"It's okay, really. If I'm honest, he was an awful lot like you."

I blinked. "Seriously?"

He nodded. "When we first got together, I was thirty-two, and he was twenty-eight."

"Then he *was* like me," I declared. Robert gave me an inquiring glance, and I grinned. "He had a thing for older guys too. Not that you were much older than him." I cocked my head. "You know I'm gay, don't you?"

"I do now. A little bird might have showed me some… photos on his phone."

It took me a moment to realize he could only be talking about Walt or Matt. "You saw my profile pics? On Scruff?"

"Uh-huh. The first moment I got to myself, you wanna know what I did?" His eyes gleamed. "I registered so I could see more."

"More guys?"

He shook his head. "More of you."

A pleasurable tingle surged through me. "Did you like what you saw?"

There was that grin again. "Do you have to ask? Of course I did. But I want more."

I arched my eyebrows. "More pics?" Hell, I had a ton of them on my phone.

"No—I mean, yes, but… what I'd really like is to *know* more."

"About me?"

He nodded.

I smiled. "Funny. I was thinking the same thing about you." Maybe it was time to lay my cards on the table. "So then if I turn up on your doorstep one evening—"

"Are you likely to do that?" His breathing quickened, and I couldn't tell if that was due to anticipation or anxiety.

"I think that's a given, don't you?" I saw little point in being coy.

He swallowed. "Good to know."

I shifted a little closer to him, and the wooden deck creaked. "You want to know more about me so that if you invite me in—"

"*When* I invite you in," he corrected, his cheeks flushed.

That tingle was back with a vengeance.

"Okay—*when* you invite me in—and just so we're clear about this, I won't be there for coffee, will I?"

He raised his chin and met my gaze head on. "No, you won't. If that's okay with you."

I couldn't help myself. I cupped his cheek, and he shivered. "I think this is the moment when I tell you what a hot, sexy man you are, and I can't wait to fuck you."

Come on, Robert. Tell me you bottom.

"You're pretty hot yourself." Another full-body shiver. "And I can't wait to be fucked."

Thank you, God.

He bit his lip. "And kissed."

Oh, I was down for that.

I leaned in, brought my mouth to his, and kissed him, no heat, just a brushing of lips. His eyes were closed, a visible calmness settling on him.

"Do that again," he murmured, and I homed in on his inviting lips, letting the kiss play out a little longer this time. Then I drew back, and he opened his eyes. "Okay… what were we talking about?"

I laughed. "Wow, I'm good. Two kisses and I've scrambled your brain."

"My first kisses since Kevin…"

I gave him a warm smile. "I get it. So now, when you invite me in, I won't be some stranger. You want there to be a… connection between us before we go any further."

Hell, we already had one.

"Yes, but…" He took his hat off and rubbed his scalp.

"You've gotten this far," I said with a hopefully reassuring smile. I knew we'd have to move at his speed.

He replaced his hat and took a deep breath. "Something I need to say here. And it's important. It might even make you decide not to proceed any further."

There was little doubt of that happening. "Color me intrigued."

"I don't know where you expect this to go—"

I chuckled. "I've got ten more days here. It can only go so far in that time."

"Is that all?"

I removed my gloves, placed my hand on his knee, and gave it a squeeze. "You were saying?" I saw once again how the physical contact relaxed him.

"I just wanted to say... I know this isn't some romance novel, okay?"

Okay, I hadn't expected *that*.

He surged ahead. "Guys can hook up without becoming emotionally attached. Sex doesn't need to be complicated. And I know that can work, because I see it here on the ranch every goddamn day."

"You're talking about Teague and Butch."

His eyes widened. "You know about them too?"

"Yeah. First night here, I woke up to find Butch sneaking out—and then I learned where he was going, what he was doing..." I grinned. "And who he was doing it with."

"They have sex for release, and they're happy with that, with just the physical side of things, and—"

"And you thought I might not be happy with a similar arrangement," I concluded.

"Yes."

I cocked my head. "How many men have you been in a sexual relationship with?" I was fairly confident it was just the one.

He flushed. "Two." I stared at him, and he shrugged. "He was years before Kevin came to work at Salvation. He's the reason I know sex doesn't have to be complicated, because it sure wasn't for us."

"Did this guy work on the ranch too?"

He nodded. "He'd been a wrangler for maybe five years before I noticed him. Except it was the other way round. He noticed *me*."

"How old were you when you and he first got together?" I bit back a smile. "He had a name, right?"

Robert chuckled. "His name was Clay. I was twenty when things first got... interesting, and he was thirty-three." He shivered. "He had the biggest hands—and a humongous dick."

I laughed. "Lucky you. And how long did you get to enjoy it?"

"Two years, almost three. Then one day, he was gone."

I frowned. "What do you mean, gone?"

"Just what I said. I woke up one morning, went down to the bunkhouse, and Butch was talking with some of the guys. He said Clay had cleared out in the night. All his stuff was gone."

"Did he ever get in contact with you?"

"Not a goddamn word." Robert glanced at me. "I didn't pine for him, if that's what you're thinking. It was—"

"Just sex, yeah." I leaned back on my hands. "And no one on the ranch knew what had been going on with you two?"

"Far as I know. We worked hard to keep it a secret." Robert smiled. "Probably the *only* secret I've managed to keep around here."

"There's a gap in your story. You telling me there was no one else from the time Clay left, to when you and Kevin first hooked up? That had to be…" I did the math. "Nine years or so."

"Yup."

"No other ranch hands caught your eye? No one in town?" There had to be a few gay guys in Bozeman.

"Nope."

I grinned. "Not even Butch?"

He laughed. "Good Lord, no." He peered at me. "Would you mind if we headed back?"

"Only if we continue with this conversation."

"I'm okay with that."

We got up, and I followed him across the creek. We untied the horses, mounted them, and then rejoined the trail. I rode beside him, the sun warm on my back, the smell of grass in my nostrils.

Robert glanced at me. "I think it's your turn. I've done all the talking so far, so why don't you tell me something about yourself?"

"What would you like to know?"

"You asked about me, so it's only fair if I ask you the same question. Have you had a lot of relationships?"

I smiled. "That depends on how you define relationship."

"Suppose you tell me how *you* define it?"

I didn't mind talking like this, not at all. There could never be too much communication as far as I was concerned, and if Robert was okay with that, all the better.

"First of all, I don't do boyfriends. I *do* have a lot of guys who I have sex with, and I'm not romantically involved with any of them." I glanced at him. "I prefer sex to be without attachment. I'm not going to explain *why* I prefer it that way—what's important is that I do prefer it."

"Seriously?"

I nodded. "So your fears that you're gonna put me off are groundless. You're telling it like it is, how you need things to be, and it all sounds pretty goddamn perfect to me."

Robert came to a halt. He leaned on his pommel, his gaze locked on mine. "Then we *are* going to—"

"Fuck?" I grinned. "Count on it."

His breathing hitched. "Again, good to know." He cleared his throat, and resumed his trot. "Then I guess there's something else we need to discuss. Protection. Unless this all sounds way too clinical and detached to you."

"Hell no." I smiled. "You're talking my language." He was a Dominant's dream—a guy who wanted to talk first—even if he did turn out to be vanilla.

And how would I feel about that?

All the guys I went with on a regular basis were kinky as fuck. Getting into bed with someone who might be vanilla… I wasn't sure if I could turn off the Dominant in me. I'd never even bothered trying.

There was a voice in my head, that of Dale Myers, the Dom who'd first showed me the ropes.

Everyone has a kink, Toby—you just have to work out what it is.

And maybe I'd have some fun trying to work out what Robert's was. In the meantime, I could do vanilla. I smiled to myself. Judging by the way my dick was growing harder by the second, a vanilla fuck would be no problem at all.

Then I realized Robert was still talking.

"Good. Because—for reasons I'm not going to explain either—I prefer to be frank and open about things like this."

This was getting better and better. "I'm all about communication. I'm going to assume you know what PrEP is."

"And you'd be right. Kevin and I discussed it once. But we didn't see the need. It was just us. Neither of us wanted to bring anyone in from outside."

"What about testing?"

"He made sure we got tested regularly, at a clinic in Bozeman. We didn't use condoms."

"I think condoms can be kinda sexy," I said with a grin. "But that's just me. I've got a thing for rubber."

He bit his lip. "Yeah, I saw the photos."

I had to think for a minute what else was in those photos—and how much they said about me. Something else occurred to me. *Did they turn him on—or off?*

I needed a hint.

"See anything you liked?"

For a moment I wasn't sure if he'd respond. Then he shivered. "You've got a thing for leather too, don't you?"

Oh, *now* he had me intrigued. "You noticed."

Robert snorted. "Kinda hard to miss it." Then he shifted in his saddle, and I had what I was looking for.

Inside I was buzzing.

"But… I don't have any. Condoms, I mean."

I smiled. "I do. I found some freebies in my suitcase, stuff they were giving out at Pride. Enough to last us one night at least."

"You went looking for condoms? When was this?"

I wasn't going to lie. "The night I discovered you were gay." I smiled. "Just in case I got lucky. A guy can dream, right?"

He shivered. "Thank God for Pride."

"But once they're gone, we'll need to go shopping for supplies." I gazed at him. "We might be talking calmly and clinically about this, but inside, your heart is pounding, isn't it?"

He swallowed. "Yes."

"And your dick is like a rock in your jeans." I didn't glance at his crotch—I didn't need to.

Another swallow, and his pupils dilated a little. "Yes."

"And right now, all you can think about is us naked."

"Oh God." A flush rose up his neck, staining his ears red.

"I'll take that as a yes. So the question is… how long do I wait before I walk up the path to your front door? And if I'm up there and not around the ranch, is that going to attract attention?" Before he could answer, I straightened in the saddle. "Tonight. I'll come tonight."

He gaped at me. "You kiss me, wind me up like some goddamn kid's toy, then tell me I have to *wait?* What are you, some kind of sadist?"

I grinned. "*Now* you're getting it. But I'll make you a promise."

He waited, his breathing erratic.

"I'll make it good for you." I gazed ahead at the trail leading to Salvation. "This'll be a new experience," I said with a rueful smile.

"What will?"

"Riding with a hard-on." And with that, I took off at a gallop.

"Where are you going?" he yelled.

I pulled on Lightning's reins, and he came to a dead stop. I twisted in the saddle to look back at Robert. "I think we should arrive separately, don't you? Don't want to arouse *too* much suspicion, do we?" Without waiting for a response, I charged off again, feeling lighter than air.

Robert's wasn't the only heart pounding right then.

CHAPTER SIXTEEN

Robert

It took me a moment to realize the sounds filtering through my head were those of Matt clearing away the dishes.

"You done, boss?"

I glanced at the half-eaten supper. "Yeah, thanks." I'd been too nervous to do Matt's casserole justice.

He peered at me. "You okay?"

Does it show? "Do I look like I'm not?"

Matt smirked. "You keep looking at the clock. You expecting a visitor?" Before I could reply, he held up his hand. "You know what? It's not my business."

"And what are you up to this evening?" Not that I was trying to get rid of him, but…

Who was I kidding? I was trying to get rid of him.

"I'm going down to play poker with the guys. Anything you need before I go?"

I feigned a nonchalance I definitely did *not* feel. "Can't think of anything."

"Then I'll see you in the morning." He paused. "You sure there's nothing you want?"

"Didn't I just answer that?"

"Then I'll see you in the morning."

I tried not to smile. "And I think *you* just said that." I cocked my head. "Something on your mind, Matt?"

He flushed. "Listen, if you want breakfast a little later tomorrow, I can do that. You don't have to be up at the crack of dawn."

Hoo boy. I guess my secret is out. I didn't bother to wonder how word had gotten around. A mouse could fart in the barn and everyone knew about it.

He coughed. "I'll go load the dishwasher, then I'll be off."

"You do that."

He disappeared into the kitchen, and I chuckled. I pulled my phone from my pocket and peered at it.

No messages.

I wasn't sure what I'd expected when I texted Toby to share my number. My thoughts veered from expecting *I've changed my mind* to *See you at seven.* And while an ETA would've been good, something told me that wasn't his style.

And what is *his style?*

Now *there* was the million-dollar question.

"Off now, boss."

I walked with Matt to the door. "About breakfast…"

He arched his eyebrows. "I guess I'll be here a little later after all. Are we talking an hour, maybe?"

I had no idea. "Sure, let's go with that." He nodded, and I watched him go down the path. The sunset was still a few hours away, and the white walls of the barns below glowed warm in the last rays. Before he went out of sight, Matt turned and waved.

He was grinning.

Yeah, he knew *exactly* what was about to go down.

That brought a grin to my face. *Me—I hope.*

I closed the door and glanced at the clock. Time for a shower. There was always the possibility Toby would put in an appearance before I was done, but maybe me opening the front door in nothing but a towel would get the evening off to a great start. I hurried up the stairs to the bathroom, flipped on the shower, and got undressed.

What came to mind as I scrubbed was Kevin's voice.

Make sure that asshole is nice and clean enough for me to eat.

I shivered as the memories claimed me. Ropes securing my arms, tied around the bed posts. Me face down, a couple of pillows shoved under me to tilt my ass, and another under my head. More rope around my thighs, attached to the posts at the foot of the bed, spreading me wide. Kevin's tongue in my ass, propelling me closer and closer to the orgasm he'd forbade me to have, because the bastard knew he could make me come like that.

Five years. Five *long* years.

I braced my hands on the tiles and bowed my head, letting the water cascade down my back.

Lord? If it's not too much trouble? Please let rimming be one of Toby's favorite things. I haven't asked for much from you since Kevin died, but I'm asking for this.

Except what I wanted was more than a tongue in my ass. I wanted a man in my life who would bend me to his will, take control, push me...

Make me his.

And until I found such a guy—because between them, Zeeb, Diana, and Teague had convinced me it was time to start looking again—I'd take as many nights with Toby in my bed as I could get.

He wants this, I want this. That had to be the definition of win-win.

I got out of the shower, wrapped a towel around myself, and went over to the cabinet under the sink. My douche sat in a box, gathering dust. I took it out, blew the dust off, and removed the contents.

A little hot, soapy water, and hey presto, you shall *go to the ball.*

Maybe the anticipation was getting to me.

Douching was one of those rituals that always grounded me in the past. Getting my head in the right space, focusing on what was to come...But now? This was different. It was a means to an end. And I was jittery as fuck.

I caught sight of my reflection. *Will you just stop? You're acting like a virgin about to get his cherry popped. Now get cleaned out.*

Pretty soon I was douched and shaved, my breath was minty fresh—I didn't want Toby knowing what I'd had for supper, thank you very much. And when he still didn't show, I went to my closet to grab clean clothes. I spent maybe ten minutes debating what to wear. Finally I settled on jeans and a tee—the less I put on, the less he had to take off, right? I opened the drawer containing my briefs and boxers, then closed it. Kevin always preferred—

I leaned against the dresser. *No more thoughts of Kevin, okay?*

The doorbell rang at seven-thirty, and I hurried downstairs to open it, almost going ass over tea kettle in the process. *Yeah, great start.* I could already hear Teague calling for paramedics. 'Man here with a broken ankle and an erection.'

Toby stood there in jeans, boots, a black T-shirt, and a denim jacket. He smiled. "Good evening."

That was all it took to get my heart pounding.

"Hey." I stood aside to let him enter, then closed the door behind him, forcing myself to breathe normally. "I'm curious. Where do they think you are?"

"Out for a walk."

I blinked. "And they believed that?"

He rolled his eyes. "Are you kidding? When I got out of the shower, Zeeb came into the bathroom and passed something to me, kind of surreptitiously. For God's sake, we were the only two in there."

"Do I want to know?"

His eyes gleamed. "Condoms. Then Matt asked if I had everything I needed for the night. I bluffed it out, but I got the feeling he knew."

"If it makes you feel better, he went through the same routine with me."

"And then there were all the glances, the snickers… I swear, the only people who *didn't* do anything were Declan and Garrett."

I laughed. "Hey, look on the bright side. At least we don't have to bother sneaking around, if everyone knows."

Toby stared at me. "You're okay with that?"

I was halfway toward being okay with it. I suspected that after a couple of similar evenings, I wouldn't give a shit.

"What are they gonna say? I'm the boss, remember?" I took a calming breath. "You haven't changed your mind?"

"Uh-uh." He took a step closer.

I wasn't done. That last look in the mirror had raised a question. "And it doesn't bother you? That I'm... older." Then I remembered our conversation that morning. "Wait—scrap that. You like older guys."

"You were paying attention. Good." There was a twinkle in his eyes. "Besides, you already know I think you're hot—and you *know* I want to fuck you."

I couldn't suppress the shiver that trickled down my spine. Fuck, there was something about him that turned me inside out. A sense that he knew exactly what he was doing. He'd promised to make it good for me, and now, listening to the quiet confidence in his voice, the self-assuredness that poured from him, I believed him.

My heart thumped. "So... What happens now?"

"Now? We do this." He stepped closer still, cupped my face, and kissed me.

God, it felt good. It started out chaste, but soon his tongue went deep, and it had been *too goddamn long* since I'd been kissed like that. His hand slid down my neck, over my shoulders, around my back, and down to my ass. He squeezed, pulling me tight against him.

Fuck, he was like a rock.

"I see you didn't lose the hard-on," I murmured when he broke the kiss.

Brown eyes locked onto mine. "I got rid of that one in the shower. This is an all new-and-improved hard-on." He took my hand in his. "Now, how about you show me your bedroom?"

I led him through the house toward the stairs, my heart hammering. "Did you bring them?" I'd searched every drawer in my bedroom.

"Yeah, we're good to go all night if we need to."

I laughed. "Can't tell you the last time I went all night." I paused at the top step. "Just how old are you?"

"Thirty-five."

I chuckled. "No wonder you can talk like that." Lord, I remembered being that age, when three orgasms a night was the norm—*if* I was allowed to come.

I pushed the door open, and he went in first, pulling me after him. He came to a halt. "Whoa. Nice bed."

I *loved* my bed. It was wide and high, made of pine, with posts that were perfect for tying things around. And then I gasped as he pushed me backward onto it.

"Good mattress too." He kicked off his boots, shrugged off his jacket, and climbed onto it. I let my knees fall apart, allowing him to crawl up my body until his face was inches from mine. He paused, his eyes on mine, watching...

Don't study me—kiss me, for God's sake.

Then I let out an internal sigh of relief when our lips met. I cupped his nape, dragging him in, wanting more. He rocked, his crotch sliding over mine again and again, until I was doing my damnedest not to whimper.

He sat upright, hauling me with him. "Arms."

I held them high, and he pulled my tee over my head before removing his own. He pushed me onto my back once more, only this time, his lips were on my neck, making me shiver. I wanted them to graze the skin, to leave a mark, but he kept his kisses gentle. When he moved lower, his tongue seeking out my nipple, I shuddered. *Suck on it, please.* Instead, he laved it with teasing flicks, until I was writhing beneath him. He traced a line from my chest to my navel, a slow, tantalizing lick that sent tingles through me.

Does he have any idea *what he's doing to me?*

He paused at my waistband, and my shivers intensified. "Want to see this." Toby unbuttoned my jeans, lowered the zip, and my dick sprang out, clamoring for attention. "Oh, perfect."

He gave it a tentative lick, and I groaned at the sensation. Then I gasped when he took the head into his mouth. I placed my hands on his head, dying to exert pressure but not daring to.

It had been more than twenty years since I'd played the feeling-each-other-out game, so I was way out of practice. I pushed up with my hips, my cock not going too deep, just enough to signal my need, praying he noticed.

Toby licked up and down my shaft, pausing now and then to suck on the head. He pulled free, his gaze locked on mine. "Time to lose the jeans—for both of us."

Thank God.

He grasped the waistband and tugged, and I lifted my hips off the mattress to allow him to slide my jeans lower. Toby shifted off the bed and grabbed the hems, tugging them off my legs, my dick smacking against my stomach. Then he popped the button on his own jeans and started lowering the zipper, stopping when the head of his dick came into view.

Shit, don't stop there.

"Oops. Can't forget the supplies." He reached into his front pocket, removed three condoms, and tossed them onto the bed.

"Lube's in the drawer," I managed to get out as he shoved his jeans to his ankles.

"Yeah, we're going to need that." He tugged out of his jeans and took off his socks.

My stomach quivered as I opened the nightstand drawer, scrabbling for the bottle. I placed it next to the condoms, drinking in the sight. His shaft stood to attention, and my first thought was that there was more of him than there'd been in the tub. The gentle ripple of his abs, the V that led the eye lower to the mass of dark, tight curls above his dick, the curve of his pecs...

Toby was a heartstopper.

He stood beside the bed, gazing at me in silence, until I wanted to beg him to do something, *anything*... He leaned forward, gripped my hips, and dragged my ass to the edge of the bed. He grasped my ankles and lifted my legs into the air.

"Hold them for me."

God, I was *so* ready to be fucked.

I hooked my arms under my knees and drew them to my chest. Toby rubbed his thumb over my hole, and I shivered again.

"It's been a while, I know, so I'm going to take things nice and easy."

Noooo, I wanted to scream. Fuck nice and easy. I wanted my ass reamed—*after* he'd loosened it with his goddamn tongue.

He squeezed lube onto his fingers, then slid them over my pucker.

Rimming was out, apparently. *God hates me, that's what it is.*

My breathing quickened as he circled my hole, but then so did his, and I realized he wanted this as much as I did. He pushed, and I welcomed the intrusion, moaning as he entered me up to the knuckle.

"Fuck, you're tight."

I glared at him. "Then do something about it."

Toby arched his eyebrows. "Temper. You have to be good if you want your oats, remember?" He didn't break eye contact as he slid his finger in and out of my ass, keeping the same, steady pace. When he added another, I felt the burn and did my best to relax. The slow and steady rhythm was driving me insane, and a couple of times I came close to breaking point.

Then he leaned over me, his fingers wedged in my hole, and I shuddered into his kiss. "I think you're ready for my cock," he whispered against my lips.

"I was ready this morning," I quipped.

He withdrew completely, then reached for a foil packet. I watched, entranced, as he unfurled the latex over his rigid shaft. He applied more lube, propelling his dick through slick fingers. And when he pressed the hot head of his cock to my hole, I resisted the urge to impale myself on it.

Dear *Lord*, that first unhurried slide into me took my breath away.

He was true to his word. He took it slow, moving in and out

of me at a leisurely pace, his hands gripping my thighs. The rolling motion of his hips was almost hypnotic, and I wanted to move with him, to urge him to go deeper, harder... He picked up a little speed, and my heart leaped—until he slowed down once more. Then he did it again, each time bringing me close to where I needed to be, only to back off at the last minute.

I was a hot mess, but I was also confused as fuck. Toby's breathing was erratic, his skin flushed... I don't know what sign he was waiting for from me, maybe a neon one on my forehead that said FUCK ME, but I sure was sensing something.

It felt a lot like frustration bound up with a whole lot of longing.

I was done.

"No, please," I begged. "I'm not gonna break, okay?"

Toby

I stilled. "Something wrong?" Oh my God, the effort it took not to move inside him.

"No. I mean, yes. I mean... it feels good, okay? Just..."

"Just what?" *Come on, Robert, tell me what you want.* I'd deliberately kept things vanilla, but I was starting to regret that decision.

He looked me in the eye. "Are you *trying* to bust my balls?" *What?*

"Because it feels like you're teasing me."

"You don't *want* me to tease your hole?"

He rolled his eyes. "Hell no."

"Then tell me what you do want."

He swallowed. "I want you... I want you to... fuck me."

"Isn't that what we're doing?"

"Yes. I mean, no. I mean—"

"Maybe what you need is something like *this*." I grabbed his shoulders and drove into him, punching the air from his lungs.

"Oh Jesus, *there* we go," he groaned.

"That better?" I slid out, only to thrust into him once more, no longer holding back.

"Again," he begged.

I filled him to the hilt. "Like that?"

"Yes," he moaned. I pulled free of him, and he raised his head from the mattress to stare at me with undisguised incredulity. "Seriously?"

I had to fight hard not to let my elation show. *Oh, now I get it. You like it rough.*

I was more than happy to oblige.

"Lie in the middle of the bed."

He shifted across, and I knelt on the bed. I grabbed his knees, spreading him, then aimed my cock at his hole, spearing all the way into him, watching his face contort, a mixture of pleasure and pain. What raced through my head was a question.

What would he do if I took hold of his wrists and pinned them to the bed?

There was only one way to find out.

CHAPTER SEVENTEEN

Robert

Fuck, his dick feels so good.

It didn't matter how realistic a dildo looked or felt—nothing compared to the feel of a warm, hard cock in my ass. Okay, maybe *one* thing, but going bare was off the menu, so there was little point even fantasizing about it.

Then my heart stopped when he seized my wrists, pushed them onto the mattress, and pinned them there, holding me down.

Holy fuck.

Toby's breathing grew harsh. "You like that."

It wasn't a question.

I nodded, unable to get the words out.

"Tell me."

"No, I don't like it—I fucking *love* it." There was an edge to my voice, just the trace of a whine.

His eyes sparkled. "Good boy. Oats for you."

I rolled my eyes, and opened my mouth to tell him he wasn't talking to Lightning, when he pulled out of me and then slammed in hard, his hips pistoning. He fucked me with long, deep strokes punctuated with grunts and the slap of skin against skin.

It was as if a switch had flicked on inside him, but whatever the reason for the change in pace and intensity, my heart was singing. He drove into me again, and I moaned—until he froze, his cock buried in my ass.

I stared at him, forcing myself to breathe.

Toby tightened his grip on my wrists. "Squeeze my cock." I blinked, and he nodded. "Come on, squeeze my cock. Show me you like it." I tightened my ass muscles around his dick, and he smiled. "Oh yeah, you like it." Then he withdrew.

I groaned. "And we're back to you busting my balls again."

Toby leaned over and kissed me, a deep, exploratory kiss that made my toes curl. "Don't worry," he murmured against my lips. "We're not done yet." He lay on his back, tugging at the latex. He tossed the condom to the floor, then spread his legs and grabbed his cock around its base. "Show me what you can do."

That was when I decided I was going to blow his mind.

I took him into my mouth, stretching my lips around solid, warm flesh, and gave a good hard suck. The heartfelt groan that poured out of him made me feel amazing, and I repeated the move, only now I was bobbing my head, taking him deeper and deeper, relaxing my throat until I'd swallowed him to the root.

"Oh my God."

Mind blown.

He shoved a pillow under his head, his eyes locked on mine. "Work the shaft with your hand." I pulled free of him, spat into my palm, and curled my fingers around his cock, sliding them up and down, while I flicked the underside of the head with my tongue.

"Fuck, yeah, just like that." He craned his neck to stare at me with gleaming eyes. "Suck my balls." I took them into my mouth, one at a time, and he dropped back onto the pillow, a shiver running through him. He grabbed his dick. "Open your mouth, stick your tongue out." When I complied, he smacked the head against my tongue.

I made sure to maintain eye contact, and that was the hottest thing ever, sucking on the head, our gazes locked, his chest heaving.

Toby shuddered out a breath. "Stand over there against the wall, facing it."

I didn't need a second invitation.

I placed my hands flat to the wall, my heart hammering, my ass tilted for the cock I knew was coming. I caught the tear of foil and the *snap* of the bottle lid. He stood behind me, spread my ass cheeks with strong fingers, and slid inside me one more time.

Dear *Lord*, it had been a while.

I loved the change of angle, the way his pubes grazed my ass cheeks once he was all the way in. Then he grabbed my hands and brought them over my head, crossing them at the wrist and pinning them to the wall with one hand, while he reached for my cock with the other.

I groaned. "Do that, and I'll come."

His breath tickled my ear. "No, you won't." It felt more like a command than an assurance. He continued fucking me, slamming into me, our bodies smacking together. Then he filled me to the hilt and did a slow grind, rotating his hips as he stirred his dick inside me.

That was beyond amazing.

"Keep your hands there," he instructed. He slid his to my hips and held onto me as he fucked me, yanking me back onto his shaft. "Like that?"

My only response was a series of grunts and moans, driven out of me with each thrust of his dick.

Then he grabbed my hands and pulled them behind my back. "This okay?"

His obvious care and concern touched me. "More than okay." My cheek was pressed to the wall, my arms were held captive behind my back, and he was spearing into me, going deep every. Fucking. Time.

I was in heaven—until he held onto my wrists with one hand, and my throat with the other. He didn't squeeze—he didn't have to. Just feeling his fingers there was enough to have me harder than I'd been in a long while. Unable to move my arms, his hand cupping my throat…And then he let go of my wrists and reached around once more for my cock.

I was amazed I didn't come there and then.

When he withdrew again, I wanted to scream at him to *put it right back in there*. Instead, he got onto the bed on his back.

"Ride me." He squeezed more lube onto his gloved cock.

I clambered onto the bed and sat astride him, reaching back to guide him to where I needed him to be. I sank onto his heavy shaft, lower and lower, until at last my body sheathed him completely. I bent over to kiss him and he tilted his hips, staying deep inside me. Then he grabbed my hips and pulled me down onto him, his cock going deeper than I'd thought possible.

I was so full of him.

"Lean back. Put your hands on my knees. I want to watch your cock bounce while I fuck you."

I put my weight on my hands and rode him, my dick bobbing so hard, it smacked against my belly. I let go with one hand to reach for my shaft, and he knocked it out of the way.

"No. No touching."

Oh my God. My heartbeat raced, my body tingled, and my belly quivered.

How does he know?

Toby thrust into me, his hips rocking up off the mattress. "You're getting closer."

I nodded, desperate to tug on my cock. No way was I about to do that, however.

Maybe he saw something in my face. He reached up and cupped my nape, drawing me to him. We kissed, a searching, claiming kiss, his tongue in harmony with his dick. My forehead touched his, and he whispered, "Now, Robert. Touch your cock."

I slid a hand between our damp bodies and wrapped my fingers around my shaft. I gave it maybe three or four tugs before I shot hard. I shuddered through every pulse of my dick, and it wasn't long before he followed.

God, I'd missed that throb inside me. It could only have been better if there'd been nothing between us, but I wasn't stupid. Going bare in my mind spoke of one thing—commitment—and a guest who'd be gone in ten days wasn't going to be interested in that.

He held me against his chest, his lips on my cheeks, my

forehead, my mouth…

"So good," he murmured.

I wanted to tell him it had been good for me too.

I wanted to tell him he'd set me on fire.

What spilled from my lips was something entirely different.

"What just happened?"

Toby

I kept my tone even. "We fucked. Maybe I should've recorded it on my phone, you know, to send to you, in case you needed reminding."

I was half-joking. I wanted to remember every minute.

My hookups and scenes followed a pattern. We'd meet, check our status, talk a while—at least until I'd worked out what they were into—or not into—we'd discuss any boundaries that needed to be set, and then it would be all systems go. There was a reason I posted photos of me in my harness on Scruff—I didn't want my proclivities to be a surprise.

Not that I'd gone into this night with Robert blind—the photos hadn't put him off, far from it. But I *had* gone in determined to keep things vanilla, because we hadn't even discussed if he *was* vanilla, and just thinking about taking the first steps into BDSM.

Then I recalled his obvious excitement when I held his throat. Breath-play wasn't something vanilla guys got off on, whereas it was definitely more of a D/s thing.

What is going on here?

He liked it rough. He got hard as a rock when I engaged in a little breath play. There'd been other stuff too, and all of it was leading me to one of two possible conclusions—either Robert fantasized about being taken roughly, or…

I cupped his bearded jaw, tilting his head to look him in the eye. "What did you like most about what we did here?"

He stared at me for a moment, then shuddered out a sigh. "The way you… took control, told me what to do…"

I stared back. "Something you want to tell me?"

Robert raised himself, and my softened dick slid from his warm body. I removed the condom, tied it up, and placed it on the nightstand along with the torn wrappers. Without a word, Robert handed me tissues to wipe his cum from my stomach. Then he leaned over and opened the drawer. When he didn't remove anything, I took the hint. I peered into it. At first, I wasn't sure what I should be looking for, until I caught sight of—

Now it made sense.

I reached into the drawer and removed the leather cuffs. "These are yours, right?" They weren't new, I could tell that much. The edges of the holes where the metal prongs poked through were worn.

He nodded.

Then I saw the cock cage. "This too?" I picked it up and laid it on the pillow.

Another nod.

I bit back a smile. "Is that it, or is there more?"

"Under the bed. Well, that's all there is here at the house."

I arched my eyebrows. I got off the bed and crouched on the rug, peering into the darkness. I spotted a clear plastic bag, and reached under to pull it toward me. It had a coating of dust, but not enough to prevent me from seeing its contents.

This gets better and better.

I tossed the bag full of coiled rope onto the bed, then got to my feet. I sat beside him on the bed, my heartbeat racing as I went through a mental check list of all the clues. Based on everything Robert had done so far, I dismissed the fantasy idea, because there was one more obvious explanation.

"You're a submissive." Not only that—he was a good, *experienced* sub.

He nodded.

"How long have you been into kink?"

His breathing caught. "A long time."

His words from our ride that morning came back to me with added significance.

'For reasons I'm not going to explain either, I prefer to be frank and open about things like this.'

Yeah, this was an experienced sub. No wonder he'd felt comfortable talking about things first.

Then it hit me. My stomach clenched.

"Oh my God. You and Kevin... You weren't just fuck-buddies."

He shook his head. "When we were around others, he was Kevin and I was Boss, occasionally Robert, because he'd been the foreman for years, and no one batted an eyelid at him calling me by my first name."

"And when you were alone?"

He swallowed hard. "He was Sir. And not just in the bedroom." His eyes glistened. "When I lost him, I lost my anchor, my weathervane, my rock... He grounded me. He took my daily worries and anxieties, and made them vanish. I gave it all to him, and he let me." Another swallow. "He took it all away."

My heart ached when I thought of him the last five years, adrift on an ocean of pain and guilt, moved by the tide, never reaching a satisfying destination.

I wanted to help him reach the shore.

"I am so sorry for your loss," I murmured, wiping his tears away with my thumbs. Then I straightened. "But now that I know everything—" I peered at him. "I do know everything, right?" He nodded. "Okay. We need to decide where we go from here."

He blinked. "Where we... go?"

I leaned back on my hands. "Let's be practical for a second. I've got a week-and-a-half left here. So as far as I see it, there are two options. One—we buy a shitload of condoms, and we fuck like bunnies."

"What's option two?"

I looked him in the eye. "You've missed it, haven't you? Submitting, I mean."

"Like you wouldn't believe."

But I would. He couldn't turn off his submissive nature any more than I could turn off my dominant one.

"So much that it hurts," I guessed.

He swallowed, then nodded.

"Then option two is… We talk. We discuss limits. We get tested, wherever it was you used to go—"

"Bozeman. There's a clinic."

The speed of his response told me that would be pretty high up the To Do list. I nodded. "That would be item one on the schedule then. We're not gonna waste time, not now I understand why you're hurting." He winced, but I knew what pained him wasn't physical.

I also knew what he needed was not some quick fix, but something more long-term. And suddenly my mind was going wild with ideas: phone sex; games of denial; putting him in restraint until I got back to—

I stilled.

I want to be his Dom.

I want to come back to visit.

He needs this, and I have the time to do it.

But *could* I do it? I'd never had a long-distance D/s relationship before. I had no idea if it could work. But would Robert be able to handle a D/s relationship without attachment? Just how close had he been to Kevin? Would he want more? And if he did, would I mind that?

I had to shut down that train of thought. It was leading down the rabbit hole, and it was way too early to be thinking about that.

What shocked me was I wanted to offer him more than whatever time was left to us.

I lifted his chin with my fingertips. "Would you like me to

make it hurt a little less?"

His breathing hitched. "Please..." Robert gazed up at me, his expression almost serene. "Sir."

He had taken one word and made it sound like a prayer.

I couldn't hold back when I saw the naked longing in his eyes, the need burning there... I leaned in and kissed him, a sweet, tender kiss not intended to arouse him, but to seal the moment.

When I broke the kiss, he expelled a breath. "Thank you."

I toyed with the idea of putting him in chastity—the cage was right there, for God's sake—but it felt too soon. We needed to talk first. And right then he seemed a little... fragile wasn't the word, but something was going on.

He froze as a mournful howl reached us, followed by another. It didn't sound too close.

"What was that?" Then the howls came again, only louder.

"Aw shit."

"What's wrong?"

"What you heard is a wolf pack. They like to hunt at night. Thing is, we can't shoot 'em like we used to. Remember we told you they're protected under the Endangered Species Act? So now we have to scare 'em off."

Then it was my turn to freeze when I heard a door open downstairs.

"Boss?"

Robert stared at me in resignation. "You need me, Teague?" he called out. He grabbed his jeans and tee, and I cursed Teague's timing. We might not have shared a full-on scene, but enough of one that I wanted to apply a little aftercare.

"Yeah." He sounded miserable as fuck. It took me a moment to realize part of that misery was down to having to disturb his boss.

I laid a hand on Robert's arm, stilling his frantic scramble into his clothing. "He's not going to be surprised to find me here, is he?"

Robert shook his head.

"Okay then. Breathe. I'll get dressed too, and I'll go downstairs with you." With all I'd learned about him—and the knowledge I was going to learn a whole lot more before it was time to leave Salvation—I figured there was little point in sneaking around.

Fuck, they all knew anyway. And if they didn't, they would by the time I got to the bunkhouse.

We finished dressing, and went downstairs. Teague stood at the foot of the stairs. He didn't even blink when he saw me. "Sorry to disturb you, boss, but we've got problems."

"I heard. Who've you rounded up to go investigate?"

"I figured me, Zeeb, Walt, and Butch."

"Figure me in there too."

Teague twisted his hat in his hands. "Yeah, thought you might." He coughed. "Everything okay here?" His gaze flickered in my direction.

"Everything is fine," Robert assured him. He'd switched into boss-mode, and I knew we were done for the night.

Then it occurred to me Teague's question had added significance.

He's making sure Robert is okay. That made sense. He'd known me for all of four days, and he didn't trust me yet. I was just a guest who was fucking his boss, and that had to be a huge development.

"Let's go." Robert and Teague headed for the front door, and I followed. As we stepped onto the path, the floodlights came on. I could see more light below, coming from the stables, and I caught the clatter of hooves on gravel and raised voices.

When we reached the bottom of the path, I squeezed Robert's arm. "I'd better leave you to it. I'll see you in the morning."

He nodded. "Sorry about this," he murmured.

I smiled. "Shit happens, right? You go be the boss." As he turned to follow Teague, I muttered, "We've got time, okay?"

He expelled a breath. "Yeah." Then he hurried toward the barn.

I walked in the direction of the bunkhouse, mulling over what had been an eventful evening. Anticipation thrummed through me at the prospect of ten days of discovering what made Robert tick. The promise of several nights of hot fucking had suddenly blossomed into something richer, more satisfying.

Tomorrow I'd share my proposal. Then it would be up to him.

And if he says no?

Despite my assurance to Robert, ten days was not a lot of time, and I meant to milk them, to squeeze every second of pleasure out of them.

Milking...

Okay, that was going on the list of things to discuss.

CHAPTER EIGHTEEN

Robert

I closed the front door, locked it, and climbed the stairs, my arms and legs like lead, but nowhere near as heavy as my heart.

What the fuck is wrong with me?

I should have felt amazing. Shit, I'd had sex for the first time in years. Having to go off on a wolf hunt had brought the proceedings to an abrupt end, but thankfully none of the cattle had been attacked, and we'd sent them fleeing into the woods. Walt and Kyle were spending the night out there in case any more showed up.

As for the rest of the evening?

I was a mess.

Toby… a Dom. Maybe a part of me had recognized that. I'd gravitated to him the way I'd gravitated to Kevin, Clay too if it came to that. They'd both shared the same kind of vibe, a self-assurance that was very attractive. And when he made the switch from gentle to *I'm gonna fuck your brains out*, I wanted to shout to the heavens, telling God He'd more than made up for the lack of rimming.

Except I was still hoping for that part.

It had been a glorious fuck. *Then why do I feel as if I want to bawl my eyes out?* My heart pounded, my stomach was tight, my palms were clammy, and my anxiety level was through the roof. Okay, my concerns over the possibility of wolves attacking the herd had exacerbated that, but the crisis had passed, for God's sake. *So why do I feel so weighed down?*

This wasn't the first time I'd felt like this—it had happened maybe four or five times in the past—except then, I'd had Kevin to turn to.

Kevin to hold me, soothe me, make it all right again.

Now? There was no one.

Sure, there was Toby, but he was in the bunkhouse, and I wasn't about to call him. Besides, he didn't know me. One fuck didn't mean we trusted each other…yet.

But you want to trust him, don't you?

Fuck yeah.

My thoughts went to the cabin. If I saddled Rusty and took a ride over there, maybe once I was surrounded by stuff he'd owned or touched, there'd be enough of Kevin's presence in the cabin to calm me, ground me…

I gave myself a hard mental shake.

I can't keep doing this.

I can't keep thinking about him.

He can't be my rock anymore, because he's fucking dead.

And since when do I believe shit like that? What am I gonna do, touch the sling he fucked me on, and suddenly feel his… spirit?

That comment to Zeeb about burning the cabin to the ground? Yeah, that had been a little… excessive. But maybe it was time to exercise a few ghosts, rid myself of my demons.

I undressed and got into bed. I was conscious of Toby's scent, clinging to the pillow, and I breathed him in. *Did it really happen? Did I dream it?* I closed my eyes, and the smell transported me back. His words played over and over in my head.

'Would you like me to make it hurt a little less?'

I'd told Kevin once that a night of him cured a lot of ills, and he'd laughed.

'There's no such thing as a magic dick.'

Toby had sounded sincere, as if he really believed he could take away my pain. But how?

Lord, I'm tired. Except it was more than fatigue. I was weary to the bone.

I had the feeling sleep wasn't going to put in an appearance any time soon.

Toby

I lay in my bunk, listening to the sound of Butch's soft snores. Zeeb and the others had returned to the bunkhouse an hour after Teague had appeared at the house. From the little conversation I heard, the wolves appeared to have been routed.

I didn't get to see Robert, which disappointed me.

I laced my fingers under my head and closed my eyes, replaying the scene, recalling the noises he'd made, the way he'd writhed beneath me, the flow of his body as he rode me...

A long-distance submissive? Now that's a big commitment.

Not only big—daunting.

Up at the house, the idea of being Robert's Dom had seemed the perfect way to go, but now that I thought about it, I wasn't so certain. Too much would depend on how badly both parties wanted it. Yeah, there was a lot of scope for scenes involving video calls, phone calls, but at least if we were in the same city—or even the same state—I'd be there if he needed me. This way, there'd be a thousand miles separating us.

But he'd have you, *which is a damn sight more than he has right now.*

I envied what he and Kevin had shared. Fifteen years, Dom and sub... I'd never had a D/s relationship that had lasted more than a few years, three tops. Then I reconsidered. Those relationships had been nothing like Robert and Kevin's. Maybe they were more... was transactional the right word? Each one had started out from a basis of 'this is what we both want from this,' and for the most part, emotional entanglement had been kept out of it. As the relationships developed, so did the attraction—I just never let it go too far. And when it did, that wasn't down to me. Tyler was the latest sub to want more than I was able—or

willing—to give.

What Robert and Kevin had shared felt totally different, and it had worked for them—I just wasn't sure if it would work for me.

It sounded as if they were more deeply involved with each other than I'd ever been with a sub. It had been more than D/s for them—feelings had gotten entangled too—and since when had I ever allowed a deeper connection with a sub?

Yeah, daunting as fuck.

Theirs had been more than a non-romantic D/s relationship. They had been all-inclusive when it came to heads, hearts, and a D/s partnership—or as close to it as they could get.

A tough act to follow.

Except I knew that was an excuse.

I'd been attracted to Robert *before* I'd known about his past, his experience. That first encounter had shown me we were a good match, and I wanted to see where the next would lead us.

I guess I've made a decision.

I'd talk to him the following day—and hope he wanted to head in the same direction.

Wednesday, June 15

Zeeb handed the coiled rope up to me. "You ready?"

"As ready as I'll ever be." In my other hand I clutched Lightning's reins. I bent over, patted his neck, and whispered, "We're going to do this, okay?"

That whinny was either him saying *Sure* or *You're gonna land on your ass, mister.*

Walt got onto the quad bike, to the rear of which was attached a metal steer that was nothing more than a head to aim for, the rest of it just flat metal. Walt twisted to glance at me. "I won't be taking it slow, okay?"

I nodded.

"Go for it," Teague hollered from the other side of the fence. Butch, Paul, Declan, and Garrett were lined up to watch, which did not relieve the pressure I'd already put myself under. There were a couple of hands I didn't recognize too.

Then I caught sight of Robert strolling toward the paddock, and my stomach clenched. I leaned over once more. "Hey, Lightning. The boss is here. Don't make me look bad, okay?" I had visions of falling off while I tried to rope the damn thing.

Walt turned the key, and drove across the paddock away from me, tugging the metal steer behind him. I waited until he'd put some distance between us, then galloped after him, the rope twirling over my head. I launched it, looped over the metal steer's head, and pulled it taut.

Zeeb was the first to applaud. "Yay. *Man*, you're good with a rope." The others followed suit.

I didn't need to turn around to know the cough I heard came from Robert.

I rode Lightning over to the mounting block. As I got off him, I patted his back. "Good boy. I'll be out with a treat for you later."

Paul chuckled. "I'll take him. And I'll make sure he gets his treat." He led Lightning toward the stable.

"Dude, you made it look easy," Garrett complained. "I'm never going to be able to do this."

"Hey, let's concentrate on one skill at a time, okay?" Zeeb told him. "We get you comfortable on a horse, that's the priority. We've got plenty of guys if we need to rope steers. At least that way, you'll be able to come on the cattle drive." He gave Garrett a warm smile. "You'll love it."

I took my hat off to Zeeb. The man was good with people.

"You sure?" Garrett's brow furrowed.

"Course I'm sure. Tell you what—how about you and me go on a trail ride this morning? A nice easy trail, just to ease you into it. We can take as long as we like."

Garrett's expression of longing told me he wanted to believe Zeeb. Then he pointed toward me and Declan. "But what about them?"

"Dec's coming with me to check on the herd," Teague

announced. He grinned. "Not like he hasn't done *that* before."

Declan laughed. "Hey, I'm hoping if I ever quit the rat race, you'll give me a job here."

"And Toby doesn't need any more lessons," Zeeb added. His eyes glittered. "You get an A."

"Thanks, Teach." I gazed at the group of ranch hands. "So what will I be doing?"

Butch snorted. "Do you *really* want us to answer that?"

I thought I'd gotten off lightly so far that morning. No one had said a word about my 'walk.' I should've known they wouldn't stay quiet for too long.

"I'm going to go up to the house for coffee. I've only had three cups this morning." Robert's eyes met mine. "You can come with me if you like."

Walt beamed. "There you go—the boss will take care of you."

Zeeb coughed and Robert aimed a glance at him. Zeeb shrugged. "I'm sayin' nothing."

Robert chuckled. "Yeah right. I'll believe that when I see it."

"I'd love some coffee." I glanced at the others, as if daring one of them to make a comment, but no one challenged me. *Give it time.* I intended spending a big chunk of my stay in Robert's company—well, as much as he could allow me—and they wouldn't pass up the opportunity to get in a few choice comments.

"Yeah, you go drink coffee." Butch waggled his eyebrows. "We'll see you later. That's if you don't find something better to do."

"I'm sure I can find *you* something to do," Robert commented dryly. "Matt said the waste in the bunkhouse sink is blocked. And that *is* your domain, isn't it?"

Butch sighed. "Yes, boss." He trudged away from us, and for a moment I almost felt sorry for him.

Almost.

I followed Robert up the hill, glancing at him as we walked. "You okay?" I hadn't looked too closely at him down in the paddock. His eyes were puffy, and his face was kind of drawn. He gave the impression he hadn't slept well.

He stared at me. "I look that good, huh?"

"You look like you feel like shit."

"Accurately put. Please feel free not to mention it again." We got to the house, and I followed Robert inside, heading for the kitchen.

"Is Matt around?"

"No, he's gone shopping. He needs to get in supplies for the weekend, and for camping out next week." Robert grabbed two cups, then peered at me. "You do want some, right?"

I smiled. "Sure. We can talk while we drink."

And there it was, the expectation of communication. He regarded me in silence, then nodded. "Okay." He filled the cups. "Cream?"

"As it comes."

He handed me a cup. "I meant to tell you. The third Saturday in every month, it's supper here for all the hands. That includes guests too. Nothing fancy. Matt does meatloaf, mac and cheese, pizza… We all sit around the dining table, eating, drinking beer or whatever…" He gestured to the breakfast bar. "Please, sit."

I pulled out a stool and perched on it. "Bad night?"

"I've had better. What made it worse was not being able to account for the way I felt. I was just so… low."

"You know what sub drop is, right?"

He blinked. "I thought I was just depressed. It's not the first time it's happened."

I nodded. "You got your head into a good place, and then Teague arrived. What with worrying about the wolves, not being able to settle naturally after we were done… Something jarred you out of your head space. But sub drop is *not* the same thing as depression, you hear? And what is more, it's totally okay to experience drop. It doesn't make you weak—it makes you human." As an afterthought, I added, "And just so you know? Dom drop is a thing too." I cocked my head. "Kevin told you about that, right?" If he hadn't, I'd have been concerned. *Just how good a Dom was he?*

He nodded. "Yeah, he did. He explained about sub drop too, but…it's been a long time." He shuddered out a sigh, and I knew it was one of relief. I also knew it told him something vital about me.

He could rely on me, lean on me.

I got off the stool, walked around the bar to where he stood, and held my arms wide. He didn't even hesitate. He walked into them, and I held him to me, aware of the odd shiver still trickling through him.

"You feel that way again, you call me, okay?" I murmured. "I don't care if it's the middle of the freakin' night." And to show him I meant every word, I tilted his head up with my fingers, and kissed him on the lips, keeping it chaste, letting it linger until he relaxed in my arms. "Better?"

He sighed, but in a good way. "Yeah. Thanks."

I went back to my stool. "So… about last night…Are you still okay with what we did?"

His eyes widened. "God yes." He took the stool facing mine.

I managed a relieved sigh. "Just checking." I'd learned never to assume.

"Can I ask questions?"

"Of course."

"That club you half own in San Francisco…the one for guys… Want to tell me what kind of club it is?"

I smiled. "I think you know."

"I see. How long have you been a Dom?" He cocked his head. "You *are* a Dom, right?"

"What gave it away?" I quipped. "And I suppose about eight years, ever since I got invited to a sex party and had my eyes opened."

That night had been like coming home.

Robert clasped his hands. "Maybe this is where I tell you what I'm into."

I'd been thinking about this all morning. "I'd like to approach this from a different angle."

He blinked. "Color me intrigued."

I leaned forward. "How about I tell *you* what I'd like to do to you?"

He flushed, his neck a lovely shade of pink. "Oh."

"This is not me giving instructions, by the way," I assured him. "I'd just like to put a few things out there to give you the opportunity to tell me if you want that too." I smiled. "Think of it as a Venn diagram. You've seen those, right? We're just going to see where our... interests intersect."

Maybe five seconds passed by before he replied. "Okay."

"First of all... Any injuries I need to know about? Medical needs? Any heart issues? Are you diabetic?"

He frowned. "No, but why do you ask?"

"Because if you're in a scene too long and your sugar drops, I need to be aware of that. I use creams to soothe welt marks or rope burns—ever had a reaction to one of those?"

"No, never. Can we get to the part where you tell me what you wanna do to me, please? Gotta say, I'm dying here."

I decided to put him out of his misery. "Top of the list would be Shibari." I grinned. "Rope bondage is my thing."

His flush deepened. "I can live with that."

"Did Kevin ever do a Shibari session with you?"

He chuckled. "If you mean all the pretty knots? No—wait a sec, that's not quite true. We tried it a couple of times, but to be honest, he was more into hog-tying me. And then when I was trussed up like a turkey, what followed was an epic fuck."

I couldn't wait to see him helpless, those intricate knots against his skin...

"And then there are toys."

"Specifically?" he inquired.

I shrugged. "Butt plugs, prostate massager... Nothing too elaborate—although the prostate massager needs to have a remote."

"Oh God." Robert swallowed.

"Not played with one of those before?"

"No, Sir."

I flashed him a grin. "But do you like the idea?"

"I'm not sure I want to answer that," Robert replied with a shiver. "Anything else?"

I'd saved the best for last. "Orgasm control. We're talking edging, milking, chastity…"

"I see. When you say 'control'…"

"Particularly prolonging orgasm—or preventing it. Either works." I peered at him. "Does all that work for you?"

"Yeah, it does. I do have another question, though." He inhaled deeply. "How often are we going to… play? I mean, there's the cattle drive next week…"

I reached over and took his hands in mine. "I will take as much time as you can give me. And about the cattle drive… I think you should go too."

He arched his eyebrows. "Oh?"

I nodded. "There are definite possibilities. I assume you get a tent to yourself?"

"Yes." That one syllable was edged with caution.

I smiled. "And when was the last time you were fucked outdoors?"

His mouth fell open. "But…the others…"

"Then you'll just have to be quiet, won't you?" I was looking forward to this.

"Jesus."

I reached under the breakfast bar, seeking his crotch. What I found left little doubt that despite his protestations, Robert liked the idea.

He groaned as I gave his hard cock a gentle squeeze. "Am I allowed a single request?"

"Of course. And if I like the idea, you might even get to experience it." There was very little I wouldn't consider doing.

"Rimming."

Heat surged through me. "Oh, I think that'll be on the menu. And maybe I should point out that in addition to those varying shades of kink, there will also be a lot of fucking." I still had a hold of his dick, and he squirmed.

"Okay," he croaked.

I let go and leaned back. "You and I need to go into Bozeman later today, if you can spare the time." I'd checked up on the clinic, relieved to see there was walk-in testing. I'd also found a store that might prove useful.

"Before we do that..." Robert's breathing quickened. "There's something I'd like to do. Actually, I *need* to do it."

"Okay." Whatever it was clearly mattered to him.

"Can... can we go to the cabin?"

I cocked my head. "'We'?" Not that I minded, but I was curious as to his motives.

He squared his shoulders. "I have to go there, but I don't want to do it alone."

A-ha. "I take it we're going inside?"

He nodded.

I didn't ask why—but I could guess.

Robert wanted to bid farewell to his past, and the least I could do was be there for him, seeing as I wanted to be part of his future—a future I hadn't spoken of yet.

Maybe a visit to the cabin needed to come first.

CHAPTER NINETEEN

Toby

"I thought we were going to the cabin," I asked as Robert drove along a little dirt track.

"We are—we're just getting there by another route."

"Okay, but why the truck? Is Rusty having an off day? Did Lightning have something better to do, like get his hooves polished?"

Robert laughed. "Now I've got this image in my head, of Lightning in a beauty parlor, his mane in curlers under a drier while he gets a manicure. Except... would that be a hooficure?"

I loved a guy with a sense of humor.

"And as for why we're taking the truck, I'll tell you when we get there."

Meadows lay on either side of the track, and above us was the sky's gorgeous unbroken hue. Ahead, I spied woodland, and when we reached the edge, Robert followed the track which narrowed, twisting and turning, until at last I spotted the cabin.

"Aha. This is the back way in."

"Uh-huh. Can you really see us carrying furniture across those stepping stones? And in the winter when the creek freezes and all the rocks are like glass?"

He had a point.

Robert stopped the truck beside the cabin, and we got out. I inhaled deeply, taking in the smell of pine and earth, and in the background, the sound of water cascading over rocks in the creek. I stood still, enjoying the moment.

"Always loved this spot," he murmured from beside me.

"It's so peaceful. Dad said Mom loved it here too." He glanced at the cabin.

"Procrastinating?"

He gave me a wry smile. "It shows, huh?" He walked toward the front porch steps, pausing at the bottom. I joined him, and on impulse I took his hand in mine.

"You can do this," I murmured.

He glanced at our joined hands, the faintest expression of surprise in his eyes.

I shrugged. "It seemed as though you needed a little support."

He squeezed my fingers. "You're right, I do. Thank you for doing this." Then he let go of my hand, climbed the steps, and removed a key from his pocket. He unlocked the door and pushed it open. I followed him inside.

Five years of dust and cobwebs decorated the interior. Ordinarily, I'd have made a joke about firing the cleaning staff, but not in the circumstances. Instead, I took a good look around.

The cabin was pretty much an open space with a vaulted ceiling. What light there was soaked into the dark logs that comprised the walls. A heavy wooden staircase led up to a mezzanine, and I noted the same rough branches design I'd seen at the big house. I peered through the railing running around the mezzanine, and caught sight of a bed. Below that was a small kitchen area, and the rest of the room was taken up with a couch in front of a brick fireplace, lamps, a couple of rugs—

And a sling suspended from a steel frame, gathering dust.

I grinned. "Nice. Now I know why no one comes in here." Some toys were definitely *not* for sharing, and needed to be kept out of sight. Back in San Francisco, my fuck machine was hidden from view in a cabinet. I had a few friends who would clutch their pearls if they saw that.

Robert pointed to the beams supporting the bed area. "Kevin didn't trust bolts to hold a sling, so he got us a portable one."

"I've been to sex parties where they erected three of these in one room. Handy little things."

"I've never been to one of those." His expression grew wistful.

"I'll tell you all about them one evening," I promised him.

I glanced at our surroundings. Apart from the sling, the cabin appeared pretty innocuous. I could imagine nights spent in front of the fire, the light from the flames playing over his body while I fucked him on the rug. Then I peered closer.

On the mantelpiece was a large tub of heavy-duty lube.

Aha.

I turned to him. "Did you like having his hand inside you?"

Robert's lips parted, and he adjusted his crotch.

"I'll take that as a yes."

"He didn't do it that often, but those times when he did… it meant something. We only started doing it in the last couple of years before he died."

I nodded. "That requires a lot of trust, but you'd had time to *build* that trust." I studied him. "So… are we here so you can say goodbye?"

"Yeah, but also…" He pointed to the window, where a squat oak chest sat beneath it. "We're here for that."

Now I got why he needed the truck. "Can I take a look?"

"Sure."

I went over to it, lifted the heavy dust-covered lid, and perused its contents.

It was a treasure chest.

There were ropes of different types and lengths, neatly coiled and tied. I smiled. I could tell a lot about a Dom by his rope collection, and right then Kevin was scoring pretty highly. I spotted coiled hemp and jute, which were good natural options for Shibari, although I preferred jute because of its tighter lay, making it more durable and less likely to thread over time and in a scene. But where Kevin scored an A? There wasn't a sign of cheap braided cotton there—that stuff was a bitch to untie all the tight knots. A lot of Doms used it because it was lightweight and a good option if you needed to carry a lot of it around.

What Kevin had was a solid polypropylene braid, an all-round rope good for most purposes outside of more intricate Shibari rope art. And it told me a lot. Kevin had a different style to me, which meant different sensations for Robert, different approaches.

That, I could work with.

One segment of the chest contained dildos—glass and silicone in varying sizes—and another was filled with butt plugs, cock rings, a ball gag, vibrators, a blindfold…

"I suppose in fifteen years, you amassed a lot of stuff."

He nodded. "I only kept the bare minimum at the house. This was where we played."

"You want to take this back to the house?"

"Yeah. It doesn't belong here now."

I surveyed the cabin's interior. "What will you do with this place?"

"I'm not sure yet. It'll come to me."

I pointed to the chest's contents. "And what about all this? You're not going to throw it away, are you? You could donate it."

He stared at them. "I'm not emotionally attached to any of it. Kevin bought it all." Then he pointed to the ball gag. "I didn't like that. We only used it the once."

"And the sling?"

"That got a lot of use." He smiled.

"What did you just think about?"

"Kevin fucked me all over this cabin—in the shower, the bed, on the couch, on the rug, against the door… And once on the porch." He shook his head. "I didn't know which was the stronger emotion—terror that guests would come along the trail and see us, or exhilaration. It was such a turn-on."

I grinned. "You do know you just guaranteed that I'm going to fuck you outdoors when we camp out on the cattle drive, right?" Before it had been a pleasant notion—now I was definitely going to make it happen. Then I realized something. "You know, that's the first time I think you've smiled when you've spoken about Kevin since I've known you. Which has been all of…" I did the math. "All of four days."

He gazed at me, and that slow smile put in another appearance. "You're right." He shook his head. "Man, talk about timing…"

"What do you mean?"

"It's just that…Kevin used to say there are no coincidences— it's just the universe making sure things slot into place. And these last few days… I suppose it started with the anniversary of his death. That was Saturday. Then a number of people decided to tell me it was time to move on."

"And then you found me at the cabin."

I didn't believe in coincidence either.

It was on the tip of my tongue to suggest me being his long-distance Dom, but I decided against it. That could wait until the end of my stay. *What if we're not as good a match as I believe we are?* Surely it was better to wait and see. I didn't want to put the proposal out there, then change my mind.

Yeah, better to wait until I was sure. Of course, this assumed Robert would be up for it, but after ten days of D/s play, he'd know if this was something he wanted too.

Enough with the introspection. There were things to be done, steps to be taken.

I pointed to the chest. "Let's take all this back to the house, the sling too. Then we'll go into Bozeman. I found that clinic you told me about. Are they pretty fast at sending results?"

"Yeah, we're talking a few minutes, unless they do swabs for chlamydia, and those get sent away. Not that I have anything to worry about on that score."

"Good. And then we'll go shopping. I found an adult store. We're going to need some new toys."

He bit his lip. "That prostate massager… the one with the remote? They might not have something like that in stock." He seemed almost hopeful.

I grinned. "They do—I checked this morning."

"Oh."

"And when we've been shopping…" I stepped closer to him, cupping his chin. "We're going to play." I leaned in and kissed him, not bothering to keep it chaste. I wanted to give him a taste of what was to come—and it might not be him. I explored him with my tongue, my hand on his neck, holding him there while I claimed his mouth.

He moaned into the kiss, and I pulled him to me, reaching around to squeeze his ass, grinding against him, my own cock meeting hardness.

"Do you have something else you need to be doing this afternoon?" I murmured, performing another slow grind of my hips.

A soft whimper escaped him. "Uh-uh."

"Good. Because I have plans for this body." I brought my lips to his ear. "No toys. No restraints. Just me getting to know your hot spots." I gave his cheeks another squeeze. "Getting to know this ass too."

"But you won't hold back, right?"

I curved my hand around his cheek. "It's been a long time since you've done this, so you need to know, I'm gonna be watching you closely. I know you're experienced, but you might need a while to get into the right head space again." I kissed him. "And that's my job—to get you there, take the heat down a notch or two if required… to make it good for you, like I promised."

"Thank you." Then he stilled. "Take the heat *down* a notch?"

I chuckled. "We're just starting out. Don't expect to hit the high notes with the first scene. Leave us *something* to work toward."

"I suppose," he said in a grudging tone.

"Hey." I cupped his nape, looking him in the eye. "You need to trust me. That might take a while, but we'll get there, okay?"

Robert nodded. "You're hitting all the right notes so far."

I smiled. "I think that was a compliment."

He glanced at the sling. "I need to find a place to put that up in the house." He flushed. "Somewhere Teague—or anyone else—won't walk in and find it."

"Yeah, I can see how that might be awkward." A thought occurred to me. "You okay going into an adult store with me? I mean, right on your doorstep and all." The ranch hands might know Robert was gay, but that didn't mean he wanted the population of Bozeman knowing it too.

He chuckled. "At the last count, there are some fifty-five thousand people living in Bozeman. They wouldn't know who I was."

"And like you said, Kevin did the shopping when it came to toys."

He nodded. "It was all online as well." Just then his phone rang, and he answered it. "Robert Thorston." He frowned. "Now? … Why am I just hearing about this?" He sighed. "And it can't wait? … Fine. I'll be there." He disconnected.

"That didn't sound good." What was more important, it sounded like something that was going to throw a monkey wrench into our plans.

"That's because it wasn't. I have to go to an emergency meeting at the Governor's office. Not just me—a whole load of landowners are gonna be there. Apparently, some assistant fucked up and forgot to call me to inform me of the fact. Someone's ass is gonna be hauled over the coals for that."

I had a sinking feeling the meeting wasn't in Bozeman. "Where?"

"Billings."

"And that's…"

"About four hours in a car, there and back, is what it is." Lord, he looked pissed, not to mention disappointed.

"Then let's do this another time."

His eyes widened. "We're not gonna—"

"Whoa there, cowboy. I was talking about moving the chest and the sling." I cupped the back of his head and gazed into his eyes.

"And whenever you get done, and you come home, I'll be waiting for you. Matt'll make sure you're fed—and then *I'll* make sure the rest of your needs are met."

I'd do whatever was necessary to help melt his tension into nothingness, even if I had to fuck his brains out to create the *right* kind of tension.

It was a dirty job, but someone had to do it.

CHAPTER TWENTY

Robert

I drove the car into the space behind the house, got out, locked it, then went back to open it again to retrieve my hat from the passenger seat. My shoulders and back were tense, and they'd been that way since about ten minutes into that fucking meeting. A soak in the tub seemed like a really good idea.

Then I remembered—Toby would be coming up to the house.

Warmth seeped through me. I wasn't sure what to expect. Our first encounter had been amazing, but the situation had changed.

Now he knows.

As I neared the front porch, I spied Teague sitting in one of the rockers, hands clasped over his stomach, his gaze locked on the horizon. I'd called him once I hit Bozeman.

He glanced up as I approached. "So how was it?"

I sighed. "Same shit, different day."

"Anything I need to know?"

"Not yet. I'll know more tomorrow, but wheels are in motion, put it that way. Everything okay here?"

He stretched his long legs out. "Yeah. We're gonna do another ride-out tonight after dusk." His eyes twinkled. "You don't need to come."

I arched my eyebrows. "Oh? And why is that?"

"Because you have better things to do. You probably just sat through the meeting from hell. Have a night off." There was that twinkle again. "Besides, you've got someone waiting for you inside."

It didn't take a genius to work out who.

"When you called, I said I was coming up here, and Toby asked to tag along. Matt's got supper waiting for the both of you."

He smiled. "I figured you wouldn't mind that." He removed his hat and turned it in his hands.

I knew my foreman. "What's bothering you?" Because *something* sure was.

"About last night. I—"

"You apologized already. Three times, as I recall."

"I felt bad about it, okay? Walking in on you like that."

"Teague… it's okay." I bit my lip. "Just… don't do it tonight, all right? Unless the barns catch fire and the stables go up in smoke. And if that happens, just break out the hoses and put the fire out."

He chuckled. "I get it. You don't wanna be disturbed."

I regarded him with amusement. "What are you grinning at?"

"Nothing."

"Bullshit."

He coughed. "Well, far be it from me to say 'I told you so' but… I fucking *told* you so."

"Told me what?"

That shit-eating grin just didn't quit. "That you'd like him." He got up out of the rocker and sauntered past me, heading for the path, singing quietly "Some-body's-gonna-get-lay-aid."

Lord, I hoped so.

I couldn't resist. "You're just jealous," I called out after him.

His laughter floated back to me. "Now why should I be that? I can get laid any night I want."

I was still smiling when I walked through the door.

Matt was on the other side of it, wearing his jacket. "Hey, boss. Supper's waiting for you in the dining room. I'll see you in the morning."

I blinked. "Good to see you too, Matt. Something I said?"

He grinned. "Have a good night." He grabbed his hat from the hook by the door, and went outside.

It was official. Everyone on Salvation would know the boss was getting laid.

I removed my hat, hung it up, and headed for the dining room.

Toby sat at the table, dressed in a black shirt, open at the neck. "Hello there."

"Hello to you too." He stood, and I caught sight of his tight jeans that did nothing to hide his erection. "I know what *I* want for supper," I quipped.

He snorted. "Later. First, you're going to eat. Don't tell me how your afternoon went. Day's over."

"Thank God."

He ambled over to me. "You're mine tonight."

I was dying to ask if he meant *all* night. I'd gotten used to sleeping alone again, but that didn't mean there weren't nights when I'd wake up in the darkness and reach for the warm, firm body that was no longer there. I wasn't about to ask Toby to stay. That felt... wrong.

He's here to play.

I'd take what I could get.

Maybe my need showed on my face, because his hand cradled the back of my head, and his lips met mine in a lingering kiss that went a long way to relieving some of the tension in me.

I knew he'd relieve the rest of it after supper. Knew that with every fiber and cell in my body.

When he drew back, I glanced at the table. There was chicken Parmesan, green beans, and mashed potato. A jug of water sat in the middle of the table. "You want a beer?"

"No. I want a clear head. And when you're done eating, you're going to go upstairs and take a shower."

I expelled a breath. "Yes, Sir." I liked that he took control right off the bat.

His eyes glittered with approval. "Good. Let's eat."

I'd been hungry on the drive home, but now? The butterflies were back.

His fingers were on my nape once more, warm and solid. "It's okay. We have all the time you need. We're in no rush."

I wanted to rid myself of the weight pressing down on my

shoulders, the ache in them, the persistent thought that I had responsibilities… Then I realized I had to let it all out, let it go…

"I need you, Sir."

Toby's eyes were warm. "You've got me."

I flipped off the shower and grabbed my towel. I'd taken longer than usual, but I believed in being thorough. How did the saying go? 'You never get a second chance to make a first impression.' Okay, so we'd already fucked but this was different.

This was a scene. An actual, goddamn *scene*.

I'd thought that part of my life was over, and now that it wasn't, I was almost dizzy with anticipation. I came out of the bathroom in my robe and walked across the hallway to my bedroom. I paused at the door.

Will he be in leather? Wearing a harness?

I rolled my eyes. Yeah, sure, Toby had packed his leather gear to go ride horses for two weeks. I pushed the door open, and my heart skipped a beat.

Toby stood beside the bed, his shirt off, his jeans unbuttoned and the zipper lowered, revealing the dark fuzz of his pubes. His feet were bare. He'd removed the comforter and sheet, and lying on the bed was a bottle of oil I didn't recognize.

He smiled. "I went shopping while you were out. Butch took me into Bozeman."

Then I saw the piece of rope, maybe a foot long. It wasn't like the rope I'd been used to. This was more like the stuff we used on the ranch. One end was frayed.

What does he want that for?

His gaze drifted up and down. "Nice robe. Take it off."

My heartbeat quickened as I shrugged out of the soft cotton garment. "What's with the rope?" I kept my tone casual.

Toby didn't reply, but came over to me. He stroked my chest, tugging on the hair and flicking my nipples with his thumbs, making me shiver. "How sensitive are these?"

"Not overly," I admitted. "But Kevin would clamp them occasionally, and then it was a whole different ballgame." *Then* he could've made me come just by sucking on them.

"Good to know." He slid his hand over my abs, and I kept still, waiting for his fingers to reach my dick, but at the last second he removed his hand, not that it was such a shock. Kevin had been a world-class tease.

"About that rope…"

Again, no response. And then I forgot all about it when he kissed me, a leisurely exploration that told me all things would happen according to his schedule, not mine.

"You're a good kisser," he murmured against my lips.

"Thank you," I whispered.

He took a step back. "A couple of things before we start… First up, safe word. Now, I don't know if you and Kevin used safe words, but you will with me. And I'm going to make a suggestion."

"Oh?"

He smiled. "Say your first name." When I stared at him, he shrugged. "In the heat of the moment, it's the only thing you'll likely remember."

I stilled. "I like that."

"Second… I know we didn't manage to get you tested today. That will have to wait. All you need to know is, my most recent test was a week ago, and I got the all-clear. I have more condoms—*if* we need them."

I didn't like the sound of that *if*.

"I thought long and hard about what I wanted to do with you," he went on. Then he smiled. "See what I did there?"

I couldn't resist. "And is it long and hard?"

"You bet. But I haven't decided yet if I'm going to fuck you. We'll see."

Yeah, Kevin had a rival for the teasing crown.

He gestured to the bed. "Lie down, please, on your back in the center."

I did as instructed, my pulse rapid, my stomach quivering.

He gazed at my already hard cock. "You look as if you're ready to pop right now."

"But I won't," I stressed. "Not until you give me permission." I knew the score, and I wasn't going to fall at the first hurdle.

At least, I hoped I wasn't.

"Now, I'm not going to tie you to the bed—unless I feel you need that. I *am* going to play with your cock, balls, and ass, and *your* goal is not to come."

There was only one possible response. "Yes, Sir."

He pointed to my legs. "Spread them, as wide as you can. Then grab the bed posts and hold on. You're not to let go unless I say so, understand?"

"Yes, Sir." I suppressed a shiver when he climbed onto the bed and slid his hand down my torso, skirting my crotch but tracing a fingertip through the crease where groin met thigh. His fingers danced over my quads, and I stifled a moan when he changed direction and inched closer to my balls.

His gaze met mine. "I want to hear you, all right? Don't hold back." Then I caught my breath when he picked up the piece of rope. He held it to my sac, trailing the frayed ends over my balls, keeping the touch light. I shivered as he moved it higher, the ends playing over my shaft that lay stiffly against my belly. Higher still, until the rope teased the head of my dick.

"That kinda tickles."

He chuckled. "It's supposed to." Then he cupped my balls, tugging them down as he rubbed the head with the frayed end, flicking it, tapping it, until I couldn't hold in my groan of pleasure. I gripped the bed posts, my back arched, and he laid a hand on my stomach and gave a gentle downward push.

"We're only just getting started." He dropped the rope onto the floor.

Oh Lord.

He picked up the bottle of oil, snapped the lid open, and held it over the head of my cock, allowing a glistening strand to descend, trickling over the taut skin and down the shaft. Then he put the bottle aside, and held my balls while he worked up and down my cock, alternating between stroking it firmly with his fingertips and grazing it with his nails. I wanted to *move*, damn it, to push up with my hips, but I fought the urge.

"Good."

That one word of praise sent my heart soaring.

He grasped my dick around its base with one hand while he rubbed the shaft, circling it with thumb and forefinger, tightening his grip with each upward stroke, looser on the downward one.

I had no idea how long he teased my rock-hard cock, but I got close to coming more than once, and each time he backed off, rubbing my belly and chest, flicking my nipples. When he reached for the oil, I knew there was more to come.

Talk about exquisite torture.

Toby

I dribbled oil over his balls and crack, my heartbeat racing as I contemplated sliding into his warm body. I rubbed my finger over his hole, and a jolt went through him. I leaned over to kiss him. "You want this, don't you?"

He swallowed. "Yes, Sir."

I stroked over his hole again and again, until he was shaking with need. I inserted the tip of my finger inside him, while I rubbed the head of his cock with my palm using firm strokes. His shivers intensified. I made sure his gaze was fixed on me when I pushed deep.

"Oh God." He arched his back, and I gave another gentle push.

"Easy now. We're not there yet." I slid out of him, watching his dick rise into the air when I penetrated him once more. I sought out his gland, and was rewarded when a strangled noise burst from his lips as I nudged it. I finger-fucked him, adding a second and noting how his calves and inner thighs trembled. He was getting close.

"Does it feel good?"

"Y-yes, Sir," he moaned, his legs shaking.

He groaned as I went deep, my thumb rubbing under the head of his cock. I'd brought him to the edge three or four times, and I knew he couldn't hold on much longer. I grabbed his balls and gave them a sharp tug, while I held his dick around the base, a rigid pole slick with oil and pre-cum. His gaze met mine, but he didn't ask to come, his body writhing constantly, his hands still clutching the bedposts.

Such behavior deserved a reward.

"You can come," I murmured, letting go of his balls and pushing my finger inside him. I massaged his prostate, and an arc of cum shot high into the air, landing on his chest.

"Oh, thank you, Sir." He gasped the words, shaking, the tremors constant through his thighs as his cock pulsed out every last drop. I worked his dick with his spunk, sliding it through the funnel of my hand, my finger still wedged in his ass.

His shudders ebbed, until at last he lay still, his chest heaving.

I bent over and kissed him. "You did good," I said in a low voice.

"Thank you, Sir."

I smiled. "You can let go of the bedposts now."

A moment later, his arms were around my neck, and he clung to me as we kissed, the smell of cum and Robert's own musky scent filling my nostrils. I lay beside him, stroking his chest, trailing my fingers through the stickiness coating his skin. His softened dick lay against his thigh, while mine was like a steel pipe in my jeans. I shoved them down over my hips, tugged my cock free, and worked the shaft, my orgasm within sight.

"Sir." It was a plea.

I knelt beside his head. He propped himself up on one elbow, and took me in his mouth, one hand wrapped around my shaft. I shuddered as I shot my load, and he took it all. He cleaned my cock with his tongue, and I shivered. I pulled free of him and claimed his mouth in a kiss, tasting myself on his lips.

"Next time, I'll be coming in your ass," I whispered.

Judging by the sigh that escaped him, he liked that idea a lot.

I held him close on the bed, stroking his head, his shoulders, kissing him, telling him how good it had been, and assuring him we'd only just begun. My thoughts went to my purchases of that afternoon. I'd already decided when I was going to use it.

This was going to be fun.

He felt warm in my arms, and I didn't want to move. Then I realized I didn't have to. No one would be concerned if I didn't go back to the bunkhouse. Everyone knew exactly where I was.

Robert craned his neck to look me in the eye. "Stay, please?"

I smiled. "Why not?" I could do that.

Except…since when did I ever do that?

CHAPTER TWENTY-ONE

Thursday, June 16
Robert

I opened my eyes, and for a moment I couldn't breathe. There was someone else in the bed, spooned around me, warm and smelling like heaven.

Then I remembered. *Toby stayed.* I hadn't expected that. I shivered as I recalled swallowing his load, sharing the taste of him in a kiss that… grew somehow, blossomed and grew into a sensual, intimate connection that left me shaking.

Lord, his arms felt good around me.

"Morning." His breath tickled my ear.

"Morning." I shuddered when his lips grazed my neck.

"I slept great."

I'd wanted to stay awake as long as possible, to burn the feel of him, the smell of him, into my brain. "Thanks for staying."

Toby chuckled, and it reverberated through me. "Well, let's look at the alternatives. I could have gone to the bunkhouse and listened to Butch's cute little snores, and tried *not* to think about what Zeeb was doing in the bunk above me—"

I laughed so hard I shook the bed.

"Or… I got to spend the night with a hot cowboy, with the promise of a slow morning fuck to start my day." Another teasing kiss to my neck. "Sounds like a no-brainer to me."

My morning wood jumped a notch or two, from *hard* to *a cat couldn't scratch it.*

I glanced at the nightstand and spotted the condom wrapper. "We can go into Bozeman right after breakfast."

"Mm-hm."

"What about that store you wanted to visit?"

He tugged on my earlobe with his teeth, and I shivered. "Did that yesterday when you went to Billings."

"Oh. I didn't get to choose anything." Plus, I'd never seen inside it.

Toby kissed my neck. "You forget, I've seen your trunk. We're not going to run out of toys. Besides, I wanted to surprise you."

"Oh Lord."

He laughed quietly. "You know, there's a tiny note of terror in your voice that is fucking adorable." He paused. "So... What time does Matt usually show up to make your breakfast?"

I glanced at the clock. "In about a half hour. Except I think he'll be late." I caught my breath when Toby wrapped his hand around my dick, moving up and down the shaft in a slow, measured glide.

"Then we've got enough time." He gave my cock a squeeze. "God, I bet you could do some serious damage with this."

My heart hammered. I'd never topped. Ever. Topping was for Doms—wasn't it? Then all such thoughts fled when Toby insinuated a finger between my asscheeks, seeking my hole. I pushed back, wanting more, until I remembered who was in my bed. I froze.

Toby let go of my dick and cupped my cheek, turning my face toward his. "Right now it's Toby and Robert, with half an hour or so to enjoy each other's bodies—so let's do that. Especially since we've got one condom left."

"You didn't buy more?"

"I can do that in Bozeman—if we need to. We *are* getting tested, right? Personally, I can't wait to drive my bare cock into you." Then he tapped his finger against the head of my dick. "Don't have to ask if you're excited about that, do I?"

I glanced at my slit, where a thread of pre-cum hung like a tiny glass rod with a clear drop at the end of it. I rolled onto my front, pulled my knees up under me, and tilted my ass. "Please..."

He knelt behind me, smacking his thick cock against my hole, the sound loud and hot. "Tell me. Tell me what you want."

"You inside me."

He reached for the lube, and cool fingers breached my pucker, making me groan. I arched my back and he slid deeper, adding a third.

"Oh Lord," I moaned.

He pulled free of my body and grabbed the remaining condom, tearing the wrapper. I rested my head on my arms as he gloved up, my breathing catching when he crouched over me, mounting me, gliding right in, all the way home. His arms caged me as he drove into me with slow, deep glides.

"Your ass feels so good," he whispered.

"Your dick feels amazing." I twisted to stare at him. "Please."

"Please what?" He withdrew, his gaze locked on my face.

"Fuck me."

He didn't break eye contact as he thrust into me, punching the air from my lungs, and I dropped my head to the bed, my fingers digging into the mattress, his body slapping against my ass again and again.

Sometimes a slow morning fuck just wasn't enough.

Toby

I walked into the kitchen. Robert was getting dressed. I might have slowed him down a tad. I'd come before him, so it was fair I sucked him off in the shower, right? Except by then we both knew Matt was in the house, so he'd had to be real quiet.

That only added to the fun.

Matt grinned when he saw me. He poured me a cup of coffee. "Good morning. Is this going to be a thing? 'Cause it makes no difference to me if I feed you here or down at the bunkhouse. I just need to know what you'd like for breakfast."

I smiled. "Whatever you've been feeding me down there was

perfect." I peered at the breakfast bar. "You want me in here or the dining room?"

"Boss usually eats in the dining room. Coffee pot's all ready for you. I'll bring the food in." He cocked his head. "How do you like your eggs? The boss generally goes with scrambled."

"Scrambled is good." And even if it wasn't—which it was— I'd have told him scrambled so he wasn't going out of his way to make something different for me.

I had a feeling I'd be having a few breakfasts up at Robert's place.

I went into the dining room and walked over to the window that looked out toward the rear of the house. I could see the entrance to the ranch.

"I like that view."

I turned around. "Who named the ranch?"

Robert joined me. "That would've been my great-great-grandfather, back in the eighteen-seventies."

I blinked. "Wow."

He nodded. "Salvation was bigger then, too."

"Do you know why he chose the name?"

"Nope. At least, I was never told the reason. I guess he must've had one."

Matt appeared in the doorway. "Morning, boss. If you two will take a seat... Breakfast is ready."

We sat, and pretty soon the center of the table was full. I grinned at Matt. "I can't wait to try your meatloaf on Saturday."

He chuckled. "If you like it, you'll need to fight Butch for a second helping. And Zeeb usually hogs all the mac and cheese." He gave Robert a nod before withdrawing.

We dug into the food, and I suppressed a moan of delight. "There's a diner near my apartment in San Francisco. I go there sometimes for biscuits and gravy. They're awesome, but *damn*, Matt's are better."

Robert didn't respond, but occupied himself with the sausage and bacon.

I laughed. "Someone's hungry this morning."

He rolled his eyes. "And you're not?" He lowered his voice. "My mornings are usually less… energetic. Not that I'm complaining, you understand."

"You think you could handle a few more energetic mornings?"

His eyes gleamed. "Oh, I could do that." Then he laughed.

I stared at him. "You have a great laugh." Not to mention an amazing smile.

He sighed. "I guess it's been MIA for a while."

That did it. I had a goal.

I was going to make sure my remaining days on the ranch were spent making Robert smile.

Zeeb's words rang in my head.

We want him to be happy again.

I wanted that too.

When we'd finished, I drank the last of the coffee, then wiped my lips with a napkin. "I need to go get a change of clothes before we head into Bozeman."

Robert let out a wry chuckle. "Ready to run the gauntlet?"

I didn't have to ask what he meant by that.

I got up from the table. "You gonna meet me down at the bunkhouse, or do I come up here?"

"We'll go in my car. Better come up here."

I walked behind him, leaned in, and whispered, "One more thing." I kissed his neck. "You make the most amazing noises when you're being fucked."

A flush rose from his chest, up his neck, and reached his cheeks. "Thank you… Sir."

That one word on his lips was enough to weaken my resolve. I wanted to drag him upstairs, strip him naked, and—

It would have to wait. Besides, the next time we fucked?

There'd be nothing between us.

The thought of shooting my load inside him was a serious

turn-on.

I kissed his warm cheek. "Later." Then I straightened and walked out of the dining room. I called out to Matt as I passed the kitchen. "Thank you."

"You're welcome."

I opened the front door and headed down the path. There was no sign of life below, so I assumed everyone was still in the bunkhouse. When I entered, Butch let out a raucous laugh.

"Look what the coyote dragged in." His eyes glittered. "You missed breakfast."

"Or did you already get your protein this morning?" Walt said with a grin.

"I'm confused." Garrett's brow furrowed. "If he missed breakfast, then how could he have had protein?"

Zeeb bit back a smile.

Teague walked in. "You're going into Bozeman this morning, right?"

I laughed. "Word sure gets around fast on this ranch."

"I've been told to have Lightning and Rusty saddled and ready for when you get back."

I arched my eyebrows. "Am I going for a ride?"

Butch snorted. "Sure, but what *we* all want to know is, who's riding who?"

Teague's eyes flashed. "Why don't you go ask the boss, seeing as you're so curious?" He pulled his phone from his pocket. "I'll call him, shall I? Tell him you're on your way up to the house?"

Butch reddened. "I guess I don't need to know after all."

Teague stared at him. "No, you don't. No one does. And do you know why? Because it's none of our fucking business. But I *will* tell you one thing for free—I've seen the boss smile more and laugh more in the last few days than in the previous five years." Another flash of those dark eyes. "So we're not gonna begrudge him a little happiness, now are we?"

Butch squared his shoulders. "No sir, we surely aren't."

"Amen to that," Zeeb echoed.

Teague addressed me. "You've paid to be here, to go on the cattle drive next week. What you do with the rest of your time is of no concern to anyone here." He glared at the hands. "Am I making myself clear?"

Murmurs rippled through the others, while Garrett looked on, clearly perplexed.

"I think I'll go get changed." I headed for my bunk.

"Good idea."

More murmurs filled the air as I grabbed a clean shirt and a pair of briefs from the drawers where I'd stored them. Suddenly, Garrett's voice rose above the others.

"He's fucking the boss?"

I burst out laughing. That was everyone on the same page, and it had only taken Garrett five days to cotton on.

Teague came over as I was buttoning my shirt. "Keep an eye on the weather while you're riding out with the boss. It's not raining here, but there *have* been rumbles of thunder."

"So that means there's rain coming?"

"Not necessarily. That's the funny thing about thunderstorms around here. They're usually dry. At this time of year, the rainfall isn't heavy." He smiled. "Now you'd better get up to the house. The boss is waiting." He stilled. "I meant what I said, by the way. You've made him smile. So whatever you're doing—keep doing it."

I grinned. "I intend to, but thanks for the permission."

He laughed. "You're okay, Toby." He strolled out of the bunkhouse.

I thought Teague was okay too, especially the way he looked out for Robert, and supported him.

Robert has a great bunch of guys here.

My phone vibrated, and I removed it from my pocket, peering at the screen. It was a text from Sean. My initial thought was that something was wrong, but the first line reassured me. Then as I read more, I smiled.

Damn it, I love being right. I re-read the text.

Hey, all is well here. Hope you're doing better.

I have news—Tyler has a new Dom, Will. Shocker, right? But you should've seen them last night after they talked. It was like something out of a Hallmark movie. I swear, Tyler didn't stop smiling all night long. Turns out Will's wanted to approach him for a while, but wasn't gonna tread on your toes. It took him until last night to get up enough nerve,

Talk about smitten—and I mean both of them. It's fucking adorable.

Watch out for grizzlies. Come back in one piece.

Warmth flooded me. *Tyler's in love—and with someone who loves him back.*

That went a long way to easing the ache that still lingered. Going back to the club wouldn't mean walking into the awkward atmosphere I'd anticipated.

Except I didn't want to think about going back, not when I had so much to look forward to right where I was.

Robert

I stared at the slip of paper they'd handed me at the clinic. It was official—I had the all-clear. The implications sent a trickle of anticipation down my spine.

Later, Toby had said. As if I'd expected anything different. He'd called it delayed gratification.

I called it torture.

I changed into my boots, ready for the afternoon's ride. Toby was waiting for me at the stables, and Paul was getting the trailer ready to hitch it up to a truck. I was going to take Lightning and Rusty out to the Spanish Creek trailhead. I hadn't done that trail in a few years, and I wanted to show Toby Mirror Lake. It was beautiful up there this time of year. There was still the odd rumble of thunder but the skies were clear, so I knew whatever was going on was far off in the distance.

My phone rang. It was Teague. "Boss... Have you got a minute?"

"I'm about to go out for a ride. What's up?"

"You've got a visitor."

It obviously wasn't Diana, or anyone else I knew, because he'd have said. "On my way."

I went downstairs, grabbed my hat, and messaged Toby as I walked down the path.

Be right with you.

As I neared the barn, I spotted Teague standing with a young woman who I didn't recognize. She had long blonde hair, and she wore jeans and a cotton shirt, sunglasses perched on top of her head. She was maybe in her mid-twenties.

I approached her with a smile. "Hi. What can I do for you?"

Teague cleared his throat. "I'll leave you to it." He gave her a polite nod before walking toward the barn.

She looked me in the eye. "Are you Robert Thorston?"

"Yes. And you are?"

"My name is Ella... Ella Kirkham."

I blinked. "Oh." I couldn't move. I wasn't sure I was even breathing.

"I think you knew my father, Clay Kirkham."

I fought to inhale. "Yes, I did. He used to work on this ranch. I haven't heard from him in a long time." *Like about thirty years.*

She swallowed. "He died last month."

Jesus. He'd have been about sixty-five. My chest tightened, but I struggled to maintain a calm facade. "I'm so sorry to hear that. But I'm not sure why you're here. Like I said, I haven't seen your dad since he left the ranch many years ago."

"My brother and I were going through his things, and I found this." She held up an envelope, and I could see my name was written on it, along with the address for Salvation. "I don't know what's in it, because I haven't opened it—it wasn't addressed to me. But you were obviously important to him." She tilted her head. "Did you know my dad well?"

"Yes ma'am, I did. I was a lot younger when he worked here, probably about your age." I held out my hand, and she took it. "I'm sorry for your loss."

"Thank you." She glanced at the envelope. "I could've mailed this, but I'll admit, I was curious to know what he wanted to say to you after all this time."

"Where have you traveled from to deliver this?"

"Elk River, Wyoming."

I stared at her. "You came all this way—to deliver a letter?"

"When did you last see my father?"

I could have told her the exact date. "I was twenty-two years old. So that would make it thirty years ago."

Her eyes widened. "And you haven't seen him in all that time? You hadn't heard from him?"

"No ma'am." I gazed at the envelope clutched in her hand, and she held it out to me with a show of reluctance.

There was no way I was about to open it and read it in front of her.

"Thank you for bringing this to me."

She glanced at her surroundings. "So my father was a ranch hand here?"

I nodded. Then I had an idea. I glanced to where Teague stood by the barn door. "Teague, can you come over here a second?"

He walked toward us at a brisk pace.

"This is Ella Kirkham. Her dad used to work here, a long time ago. Would you take her to meet Butch? He and Clay worked together for a while." I glanced at her. "Would you like that? I don't mean to be rude, but you'll have to excuse me. I have a lot of work to do today, and I thought you might like to talk to someone who knew your dad."

Her cheeks pinked. "I'd like that a lot."

I extended my hand once more. "Again, my condolences."

She thanked me, and Teague led her toward the bunkhouse.

I sagged against the wall of the bunkhouse, clutching the envelope.

What on earth did you want to say to me, after all this time? And why couldn't you say it in person? I had so many questions.

Why did he leave?

How did he end up in another state?

Why didn't he contact me?

Why did he leave without a goddamn word?

I hoped the answers lay in his letter.

Teague walked over to me, his gaze alighting on the envelope. "Who was he?"

"He was a ranch hand here. When Butch came to work at Salvation, Clay had been working here for about a year."

"What happened?"

I managed a nonchalant shrug. "He moved on. Not *everyone* stays at Salvation." I pocketed the letter and walked toward the stable. It would be quiet in there.

I wanted to read it undisturbed.

CHAPTER TWENTY-TWO

Toby

Robert's text had arrived an hour ago, and since then I'd heard nothing.

Has he canceled the ride? If that were the case, surely he'd have messaged. Zeeb said he'd spotted Robert near the stables, but that had been a while back. And something was going on. Butch was in deep conversation with a young woman, and when she left, he seemed sad. I wasn't about to ask why—sharing Robert's bed didn't afford me any privileges.

When it got to two-thirty, I figured that was it, plan canceled. Then my phone pinged.

Be ready in ten minutes.

I'd been ready since lunch.

I walked over to the stables. At least we'd gotten the visit to the clinic done. Robert's results were no surprise, given his lack of activity, but having his status confirmed had clearly been important to him. I'd felt the same way. It had only been a month since my latest test, but that didn't matter—it was a question of trust.

If things worked out and I did make my suggestion, I wanted him to trust me.

Paul led Lightning and Rusty out of the stable, all saddled up. Across their backs lay a cotton-covered roll, attached to the saddle. I was no expert, but they looked like bedrolls to me. The thought made me smile.

Just exactly what is Robert planning?

I had no idea, but I liked it.

Paul led the horses toward a trailer, its ramp lowered. I went over to him and took Lightning's reins. "I take it wherever we're going isn't close." We walked the horses up the ramp, slipped halters over the bridles, and tethered them to the bars that ran along the inside of the trailer. It was plenty big enough for the two of them. The floor of the trailer was covered with rubber matting.

Paul smiled. "The boss is taking you to Mirror Lake. That means a drive to the Spanish Creek Trailhead. The trail isn't that long, but it climbs a lot, especially in the last few miles. Make sure your phone is fully charged. You'll want to take photos." Then he stilled. "Damn it. I wasn't supposed to tell you where you were going."

I bit my lip. "Don't you worry. I'll act all surprised when I get there."

He laughed. "Thanks, Toby." We got out of the trailer and he closed it up. Paul glanced toward the house. "See if you can get him to unwind a little. Earlier, he seemed... I don't know... stressed about something."

I wondered if it had anything to do with the visitor I'd seen with Butch. "I'll do my best."

Paul's eyes gleamed. "Yeah. I'm sure you'll think of some way to relieve his... tension."

I could think of a lot of ways—and most of them required Robert being naked.

Hey, he asked for the bedrolls to go with us, right?

Paul straightened, and I knew Robert was walking toward us. "All ready, boss."

Just then, I caught the rumble of thunder in the distance. I glanced at Robert, who shrugged. "It's nothing. There are no forecasts for rain where we're headed."

"One of those dry thunderstorms, huh?"

He smiled. "Yeah, we get those. True, storms *can* come up out of nowhere, and you can't always trust the forecasts, so we'll keep an eye out for the weather." He inclined his head toward the truck to which Butch was attaching the trailer. "Let's go.

Otherwise, we won't be back in time for supper."

"Enjoy yourselves," Paul called out.

I waited for Butch to add one of his usual snarky comments, but he didn't utter a word.

Maybe Teague had really gotten to him.

I climbed into the passenger seat, relaxed and content. A sunny afternoon, a beautiful lake, and the company of a sexy man.

Things didn't get any better than this.

Robert pulled into the parking lot at the trailhead and switched off the engine. "This is as far as we go in the truck." The lot was full of cars, and everywhere I looked there were hikers in stout walking boots, armed with sticks, backpacks, and hats.

"Obviously a popular destination," I commented.

"For walkers *and* riders, yes." We got out, and went around the trailer to let the horses out. Robert pointed to the horizon. "That's where we're going. Up there are the Spanish Lakes, and we're following the trail to one of them, Mirror Lake. It's not a long trail, but the view when we get to the top is amazing."

"How long is it since you were last there?"

He gave a wistful smile. "Too long."

We walked the horses over to the mounting blocks thoughtfully provided, and saddled up. It wasn't long before we were in open country, vast stretches of meadow with much more space than the first trail we'd done. Now and then we spotted a couple of hikers, but apart from them, there wasn't a soul in sight.

Tall pine trees reached into the sky on either side of the meadow. We didn't speak, and that was just fine. I wanted to enjoy the peace of the place, the gentle movement of the horse, the smell in the air, and the breeze that teased my hat and cooled my face.

We drew closer to the trees, and the trail crossed a creek into woodland. The ground was rocky, with roots snaking across it, and the horses had to step carefully. I lost count of how many creeks we crossed, each one wider than the previous one. At one point we reached a fork in the path, and Robert pointed left to where water cascaded down over rocks, a kind of mini waterfall.

"We go that way."

We trotted across the top of it, the water louder than before. And then we were back in the trees, riding in shadows, the trail narrowing as it climbed, the wind whistling through the forest.

"No bears in here, right?" I quipped.

He laughed. "There's always the possibility of running into a grizzly. That's why I came prepared."

I gave a mental eye roll. *Sure, Toby—notice the bedrolls and completely miss the rifle.* I knew where *my* head was at.

The hills climbed steeply to the left of us, and the terrain grew rockier. There was yet another creek to cross, and another. In the distance I heard the rumble of thunder again.

"You sure that weather report is reliable?" I had visions of lightning striking the trees around us.

"Yeah. Don't worry."

The trail continued to climb. "Just how high are we?"

"This trail climbs two thousand feet in about three miles." He pointed ahead of us. "We're almost there."

When we reached Mirror Lake, I was blown away by the view. "This is beautiful." I could see why it got its name. The lake nestled in a valley. The mountains in the distance, the line of trees surrounding it... all were reflected perfectly in its calm waters.

"This is the Lee Metcalfe wilderness area," Robert told me.

"Who was he?"

"A Montana congressman. He's dead now." He came to a halt. "We'll stop here." He dismounted, using a tree stump, and once he'd led Rusty to the water's edge for a drink, I dismounted too and followed suit. Lightning bowed his head and drank, and I stroked his neck.

I gazed at the lake, soaking in the tranquility. The sun was warm on my shoulders, and suddenly I wanted to feel it on my bare skin. I smiled. "What is it about nature that makes me horny?"

Robert laughed. "I get the feeling you're always horny."

I raised my eyebrows. "Something wrong with that?"

"Nope, I feel the same way."

I grinned. "Then let's go for a swim."

He gaped. "It'll be freezing in there."

"So? It'll get your blood flowing. Come on… You *can* swim, right?"

Robert rolled his eyes.

I decided actions spoke louder than words.

I tethered Lightning to the nearest tree, and began to strip, pausing when I noticed Robert hadn't moved. "You know you want to," I teased. "And I'll give you an incentive. Swim with me, and after, I'll let you come."

His eyes widened. "You fight dirty."

I laughed. "And you're only learning this now?" I finished my strip tease, leaving my boots and clothing in a pile under a tree, and then launched myself into the water before I could change my mind. "Holy fuck, it's cold." I dipped my head below the surface, then stood, shaking the water from it. Robert was undressing—slowly— and I crooked my finger. "Come here. It's not so bad once you get over that first shock."

He edged into the water, and I took advantage of the moment to study him. He wasn't lean—not that I minded the gentle swell of his belly—but it was obvious he worked out. His upper arms and thighs were muscular, his dick long and thick even when half-soft, pointing downward from its nest of unruly dark curls.

"You are one sexy man," I murmured as he drew nearer. I looped my arms around his neck and we kissed, water up to our waists, the sun warm on my back and head. Then I released him and swam away toward the center of the lake, the temperature dropping. He followed, and I came to a stop, treading water. We kissed again.

"Christ, my nipples are like bullets," he muttered, his teeth chattering.

Yeah, maybe it was a little too cold.

"Then let's get out. We'll be dry in no time." Besides, I had plans for those bed rolls.

We swam to the shore, and as we approached it, I grabbed him. "Wait a second." I reached around him, brushing my fingers through his crack.

His breathing hitched, and his gaze locked onto mine, but he didn't say a word.

I leaned in and kissed him on the mouth. "Gotta make sure you're nice and clean back there," I murmured. A violent shiver coursed through him, and I had the impression it was nothing to do with the cold.

Then we clambered out, water beading on our bodies. I dripped my way to the horses, the ground firm beneath my feet, littered with pine needles that had long since faded to a warm brown. When I reached Lightning, I pointed to the cotton-covered rolls.

"So… wanna tell me why you brought these?"

Robert flushed. "I thought we might need them."

I grinned. "Then you'd better take one off the horse, unroll it, and get on all fours." Robert's pupils enlarged, and I nodded. His fingers trembled as he loosened the loops that fed through the D-rings on the saddle, removing the roll. He handed it to me, and I slid the roll from its covering, unfurled it, and laid it on the ground under the tree.

I didn't need to give further instructions.

Robert knelt on the roll, then leaned forward, his weight on his hands, his back arched, the hair on his ass flattened by the water. I got on my knees behind him, pulled his asscheeks apart, and dove in, my tongue seeking that hot little pucker.

"Oh Lord," he groaned, his head dropping to the roll.

I paused. "Just so we're clear? You have permission to touch your cock, and you can come whenever you're ready."

Judging by the way his dick lengthened and stiffened, that wouldn't be long.

I played with his hole, applying lips, tongue, and fingers, until he was in constant motion, rocking back and forth, and reaching behind him to press my face deeper into his crease. Now and then I straightened to scan the lake's perimeter, but there was no one in sight, so I went right back to sending Robert over the edge.

I tugged on his sac while I pushed my tongue into that loosening entrance again and again, his moans increasing until I knew he was about to pop. I spread his cheeks, stretching his glistening hole, relishing the sight of him wide open, the muscle contracting, ready for me.

I wanted so badly to be inside him, but I wasn't about to penetrate him without lube. Instead, I sucked on a couple of fingers, slid them into his warmth, and fucked him with them until he came with a cry, shaking, pulsing onto the roll, spatters of cream against dark blue. I covered him with my body, kissing his shoulders, his back, his neck, and he turned his face toward mine, our lips meeting in a fervent kiss.

We lay on the bed roll, my arms around him, the sunlight falling onto our bodies, its warmth battling the breeze off the lake, coaxing my skin into a carpet of goosebumps.

"I don't want to move," he said in a low voice, his head resting on my chest.

"We don't have to go just yet, do we?"

He craned his neck and smiled. "No, we don't."

"Then let's lie here and enjoy it." I loved that sated feeling, as if warm cream flowed through my veins, my mind at peace.

It took me a moment to notice the change in Robert's breathing.

Let him sleep. If Paul was right, he needed it.

Robert

As we descended the trail, an uneasy feeling settled over me. "Something is wrong."

Toby frowned. "What do you mean?"

"Listen."

He tilted his head. "All I hear is the sound of running water. There's a creek coming up, isn't there? Just around this bend?"

I frowned. "That sounds way louder than it should." We rounded the slope, and I froze. "Oh good Lord."

The creek was fuller than it had been a few hours before, but its color had changed too, from clear to a light brown, due to all the dirt, sediment, debris, and mud it carried along with it. What had been a narrow stream had swollen into a fast-moving torrent.

Toby's eyes widened. "What's happened?"

"It's a flash flood."

He peered at the sky. "There isn't a cloud to be seen."

"All that thunder we heard in the distance this morning? Maybe there *was* rain after all, just nowhere near us. And somewhere upstream from this, there's a whole lot more water than there should be."

Toby stared at the creek. "It's gotten so much wider than before. We can't cross that."

"No, we can't."

"Well, is there a way around it? Another route?"

"Remember how many creeks we crossed to get here? Most of them are probably like this." I reached into my saddlebag, and pulled out my satellite phone. I fired it up, then punched in the numbers.

Teague answered instantly. "I was about to call you. There are reports of flash floods near Billings, but some are closer to home."

"I know, we're looking at one."

"Already? How's the weather?"

"Not a goddamn cloud in the sky."

"But there was heavy rainfall in the east, about six hours ago.

I think you should come on home."

I sighed. "That might prove a little difficult," I said dryly. "We're on the wrong side of the creek."

"Aw fuck."

This wasn't my first experience of flash floods, but I didn't remember one this severe. "It can't last that long. A few hours maybe."

"So what are you gonna do?"

"We'll wait it out. We've got water, and I think there are a couple of protein bars in my saddlebag. Plus, we have…bed rolls, in case we can't get back tonight."

Yeah, that sounded totally plausible.

Teague chuckled. "Oh my, that was forward-thinking of you." He paused. "It *was* forward-thinking, right?"

"You hush. If the floods haven't receded by nightfall, we'll have to stay here. I'm not gonna risk riding back in the dark."

"No, you're not. You'll break your damn neck. Stay safe. Remember your Boy Scout days."

Before I finished the call, I chuckled. "I was never a Boy Scout." I twisted to look at Toby. "We're gonna wait it out. Nothing else we can do."

"In that case, can we wait it out by the lake? At least there are trees there for shelter if we need them."

It was a good idea. We headed back up the trail toward the lake, and skirted around it until we found a spot where we had shelter beneath trees. I got off Rusty and tied him to a tree, and Toby did the same with Lightning. I stood at the lakeside once more, gazing out at its calm waters.

"I didn't expect to see it again *this* soon," I joked. "And before you ask, no, we are *not* going swimming again." I was trying to make light of the situation. We weren't in any real danger. The waters would recede, but it might take a while, and in the meantime we'd be okay under the trees. If we were still there by nightfall, I'd make a fire.

Toby hunkered down at the water's edge. "I thought you'd changed your mind about this afternoon."

"Why would you think that?"

"One minute you're telling me to be ready, the next... You kinda disappeared on me."

"Ah." And just like that, my chest tightened a notch or two.

"Paul was worried about you," he added.

"There was nothing to worry about. I... I just had stuff on my mind, that's all. Something I had to work through first."

He stood and walked toward me. "Did it have anything to do with that girl? The one Butch was talking to?"

I stared at him. "You don't miss much, do you?"

He smiled. "No. It comes with the job description. *Doms see stuff.* It says so in the rule book. Didn't Kevin ever tell you that?"

I chuckled. "Once or twice. He didn't miss much either." But that had been a comfort.

It seemed Toby was looking out for me too.

Then I realized it went both ways—I'd looked out for Kevin.

Lord, when it came to a Dom/sub relationship away from the bedroom? I was rusty as fuck. Not that I was surprised by that. The ranch took priority, and that meant everything else had to take a back seat. Kevin had gotten that.

But will Toby?

What if this pushes him away?

I struggled to breathe. I was looking at this all wrong. Toby was a professional Dom, right? He was used to working around subs' needs.

And what does that make me? Just another sub?

Christ, that stung.

And just like that, I knew I wanted to be more than the next-in-line. Except wanting it didn't mean I'd get it.

"Wanna talk about it?"

For a moment, I felt certain he'd seen the turmoil inside my head, until it hit me.

He's asking about what happened this morning.
I could talk about that.

CHAPTER TWENTY-THREE

Robert

"Remember I told you about Clay?"

"The guy who worked here… the one who up and left?"

"Yeah, that was him." I reached into my jacket pocket for the folded paper I'd placed there. "That girl was Clay's daughter. He died last month."

"I'm sorry." Toby's voice was soft. "I know it was a long time ago, but…"

"I guess you never forget your first, right?" Clay had been gentle, until he realized that was *not* what I'd wanted—or needed—and the heat level had risen exponentially.

"So why did she visit you?"

I held up the sheet. "She came all the way from southern Wyoming to deliver this letter he wrote to me."

Toby blinked. "They don't have a postal service in Wyoming?"

"That was my first reaction. I guess she thought I might tell her what was in it." I shook my head. "I wasn't about to do that. I didn't want her to think differently about her dad."

"Then you *have* read it?"

I nodded. "Yeah. It answers a lot of questions." I unfolded it.

"Robert… you don't have to tell me, you know."

Of course he'd say that. He didn't want to go beyond professional, right? He wanted to keep his emotional distance.

Then Toby's eyes softened, and my heartbeat quickened.

Maybe he does want to know, to go that little bit deeper.

Lord, I was *so* in the dark here.

My gaze met his, and the warmth in those brown eyes settled my mind. "But I want to." I cleared my voice, and began to read aloud.

> *Robert,*
>
> *If you're reading this, then I'm gone. The first thing I have to tell you is, I've always felt guilty about leaving the ranch without saying a word to you— without saying goodbye. I'm so sorry, but not contacting you was part of the deal, and I had to abide by that. I guess now it's safe to tell you.*
>
> *The night I left, your daddy came to see me. He asked me to go into the stable with him, and there was no one else around. He told me he knew about us, that we were fucking. Then he handed me a wad of cash, and told me I was to leave, to stay away, and never to contact you again. And if I did, he'd hear about it, and he'd come looking for me. Then he told me to pack my stuff, and he drove me to West Yellowstone, all the way to the border. He told me to get out, pointed to Wyoming, thanked me for all I'd done on the ranch, and said, Have a good life. Then he got back in the truck, turned around, and headed home.*
>
> *What was I supposed to do? He was your daddy, doing what he thought was right. Okay so he was firing me, but he was also giving me the means to move away and start a new life. And that's exactly what I did.*
>
> *I got a new job, a wife, and eventually kids. I have a son and a daughter. Next to my wife Louisa, they're the most precious thing in my life. None of them ever knew I'd fooled around with guys, and I wanted it to stay that way.*
>
> *But…*
>
> *When I found out I was dying, I knew I had to set the record straight. I know it was a long, long time ago, but I've never forgotten you, and I hope I didn't hurt you too badly when you discovered I'd gone. I know your daddy probably did it out of love, but that wasn't how it felt at the time.*
>
> *I hope you've been happy. I hope you found someone who was a better fit than me. I tried, but I think you needed more than I could give.*
>
> *You were one special man, and I was proud to know you.*
>
> *Be happy.*
>
> *Clay*

My voice cracked on his name.

"Oh my God." Toby's arms were around me in a heartbeat, and I was grateful for them. "You okay?"

I leaned on him, breathing in the smell of clean hair, sun-warmed skin, and cotton. "When Clay left, I was lost for a while. Dad involved me more and more with the ranch. Only now, I realize it was his way of keeping me on the straight and narrow. I guess when Kevin came along, he decided he couldn't keep paying off the hands and decided to let me be."

Fuck, it *hurt*.

"What do you need?" Toby's hand was on my cheek.

"For you to take away the ache, the pain." I swallowed. "I know you can't take it all, but—"

"But I can make it hurt a little less." He released me, went over to Lightning, undid the knots securing the bed roll, and stretched it out under the tree. He sat on it, his arms wide. "Come here."

I went to him, sank to my knees on the roll, and he held me to him, warm and solid.

He kissed my neck, then murmured, "If I'd known we'd be out all night, I'd have packed lube."

I stilled. "There's some in my saddlebag."

A moment later, his body shook with laughter. "You really did think of everything." Then he got busy with his hands, taking my clothes off, touching me—making me hard.

"You want to know what I *didn't* bring?" Toby whispered.

And just like that, I remembered. *We got tested this morning.* "Condoms."

His lips were on my neck, making me shiver. "You know it. So right now, all I can think about is coming in your tight ass. Filling you up with my cum. Feeling your body grip my cock."

And once he'd said it, that was all I could think about too.

It was as if someone flicked a switch, and we went from *lukewarm* to *inferno.* That first slow penetration, the heat of him, the way he filled me, stretched me… I couldn't get enough. I rode him, my hips bucking, rocking back and forth, impaling myself over and over on his rock-hard dick, loving the way he pistoned into me, his cries mingling with mine, no one to hear us, see us, nothing but the lake, the trees, and the sky above us…

As we lay beside the water, naked and covered with sweat, the sun setting as Toby came inside me for the first time, I realized two truths.

Kevin was right—there was no such thing as a magic dick— but Zeeb had been right too. *"A little fuckin' is good for a lot of what ails ya."*

But it was more than that.

I'd gone into this determined to guard my heart, to build a wall around it, one that was impervious to emotions, but there were already cracks forming.

Toby was slowly but surely working his way through, and the shocker was, part of me wanted that connection.

When the sun went down and the air grew too cool to stay like that, we got dressed and I lit a fire. We put the bed rolls together and lay in each other's arms, watching the flames, and listening to the water lapping at the shore.

"Can I ask you something?"

I chuckled. "Just ask. I have no secrets from you." Glib words, but they were the truth.

"Have you ever topped?"

I stiffened. "No."

Toby pushed me gently onto my back, and leaned over me, the firelight dancing over his face. "Why does that question make you uncomfortable? And don't say it doesn't, because I can feel it. Your belly is quivering right under my hand. You're swallowing."

I coughed. "Topping is… it's something a Dom does."

Toby blinked. "You believe that, don't you? Kevin never let you top? Clay neither?"

I shook my head. "I don't think either of them had ever bottomed. But to be honest? I'm not sure I could. It… it wouldn't feel right, taking control like that." Not that I hadn't thought about it. I held my breath, uncertain if I'd angered him.

To my surprise, he smiled. "First of all, you're not alone, okay? I've met other submissives who felt the same way. And secondly, I think it's something you should experience, if only once. But we'd have to agree on the circumstances."

I stared. "You... you'd let me fuck you?"

The light from the fire glinted in his eyes. "I love being fucked. But only if *I'm* the one calling the shots."

I struggled to get my head around the concept. "I'd top—but you'd be telling me what to do?"

"Exactly. Think you could do that?"

I smiled, relief flooding through me. "Yes, Sir."

Toby leaned over and kissed my forehead. "Then that's what we'll do, Only, not tonight. We'll reserve that scene for when we have a bed." He curled around me once more, his arm across my chest. "Now get some sleep. When it's light, we'll head back down to the trailhead." His stomach grumbled. "And when we reach Salvation, we'll both need feeding."

I knew Matt would take care of that, just like I knew Toby would take care of me. I closed my eyes, aware of his warmth surrounding me, his breath stirring the hairs on the back of my neck, his hand pressed over my heart.

I'm safe.

The realization warmed me. Then I stilled.

"What is it? What's wrong?" Toby stroked my arm.

I rolled to face him. "You know what I didn't do this morning?"

"What?"

I smiled. "I didn't go to the cabin. The first time in five years, and I didn't feel the urge to ride over there."

Toby pulled me to him, pressing his lips to my head. "And how does that make you feel?"

"As though I've finally got something within my grasp, something that's eluded me for so long." I tilted my head to gaze at him. "Closure."

He smiled too. "I know how that feels. I got to experience a little of that myself earlier today. Feels good, doesn't it?"

I sighed. "So damn good." I lowered my head to his chest, listening to the beat of his heart.

I was asleep within minutes.

Friday, June 17

Toby smiled when the ranch came into view. "Well, that was an unexpected adventure."

"I think we got off lightly." From my phone call with Teague that morning, I'd learned the extent of the damage caused by the flash flooding. Eastern Montana had been worst hit, the first of the floods occurring six hours after the heavy rainfall. The ranch had been unaffected, thank God.

Toby had provided the alarm call—I'd awoken to his mouth on my cock.

My stomach let out a loud growl, and we both laughed. Matt was already at the house, Teague had told me, cooking up a storm.

I drove the truck to the stables, and Paul was there, waiting for us. "Thank God you're safe," he said as we got out and walked to the back of the trailer. "Are the horses okay?"

"They're fine," I told him. "But in need of a good feed."

"So are we," Toby added with a grin. "Not to mention a hot shower and clean clothes."

"Go get a change of clothing," I told him. "I'll wait for you. Then we'll go up to the house. Food first, then shower."

"Don't suppose I could use your tub again?"

I smiled, and waited until Paul had led the horses into the stable. "Only if I get to share it."

Toby's eyes lit up. "I think it's big enough, don't you?"

Then all talk ceased when the bunkhouse door opened, and

Butch, Zeeb, Walt, Declan, and Garrett came hurrying out.

"Hey, boss."

"You made it back, then."

"You look tired."

Butch snickered, and I arched my eyebrows. "Nothing, boss."

I grinned. "Glad to hear it. And now that you've seen we're both in one piece, we're going to go eat." My phone vibrated in my pocket, and I took it out. When I saw Errol's text, I scowled.

"Something wrong?" Toby asked in a low voice.

"Just something I'll need to take care of once we've eaten."

"Is it anything that can wait? At least until you've had a bath."

Fuck it. "Yeah, it can."

I paid the accountant well—he could dance to *my* tune for once.

I shook Errol's hand, and he walked down the path. He passed Teague on the way up, and dipped his hat toward him.

Teague strolled toward me. "I didn't know Errol was due here today."

Neither had I. "Just a few things to sort out."

He peered at me. "Everything okay?"

The thought crossed my mind to lie, but I was way past that, after the night I'd had. It had been many years since I'd slept on the ground, but my bones had known about it when I woke up. "No, it is not. I'm sick and tired of dealing with shit I can't control."

Teague's eyebrows shot up. "We gonna talk on your doorstep, or am I invited to sit?"

"We can sit out here. Go grab yourself a beer from the fridge. You know where they are. It's almost the end of the day anyway. You can bring me an iced tea while you're at it."

Teague headed toward the front door, pausing at the threshold. "Toby in there?"

I chuckled. "He went into Bozeman with Matt. He offered to help with the grocery shopping for tomorrow's supper."

Teague's eyes twinkled. "Helpful soul, isn't he?" Then he disappeared indoors.

I sat in one of the rockers, staring at the ranch below.

I love you, I've spent my life building you up, but you're driving me crazy.

"Here." Teague handed me a glass of iced tea, then sat beside me. He pulled the can open. "Okay, what's all the shit you can't control?"

Fuck, where do I start?

"For one thing, I can't control the price of beef or hay. Then there's the price of diesel. Without that, cattle don't go to auction, and hay doesn't come to the cattle. Then we have all the fucking regulations—federal, state, county… Seems like every day, a new regulation pops up to make our lives more interesting. Next, we have the protesters, complaining about the way we raise our cattle, you know, the stuff they eat. Then we've got blizzards and droughts. And let's not forget the herd. If they're not looking for a hole in the fence, they're finding one and getting out onto the highway and getting hit by a car. Or they're wandering into the forest where they meet a wolf or a grizzly." I took a long drink.

Teague stared at me. "Is that it?"

"What?"

"I was sure the next thing out of your mouth was gonna be you announcing the Apocalypse was any day now." He frowned. "The dude ranch is doing well, isn't it?"

"The dude ranch? Sure, *that* part's okay. But everything *else* revolves around the herd, our main source of income—and the main source of uncertainty."

Teague huffed. "None of this is news, so what's *really* bothering you? You've been happy these last few days."

I took a moment to reflect on his words. "You're right. I *am* goddamn happy. So why do I have a problem with that? Why can't I just *enjoy* being happy?"

Teague said nothing for a moment. He took a few gulps of his beer, then leaned forward, his elbows resting on his knees, his gaze fixed on the ranch.

"Robert... I get it."

I gaped at him. "You do? Then for fuck's sake, explain it to me, because *I* sure don't."

"You know I don't talk about my childhood—for obvious reasons—but it wasn't always the way it ended up. When I was twelve, I went to summer camp for the first time. Eagle View Ranch, Wyoming."

I bit back a smile. "I'm having a hard time picturing you at a summer camp, doing archery, canoeing, shit like that."

"It was okay," he retorted defensively. "Dad didn't want me to go, but Mom insisted. That was before, when she wouldn't back down—when she still had some fight left in her."

I had to steer the conversation in a safer direction, one that didn't torment him. "Okay... camp... Where are you going with this?"

"Just hear me out, all right? I got a whole month at camp. I went back there three times. And okay, I'm not ashamed to say, I loved it. I was away from home—from him—I could be myself... But that final year? The time arrived to go off to camp—and I didn't want to go."

"Why not?"

"Because I was already dreading the end of the summer, when I'd have to go back home. I was already anticipating camp coming to an end. Mentally preparing myself to return to the shit show that was my regular life. It was as if I was denying myself permission to be happy. Why be happy? It was all going to end, right?"

All of a sudden, I saw where he was going, and he was skirting way too close.

Teague fixed me with a stare. "You know I'm right, don't you? You're anticipating Toby leaving. You didn't grieve for Kevin—not properly anyway—for five years, but you're *already* grieving for the loss of Toby. You're mentally preparing yourself for his departure." He glared at me. "I'm right, aren't I?"

I couldn't say one goddamn word.

Teague sat back in his chair. "Now, tell me about that letter you got yesterday. We didn't get a chance to talk about it before you left to go on the trail to the lake."

It took me a moment to breathe normally. "Not much to tell. I learned my dad knew I had a thing going with a hand, Clay—and he paid him to leave. All this time, I thought my dad didn't know about me. But he did—and he didn't like it."

"Clay made you happy?"

"He was my first."

"Oh wow."

"And after he went, there was no one. Dad tightened the leash. I thought he was getting me ready to take on all the responsibility of the ranch, that he trusted me to carry on… But that wasn't it at all. He wanted to keep me busy, occupied…"

"So why didn't he buy Kevin off too?"

"Maybe he figured it would be a waste of money. It hadn't worked the first time. I was still fucking *gay*, right?"

"You don't know that for sure. I knew your dad—"

"I think I knew him a little better, don't you?" That came out harsher than I'd intended, and I winced. "I'm sorry. I shouldn't have bitten your head off like that."

"All I'm saying is… maybe… maybe you've got this all wrong."

I stared at him. "How? How could I interpret his actions in any other way?"

"Hey, let me finish, all right?" I fell silent. "Okay… Maybe he paid Clay to leave, not because he wanted you to be straight and he thought Clay was tempting you from the *path of righteousness*…" he air-quoted. "But because he didn't want you to be gay."

"Huh?"

"He didn't want you to face all the shit he knew would be out there—all the haters. And when Kevin came along… You were older, stronger, and he knew you'd be okay. So maybe he figured, 'What the hell? If Kevin makes him happy, why the fuck not?'" Teague stilled. "There *is* another possibility. Maybe your dad felt Clay was too old for you at the time. *You* know, right person, wrong time kinda thing? And when Kevin came along, it was the right person, right time, so he let you be."

"Maybe." I heaved a sigh. "And maybe you're right about the other stuff too."

"You want my advice?"

I smiled. "Do I have a choice? Because I think you're going to give it whether I want it or not."

"Stop wishing the days away, forget about him leaving, and just… enjoy each day as it comes. Enjoy *him*. You can do that here, you know that, right? Hell, everyone who works for you is probably rooting for you right this second, wanting you to grab a little happiness." His eyes sparkled. "And speaking of happiness… When Toby gets back from the grocery run? Don't send him to the bunkhouse. I'm sure there are a lot of things you two can… discuss, right?"

"A few things, yeah." Lord, the effort it took to keep a straight face. "I've invited him to the Saturday night supper. Along with Declan and Garrett, of course."

Teague laughed. "Dear Lord, that might prove an interesting evening." He got up. "I'll say goodnight, then. But Robert?"

I gazed at him. "Yes?"

"Life is too fuckin' short to waste it on thinking about what's going to happen. Live for what you've got *right this second*. Hold on to it." He dipped the edge of his hat, went down the porch steps, and onto the path, whistling a tune.

It took me a moment to recognize it.

Don't Worry, Be Happy.

"Thanks for the advice, Teague," I murmured. I pulled my

phone from my pocket and composed a short text.

When you get back, my place. As an afterthought, I added three words.

Need you, Sir.

CHAPTER TWENTY-FOUR

Toby

"Supper's almost ready," Zeeb called from the bunkhouse.

"Be right with you." My phone vibrated and I peered at the screen.

Need you, Sir.

My heartbeat quickened. Supper could wait.

I heard footsteps behind me and Zeeb joined me. "Anything wrong?"

I pocketed my phone. "No, just need to go out for a—"

"For Christ's sake," he interjected, "Don't say you're going for a walk. We're not idiots. We all know where you're going." He glanced at Garrett who was leading Lucy back toward the stable. "And I *do* mean all of us."

"Yeah, I got that part yesterday morning. Only sorry I didn't see the aftermath."

Zeeb cackled. "Oh, I think he was pretty shocked. Not about you and the boss, mind you—it was more the idea that gay cowboys were a thing."

"He never saw *Brokeback Mountain?*"

"Sure, but he thought that was just Hollywood. So we kind of—"

"Dropped him in the deep end," I said with a smile.

Zeeb guffawed. "Hey, it's like you know us or something. But yeah. Walt started talking about some guys he follows on Instagram, and then he and Matt shared pics of their favorite hunks. I guess by the time they were done, Garrett's eyes had popped out of his sockets and his ears were bleeding, but at least now he knows how the land lies. Thankfully he's okay with queers." He inclined his head toward the house on the hill. "He okay?"

"You're asking me? He's *your* boss."

Zeeb locked gazes with me. "Yeah, and you've seen more of him this past week than I have, so let's cut the bullshit."

I stared at the house. "I don't know. That's why I'm going up there—to find out."

Except that *was* bullshit, but Zeeb didn't need to know that.

He tugged the strap of the backpack over my shoulder. "Got your toothbrush in there? Your PJ's?"

I laughed. "None of your goddamn business. See you tomorrow." Zeeb laughed too as I headed for the path.

I strolled up, my mind going over what I had planned. When I reached the door, Robert opened it before I could knock. "Hey."

The first thing I noticed was a tightness around his eyes, a hand rubbing the back of his neck.

He needed me, all right.

"Is it just us?" He nodded, and I remembered—Matt was getting supper ready down at the bunkhouse. I didn't hesitate. I went inside, removed my boots and jacket, walked into the living room, headed for the nearest armchair, and sat, gesturing to the rug in front of me.

"On your knees, hands on your thighs." He did as he was told, and I could almost see the layer of calm settling on him. "Take a breath." I watched as his chest rose and fell, and I breathed with him. "Okay. Talk time. Seeing as you sent out the equivalent of the bat signal." Not that I minded in the slightest.

He tapped his temple. "There's a lot going on in my head right now."

"Getting crowded in there?"

Another nod.

"Then let's do something about that." I cocked my head to one side. "Have you eaten?"

"I grabbed a bite. I... I wasn't hungry."

We could always eat after.

I leaned forward, lifted his chin with my fingers, and kissed him on the mouth, loving how he melted into the kiss. "Just so you know? We've got all night."

His hands trembled on his thighs, and he sagged a little.

"Got a bottle of water you can take upstairs?"

"Yes."

"Good. Then go grab two of them." He went to rise, and I cupped his face. "I've got you."

He swallowed. "For the next seven days."

I frowned. "Don't be thinking about that now. Let's concentrate on what we have, okay?" He gave a nod, albeit with a little reluctance. "Now go get the water."

He got up and went to the kitchen. I waited for him at the foot of the stairs, and we climbed them, my heart pounding.

Whatever troubled him, I wanted to take it all away—for the next seven days.

My thoughts went to my original idea of a long-distance D/s relationship. I'd wanted to share it with him, but now I had my doubts. *Would it work?* The arrival of Clay's letter had disturbed things. It was right that Robert knew the truth, but he hadn't sent a text to let me know there was an issue, he hadn't told me he'd be late… Small things, yes, but what did they imply about the possibility of making a long-distance relationship over the phone work in the long run?

Will I be forgotten?

Now *there* was a sobering thought, one that poured ice water onto my resolve.

Don't think about it now. Focus on Robert. He was my priority. He needed me.

We entered his bedroom, and I pointed to the nightstand. "Leave the bottles there." Then I dropped my backpack to the floor, and undressed him, keeping my own clothes on. I caught a whiff of body wash and smiled. "Good boy." I took him in my arms, burying my face in his neck, breathing in his clean, masculine smell. I slid my hands down his back, until I cupped his asscheeks. I gave them a rough squeeze, and he shivered.

I pointed to the bed. "Bend over." He did as instructed.

I knelt on the floor behind him, spread him wide, and went to work on his hole with my tongue. Within seconds he was writhing, and I held him down while I tongue-fucked him.

"L-love it when you do that," he stammered.

I chuckled, knowing the vibrations would only add to the sensations. I loved how he grabbed the comforter, clutching it. When his movements grew more frenetic, I figured he was getting close.

Not yet, Robert.

I pulled back. "You could come from this, couldn't you?"

"Yes," he moaned, attempting to get my tongue deeper.

I held him steady. "Well, you won't tonight. I have something else in mind. A couple of somethings, actually." I picked up the backpack from the rug where I'd left it, opened it, removed the massager, and set it down in front of him where he could see it.

Play time.

Robert

Oh Lord.

It was black, shaped like a weird letter L. There was a curved piece at the bottom, and sticking up from it at one end was another piece with two bulbous parts.

Toby leaned over me, his shirt brushing against my back. "You know what this is?"

"Sure. A torture device."

He laughed, then tapped the bulbous part with his finger. "This bit goes inside, snug up against your prostate. This bulge here means it won't pop out. And *this* part—" He indicated the long curved bit. "—rests under your balls. Now, onto the bed, on your back, legs in the air."

My heart thumping, I rolled over, pulling my legs toward my chest. Toby opened the nightstand drawer, removed the lube, and handed both the bottle and the massager to me.

"Okay, put it in."

I slicked up the silicone and eased it inside me, moaning at the stretch as the fat bulge popped through the ring of muscle. The curved part pressed against my taint, the round end pushing into my sac.

Toby held up his phone. "And now we play. Let's see what it can do."

"I'm guessing it vibrates."

He chuckled. "Oh sweetheart, it does so much more than that. It has different vibration levels, sure, but it can also be activated by sound. I can even synch it to music—that is *amazing*, by the way— and there are different patterns of vibration." His eyes gleamed. "But you know what I like most about it?"

"I'm sure you're gonna tell me." My muscles clamped around it, my stomach tense, awaiting whatever was coming.

"I can control it from across the room, sure, but I can also control it from a different location—a different state…"

I widened my eyes. "Internet?"

"You know it."

I wet my lips. "That's… diabolical." And *oh my God*, the possibilities…

And just like that, my mind veered away from the scene, and hurtled in a new direction.

We could play even when he's in San Francisco.

My heart hammered, until reason took over. *Don't get your hopes up. Toby has a life in California, one you don't figure in.*

That didn't mean I couldn't cling to just the tiniest bit of hope.

Then Toby tapped his phone and a tingle went through my balls, a vibration inside me that made me ache, but it was a good ache, one that made me want more of it, that made me forget fantasies about the future.

"Fuck."

He chuckled. "Well, I guess there really is no truth in advertising." When I frowned, perplexed, he grinned. "*Whisper-quiet,* my ass."

I don't know how long he played with the different levels and patterns, stroking my cock as he slid his finger across the phone screen. I only knew that by the time he came to a stop, my dick was leaking pre-cum like a faucet.

Wait—he's stopped.

It was a no-brainer something else was about to happen.

Panic stole over me. "You're not going to take it out, are you?"

Toby smiled. "You like it."

"Fuck yeah."

"In fact, if I carried on playing, you'd probably come, right?"

Oh Lord.

He stroked my stomach with a soothing motion. "Don't worry. I'm gonna leave it in—while you fuck me."

Holy fuck.

"You can rest your legs for a moment." Toby unbuttoned his shirt, taking his time, and I watched, rapt, as he removed it and tossed it to the floor. His jeans were next, and as he lowered the zipper, his dick stood to attention.

It took me a second or two to realize he was talking.

"I know you love getting your ass eaten—did Kevin ever get you to eat his?"

"No." Asking him for permission to rim his hole had always felt wrong.

His eyes focused on me. "Want to try it?"

Oh Lord. "Yes."

"Then get in the center of the bed."

I shuffled backward, and he knelt between my thighs, gently pushing them apart. He stroked my dick, then bent over to take it in his mouth, and I groaned. I closed my eyes, only to open them a second later when a new burst of vibrations pulsed through my ass. My cock rested in his palm while he licked up and down the shaft.

"Can't wait to have this inside me." He held my dick upright, gave it another hard suck, then grinned. "Now it's my turn." He tossed the phone aside, lay on his back, his knees toward his shoulders, presenting his hole. "It's all yours."

I got onto my knees, my heart beating so goddamn fast. I reached out to rub a finger over his pucker, feeling the warm skin contract, then relax.

Toby propped his head up with a pillow. "You're gonna lick my hole. Work it open with your tongue."

I lay on my front, my hands on his ass, and teased his entrance with my tongue. He moaned. "Yeah, just like that." I did it again, but this time I applied a little more pressure, and the muscle let the tip of my tongue in.

Toby shuddered. "Slide a finger in there. Tease my hole open."

I did as I was told, my chest swelling with each new groan that fell from his lips.

"Another."

His ass was tight around my fingers, clinging to them, but it wasn't long before I found it easier to penetrate him.

"Want your tongue again."

I slid my fingers free of him, and licked over his entrance. My tongue danced inside his hole, and it felt amazing.

"Get your face in there. Rub your beard over my hole."

I did as instructed, loving the shudders that multiplied with each pass of my beard through his crack. He shivered. "Feels so good." Toby glanced at his phone, then back to me. "I figure you don't need any more distractions, not once you're inside me."

Dear Lord, I wanted that. "Should I take it out?"

"No—in case I change my mind." A flash of a smile. "Ready?" He gazed at my dick. "Stupid question. You're like a rock."

We both were.

I shuffled forward, working my shaft. He grabbed the lube and handed it to me. I coated it liberally, then brought the head to kiss his hole, my heartbeat racing.

"Slow and steady, okay?" His eyes met mine. "You've got this." He lowered one leg to rest against my shoulder, and I popped the head in, encountering little resistance as I slid all the way home.

"Is that okay?" I asked. Lord, he was so tight.

He grinned. "More than okay. You're thick—my favorite kind of cock."

I didn't want to think about him writhing on someone else's shaft. I started with slow thrusts, and he nodded, his lips parted, his breathing a little ragged. Soon I picked up the pace, my hips creating their own rhythm as I slapped against him. I couldn't tear my gaze away from the sight of my shaft sliding in and out of his body, hard and glistening.

It was mesmerizing, but I needed more.

"Can we change position?"

"How do you want me?" Before I could respond, he flipped over onto his belly, his legs wide. I was back inside him in a heartbeat, returning to my previous speed and rhythm, my hips pumping, his asscheeks rippling with each impact.

"That's it," he gasped. "Grab my shoulders, get a good grip."

I anchored myself and shifted into a higher gear, fucking him, slamming into him, my heart singing as I filled him again and again.

"Oh, perfect," he moaned.

I propped myself up on my hands, my weight resting on them and the balls of my feet, and thrust into him. "Oh my God." My pulse raced, sweat broke out, and I knew I was getting close.

"Let me get onto my back," Toby implored.

I withdrew, and he rolled over, his ankles coming to rest against my shoulders. I pointed my dick at his hole and drove it home.

He reached up and cupped my cheek. "Come inside me. Fill me up."

I swear, I nearly came at those words. I picked up speed,

slamming into him, and then I was there, throbbing inside him, my body shaking with each spurt of my cock.

"Oh fuck." He tugged on his dick, cum pulsing from the slit, landing in spatters on his stomach and chest.

With a shudder, I fell forward on top of him, my cock still buried inside him, and we kissed. He held my face in his hands, and I felt the stickiness of his release on my cheek. "That was incredible," he murmured. Then his arms were around me, his legs gripped my body, and he kissed me over and over, on my head, my brow, my cheeks, my mouth, words of praise tumbling from his lips, making me feel...

Precious.

I pulled free of him, and the sight of my cum trickling from his hole left me energized and lightheaded. He reached down, scooping it onto his fingers before bringing them to my lips. "Clean them."

I sucked on them, my gaze locked on him, adrenaline surging through me. And then I was in his arms again, my head on his chest.

"So... is that something you might want to do again?" His voice rumbled.

I craned my neck. "*Can* I do it again?"

He smiled. "Yeah, you can. But right now there's something else we need to do." I gave him an inquiring glance, and he smirked. "Unless you want to leave the massager in there?"

I reached back and eased the silicone toy from my ass, feeling its loss instantly.

"I have a confession," he murmured. I glanced at him, and he bit his lip. "I thought about using the massager on you while you fucked me."

I caught my breath. "Oh Lord, I am so glad you didn't. That would've been a bit too much. In fact, I'm not sure I could've stayed hard if I'd had to cope with all those vibrations, and the feel of your body wrapped around my cock." I looked at the toy. "Okay, it's not quiet, but fuck, it's powerful." And I couldn't wait to play with it again.

"You can clean it later, so it's ready for the next time."

I bit my lip. "Any idea when that's likely to be?"

His eyes glittered. "Yes, but I'm not sharing that information. Right now I want to get into the bed and hold you." My stomach growled, and he laughed, until a similar noise came from his belly. He grinned. "*After* we've eaten."

"And then?"

He kissed me on the lips. "Then I hold you all night long."

Perfect. "Thank you."

He stroked my beard. "No need. I get to spend the night with you in my arms. I think that's what you call a win-win." His fingers caressed my temple. "Less crowded in there now?"

"Definitely." There was only one thing on my mind.

Toby.

CHAPTER TWENTY-FIVE

Saturday, June 18
Robert

I opened the door to find Toby standing there. I blinked. "You're early. Supper won't be ready for another fifteen minutes. No one else is here yet."

"I know. That's why I came now." He stepped inside, and closed the door behind him. "Where's Matt?"

I frowned. "In the kitchen. Why?"

"Just checking on his whereabouts." Toby lowered his voice. "Where's the prostate massager?"

I stilled. "In the nightstand drawer where you left it, but... ranch supper, remember? All the hands? Not to mention Declan, Garrett?"

He stared at me. "Go upstairs and put it in."

Shock thrummed through me. "There's no time. They'll be here any minute."

"Kind of my point tonight." That stare softened. "Two-way street, remember? Now's the time to say no—"

"Wait." Fuck, my heart was pounding. "No... to knowing I've got something up my—"

"Ass?" he proffered.

"Sleeve," I said, laughing. "I was going to say sleeve." Then I swallowed. "But with all the guys here?"

Toby studied me. "That scare you a little?"
Another hard swallow. "Yeah. I'm their boss." And while they all knew what Toby and I got up to—or at least they could guess—that didn't mean I wanted them knowing just how far we went.

For God's sake, let me keep one *fucking secret.*

He came in close, his breath warm on my neck. "I won't embarrass you, because I know there are some things you want to keep private. And if this is forcing you out of your comfort zone, then it's okay to tell me that." He kissed my neck, and I shivered. "But living is more than just breathing, all right? Now and then you need to do something that scares you a little—preferably with someone you trust. So I guess what I'm asking is... do you trust me?"

Now *there* was the million-dollar question.

I licked my lips, my mouth dry. "Yes, Sir," I whispered.

Lord, his smile... It could fuel the state, let alone a small town.

"Good boy." He kissed me on the lips. "So... here's what we'll do. Your water glass during supper—or your glass of iced tea, whatever. One tap on it with your finger means stop, okay? And two means ease off."

"I guess three means keep doing what you're doing." My cock filled at the idea of Toby edging me while everyone around us ate supper, blissfully unaware.

Yeah, this was truly Dom and sub territory, and I was delighted to be back in it.

"Then we're good to go?"

"Yeah." I took a deep breath. "I want this." I bit my lip. "I'd better go upstairs and put it in, then."

He beamed. "Good boy."

I went upstairs to my room, grabbed the lube and the massager, and laid them on the bed while I shoved my jeans to my knees. I got on my back, drew my legs toward my chest, and slicked it up. My hole had tightened a little since our slow morning fuck—except that had turned into a fast, hard fuck within minutes—so I slid the toy inside me with care.

My phone pinged in my jeans pocket, and I peered at it.

Come downstairs.

I pulled my jeans up, expecting the massager to burst into life, but nothing happened.

I knew it.

I'd been right all along. It was an instrument of torture. As I left my room and headed for the stairs, I heard voices below. I walked into the living room to find all the hands had arrived, Declan and Garrett too—and there was Diana, standing next to the fireplace.

Oh hell no.

I gaped at her. "You didn't tell me you were coming."

Toby's watchful gaze let me know he was looking for any sign that whatever play he'd had in mind needed to stop before it even got started.

Damn it. Where was a glass when I needed one?

She grinned. "Surprise. I haven't been to one of these in a while." She arched her eyebrows. "You don't mind, do you?"

And what was I supposed to say to that? *'Yeah, actually, I do mind, because the thought of sitting at the same table as you while Toby sends vibrations buzzing through my ass and balls is horrifying.'* Especially now I knew that thing was definitely *not* quiet.

Fuck. My dick was like a rock at the prospect, and that wiped away any doubts I had that I wasn't kind of… excited to be doing this.

I glanced at Toby, then back to Diana. "No, of course not."

Toby was grinning, the bastard.

Yeah, you can see I'm not backing down, can't you?

Bring. It. On.

"Supper's on the table, guys," Matt called out. "And there's plenty more in the kitchen."

"Great. I'm starving," Butch declared.

"You're always starving," Teague said with a grin.

"And your point is?" Butch gestured to his large frame. "You wanna know how much food it takes to keep me looking this awesome?"

The rest of the banter went pretty much over my head. All I could think about was that massager wedged in my ass—and what

Toby was going to do with the remote.

The food was excellent as usual, the conversation just as lively, but all the same, it was excruciating torture. I kept waiting for that initial buzz, those rhythmic pulses. I even wondered if he'd switched it to voice activation, but there was zilch. Toby didn't sit near me, but at the other end of the table, watching me. Every now and then, his hands would dip under the table, and I'd freeze, but nothing happened. Half an hour after we'd sat to eat, I was still anticipating.

Yeah this was torture.

Toby

I was so fixated on Robert, I didn't realize I was being addressed by his sister. "I'm sorry," I apologized. "I must have zoned out for a moment there." *I was too busy watching your brother.*

Damn, this was fun. My game of *now you see them, now you don't* with my hands must've driven him to distraction.

"So… you're from San Francisco?"

"Yes, ma'am."

She snorted. "I'm Diana, okay? *Ma'am* makes me feel as old as Methuselah."

"Trust me, you don't look it."

Diana chuckled. "And you have a smooth tongue." There was a look of Robert about her, and I got the impression they shared a similar sense of humor. "How's your stay been so far?"

"It's been great, although I'm sure the best is yet to come." When she gave me a speculative glance, I smiled. "The cattle drive next week."

"We leave on Monday, early," Teague told her. Then with a smile, he added, "Robert's going too."

Diana turned her head slowly to stare at her brother. "Oh really?"

"Yeah." Butch helped himself to the last hunk of cornbread.

"Maybe not being carried off by a flash flood has given him a new lease of life. Because *something* sure has." His eyes twinkled. "Wonder what that could be?"

Her eyes widened. "What's this about a flood?" She glared at Robert. "Did you get caught up in that? You didn't tell me."

"That's because there was nothing to tell," he retorted.

Zeeb gave her a précis of what had happened on Thursday, and all of a sudden, all traces of anger and concern faded. She regarded Robert, her eyes dancing with amusement. "So you and Toby got stranded up at Mirror Lake all night? How… cozy."

Robert coughed. "I think supper's over, don't you? Besides, you've eaten every scrap of food. And if Butch licks his plate any cleaner, he'll bring the pattern off the china."

Diana's eyes sparkled. "And why are you in such a hurry to go to bed?" Then she glanced at me and her face lit up with another grin. "Oh, I see."

She didn't seem unhappy about the idea.

A muted howl rose up outside, followed by yet more, and I froze. "That's not good." Around the table, all eyes went to the windows.

"No, it sure isn't." Teague stood, the others with him. "Walt, you take Declan and Garrett down to the bunkhouse. Toby, you stay here with the boss. Me, Zeeb, and Butch will take care of this." He gave a grim smile. "Let's go, boys, before those wolves decide it's their supper time too, and the cows are the entrée." He glanced at Robert. "Thanks for supper. I'll call you with an update."

The others murmured their thanks before following Teague out of the house.

Diana stood too. "I'd better go. I told Newt I wouldn't be back late." She gave me a sideways glance. "At least I know you'll have company." She walked to the end of the table where Robert stood, and kissed his cheek. "Have fun. Don't do anything I wouldn't do." Another grin. "On second thoughts…"

He let out a low growl. "Diana…"

She flashed me a smile. "Good to meet you, Toby. I hope to see more of you." She bit her lip. "I only wish I got to see as much of you as my brother gets to see." Then she headed for the door.

I grinned. "She can be a handful, can't she?"

He rolled his eyes. "You have *no* idea."

Matt wasn't long after her. "Just going outside for a smoke, boss." He grabbed his jacket and hat, and followed Diana.

Then it was just the two of us.

I estimated there'd be a delay of maybe five seconds before Robert exploded.

He didn't even make it to two.

He glared at me. "You didn't turn it on."

"Of course not," I said calmly.

His eyes widened. "What do you mean, 'of course not'?"

I went over to him, and laid my hands on his shoulders. He was trembling. "It would have been wrong," I said in a low voice. "It would've opened you up to humiliation, especially when Diana turned up." I stroked a finger over his cheek. "You said you trusted me, remember? You consented to our play, but your ranch hands and Diana didn't." I smiled. "Sometimes pleasure doesn't come from flicking a switch…" I kissed him on the lips, slow as you please. "It comes from the private anticipation of seeing how it plays out."

He gaped at me. "So you never intended using it in the first place? It was just a mindfuck?"

I beamed. "And a *wonderful* piece of mindfuckery too. So I guess that means…" I leaned in and kissed him, and he sighed into it.

"What does it mean?"

I kissed his forehead. "You get a reward. So let's go upstairs and take out the massager. I've got something else that'll feel so much better in there." I grabbed his hand around the wrist and drew it to my crotch. "Because watching you all night got me *so* fucking hard."

"But… Matt'll be back."

I snorted. "Trust me, after that supper, he'll know exactly where we are—and what we're doing. And if I think you're getting too loud?" Another kiss, this time to the tip of his nose. "I'll gag you."

Robert

Sunday was spent mostly in preparation for leaving the following day. The men gathered the tack and the grub, then packed the chuckwagon with the supplies, including all Matt's food and cooking utensils. There were cool boxes filled with meat and other food that needed to be kept fresh. Bedrolls were added, stuffed into crevices and any space that would take them. Declan and Garrett groomed the horses, and Paul cleaned all the saddles and bridles. It would be an early start, but by late afternoon we would reach the camp.

I was looking forward to it. It had been awhile since I'd done this, and the prospect of a gentle ride, the herd moving forward in a slow wave, was a pleasant one.

I've put too much on Teague's shoulders the last few years. That would stop.

I was back.

Sunday night was also the last chance I would get to be alone with Toby, and I took advantage of the fact, begging him to fuck me. We were alone in the house, so he obliged, letting me make as much noise as I wanted—but not before he'd cuffed me to the bed posts, ropes around my thighs, pulled them up toward the bed rail too. I was spread wide for him, unable to move, and I loved every fucking minute. When he was done, he untied the ropes, removed the cuffs, checked my wrists, and then held me while I came down from my orgasm, my mind at peace.

I didn't think I'd slept that well in years.

Monday morning, it was still dark outside when I awoke to his mouth on my cock. I shivered, arching my back, pushing deeper. "I wish all mornings could start this way."

He chuckled around my dick, and the vibrations were exquisite. He pulled free and glanced at me. "Enjoy it while it lasts. No more coming for *you* for a while."

I didn't like the sound of that.

Then I forgot everything except the feel of his lips and tongue, and I shot my load, shaking with each pulse into his mouth. He lapped up every drop, then cradled me in his arm while he stroked my limp dick.

"I told Teague I wouldn't be staying in the same tent as Declan and Garrett."

I chuckled. "I think he'd have guessed that already."

Toby stretched over me toward the nightstand drawer, and opened it. I wondered what he was searching for—until he held up the cock cage. "I thought I'd give you something else to think about while we're moving the herd."

Now I understood the comment about enjoying it while it lasted. "You want me to wear that? But… everyone will see it."

"No, they won't. It'll just be like a weird bulge in your jeans. You can hide that, right?"

You're damn straight I'm going to hide it.

Toby regarded me steadily. "Consent, remember. You can say no."

I raised my chin. "Not saying no."

He beamed. "You know what I think? Eventually you'll just accept it and quit hiding it."

Yeah, right.

"Of course, once we get to the camp, I might ask you to do something."

"Do what?"

He grinned. "Anything that makes it a little more obvious. But that would only be some of the time. *Most* of the time you'll be able to hide it—maybe."

I gave him a mock glare. "When you were listing all the things you wanted to do to me, I don't recall mindfucking being one of them."

He grinned. "Surprise."

CHAPTER TWENTY-SIX

Robert

It was still dark when we rolled out of Salvation, heading for the pasture where the herd awaited us. Paul rode in the chuckwagon with Matt, and Kyle and Owen joined us, bringing along two more horses.

Toby wasn't far behind and I knew once we got going, he'd ride alongside me.

I'd forgotten how many of these I'd participated in over the years. Except this one was different. This cattle drive was a first, a fact that was brought home to me every time my caged cock shifted against the rough of the saddle. It served as a reminder. Toby hadn't locked my dick into its metal prison to degrade me, or deprive me of pleasure—although he might have teased that was its purpose. No, wearing it created a sensation of permanent pleasure, a link with him.

It was our secret, and promised even greater pleasure when removed.

Zeeb trotted up to join me. "You okay, boss?"

I smiled. "I'm fine." Then I reconsidered. "No—I'm *more* than fine."

He nodded. "That's what I thought. It's a good look on you." Then he moved away, picking up speed to catch up with Butch and Teague.

When was the last time I'd been this happy? Yet it was a weird happiness, tinged with a sense of… I wasn't sure what it was. Impending doom was far too strong a term, but yeah, I felt as though something was hovering over me, ready to drop, to push me into the ground. I knew what lay at the heart of it, and although my scenes with Toby pushed my anxiety into the background, they didn't stay gone. All it took to bring it back with a vengeance was the thought that I needed to make the most of the good feelings, because when he left, they'd leave with him.

It was more like a *Happy—for now.*

But is that enough?

And what the hell do I have to be anxious about? Why is it manifesting now?

I considered the last five years. I'd spent most of them feeling depressed, not that I'd ever sought medical help, so maybe my anxiety hadn't come to the surface. But now, with the depression having lifted to a point, it was possible that had allowed other emotions to rise to the surface, to become more pronounced.

Lord, the irony... The one thing I knew would relieve my anxiety was about to get on a plane and head back to San Francisco, and I couldn't do a thing about it.

We were finally on our way, about six hundred head of cattle moving south, mooing constantly. As we rode along, I watched the sun rise over the mountains to our left, spilling its light onto the land before us.

"That's so beautiful," Toby said as he caught up with me.

"Wait till you watch the sunset tonight. I swear, the way it catches the snow-capped peaks, it looks as if the mountains are on fire." I glanced at him. "Is it what you expected?"

"It's so much more. I can see why Declan keeps coming back." He flung his arm out. "All this wide-open space. Beautiful country." He sagged in the saddle. "A man could be truly happy here."

I disagreed. It was a great life, sure, but it wasn't enough. For a while, I'd gotten awful close to being truly happy, but it had slipped through my fingers.

I had the feeling it was about to get slippery again.

He gestured to the hands, riding in formation. "Do they all have assigned positions, or is it more random than that?"

I chuckled. "Okay, cattle drive 101." I pointed way in front, to where Teague and Butch rode out ahead of the herd. "Those two are point men. They determine the direction of the herd, they control its speed. Plus, they give the cattle something to follow. And they're point men because they have the most experience."

"Gotcha. Okay, what about the others?"

I pointed ahead. "Walt and Zeeb are swing riders. That means they ride on either side, about a third of the way behind Teague and Butch. Their job is to keep the herd together. They're basically on the lookout for any animals that might try to break away. Zeeb's been doing this for nine years, Walt, maybe four years."

"And what about Declan and Kyle, farther back from them?"

"They're drag riders. They keep the herd moving, pushing the slower animals forward. Declan's done this before. And right at the back we have Matt driving the chuckwagon, and Paul who rides with him. Oh, and Garrett is riding alongside."

"Paul's the wrangler, right?"

I smiled. "You're learning. We'll make a cowboy out of you yet."

He peered at the line of cattle that swelled in the middle, its widest point. "They seem to know where they're going."

I chuckled. "The reason we have all these riders? Cows don't always go where you want them to." I glanced at his clothing. "You've come prepared for the weather, at least." Clouds hung heavy over the horizon, and I knew we were in for rain. The forecast promised a break in the weather the following day, however.

Toby watched the dogs as they sprinted alongside the herd. "I haven't seen them before."

"The two Border Kelpies belong to Kyle, and the Australian Shepherd is Owen's. A maverick steps out of line, and they're on it."

"Maverick?"

"That's an unbranded calf."

Toby frowned. "Are there any bulls out there?"

I laughed. "Hell no, just mothers and their calves. The only procreation on Salvation happens when *we* want it to happen. That's why we're careful not to let a bull anywhere near the cows. You think about it. If someone told *you* when you could fuck, and kept you—"

"In a cock cage," he said with a smile.

I gave him a mock glare. "Yeah, exactly. Well, how do you think *you'd* react if you got loose among a herd of cows?" I sighed. "This is nothing like the cattle drives of the past, but we'll keep doing what we're doing. We have to leave something for the next generation, right?"

"How long do you think you'll keep doing this?" he asked.

I smiled. "Put it this way. Hank Quaid's father still goes on cattle drives, and he's in his eighties."

He chuckled. "So you're in it for the long haul."

"I'm in it until it's time to stop."

When that might be, I had no idea.

Toby picked up a little speed. "Think I'll mosey on up to the front and talk to Teague." He grinned. "Well? Do I sound like a cowboy?"

I chuckled. "No, you sound like you've been watching old westerns."

He waved a hand, and took off. I kept Rusty at a steady trot, my mind at peace.

It felt good to be doing this again.

A short while later, Garrett joined me, looking at ease in the saddle. "Hey," he said with a smile. "I wanted a word while no one was around."

I arched my eyebrows. "Everything okay?"

"Oh, sure. It's just that…" He flushed. "I wanted you to pass on my thanks to your hands. They've been very patient with me, and I do appreciate that."

"They were just doing their job. Not every guest takes to this as easily as Declan or Toby." I smiled. "You look great on a horse, by the way. No one would ever guess you'd never ridden one before last week."

"Declan kept telling me, all I had to do was keep at it, and he was right." He sighed. "This was exactly what I needed."

"What do you do for a living, Garrett?"

"I'm a financial consultant. Only, I'm under a lot of pressure right now. Deadlines, targets…" He swallowed. "And I'm dealing with other stuff too."

"None of which you have to tell me, all right?" I assured him.

He nodded. "I wasn't about to. But I had to tell you… this vacation has made me look at my life, at what's important." He gazed ahead. "Life's too short to keep doing the same old thing if it makes me unhappy."

"I agree." My thoughts went to my habitual morning rides to the cabin. "Sometimes you just have to let go and move on."

He tipped his hat. "I think *you've* done that." His smile lit up his face, and for the first time since I'd laid eyes on him, Garrett seemed happy. "You two are a good fit."

I forced a smile. *Sure—and he's leaving at the end of the week.*

Before I could say another word, Garrett dropped back toward the rear.

I stared forward to where Toby rode alongside Teague, the pair of them laughing at something.

He's a damn good fit.

Then I pushed the thought aside. Torture was not good for the soul.

Toby

That first night, the camp was not what I'd expected. I'd imagined bedrolls, campfires, tiny tents... The tents were big enough to sleep five or six hands. There were several fires going, illuminating the surroundings. Matt was busy, stirring a huge pan of something that smelled delicious. Supper would be late. We'd had to deal with more than a few strays long the way, but at last we'd arrived at the first camp. Robert and Teague were riding the perimeter, checking for wolves.

Supper was chicken soup, with abundant chunks of meat and vegetables, and there was plenty of it. We sat around the campfires, drinking it from metal cups, and once we were done, Matt and Paul collected them and went to wash them in the river. Everyone seemed quiet, but it had been a long day.

I sat in a camping chair in front of the tent I shared with Robert, watching daylight give way to inky blackness, the stars winking into existence until the sky was strewn with them. We were camped at the foot of a mountain, moonlight tinging its snow-capped peaks with a bluish hue. I could hear running water: the river snaked its way through the valley, too wide to cross, but with banks accessible enough that the cattle could drink from it.

The wind picked up a little, and I shivered. I was glad I'd followed advice and worn several layers: the night air had a definite chill to it.

Zeeb ambled over to me, a cup of coffee in one hand. "So how's your ass after the first day?"

"Why do you think I'm sitting?" I chuckled. "Lord, I ache. No one thought to bring a tub so I could soak in it, however," I quipped.

He rolled his eyes. "I'll be sure to bring it up with the management," he said dryly. "And come morning, we take everything down and move on. At least you'll get two nights after this before it's time to head back. My advice for tonight? Get some sleep."

I was actually too tired to even think about sex. "Sounds like a plan." When he didn't make a move, I peered at him. "Something on your mind?"

"I see you followed my suggestion after all."

"Excuse me?"

He pointed in the direction Robert had taken. "The light's back in his eyes. He smiles more, laughs more."

"That *was* what you wanted, wasn't it?"

"Sure. Except *now* what concerns me is, you'll go too far."

I stared at him. "You've lost me."

His face fell. "This is all my fault. I didn't think it through."

"What do you mean?"

For a moment he didn't reply. "You obviously give him what he needs. But you're gonna leave Saturday."

"I can't change that. And you always knew that would happen."

I'd always known it too, but with the day for my departure drawing closer, what surprised me was the feeling of... sorrow wasn't quite the word. I certainly wasn't happy about it.

But you've decided it's not going to end. You're going to be his long-distance Dom, remember? If he agrees.

Maybe I was having second thoughts.

Maybe doubts were setting in that this could work.

"Sure I did. I just didn't anticipate the effect you'd have on him."

I arched my eyebrows. "I hate to break up your pity party, but did it ever occur to you we'd have ended up in this situation *without* you pushing me in Robert's direction?" The spark was already there the first day we'd met—we'd just fanned the flames.

He stroked his jaw. "Maybe. Anyway, we're here now, so it's no use debating how it got started. But if you wanna make me happy, there's something you *can* do."

"And what's that?" I was intrigued.

He locked gazes with me, his eyes like steel. "Don't break his heart."

I blinked.

Zeeb nodded. "Because you do *that,* and I'll come out to California, and I'll find you." There was a hard edge to his voice that made me believe him.

I frowned. "You know, for a man who professes to like me, that sounds like a threat."

He gave me a cool smile. "Good. I wouldn't want there to be any… misinterpretation. Now get some sleep. Tomorrow's another long day." He wandered off in Matt's direction.

I supposed it was kind of sweet. And then I realized he was just the first—Butch was walking toward me with a purposeful stride.

Now what?

"Hey, Butch."

He hunkered down next to me. "I like you, Toby."

Obviously not a man for small talk. "You're not so bad yourself."

"So this is gonna be said with love, okay?"

I stared at him, my eyebrows arched.

Butch squared his jaw. "Break his heart, and I'll break you." And with that, he stood and walked off.

Oh my God. I felt like some kid who'd asked a girl to the prom, only to be threatened with bodily menaces by her dad, if I dared bring her home in a less than perfect state—or broke his little girl's heart.

Is anybody else *going to threaten me?*

Then I realized that was a dumb question—Teague was back in camp, and he was heading my way.

Before he had a chance to open his mouth, I surged to my feet and got in first. "Look, if you're here to tell me not to get too close to Robert, a couple of guys already beat you to it."

That didn't slow him down for an instant. "He's had enough heartache. He's already dreading you leaving."

I glared at him. "There's not a lot I can do about that, now is there?"

Except there was.

Maybe it was time to discuss my plans. Because if his *hands* were thinking this way, Robert had to be too.

That was it. My mind was made up. I'd make the long-distant D/s relationship work—for both our sakes, because I needed this too.

I sighed. "I will do everything I can to ensure he isn't hurt. Is that good enough?"

Teague frowned. "I don't see how you can do that when you're in San Francisco and he's here, but I suppose we'll have to see."

"Let me guess. If I don't come up with a solution, you're going to talk with your fists?"

"No, I won't lay a finger on you." His eyes sparkled. "I won't have to. There'll be guys lining up to do that for me."

He strode off, leaving me with my jaw on the ground.

This is so fucked up.

I knew what the problem was. If this had started out at the club, or via Recon, that would've been fine. All the club guidelines were in place, our roles would've been discussed...

But this *wasn't* a normal D/S relationship.

I'd gotten to know—was *still* getting to know—Robert outside of all that. There'd been mutual attraction from the beginning, and we both knew it, and that was growing kind of naturally. Damn it, I hadn't come to Salvation as a Dom—I was just a guy going to a dude ranch, who happened to like its owner, and D/s had progressed from that.

But I *could* steer it back onto a path I was more familiar with—right?

Then I saw Robert coming my way, and my heart thumped.

This was *way* outside of my agreed *no emotional tie* comfort zones in a D/s relationship.

I went into the tent and grabbed the bedrolls, more with the thought of comfort rather than activity in mind. As an afterthought,

I rummaged through my toiletries bag, removed the lube, and shoved it into my jacket pocket.

It never hurt to be prepared for any eventuality.

I went back outside and waited. When he came to a halt, I sighed.

"Let's go for a walk."

His gaze drifted lower to the bedrolls tucked under my arm, and the bulge in my pocket. "Oh, I see. *That* kind of walk." His lips twitched.

I was too wound up to smile. "Maybe. That'll depend on how the conversation goes."

All trace of humor vanished. "'Conversation'?"

I nodded. "We need to talk."

He squared his shoulders, and it was as if he'd been expecting this. "Fine. Let's go." I made as if to move, and he held up a hand. "Wait." He dove inside the tent, and returned with a flashlight.

I had to smile. *Gotta love a practical man.* Then I took the flashlight from him and fired it up, illuminating our path as I led him away from the camp, closer to the mountain, and out of earshot of the others, my heartbeat racing.

It wasn't until that moment that I realized how badly I wanted him to accept my proposal.

Robert

As we walked, I grew aware of all the sounds of life around us—the cicadas, the rustle of… something running—or slithering—over the ground, the call of birds…

"This place is alive," I murmured. Not that I was paying all that much attention—I was too preoccupied with the upcoming conversation.

What does he want to talk about?

Toby came to a dead stop. "Here. This'll do."

I glanced at the dark shapes surrounding us, the deep shadows created by moonlight. "There could be anything out there."

"Anything?"

"You know… creatures… with teeth… claws… fangs…"

Toby laughed. "We're not staying long." He unfurled the bedrolls and laid them on the ground, side by side, then gestured to them. "Let's sit."

I got onto the bedroll. "Could we lie down? I want to look at the stars."

He smiled. "Sounds like a great idea."

We lay on our backs, staring at the night sky, vast and black over our heads, so many stars they appeared like dust.

"Never seen so many stars," he murmured. "Not surprising, given the light pollution in San Francisco."

"When I was fourteen, Dad brought me here on the cattle drive. We spent every night looking at them. He taught me their names, something I've never forgotten."

"You miss him."

It wasn't a question.

I sighed. "Yeah, I do. He was all the family I had. My aunts and uncles rarely visited, so it was just him, me, and Diana—and the ranch hands, of course."

"But they're your family too."

I smiled. "Yes, they are." I gazed at the huge, twinkling canopy above us. "Kinda makes you feel so small, doesn't it?"

Toby rolled onto his side, his head propped in his hand, and I knew it was time to talk.

"I asked you this once. I guess I need to ask it again. Where do you want this to go?"

I'd thought of little else the past few days. My dad had said owning a ranch meant having to be a realist, something that had stuck with me ever since. "It's okay. I know everything ends on Saturday. I'm just trying not to think about that."

Trying—and failing miserably.

Toby fell silent, not that I'd expected any other response. Then he cleared his throat.

"And what if it didn't?"

For a moment there I didn't understand. "What?"

"What if... I went back to San Francisco, but I visit as often as I can, and we carry on." He locked gazes with me. "With you as my submissive."

Oh Lord, my heart.

"You mean it?"

"I wouldn't suggest it if I didn't."

My mind was already calculating. "But... could it work?" I sent up a silent prayer. *Please, let it work. I need this to work, Lord.*

Toby widened his eyes. "You're asking *me*? I've never done this."

"But you want to." Hell, he'd come up with the idea, right?

"Okay, let's be practical. There'd be a lot of distance between us."

"Like a thousand miles at least." I'd looked it up.

He nodded. "But if we want this to work, there are ways and means, all right? Phone sex, for one thing." He peered at me. "You ever do much of that?"

"Never." But Lord, I liked the prospect.

"Then there are video calls." He grinned. "Calling you up on Skype, telling you to put in the prostate massager—then watching you squirm when I turn it on. Talking you through masturbating—"

"I do know how to do that," I commented. "I was probably doing that before you were born. No—I *was* doing it before you were born."

"But you'd be following instructions. I could always leave you in restraint until I got back." My mouth fell open, and he chuckled. "No, I will *not* be leaving you in a cock cage for weeks on end." He grinned. "Although I love the idea."

"Just how long were you planning on leaving between visits?"

"I don't know, okay? I only know, I've been thinking about

this for a while."

"How long?" I demanded.

His eyes met mine. "Since the first time we fucked."

My skin tingled, and something fluttered deep in my belly. "That long?"

Another nod. "I wanted to see how things panned out between us before I mentioned the idea. But I don't want you to be under any illusions here. It would take *both* of us to make this work. Okay, so I won't be here, but I *will* be your Dom—if that's what you want.

Warmth radiated through me. "You have to ask?"

Even in moonlight, I could see Toby's smile light up his face. "Then that's what we'll do."

I brought my hand to his neck. "Kiss me, Sir?"

Toby didn't reply, but leaned in, and our lips met in a slow kiss.

Kind of a sealing-the-deal kiss.

"I brought lube," he murmured against my lips.

"I noticed."

He chuckled. "But if I'm honest, I'm too exhausted to fuck."

"That's what all day on a horse will do for you," I told him. "And you'll feel no better tomorrow when we reach the final camp."

"Then why don't we go back to our tent, zip our sleeping bags into one giant bag, get naked, and cuddle up? Let's save the more vigorous activity for Wednesday night." He grinned. "My body might have recovered a little by then."

The idea of lying naked in his arms sent yet more warmth flooding through me.

"Sounds good to me." Then I remembered. "What about the cock cage?"

"What about it?"

"You're leaving it on?"

He kissed me. "You *can* wash with it on, you know."

As if I'd expected anything different. "Yes, Sir."

That earned me another grin. "And when Wednesday night comes, so will you."

That was going to be one explosive orgasm.

It still hadn't sunk in.

I'm not losing him.

I've got a Dom.

He's leaving—but he's coming back.

I intended to do everything in my power to make this work, even if that meant ignoring the voice at the back of my mind, the one that kept repeating the same question over and over.

Will it be enough?

CHAPTER TWENTY-SEVEN

Wednesday, June 22
Toby

It was late afternoon, and I'd spent the day walking through the camp, watching the herd from a distance, listening to the sounds they made as they fed on the lush green grass. Kyle and Owen were on horseback, trotting around the camp perimeter, keeping an eye on things, and armed with rifles in case of predators. The others sat in front of their tents, playing cards, reading, and enjoying the sunshine now that the rain of the previous night had finally stopped. I'd loved lying beneath canvas, listening to the almost cozy sound of rain drumming against it. When it didn't abate, I'd grown concerned, until Robert snuggled closer, and told me to quit worrying, that we weren't about to become embroiled in another flash flood.

Then we'd kissed, a leisurely rolling together in our giant sleeping bag, naked bodies entwined, warm skin, warm breath, hands that stroked, caressed, teased…His breath had caught when I touched the cock cage, only to leave him in a sigh when I left it in place.

"Tomorrow," I'd whispered.

I'd fallen asleep with him in my arms, and that had felt… right.

That first view when I'd emerged from the tent that morning had been glorious. It was as if God had washed the sky. It was a beautiful clear blue, not a cloud to be seen.

"I envy them," I murmured, gesturing to Kyle and Owen.

"Why?" Robert asked.

"They get to stay here until the herd returns. Although I suppose it could get a little lonely."

"That's why I always make sure I leave at least two guys up

here, and rotate them. And the dogs make for good company too."

I turned toward the sun, feeling its warmth on my face.

"You look good in this light," Robert said in a low voice.

I glanced at him and chuckled. "They can't hear you. Our tent is nowhere near anyone else's." I suspected that had been his decision. Sure, he liked his privacy, but I also knew he didn't want any stray noises reaching the others.

And then I had a delicious idea.

I ducked into the tent and grabbed the lube and the bedrolls.

"Going somewhere?" he asked from the tent flap.

"Yup. *We* are going for a walk. Bring that blanket."

He frowned. "A walk? But—"

I strolled over to him. "Supper won't be for a few hours. Everyone's occupied. Teague's in charge." I locked gazes with him. "And I want you."

Robert

Someone somewhere had just turned up the thermostat.

"How can I say no to that?" At least he was planning on us fucking away from the camp. "So where are we headed?" I picked up the blanket. Then as an afterthought, I dug down into my toiletries bag and fished out the packet of wet wipes.

Toby laughed. "That's what I love about you—so goddamn practical." Then he strolled out of the tent.

My heartbeat quickened.

It was just a turn of phrase.

Everyone says stuff like that.

What shocked me was I wanted to believe it.

I went outside to find him scanning our surroundings. He pointed toward the foot of the mountain. "Thataway."

The farther from the camp, the better.

The terrain grew rockier as we neared the mountains. Huge

boulders seemed to spring up out of nowhere, great slabs of beige-colored rock that soaked up the sun's rays. Narrow paths twisted around them, and here and there, trees grew, not as lush as the ones along the river, but wiry with fewer leaves.

We'd been walking for maybe five minutes when Toby came to a halt.

"Why here?" The sounds of laughter from the camp were carried on the breeze. We weren't *that* far from them.

He pointed to a boulder. "That'll do."

"Do for what?" Dumb question. I knew why we were there, didn't I?

Toby patted a flat ledge of rock. "Perfect." His gaze flickered in my direction. "Clothes—off. You can leave your boots on."

I stared at him. "They'll hear us."

Okay, so it wouldn't be the first time some of them had heard my goings-on—that didn't mean I wanted to give a repeat performance. Besides, that had been a long time ago, when I was a hell of a lot younger, not their boss, and didn't give a flying leap who heard. And then we'd had the cabin, safely out of earshot and away from prying eyes.

Toby grinned. "The noises you make when you're getting fucked? I'm not surprised. I *could've* brought a ball gag—but I didn't."

He'd planned this. "So the object of the scene…" I swallowed.

"Is not to get caught." He dropped the bedrolls to the ground, and held his arms wide. "Come here and kiss me."

An invitation I had no desire to refuse. I placed my blanket on top of the bedrolls, and walked into those waiting arms.

His mouth was gentle at first, a brushing of lips against mine, whisper-soft on my cheeks, my forehead. But I didn't want gentle. I wanted to *feel*.

I grabbed his head and deepened the kiss, opening for him, and he responded with a hunger equal to mine. Our kisses intensified, the heat spiraling between us, and I knew it was the thrill of having the others so close by. Toby took off his hat, then mine, set them on the boulder, and then his hands were on my face and neck, pulling me in, devouring me, letting me know his need was white-hot too. Fingers fumbled as we undressed each other, shirts tossed to the ground, the sun warm on my bare skin, until all we wore were our boots, his hard dick pointing upward, pre-cum already descending in a thin glistening rod from his slit.

I glanced at mine, encased in its metal cage, and he chuckled. "I promised, didn't I?" He picked up his jeans, reached into the pocket, and slid the key into the little gold padlock that secured it. He eased my soft dick from its constraints, and I shivered. Toby lowered his head as if to lick it, and I stopped him.

"No," I begged. "Do that and I'll come."

He chuckled, his breath warm on the head. Then he straightened, cupped my face, and looked me in the eye. "Want you."

He'd already said that, but what hit me was the tremor in his voice, the feeling this wasn't Toby the Dom, but Toby the man, aroused, needing...

Lord, I needed him, too.

"You have me," I whispered. Emboldened, I grabbed the blanket, laid it at his feet, sank to my knees, curled my hand around his thick cock, and took him into my mouth. He leaned against the boulder, his eyes closed, and my head bobbed, his shaft sliding in and out. He didn't bother holding back, his hands on my head, as he pumped his hips, going deeper, faster, until saliva coated his dick, *dripped* from it, and all I wanted was to feel him inside me.

Toby

Dear God, the *sight* of him, swallowing my cock to the root, his eyes meeting mine, the longing in them...

A longing I recognized, the same longing that burned inside me right then.

This was a scene, remember? Fucking him within earshot of the camp?

That might have been the plan, but somewhere along the way it had developed into something else, a desire to feel his body against mine, to experience that intimate—

Connection.

For a moment, I didn't know myself.

Get back on track.

I pulled free of his mouth, then hauled him to his feet and spun him around. "Hands on the rock. Bend over." He braced himself, trembling, and I knelt behind him. I pried his cheeks apart and went to work with my tongue, licking, teasing, probing, until he was pushing back, his hand reaching for my head to keep me there, my face buried in his crack.

I drew back. "Hands—on the rock." I delivered a slap to his ass, the sound loud and sharp, and I knew exactly what went through his mind. He obeyed, but the noises tumbling from his lips swelled in volume and number, and his body danced on my tongue.

Lord, I wanted in there.

I stretched out my hand for my jacket and fumbled in the pocket for the lube. Then I stood, my chest pressed against his back as I swiped slick fingers through his crease and over his pucker. "That's all you're getting. You're loose enough." I applied lube to my shaft, dropped the bottle onto the blanket, spread his cheeks, and slid right in in one hot glide.

"Oh fuck." He shuddered, stilling as I leaned in to kiss his neck, his body so goddamn tight, wrapped around my dick. He turned his face toward me, and we kissed, his tongue seeking mine.

There was something about kissing him when I was so deep inside him that answered a need in me I'd had no idea even existed.

And there it was, that connection again, only this time, I went with it, chased it, wanting more.

"Now," I whispered. I gripped his shoulders and powered in and out of him, my hips pistoning, my body slamming into his. "Fuck yourself on my cock."

He pushed back, his asscheeks rippling as I smacked into

them, his moans building with every thrust.

It wasn't enough. I needed to be deeper.

I pulled free, and he groaned. I spread the blanket on the ground. "On your back, legs in the air." He didn't hesitate, and I got on my knees, aiming my dick at his hole and spearing into him, his boots resting on my shoulders, his gaze locked on mine. I propped myself up on my hands, my legs wide as I moved in and out of him.

"Mine," I said, my hips rolling as I buried my shaft all the way inside him. My movements became jerkier as my thrusts multiplied, and I knew I was getting close. Robert kept his hands away from his thickening cock, as if the slightest touch would make him shoot, but also because I hadn't told him he could touch it. I slowed to a crawl, leaning in to kiss him, our breath mingling.

"Your hole is so open right now. I can just slide in and out."

He nodded, his lips parted, his breathing ragged.

I couldn't maintain this pace any longer. I picked up speed, and the wet sound of my cock filling him over and over was so fucking erotic. "Oh, God, listen to that."

"Sir… please…" The entreaty in Robert's eyes unraveled me, and I nodded.

"Touch yourself."

He wrapped his fingers around his leaking shaft, and tugged on it as I rocked into him, ready to send both of us over the edge. All too soon, I shot my load deep inside him, and seconds later he came too, more cum than I'd seen in all our encounters.

I buried my face in his neck with a groan, my cock throbbing as I spilled into him, his arms locked around my neck as he clung to me, shaking, gasping, lost in his own explosive orgasm. And when we were both done, I lay on him, his legs caging my waist, and we kissed, the heat receding, my sweat chilling in the breeze.

Oh Lord, that was…

I gazed into his eyes. "That was epic." Except the words felt cheap.

It had been amazing, veering away from a magnificent fuck

into far more complex territory, leaving me a little lost and dazed.

He chuckled. "I think I'm getting too old for fucking on the ground, even with a blanket." He winced.

I helped him to sit, then shifted position to sit behind him, leaning against the solid warm rock, his head against my shoulder, my legs holding him, one arm around his front across his collarbones, the other across his chest, my hand over his heart.

It was perfect. I cradled him, listening to his breathing as it slipped back into his normal rhythm, feeling his heart beating. I brushed my lips against his ear.

"So... do you think they heard that?"

Robert laughed, and it vibrated through him.

I figured that was a yes.

Supper was over, the sun had set, and everyone was seated around the campfires. Walt had brought along a guitar, and was strumming it softly. The others stared into the firelight, some deep in thought, others talking quietly.

Robert sat beside me, lost in his own contemplation. Unseen by the others, I took his hand in mine, and he gazed at me, lips parted. I smiled and tightened my fingers around his.

Then we heard it, the mournful cries I recognized instantly.

Teague moved swiftly, sending out four hands armed with rifles. Robert didn't shift from my side. I heard the sound of hooves as the riders headed out, and a while later, a few shots rang.

About fifteen minutes after that, Teague and one of the hands returned.

"We've routed them," he told Robert. "Kyle, Owen, and Declan are keeping watch, in case they return." He rejoined us around the fire.

I glanced at the faces lit up by the firelight. "Where's Garrett?"

Butch chuckled. "Asleep. I think the last three days wore him out."

"Hey, he did good," Zeeb remonstrated. "He's a helluva lot more confident than he was when he first came to Salvation."

"I agree." I smiled at Zeeb. "And most of that is down to you."

"I second that," Teague added.

"Me too," Robert said with a smile. "You did a really good job."

Zeeb's eyes lit up and his face glowed.

Matt got up from his camping chair and went over to the chuckwagon to bring us a fresh pot of coffee. When he'd refilled the cups, he sat down.

I gazed at the men sitting around the fire. It had only been two weeks—well, almost—but I felt as if I knew them so well.

Robert's family.

I sipped my coffee before speaking. "So… you think you'll stay at Salvation for a while?" I aimed the question at the assembled men.

Butch snorted. "Until he fires me." He pointed at Robert, who laughed.

"Don't go busting any more heads with pool cues, and I'll think about it."

"Seriously though…" Butch's face grew solemn. "These guys are my family." He stared at them. "Hey, you know you are. Some of you have been around a while—" He glanced at Paul, Zeeb, and Teague—"And some of you are new—" Another glance at Matt and Walt—"but of all the guys who work on the ranch? Yeah, you're my family."

Beside me, Zeeb sighed. "I'm not usually the kind of guy who gets sentimental, but yeah, Butch nailed it."

Paul nodded. "A piece of my heart belongs here."

Teague stared into the flames. "Salvation has been my home since I was sixteen. It's also been my family—a far better family than the one I left behind in Wyoming."

Zeeb peered at me. "And what about you?"

"What about me?"

Butch cleared his throat. "I think what he's asking is, if we're gonna see you around here again."

I glanced at Robert, and my heart skipped a beat. "I'm going to try to visit as often as I can."

"Is it me, or has the Salvation family just grown?" Zeeb said with a chuckle.

I smiled. "I'd say yes." I was still gazing at Robert.

Teague let out a snort. "Okay, I'll say this if no one else will. You two—get a tent." Everyone laughed.

Robert grinned. "You know what? That's a damn good idea." He got to his feet—then looked me in the eye. "You coming?"

And then it hit me. We were out in the open. No more hiding, no more pretense.

I beamed. "Yes, I am."

He pulled me to my feet, and I grinned at the hands. "Night, boys. Don't let the mosquitoes bite."

As we strolled toward our tent, I caught Zeeb's mutter.

"Damn, I *knew* I should've brought ear plugs."

Thursday, June 23
Toby

Robert rode alongside me as we headed back to Salvation.

"It took us two days to reach the south pasture," I remarked. The second group of cattle and riders had reached us late Wednesday. "Can the horses make it back in just one day?" It had to be more than thirty miles.

He chuckled. "A good trail horse in decent shape can manage fifty miles in a day."

"Can't believe this week has gone so fast."

Robert lapsed into silence. Come to think of it, he'd been quiet all morning.

"What's wrong?" Not that I didn't have a good idea.

"We've got two nights left. And yeah, I know what you said, about coming back and all, but that doesn't mean I'm not going to miss you."

"I know. I'll miss you too."

He glanced at me. "Really?"

My chest tightened, and it came as something of a shock to realize I'd spoken the truth. "Yes, really."

"Then…" He bit his lip. "Would you do something for me?"

I blinked. "What did you have in mind?"

"Give me tomorrow. Just us. A whole day with nothing but touching, fucking, sleeping…"

Oh God, I loved the sound of that.

"You got a guest room I could use?"

His eyes widened. "You don't want to sleep with me?"

That earned him an eye-roll. "No, I was thinking of putting the sling up in there. It could be our playroom for when I visit. The chest could go in there too."

His smile made something inside me turn over. "I like that. Our room."

I liked it too.

Except it was more than liking the idea of having our own space. What surged through me was warmth at the prospect of seeing him again, spending time with him, talking with him…

Avoiding emotional attachment seemed to have fallen by the wayside, and I didn't know what to make of that.

CHAPTER TWENTY-EIGHT

Friday, June 24
Robert

I tapped on the bedroom door. "Can I come in now?"

From inside, I heard Toby's laugh. "Did anyone ever tell you patience is a virtue?"

"Yeah, but it's not one of mine."

More laughter.

"You've been in there for an hour," I groused. Not only that, he'd taken delivery of a mysterious package that morning, and I was dying of curiosity.

"More like forty-five minutes, but who's counting? And we just spent all morning in bed, so you have nothing to complain about."

All I knew was, the precious minutes I had left with him were slowly ticking away.

Then the door opened, and he stood there in nothing but a pair of jeans, his feet bare. He grinned. "Okay—*now* you can come in." He stood aside and I entered, noticing the black tarp under my socked feet, covering most of the wooden floor.

"Is this what arrived this morning?"

"Uh-huh. I ordered it before we left for the south pasture." Another grin. "Once I saw *that*, I knew it'd come in handy."

That was the sling, set up in the corner, its chrome bars and metal chains gleaming, the leather seat cleaned. Then I noticed the chest below the window. Against the opposite wall stood a table, on which sat ropes, lube, cuffs, a blindfold... The bed had been stripped back to the mattress, folded towels at the foot of it.

Now it looked like a playroom.

Toby closed the door behind us. "Matt won't be here for hours. Lunch is already made, waiting for us in the fridge. So it's just us." He took a step toward me. "Okay… We started the day with a sixty-nine. I fucked you in the shower. I ate your ass… Have you thought about what else you'd like to do? I mean, I have an idea what *I'd* like to do but this is *your* day, after all."

I wanted it to be *our* day.

And suddenly, I knew how I could make that happen.

My heart pounded. "Yes, I *have* thought about it. I want you to… to fist me."

Then my heart sank as I watched his expression change.

Toby

Oh fuck.

I needed to tread delicately, but he had to know the truth. Fisting? I have to be in the mood to do that. And it wasn't something you could just spring on someone at the last minute before a scene.

I took a deep breath. "To be honest? I don't think I'm up for that." He swallowed, and I let out a sigh. "I'm sorry, but that's a session that requires planning… I had something more relaxed and… sensual in mind."

Robert said nothing for a moment, and then he nodded. "You're right. I should've mentioned it before now."

Yeah, he was a good experienced submissive, even if he was still a little rusty. I'd known a few who would've thrown a hissy fit— for all of five seconds before they could either control themselves or find their way back to the door.

He gave me an inquiring glance. "Sensual sounds good though. What were you thinking of?"

I pointed to the table, where the rope lay in a coil. "Shibari." I searched his face for a sign.

Robert shuddered out a breath. "Actually? That sounds exactly what I need right now."

I smiled. "I think I already knew that." I gestured to his clothing. "Undress." I could have done it myself, but I liked to keep bodily contact to a minimum prior to a Shibari scene. It lent greater impact to those times when I did touch the sub's body. I maintained eye contact, waiting for him to begin.

Robert breathed deeply, then unbuttoned his shirt.

I stood motionless as he undressed, watching as he folded his clothes and placed them in a pile on the floor. He was quiet, as if contemplating what was about to happen.

Perfect.

When he was naked, he stood before me, his head bowed, arms by his sides, waiting for me. I picked up a fifty-foot length of jute I'd found in the chest.

"So… I'm going to be decorating you."

"Do you have a particular pattern in mind, Sir?" His voice was low.

I nodded. "Nothing too elaborate. Hishi Karada." He smiled. "Aha. You're familiar with that." It was a simple technique that could be used to make all sorts of designs.

"Yes, Sir. It's been a while, though, and he only did it the one time."

I looked him in the eye. "If something feels a little off, or uncomfortable, if you experience any tingling sensations, then you tell me." I lifted his chin with my fingers. "I'm going to be focused on *you*—your body, your posture, your breathing. I want to hear every noise that comes out of here." I touched his lips. "I want to feel the goosebumps that crawl over your skin. You'll have my full attention. There won't be any distractions." I kissed him on the lips. "And most of all, I want you to enjoy it." I cocked my head to one side. "Have you ever watched yourself get tied up?"

His eyes widened. "No, Sir."

That decided it for me. Forcing a sub to watch himself be manipulated was such a power move, and most subs loved it.

I hoped Robert would too.

I led him toward the free-standing full-length mirror. I'd left it there, knowing it would come in handy. "You don't have to watch all the time, but when I tell you to open your eyes, do as I say, okay?"

Another soft sigh. "Yes, Sir."

I could tell by his stillness he was ready.

I began by creating the core harness. I loved the simplicity of the Hishi Karada, a diamond-based pattern that encased the body, created from one single long rope. I pulled the rope over Robert's head, leaving a loop between his shoulder blades, one that I would come back to in order to ensure it remained in the right position. Above the loop was a knot.

I tied the first overhand knot, positioning it below the clavicle, and yet another layer of stillness settled on him. "Good boy." I added knots down the front of his body, making each one in the same way, maintaining the spacing between them. He held himself so still, his breathing steady, calm, his eyes closed.

I took a moment to study him, the man ready to submit himself to me, to trust me enough to relax and enjoy the sensations. This was always a special moment.

Robert's submission was as heady to me as it was to him.

Then it was time to slip the tails of the rope between his legs, on either side of his balls, and up his back to pull them through my first loop. I gave it a tug, knowing he'd feel it tighten against his skin, then loosened it a little. I didn't want too much tension around the groin area. It also gave me scope to move the tails out of the way, for reasons I was keeping to myself.

Once I'd repositioned the knots on the front, I stepped behind him, leaned in, and whispered, "Open your eyes."

Robert stared at his reflection, and a shiver rippled through him, accompanied by a moan.

The sound of that keening groan was music to my ears.

How does he see himself in this moment?

Then his eyes met mine in the mirror, and I knew.

The rope that bound him also freed him. It represented all the physical and mental ties that made up his life—the ranch, loss, need, longing, sadness, grief—but in that one heart-stopping moment, in that brief span of time when our gazes met, I knew he owned every one of those ties in ways only a sub could.

Control was as much his as it was mine.

Then I gave myself a mental shake. There was a beautiful man waiting for me to finish decorating him.

I was now ready to add the back and sides. I split the tails, bringing each one around to the front on either side of his body.

I met his gaze. "Arms out to the side, straight. Keep them there. And if they dip, you'll know about it." He'd feel my hand on his ass.

I hooked the tails through the center line, allowing the rope to glide over his nipples, eliciting a shiver. I loved to hear the hitches in a sub's breathing, those quiet little moans they couldn't suppress. There was nothing sexual in what I was doing, yet I knew the feeling of rope sliding over Robert's body, my hands on him, my nails grazing his skin, my lips or breath caressing his neck or back as I tied him, all of it would combine to send him into a state of arousal. I rarely talked while I did this, but that was because I couldn't think of anything else, anchored as I was in the moment. I watched his reactions, knowing the feel of the ropes would ground him, sending endorphins rushing through his head and body. Shibari wasn't fast, or passionate. If anything, it was more of a meditation, for both Dom and sub alike.

His eyes were closed once more, and his almost meditative expression, along with the goosebumps that bloomed over his skin when I trailed fingers over it, spoke louder than words ever could.

As I fashioned the harness around him, I noted yet more goosebumps. "Watch me," I said in a firm tone.

He opened his eyes, and his nipples grew taut, standing proud, his shivers multiplying. I didn't need music—I was creating my own. Tying up a submissive was like playing the cello, finding the right speed with which to move the bow across the strings, to provide the most natural resonance, without it being too loud or too soft, where it might disrupt the flow. I was aiming for a perfect level of continuous stimulation, building the intensity of the moment with him. I wanted him to mentally let go of everything else—even for a short while. I wanted him to feel only my body, my hands, my physical warmth as I moved around him, my breath on his skin.

Robert's breathing caught and he closed his eyes as I pulled the rope tight. I knew he was relishing the squeeze, the feeling of being held, comforted… I loved the shuddering breath that escaped him when I looped the rope through the center line, adjusting it, then tightening, as the hug started to set in. His breathing became more controlled, but the sight of his closed eyes, the unconscious smile that played about his lips, his utterly relaxed posture… all of it pointed to a state of heightened arousal. He seemed to be deep into what I called rope space, and that was confirmed when I touched him to turn him around. The sudden feeling of my warm hands on him made him moan.

When I was almost finished, I stood back to admire my handiwork. He'd kept his arms rock steady. "You can lower your arms now." When he did so, moving slowly, I shifted closer, letting him feel the warmth from my body. I leaned in and whispered, "Open your eyes, boy. See how I've used your body for my designs."

His eyes popped open, then I watched in the mirror as his pupils dilated.

"Oh fuck, that's hot," he groaned.

I had to agree. The tight lacing of the jute rope made a mosaic around his body, finished with an intricate diamond pattern down the center of his abs, the final one shaping his cock and balls.

He trembled, and I pressed my lips to his shoulder, feeling the shudder that ran the length of his body. I dragged my nails over his arms, down his back, then reached around from behind him to play with his nipples, teasing them, flicking them. His shaking intensified, as did his moans. His cock was rock-hard, leaking pre-cum, and when it lurched, I knew he was probably one good stroke from coming right there and then.

I had to work fast.

I seized the lube from the table, unzipped my jeans, freed my dick, and slicked it up. I slid my arm around his torso, my hand to his neck, firmly pressing into his pulse points, while with the other, I grabbed the rope through his crack and hooked it around his ass cheek. With that out of the way, I reached around him to his nipple and gave it a firm pinch, pulling a groan from him. Then I pressed the head of my dick between his cheeks and slid into him in one smooth glide.

The swift penetration, combined with watching himself get fucked, was the overload I'd hoped it would be. Robert shot his load all over the mirror, violent tremors shaking him with each spurt of his cock, until I had to hold him upright because his knees gave out, my own dick throbbing inside him, filling him.

As the tremors ebbed, I kissed his neck, holding him to me, aware of his pounding heart, his staccato breaths. "I've got you," I murmured. When he could stand, I kissed him on the lips. "You were awesome." I eased out of him, stifling a moan at the sight of my cum dripping from his hole.

He turned his head to stare at his reflection. "You don't have to take it off right away, do you?"

I laughed. "No, you get to admire yourself for as long as you like. And when you're done, I'll remove the rope nice and slow, and you'll get to see my marks on your skin." I loved seeing the beautiful patterns produced by the snug rope.

Then I'd hold him, stroke him, kiss him, and maybe even take a nap with him.

Perfect end to a wonderful scene, and an amazing vacation, one that promised so much more to come—provided we could make it work.

I was determined to give it one hundred percent. I didn't want to lose this—to lose him.

Chapter twenty-nine

Robert

I opened my eyes and stretched. I loved a Shibari scene once things started getting tight. Yes, there was the hug, but I associated that sensation with being an extension of Toby, knowing he was transforming my body into a work of his art, his design. I willingly gave myself into his control because I knew, instinctively, the result would be beautiful.

And because his hands on my skin? Hot as fuck.

Toby lay next to me on his back, still sleeping. He seemed to be dreaming, and it was obviously a good dream—his dick twitched, jerking up from his belly. The temptation to take that firm head into my mouth was huge, but I pushed it aside.

Not without permission.

I had to admit, when it came to rope, Toby was way better than Kevin. The rope harness didn't look all that different to when Kevin had done it, but the way he'd applied it, the continuous stimulation, nothing overtly sexual but everything conspiring to heighten my arousal.

And yet…

Yes, it had been an amazing scene. *So why do I feel so fucking low?*

Toby stirred, and I froze. When it became clear he wasn't about to wake up, I eased out of the bed as carefully as I could. I needed to think, and I couldn't do that when he provided such a delicious distraction. I grabbed a pair of sweats and a tee, and crept out of my bedroom.

I went downstairs into the kitchen, and put on a fresh pot of coffee. I stared out of the window, my head in turmoil.

Why can't I just be happy?

The scene had been wonderful, the cuddling afterward just as good. No, it was *all* good—and it was about to be over.

Toby's plan sounded awesome, but… *He won't be here. It won't be the same. Yes, the scene was amazing, but I won't get that again until his next visit—whenever that may be.*

I wasn't an idiot. I knew I was falling for him. I'd known that for a while.

Falling? Who was I kidding. Fallen, smitten…

I poured myself a coffee, and went out onto the front porch. I sat in a rocker, gazing at the ranch. What I'd had these past five years? I really couldn't call it living. And what Toby was offering… I wasn't sure I wanted that if there wouldn't be a deeper connection between us. I already knew avoiding emotional attachment was a lost cause. I also knew what lay at the root of my concerns.

I'm putting too much emphasis on Toby.

I'm attaching too much importance to what we have.

I'm becoming codependent.

I couldn't keep doing this. I couldn't keep thinking of *every single* possibility, and analyzing it. *Is it good? Is it bad?* Lord, I felt like Voldemort, living a half-life.

The door opened and I froze. Toby stepped out onto the porch, dressed in his jeans and a shirt, a cup of coffee in his hand.

"I was surprised not to see you when I woke up. How long have you been out here?"

"Long enough to do some thinking."

He gazed at me, suddenly still. "That sounds ominous."

There was so little time left. If I was going to say something, it needed to be soon. I couldn't leave it until he was getting into the truck to head into Bozeman for the shuttle. Even worse—until he was home in San Francisco, and I dropped it all on him via a phone call.

I pointed to the rocker. "Sit. We need to talk."

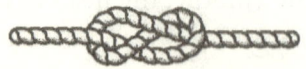

Toby

All of a sudden I had a severe case of déjà vu. *This is not going to be good.* "Okay."

Robert wasn't looking at me, and that was a bad sign right there. "This... this isn't going to work."

Oh fuck.

"Excuse me?" I fought to maintain a facade of calm. *Don't do this. Please.*

"This whole long-distance thing."

The temptation to contradict him and tell him yes, it *could* work was huge, but instead I bit my tongue. "Tell me why." *Give me something to work with, so I can prove you wrong.*

It was nothing like the conversation with Tyler—my heart hadn't been involved then, I'd remained cool, objective...

That had vanished the moment Robert said *this isn't going to work.*

"When we started this, you were honest. You don't do boyfriends. You prefer sex without attachment."

"I thought that was how you felt too."

"It was," he protested. "But... it isn't now."

"And that changes things?"

He nodded. "If I'm honest, I don't feel you're in this for the long haul. And now I've had time to think about it, a virtual relationship—a relationship by remote—is not sustainable in my opinion. Nor do I think it would be satisfying." He gazed at me with stricken eyes. "So why do it? Why torture ourselves?"

Aw shit.

I wanted to reply, to tell him it was okay, that I really *was* in this for the long haul, but... How much faith would he lose in me as a Dom if he saw me supposedly break one of my own rules? Robert craved stability in his Dom, and rule-breaking would only tell him I couldn't promise to be what he needed.

That wasn't stability.

My head was spinning. I'd come to Salvation to experience a life far removed from my own, and Robert had… well, he'd snuck up on me. I hadn't seen him coming. And now he was here, a part of me, what burned between us was so different to what I was used to, and for once I didn't know how to make it all better.

I forced myself to remain calm. "Do you want time to think about it?"

"That's the point. I *keep* thinking about it. That's all I do. I think… I think I need to take a step back."

No, this was definitely *not* going to be good.

He shuddered out a breath. "Would you… would you spend tonight in the bunkhouse? I need some space, some time to think."

I inhaled deeply. "Okay. I respect the fact you need some thinking space. So I'll take a page out of your book. I'll take a step back."

This was not looking hopeful.

"You put your cards on the table," I continued. "And you've given me something to think about." Only I didn't *want* to think about it, because doing that made my stomach roil. "But I *will* say this. You've got me all wrong." That part about me not wanting to be in this for the long haul? Yeah, that hurt. "So fine. I'll go down to the bunkhouse. I'll give you tonight. But I'll be back in the morning before I leave, and we can talk again."

The expression in his eyes told me there was little chance of any change of mind.

I got up, and walked down the path toward the ranch, my head in a mess.

Now what?

I couldn't think straight either. My mind kept replaying his words, over and over, and underneath it all was that quiet voice, the one that told me not to let go, to hold on to him, because I *needed* him.

There was no one around, so I figured everyone was in the bunkhouse. The last thing I wanted was to be around people, but I had little choice if I was going to sleep there tonight.

Let's get this over with. After the thinly veiled—and outright—threats during the cattle drive, this was not going to be pretty.

As I walked in, Matt glanced in my direction. "How was lunch?"

"I wouldn't know. I didn't eat it. We fell asleep." And that empty feeling in the pit of my stomach could have been hunger, but I knew better.

Butch snorted. "The conversation was that stimulating? Or did he wear you out?"

His snark went over my head. There was too much going on in there.

Zeeb regarded me thoughtfully. "What's wrong?" His voice was quiet, nothing like his usual loud outbursts.

And just like that, a hush fell, and all eyes turned in my direction.

Fuck.

Teague's gaze flickered in the direction of the house. "Is Robert okay?"

"He's fine. But don't go up there right now," I added quickly. "He needs some space. I'll be eating down here this evening."

Teague's face fell. "Shit. I knew it. I *knew* this would happen."

"*What's* happened?" Butch demanded.

"Whatever it was, it's none of your fucking business." I put a rein on my emotions. "Look, your boss needs time to think. I'm willing to respect that, to give him some space—you should too."

"What does he need to think about?" Paul's brow furrowed. "What did you do?"

"Me? I… I didn't do anything." All I'd done was make a suggestion, one I thought had been enthusiastically received—until Robert's mind had kicked in and analyzed the fuck out of it.

I couldn't blame him for that. All I could do was hope.

"But…" Walt appeared confused. "It was going so well. He was *happy*, goddammit."

"Yeah, he was," Butch confirmed. His gaze narrowed. "So why isn't he happy now?"

I lost it.

"For Christ's sake, anyone who thinks two people from totally different worlds can make it work just like that is delusional, okay?"

Butch looked as though I'd just kicked his puppy. "So it *is* over?"

No, it isn't, I wanted to yell. *I just need to give Robert time to realize that.*

"I'll talk to him again tomorrow before I leave." I wasn't answering his question, but it was the best I could do.

Zeeb stared at me. "Then you *are* leaving."

"Yes. I have a life in California. He has his life here." I couldn't take anymore. I walked out of the bunkhouse and headed for the paddock. I needed air.

Fuck. Robert was up there, hurting, and here was I, hurting people I'd come to like and trust, and that wasn't good.

From behind me came footsteps and the sound of hooves on gravel. I turned to find Paul leading Lightning toward me, saddled. "Here." He held out the reins. "Go for a ride. You need him right now."

"Are we talking about the horse—or the boss?"

"Both?"

I wasn't in the mood, until it struck me Paul was right—I needed this.

I led Lightning to the mounting block, and got on. "Come on, boy, let's get out of here." I trotted toward the meadow, heading for the trail that led to the creek. It felt good to be riding, to feel Lightning move beneath me, to feel the wind in my face.

I missed this so much. These last two weeks had given it back to me, and I'd rediscovered the joy I'd once felt.

And if I didn't do something, I'd lose it all over again.

When I got to the creek, I dismounted, and stared across at the cabin.

You may be gone, Kevin, but you sure left a mess behind you.

It all came down to one thing. I wasn't ready to let it—let *him*—go.

I stroked Lightning's neck. "What do I do, boy? Tell him he's wrong? Because I don't think his head is in the right place to accept that."

There was nothing for it but to go back to California—after one last attempt to talk to him in the morning before I left.

I'm not giving up.

Saturday, June 25

I threw my bags into the trunk. "I guess this is it." The atmosphere over breakfast had been distinctly frosty. My flight was the first to take off: Declan and Garrett wouldn't be leaving until the afternoon. The way I was feeling, I was glad to be getting out of there.

Zeeb and Butch strolled out of the bunkhouse to join us.

"You going up to the house before you leave?" Teague asked.

I nodded. "I said I would." *And if Robert has slept well, he might be thinking more clearly.*

He gestured to Butch. "Okay then. Butch will drive you up to the house, and when you're done, he'll take you to the airport. Forget about the shuttle."

"You just want to make sure I get on that plane, don't you?"

Zeeb huffed. "Actually? You've got it backward. I think the idea is to make sure Butch is available to bring you back in case you change your mind."

That knot in my stomach tightened. "Not gonna happen. I have things to do back home."

Except that was a fucking lie. Sean didn't need me. He could run the club single-handed.

So why am I going back there?

I handed my hat to Paul. "Thanks for the loan."

He smiled. "You look after those cowboy boots. And this isn't goodbye. We're going to see you again."

I loved his conviction.

I got into the truck, but none of them waved me off. I didn't blame them. They thought I'd broken their boss's heart. Butch drove along the back road that led up to the house. "I'll wait here," he said as I got out.

I walked around the house to find Robert waiting for me on the front porch.

I wasn't about to waste time. "Have you changed your mind?"

He shook his head. "No."

I walked over to him. "This is *not* over, okay? I don't know when this will be resolved, but it's not over." I couldn't help myself. I leaned in and kissed him on the lips. "Goodbye—for now," I whispered. And before he had a chance to say anything else, I turned and walked back to the truck.

Butch glanced at me. "We still going to the airport?"

"Yes, we are." There was only the slightest tremor in my voice.

He drove in silence, and I stared out of the window, my chest tight, feeling miserable. Could I have reacted differently? Possibly. All I knew was, I had to respect his wishes.

We'd been driving for about ten minutes when Butch cleared his throat. "You wanna know what I think?"

I was amazed he'd kept silent for that long. "No, but I'm sure you're going to tell me."

"You and the boss... You may be from different worlds, like you said, but you're still meant to be together. I feel that in my bones."

Lord, I wanted to believe that too.

"Our differences are significant, but they're not insurmountable." I sighed. "Sorry, Butch, but this situation can't be fixed with a magic wand or even wishful thinking. Thanks for the advice, but you need to let us figure it out."

"As long as you *do* figure it out."

That was the hope I was clinging to.

Robert

I went into the playroom, where the chest sat below the window.

That's it. He's gone.

I felt as if I was strapped to a teeter totter, vacillating between my emotions telling me I'd just made a big mistake, and logic assuring me I'd done the right thing.

I didn't know which to believe.

I pulled my phone from my pocket and hit speed dial. Diana answered within three rings. "What's up?"

"Toby just left."

"Well, that's what guests do when their vacation comes to an end."

I said nothing.

"Wait—am I missing something here?"

"You know that 'power dynamic' you were talking about?" I let her do the math.

There was a pause. "Toby? And you let him *leave?*"

"It's not that simple, okay?"

"Well, couldn't you have... I don't know... tied him to the bed, or something? That's what you *do*, right?"

Despite my aching heart, I had to laugh. "You might be a woman of the world, sis, but you don't know as much as you *think* you know." *Besides, I wouldn't be the one with the rope.*

"And now you're miserable. Don't try denying it—I can hear it in your voice. Damn him for leaving."

"Don't... don't say that, all right? It's not just Toby leaving, okay? I... I've been unhappy for a while now. This life... It's getting me down. Maybe it's time for a change."

She went quiet for a moment. "Okay, I'm going to tell you something that maybe I should have told you a long time ago."

My stomach clenched. "Just tell me it's not bad news." I didn't think I could cope with that.

"Newt is seeing a therapist. He's taking meds—for depression."

"Aw sis." She didn't need to hear my problems. She had plenty of her own.

"Do you know what I never understood until recently? Depression doesn't just affect the sufferer—it affects everyone around them. So yeah, I'm living with it too. There are days when I can't get a smile out of him, and while I might've woken up happy, his mood kills all my joy. Not that he can help it, okay? It's not his fault. And he will *never* learn how this makes me feel. I've been to a few sessions with him, and he's getting there, slowly. The meds help. But..." She paused. "For a while there, Newt was talking about selling the dude ranch, about moving..."

Shit.

"And the thought of you selling up too? Okay, I know you haven't said that, but you're *thinking* about it, right? Well, that makes me miserable. When Dad left us the ranch and you bought me out, that was a key moment. It meant we could open the dude ranch. But Newt wasn't thinking straight when he talked about selling up, just like I don't think *you* are right now. So I'm going to give you the same advice his therapist gave him. Do *not* make any major decisions based on emotion, because right now? Your head is not in a good place. Give it some time."

I breathed a little easier. "That makes sense."

Another pause. "Are you two really over?"

"I don't know. We'll have to wait and see. I went into this determined to stay detached, to keep my emotions out of it, to keep it just about the—"

"Power dynamic—or the sex?"

I huffed. "Both. But it didn't matter in the long run, because I fell for him, so fucking hard."

"You'll bounce back."

"We'll see." Lord, I loved her optimism. I wanted to believe her. Maybe I *would* bounce back. But would Toby be there when I did?

Chapter Thirty

Friday, July 8
Toby

I crossed the street and stopped in front of the blacked-out windows of the club.

Why does he want to see me?

I'd phoned Sean on my return, but as yet, I hadn't been anywhere near the club. My head was too full of Salvation, the hands, the landscape, the vast skies… Robert.

I miss him.

Two weeks. Two whole weeks and I still fucking *ached*. The last thing I wanted was a business meeting, but Sean had insisted.

Let's get it over with.

I walked into the club and headed for the office. It wasn't long before the comments started.

"Hey, where have *you* been?"

"We thought you'd been eaten by a grizzly."

I ignored them and pointed to the office door. "Is he in there?"

Casey nodded. "He said he was waiting for you." He cocked his head to one side. "You okay?"

I was far from okay, but I wasn't about to tell him that. "I'm fine," I lied. I opened the door and went inside. Sean was at his desk, his phone pressed to his ear. He glanced up, and waved me into a chair. I sat, and he continued his conversation.

I had to admire him. Sean knew how to run a club. That was the whole reason we'd gone into business together. I was the silent partner who'd come up with the money, and so far I'd made back my investment and then some. Sean did all the day-to-day stuff, but he didn't play. He left that to me.

I hadn't played for a while.

Not since a certain Shibari scene.

He finished his call and leaned back in his chair. "So… you're alive."

"We spoke, remember? You knew that already." I gestured to the door. "I didn't see Tyler out there. He and Will still loved up?"

"Tyler's fine—no, he's more than that. I don't think I've ever seen him this happy."

"Well, that's what love'll do for you."

"But I didn't get you in here to talk about Tyler." His eyes widened. "Unless he's the reason you're all bent out of shape. That's not the problem, is it? You're not pissed because he's found someone who fits him better than you did?"

I barked out a laugh. "For God's sake, why would I be pissed? I fucking *told* him he'd find a Dom who'd love him the way I couldn't."

"Then what the fuck is wrong? I haven't seen you since Memorial Day. You've been back from Montana for what, two weeks?" I nodded. "And in that time, all we've done is talk on the phone—once. You haven't been to the club. Hell, you were missing in action for the Fourth of July party. Epic night."

"What did I miss? Did someone tie Deke up in a Star-Spangled Banner?"

He frowned. "Okay, something's *not* right. What the fuck happened in Montana?"

I blinked. "Who said anything did?"

Sean got up from his chair, went over to the filing cabinet, opened it, and removed a bottle and two glasses. He peered at me. "You want one?"

"Sure."

He poured about a finger's width into both glasses, then handed me one. He retook his chair, his elbows on the arms, his glass in both hands. "Okay, so Tyler's not the problem. Let's cut to the chase." He stared at me, his eyes flinty. "You're not happy here. Any moron can see that. Before you went off to be a cowboy for two weeks, I saw you occasionally. Okay, so you don't *have* to be here—but at least you showed your face—or your ass, sometimes, especially when you wore those chaps." His eyes widened again. "Did you get to wear chaps down on the ranch?"

I glared at him. "Christ, you're like that dog in that movie, *Up*. I expect to hear you yell 'squirrel' any second now. Where is this going?"

That flinty stare was back. "I thought we were friends."

I arched my eyebrows. "Have we broken up or something? Did I miss a memo?"

He sighed. "Look, I know you put up these walls to avoid close intimate relationships, but you know what? People *do* have them. And they are *not* a bad thing."

I went cold, because *fuck*, he'd nailed my existence so far on this fucking planet—well, at least until a cowboy with a gray beard and a mat of salt-and-pepper chest hair rode into my life. Because what we'd shared was *definitely* close and intimate.

"I've always wondered, you know," Sean murmured.

"Wondered what?"

"Why you are the way you are. You know, no attachments… There must be a reason for it."

I arched my eyebrows. "Why does there need to be a reason? How many gay men do you know who sleep around, with no desire for any attachments? And it's the same in the BDSM community… Not everyone wants a full-on relationship. Not everyone meets that special someone."

"So are you going to tell me what happened in Montana or not?"

God, the irony.

I coughed. "I seem to have met that special someone."

Sean's jaw dropped. "Whoa. Okay, *that* I did not expect. And?"

"And nothing." I didn't want to discuss it.

He took a sip from his glass. "This ranch you went to—what was it called again?"

"Salvation." I narrowed my gaze. "What's this 'again' crap? I never told you its name."

"And this guy you met… he works at the ranch?"

"He's the boss." I paused. "And he's submissive." I told him about Robert, his past…

"I never thought I'd see this day." I gave him an inquiring glance, and he grinned. "Those walls… They came tumbling down, didn't they?"

I shivered. "With a vengeance."

"What happened?" His voice softened.

"I suggested we could have a D/s relationship, long distance. I thought with enough determination, we could make it happen. Hell, I *so* wanted it to happen." I swallowed. "Then he changed his mind. He doesn't think we can make it work." I sighed. "You know what? I never saw him coming."

"From what you've said, he's a little messed up right now, so I get why you didn't want to screw with his head even more by telling him you'd fallen for him, not when you'd already told him that was something you didn't do. That's not a good base to start a more involved D/s relationship, not when his head is already all over the place over losing his precious Dom." I gazed at him incredulously, and he smiled. "Don't look so surprised. I might not play anymore, but I did once. You don't forget shit like that. And I'm not sure a long-distance relationship would work either. I knew a guy who tried that. Said his sub was making all the right noises on the phone, in texts, etcetera, but… his heart wasn't in it, and it didn't last." He leaned forward. "You know what *really* gets me? You didn't have to come back here, so why did you?"

I arched my eyebrows. "Excuse me?" Except hadn't I had that same thought, the day I left Salvation?

"You heard me. Your future does *not* revolve around this place. You invested in it, sure, but—"

"I get it. You want to buy me out? Is that it?" *And what would I do if he did?*

The thought was there in my head in a heartbeat.

Go back to Montana, you dumbass.

He scowled. "*Jesus*, you're prickly."

My head was spinning, and I had to get out of there.

"You know what? I don't have to listen to this." I got up and went toward the door.

"You wanna know something, Toby? You've changed."

I already knew that—I didn't need Sean to point it out.

I wanted to head back to my apartment, shut the front door, and not think about fucking Montana.

Yeah right. Fat chance of *that* happening.

Friday, July 15

I sprawled on my couch, my phone in my hand, scrolling through my photos: Mirror Lake, with its calm waters and lush trees; Paul smiling as he groomed Rusty; Zeeb pulling a funny face; Butch posing; and Robert...

The sight of him made my stomach clench.

Should I call him?

I wanted to hear his voice, his laugh. More than that, I wanted to see that familiar twinkle in his eye, the one that reflected his sense of humor, his wit...

The door buzzer sounded, and I sighed. *Now what?* I went over to it and pressed the intercom. "Who is it?"

"It's Sean. Let me in."

I deliberated telling him I was busy for all of three seconds before pressing the button. Then I opened the front door and waited for him to climb the stairs. When he came into sight, I plunged ahead. "If you've come to have another go at me..."

He held his hands up. "Hey, I come in peace."

I let him into the apartment and closed the door behind us. "I just made some coffee. Want some?"

"Please."

I went over to the coffee pot and poured out two cups.

Sean sat on the couch, glancing at my phone. I placed the cups on the coffee table, then snatched up the phone.

He crossed his legs at the ankles. "Tell me about Salvation."

I arched my eyebrows. "Google it if you're so interested."

"I'm serious. Tell me about the place."

He wasn't going to budge an inch.

I sat on the arm of the couch. "It's… less of a business, and more of a family. Some of the hands have been there for decades. You get the feeling they all have a story to tell."

"These guys have names?"

I pulled up the photos on my phone, and showed him each man, with the exception of Robert. "They're a mixed bunch. And maybe *Brokeback Mountain* was on the button, because most of them are queer."

"Seriously? You mess around with any of them?" He pointed to Paul's picture. "Because *that* guy is fucking hot."

"No! Nothing like that. They… they were fun to be around. We had a laugh. I only fell for one of them."

"Wow." I gazed at him inquiringly, and Sean smiled. "Sounds to me like you connected with these guys."

I rolled my eyes. "I *connect* with people," I air-quoted.

"*Sure* you do—and you're usually wearing leather at the time. This sounds like a whole *new* set of connections, one that doesn't involve D/s. What about Robert? What does he look like?"

I hesitated before scrolling to a photo of Robert I'd taken at Mirror Lake. Sean studied it for a moment. "How old is he?"

I stared at him. "Does it matter? Because *I* don't care how old he is, so why should you?"

And suddenly he was studying me. "You really do feel something for this guy, don't you? Which reassures me I'm doing the right thing."

"What are you talking about?"

He reached into the pocket of his jeans, and removed a folded envelope. He handed it to me. "This is for you."

Frowning, I opened it and removed its contents. I unfolded the sheet of paper and gaped.

What the everloving fuck?

"But… why would you do this?"

"Because you needed a push in the right direction. Call it my good deed for the day. However, you do need to move fast."

I looked again. "You're not fucking *kidding*."

He grinned. "Then don't waste time talking to me. On second thoughts, I'll skip the coffee." He got to his feet, and patted my arm. "Good luck. Let me know how things work out." And with that, he walked out of the apartment.

My heart pounded.

This is crazy.

This is really *fucking crazy.*

And Sean was right. I didn't have time to waste. I had stuff to do.

Saturday, July 16

Robert

I called Teague on the phone. "Have all the guests arrived?" We were expecting four, all keen to spend a week or two riding the trails.

"All but one."

"That the guy who didn't want picking up from the airport?"

"Yeah, that's him. He said in his email he was renting a car. He's not late yet, though. Wait… Hang on…"

"Look, if that's him, you'd better go deal with him, I'll—"

"What the *fuck*?"

I stilled. "Teague?" In the silence that followed, my mind went on a wild sprint through all the possibilities.

"Boss? I think you'd better come down here."

"What is it? What's wrong?" He didn't sound panicked. If anything, I could've sworn I detected amusement.

"It would be easier to show you than explain over the phone."

"Fine. I'll be right there." His tone went a long way to alleviating my concern. I grabbed my hat, and headed for the kitchen. I poked my head around the door. "We all set for supper tonight?"

Matt was on his phone, grinning.

I arched my eyebrows. "Am I interrupting something?"

He jerked his head up. "What? Oh. Sure, I've got everything ready." That grin hadn't faded. "And there'll be plenty—for everyone."

I went to the front door, shaking my head.

The world's gone nuts.

As I walked down the path, I noticed a car parked beside the bunkhouse. Our last guest had apparently arrived. I crunched my way across the gravel, wondering where everyone was. As I approached the door to the bunkhouse, I heard raised voices inside.

Teague appeared at the door. "You'd better get in here."

I walked in to find all the hands standing in the middle of the floor in a huddle, talking loudly. I guessed the three guys standing to one side, all wearing puzzled expressions, were the guests.

"What the hell is going on here?" I demanded.

Everyone froze, and the knot of ranch hands dissolved to reveal—

Oh my God.

It was Toby.

He gave me a warm smile. "Hey."

I didn't take my eyes off him, my heart racing. "Teague? Could you take everyone to the stables, please?"

"But—"

"Now, Teague. Give them a tour of the ranch. Whatever. Just... take them out of here?"

Butch snorted. "Yeah, good idea. We don't wanna be around for the next part."

They filed out of the bunkhouse, until it was just me and Toby.

I stared at him. "What are you doing here?"

"My business partner booked two weeks here—for me. He bought the air tickets, rented the car... all in my name. I only found out yesterday."

I was trying my best to remember how to breathe.

"And as for why I'm here? Why I decided *not* to refuse his generosity? I...I broke my own rule."

I frowned. "What rule? The not-doing-boyfriends rule?"

"It's more of a don't-fall-for-me kinda rule. And—you know what? It doesn't matter. All you need to know is... I've fallen for you. And I left without telling you because... I thought if I shared that, you wouldn't trust me as your Dom. How could you, if I broke my own rules?"

Oh God. He'd thought...what?

Then I thought about it. I'd knocked his confidence when I turned him down for the long-distance D/s relationship, not that I'd meant to do such a thing. But once I'd done that, he'd have found it even more difficult to tell me he'd broken his own guideline as a Dom, thinking I'd...

My brain wouldn't cooperate. "You've..."

He walked up to me. "All the way here, you know what I was thinking about? Lobsters."

I blinked. "Now you've lost me." He was close enough that I could smell him, that familiar scent that had clung to my pillowcase, the same pillowcase I'd refused to wash for a week after he left.

"Put a lobster in boiling water, and it'll fight, but put it on slow cook, raise the temperature, and that lobster won't even know it's being boiled."

"Please, tell me there's a point to all this."

"You put me in the club, introduce me to a sub, and I'll stick to my rules. I'll avoid getting entangled—falling in love..."

Lord, my heart...

"But take me away from D/s, put me on a ranch where I'm just getting to know someone, and I won't even notice I've fallen for them until... well... until it's too late." He looked me in the eye. "I want to stay—if you'll have me."

"But what about San Francisco? The club?"

"My business partner will run it. I'm a silent partner anyway. But... I'm not looking for a twenty-four/seven submissive. I want a partner who'll share my lifestyle, sure—but also my life." He smiled. "And this is the part where you kiss me."

I didn't hesitate. My hands were on his face, his beard, my lips locked onto his, and I kissed him with all the vigor of a drowning man who'd just found a lifebelt.

"You're sure?"

"Yeah. I'm not certain I'll be any good at helping run a cattle ranch, but I had a few ideas about the dude part of it."

"The dude ranch is what supports the rest."

Toby's eyes lit up. "Then maybe I'm on the right track."

"What do you mean?" *And why are we talking, when we could be kissing... and touching?*

"How about offering a different sort of experience?"

I stilled. "Such as?"

"What if one week out of every month, Salvation opens its doors to people like us?" When I arched my eyebrows, he grinned. "Kinksters. Doms. Subs."

"Why would they come here?" Despite my need to hold him, to convince myself this was real, he was *really there*, my curiosity got the better of me.

"There'd be guys who want to push their boundaries, in a place where they can focus, relax, set aside their day-to-day worries."

"I like the idea in principle, but... I'm not sure there'd be enough interest."

He smiled. "Trust me, I have enough connections to get the word out. We could bring in… guest speakers, I suppose you'd call them. Someone to talk or demonstrate whips, Shibari, sounding, wax, you name it. We get people here to try something new. And you know what? It'd be profitable too. Gay guys with no families? We're talking a *lot* of disposable income."

Okay, now he *really* had my interest. "I love it. But…"

"But?"

"We have to put it to the hands. I know it wouldn't impact *them*—they'd still work with the cattle and the horses—but—"

"But they're your family. I agree. When?"

"You've arrived in time for Saturday night supper. How about then? Once everyone's eaten, and the guests return to the bunkhouse, of course." This called for a special kind of staff meeting.

"Sounds great. No time like the present." Then he grinned. "I'd better make sure you're wearing the prostate massager before they all arrive."

I swear, all the blood in my body headed to my dick. "I think we'd better go up to the house and make sure it works… You know, to be on the safe side. I mean, it hasn't been used for a while."

"How long do we have until supper?"

I smiled. "Hours."

He kissed me, not bothering to keep it chaste. "Then what are we waiting for?" Another heated kiss. "We've got some catching up to do."

And I knew exactly where we'd be doing it.

Toby

I gazed at the faces around the table. Robert had made the pitch, and now it was up to them. "So, what do you think?"

Butch stroked his chin. "Let me see if I've got this right. You wanna bring a load of gay guys to Salvation, to get up to a load of kinky shit?"

Robert coughed. "Pretty much, yeah."

"But we wouldn't have to *see* the kinky shit, right? Or participate in it?"

"Absolutely not."

I grinned. "Unless you wanted to."

Butch's lips parted, and I would have given anything to know what passed through his mind right then.

Zeeb looked me in the eye. "So this means you'll stay?"

I smiled. "It does."

He mimed mopping his brow. "Well, thank fuck for that. Looks like I don't have to kill you after all."

"I like the idea," Teague announced, putting his phone down on the table. He grinned.

"What are you thinking?"

He'd been on his phone as soon as Robert had shared my proposal.

"Oh, just imagining this place, with guys walking around in leather, or jocks, or nothing but boots and a leash."

I arched my eyebrows. "*Someone's* been doing some research."

He flushed.

Walt chuckled. "Wow, things sure could get interesting around here. One week per month? It'll make the rest of the month seem tame in comparison."

"So you're all with me on this?" Robert asked.

"With *us*," I amended, and he gave me a grateful smile.

"With us," he echoed.

Teague looked around the table as everyone nodded. "Yeah, we are. I guess Toby will be living here?"

"Yes, he will." Robert took my hand in his.

"Oh Lord, that's our cue to leave." Butch pushed his chair back. "Any more displays of public affection, and I might heave."

I caught his eye. "Just so you know? You don't fool me for a second."

He blinked.

"We'd better get down there." Teague stood. "We've left our guests alone long enough."

Zeeb heaved a sigh. "Thank God you both came to your senses. Now maybe we'll get a smile outta this guy." He patted Robert on the back.

When everyone had left, I took Robert in my arms. "Was it that bad?"

"Pretty much."

I kissed him on the lips. "I'm not going anywhere. And to prove it... I've got something for you." I grabbed my jacket from the hook by the door and reached into the inside pocket. I removed a small box.

"What's this, a present?"

"Yes... well... sort of." I took the lid off, and Robert's eyes widened when he saw the gleaming straight metal chain composed of small, thick links, the gold padlock nestled in the center of it.

He swallowed. "Is this... what I think it is?"

I nodded. "You won't believe the panic I got into yesterday, trying to get to the store to buy this. Sean left it kinda late to spring the surprise on me—I think that was the whole idea—so I was a little... rushed." I gazed at him. "So... do I put it on?"

He shuddered. "Yes, Sir. I want this."

I placed it around his neck, passing the bar of the chunky gold padlock through the two end links. I clicked the padlock shut. I kissed him again, my heart soaring as he brought his fingers to it, stroking it, his breath hitching.

"Only I have the key to this," I told him.

Robert's smile was almost serene. "That works. You're the only one who has the key to my heart."

THE END

Well… for now.

THANK YOU

As always, a huge thank you to my beta team.

Special thanks to Jason Mitchell – it was so good to be plotting with you again!

Extra special thanks to Jack L Pyke and Blake Lockheart, for their BDSM-related expertise. This book is all the better for your wonderful input.

ALSO BY K.C. WELLS

<u>Learning to Love</u>
Michael & Sean
Evan & Daniel
Josh & Chris
Final Exam

<u>Sensual Bonds</u>
A Bond of Three
A Bond of Truth

<u>Merrychurch Mysteries</u>
Truth Will Out
Roots of Evil
A Novel Murder

<u>Love, Unexpected</u>
Debt
Burden

<u>Dreamspun Desires</u>
The Senator's Secret
Out of the Shadows
My Fair Brady
Under the Covers

<u>Lions & Tigers & Bears</u>
A Growl, a Roar, and a Purr
A Snarl, a Splash, and a Shock

Love Lessons Learned
First

Waiting for You
Step by Step
Bromantically Yours
BFF

Collars & Cuffs
An Unlocked Heart
Trusting Thomas
Someone to Keep Me (K.C. Wells & Parker Williams)
A Dance with Domination
Damian's Discipline (K.C. Wells & Parker Williams)
Make Me Soar
Dom of Ages (K.C. Wells & Parker Williams)
Endings and Beginnings (K.C. Wells & Parker Williams)

Secrets – with Parker Williams
Before You Break
An Unlocked Mind
Threepeat
On the Same Page

Personal
Making it Personal
Personal Changes
More than Personal
Personal Secrets
Strictly Personal
Personal Challenges
Personal – The complete series

Confetti, Cake & Confessions
(FREE)

Christmas
Connections
Saving Jason
A Christmas Promise
The Law of Miracles
My Christmas Spirit
A Guy for Christmas
Dear Santa
Santa's Secrets

Island Tales
Waiting for a Prince
September's Tide
Submitting to the Darkness
Island Tales Vol 1 (Books #1 & #2)

Lightning Tales
Teach Me
Trust Me
See Me
Love Me

A Material World
Lace
Satin
Silk
Denim

Southern Boys
Truth & Betrayal
Pride & Protection
Desire & Denial
The Southern Boys Trilogy

Maine Men
Finn's Fantasy
Ben's Boss
Seb's Summer
Dylan's Dilemma
Shaun's Salvation
Aaron's Awakening
Levi's Love
Maine Men – the Complete Series

Salvation
Wrangled

Second Sight
In His Sights
In Plain Sight

CrossBow Protection
Broken Warrior

Standalones
Kel's Keeper
Here For You
Sexting The Boss
Gay on a Train
Sunshine & Shadows
Double or Nothing
Back from the Edge
Switching it up
Out for You (FREE)
State of Mind (FREE)
No More Waiting (FREE)
Watch and Learn
My Best Friend's Brother

Princely Submission
Bears in the Woods
Holy Hell – with Parker Williams
Teasing Tim
Str8 B8

Anthologies

<u>Fifty Gays of Shade</u>
Winning Will's Heart

<u>Come, Play</u>
Watch and Learn

<u>Writing as Tantalus</u>
Damon & Pete: Playing with Fire

ABOUT THE AUTHOR

K.C. Wells lives on an island off the south coast of the UK, surrounded by natural beauty. She writes about men who love men, and can't even contemplate a life that doesn't include writing.

The rainbow rose tattoo on her back with the words 'Love is Love' and 'Love Wins' is her way of hoisting a flag. She plans to be writing about men in love - be it sweet or slow, hot or kinky - for a long while to come.